Butta'
WORLDWIDE

DESKTOPEPICS

Corey A. Burkes

Butta'

- The Series -

Episode II
Butta': Worldwide

Corey A. Burkes

Paperback Edition PUBLISHED BY DESKTOPEPICS
Entertainment
PO Box 1841
Marietta, GA 30061
http://butta.desktopepics.com

Cover design by Corey Aaron Burkes

Photography by Kim Cantey-Davis of
www.mystiqphotography.com

Featuring promotional models:

Doris Morgado
Samantha Murdock
Kida Davis
Kandiss Lewis
Christina Boykin
Haji Abdull
Roxzane T. Mims
Christina Boykin

Make-up and Hair by Sharitta Ann Baker and
Nakia Boykin

Spanish Translations by Lissette Espaillat

Also from Corey A. Burkes
Butta'
Toasted!
Gravity Gone
Emotionally Compromising
Scratch
Sleight of Death

My Pledge to You & Warranty

This novel, except for the physical or digital printing, binding and professional editing, was handcrafted in every detail by the author, *Corey Aaron Burkes*.

From the first word to the last, this novel—the cover design, story, and embodying marketing that led you to bring this book home—was made from *the heart* and carries with it a dedication to quality and superior *storytelling* without third party interests, research marketing teams or based on the temperature of public opinion. This is storytelling in the purest form—with *care* and with the sole interest of *entertaining you*.

As time and usage wears down these pages, or if you should lose your eBook version, you are assured a *Lifetime Replacement Guarantee*. Should, at any time, your book becomes damaged for *any* reason, send the damaged copy back to *me* and *I* will replace it *free of charge*[1] ... *free shipping*. No questions asked.

Register your novel at www.desktopepics.com to receive your Owners Privilege Pack.

Join Butta's Clique on Facebook!

---

[1] Please visit desktopepics.com for further information on our lifetime replacement warranty. Register immediately!

Corey A. Burkes

For
Johanna Haberman
1944-2012
Ma … Please be proud of me.

Acknowledgements

Earlier on in my career, I had received many touching reviews for Butta', and when it is your first time out the gate, it's not something you take lightly. Because, quite frankly, it could have went a completely different direction.

First on the list is **everyone** that bought, read and enjoyed the first novel. Thank you for making the second one a pleasure to finish. I pray it maintains the quality you deserve. The time you give to read my work is valuable and I *do not* take it for granted.

I wish to extend a special heartfelt thank you to RJ of **3Rs Den**. Your words were eloquently received to help me define who I am in this industry—and confirmed how comfortable I can be in my style of writing and still entertain the reader. Thank you very *very* much.

Naturally, I thank my family and my children for reasons I need not have to explain.

To John and Andrea Jackson and their daughter, Amber: Once the perfect neighbors and now some crazy Boston fans. Not everyone is perfect (smile). A pleasure to know and share times with you guys.

To Samantha Lawrence and her family. Andrea Johnson and her family. Jackie Hopgood, Deloris Capehart and Regina Camp-Brantley.

To Nicole M. Grant, who was the first to read and edit this novel back in 2009! Thank you for reminding me where I came from—thus assisting me on where I'm going.

Amy Kolo and her family, LaChandar Ross, Monica Lewis (*Scorpio Queen*), Trenae Hunt and Fatisha Christianson … 2008 was a better year knowing each of you. The BBQ is still on and poppin'.

To Joe and Ann-Marie Bopp and their children. I missed thanking him in book one—Joe is very much considered part of my 'usual suspects' group and is one of my oldest friends. I've come to understand that he will never change—thank god for that. He's my brother till time concludes. But I suspect we'll still be hanging out thereafter.

Gail Augustus and her family. Thank you for your time and interest in the book, the characters and the story. Come to think of it, I can honestly say Ms. Augustus was a definite contributing factor to writing the next story at all. Thank you so much.

To John and Shelita Compton, with children Mason and Kendal: Thank you for welcoming us to Georgia. You made the transition from New York to Kennesaw a pleasure. Gotta do it again!

John and Rikia Owens, with Jayla, Amari and Khalil: Family friends that also contributed to our *Georgia state of mind* living. Thank you for the welcoming and hospitality. John, we'll get that basement together one of these days.

Seth Harwood of Jack Wakes Up … the master storyteller, book promoter and a helpful friend. Thank you for taking the time to pass on your wisdom. A strong percentage of the reason this book is in your hands right now is because of the teachings I've learned from Seth—the online book developer/marketer, audio book producing guru. *Jack Wakes Up* is a necessary read for everyone who loves crime fiction and can be found at all bookstores nationwide and online. Visit sethharwood.com and tell him *Butta'* sent you.

Kim Cantey-Davis, her husband Terry and daughter Symone. Kim, you welcomed me to Atlanta with open arms and included me into the tight union of talented friends and I can't thank you enough for making me feel like I never left home at all. Watching your daughter grow artistically must be the icing on the cake for you. I am very proud of her and your family. Thank you for taking such great pictures (mystiqphotography.com)

Naomi Lavette and her family—thank you for showing me what endurance and focus on your one talent can achieve. Say hi to *Tyler Perry* for me as your fan club is continuing to increase.

Corey A. Burkes

To the cast and crew of the Butta' Podcast: Kim Cantey-Davis, Naomi Lavette, Tony Johnson, Santino Shepherd, Adair Lawrence, Sanedria Potter, Loretta Pinkney, Kitti and Ben Sims … thank you for providing your incredible talents to the process. Thanks to each of you, the online audio drama bar has been raised.

Daphine Glenn Robinson for being a great *virtual* friend. An online buddy.

All said and done.
The lights dim and the adventure *finally* begins …

Corey A. Burkes

Previously in Butta'

Brooklyn, N.Y. – Hibiscus Day Spa - 2 P.M.

Butta', Kasey and Trigger were just finishing the *Sea Salt Body Scrub* portion of their *day of indulgence*—potentially their last, if things didn't go as planned. Starting with the world-class, Swedish Massage and the Hibiscus Signature Facial, the body scrub was the highlight of the past twenty-four hours. Lastly, the Citrus Punch Manicure and Pedicure would punctuate the spa treatment.

With a towel wrapped about her head and one about her body, Trigger always knew how to sum up a collected feeling. "Ladies— we are *chillin'*."

All three women were tended to by the finest pamper-professionals in town. It took all of Kasey's strength to stay awake; this was the best massage she ever had—and that was coming from a world traveler.

"Bee?" Kasey called out, shocking herself awake.

"Hmmm," Butta' replied blissfully.

"We have to talk about some things."

"Can it wait?"

"The *guild* has a few issues with this operation."

Butta' peeked with one eye at Kasey and the manicurists about them. As long as no one mentioned names, places or things, this conversation could possibly carry on. "What about them?"

"They say it's too personal and they suggest you apply your efforts somewhere else. Now, you know I defended your actions of course."

"*Um hmm*—of course you did."

"Don't sound like that."

"Like what?"

"Like you don't trust that I had your back."

"*Did* you have my back?"

Kasey fell silent and then sighed. "The fact that I'm sitting here should be your answer. You know, I was supposed to be assigned in London for that *Franco* thing."

"You're telling me you'd rather do a job in merry old England, under some rich old farts arm spending his money and drinking his champagne than here in New York?"

"Exactly *what* will I be doing any different tonight?"

"Doing me a favor." Butta' shut her eyes, leaning back; secure with the knowledge that she had given more of her time and energy to Kasey than tonight would ever repay.

Kasey knew that as well.

"What's the guild?" Trigger asked.

"Kind of like a union for the work we do. They pass out assignments; we get a percentage—the world goes round and round."

"Am I in the guild now? How do I get down?"

Good question. Butta' never made the effort—nor had the time—to pursue what place Trigger had with them. The *little sister-thing* wouldn't swing for too long.

"The guild doesn't know who you are, Trig. It might be the best thing for you. Getting in is not a two-way street. It's not easily reversible."

"I can do what you guys do. *I'm grown.*" Her age was talking. She sounded defiant—maybe because she was inherently rebellious.

"Not grown enough for the guild, baby," Kasey tapped her hand. "Don't ask for things you know nothing about."

"You know," Butta' started, "The guild has a vested interest in what's going on."

"I know," Kasey nodded. "Why else have you gotten this far? They know you're looking to settle up with that guy. They know about your … *problem.*"

"Then why are they complaining?"

"They are quite firm with one request."

"And that is?"

"Your *problem* cannot die. They said they are permitting you do anything else, take whatever you need—but should the problem wind up dead—you may have another problem. He's too big—too many fingers in too many dealings that require him to be around for *a lot* of people."

"They supplied us with the invitations!" Butta' was incensed. "What did they *expect* me to do? Walk up in there and just slap him? This isn't a game."

Kasey hushed Butta' down, making sure the spa workers didn't know more than they had to.

"I'm not trying to stop you. We've worked together too long to know that won't do any good. I still need to tell you the truth once in a while. I'll let Munchie *'yes'* you to death. He's better at it."

Butta' learned to listen to her only friends. Doing what she was told was another story. Was she the only one who believed Lingo needed to die? While her nails were being buffed and cleaned, she felt alone again.

Still in solitary confinement.

Later … Stein Tower – View from Ventilation Shaft

The lab man rushed back to the screen. The light was getting brighter and more steam was spreading everywhere around him. Electrical interference was creating static in the camera view. "Do we pull it at four-eighty?"

"No!" The Red Bull drinker stood and thumbed through sheets of paper on a clipboard.

"What are you doing? Dale—we pull at 480 like we're supposed to." The other control room person had problems with the latest decision.

"No! Keep it going. I want to see—" he trailed off, watching the screen; full of thoughts running through his mind.

"But—"

"Sshh!" He waved down his companion, looking at the on-screen lab man who was smiling back, nodding. "Right. Nothing ventured—"

"—nothing gained," Dale finished. His heart was racing.

"Four hundred and eighty carats. Four hundred eighty-one … four-eighty-four …, four-ninety—*Dale!* We can't push it! Stein will—"

"Stein will *applaud* us, goddamn it. Let it do its thing!"

By now, the on-screen lab people had backed from all the steam and rocking machinery, fearful of a possible explosion. The image was almost incomprehensible; filled with static and a flickering screen.

"Another jump! *Eight hundred carats*! Dale, pull it!"

"It can go higher!"

"Pull the damn thing!"

Someone on-screen heard him and the machine slowed down. Smoke and steam billowed around the technicians on screen, blanketing the lab floor. Slowly, cautiously, everyone motioned to the large machine.

"Well?" Dale asked of his small crew.

One of them scratched his head, looking up in wonder. "*Goddamn, man*. Pure uncut diamond—weighing in at—*shit*! Nine hundred and twenty carats. That's bigger than the damn—that one by that guy—the one who built the Taj Mahal—you know!"

"Donald Trump?" Someone offered.

"No, you idiot! The *real* Taj Mahal."

The lab tech on the screen helped them out. "He's referring to the *Great Mogul*, discovered in the 17th century and named after Shah Jehan. It was 793-carats. By now, we've reached the level of ultra-priceless proportions, gentlemen. Not even the richest man on Earth can afford this diamond."

"Stein'll find a price, that much I'm certain." Dale popped open a bottle of water, putting his papers together. "Alright. Our systems are monitoring any latent formations. We have the creation on record and logged the time. We're done here in the states unless you plan to make another."

"*No, sir.*" The lab man removed his mask and gloves, evidently worn out. "Two today is our limit and we have family to attend to. Give our regards to Mr. Stein and tell him we greatly appreciate his most *generous* bonus."

"You guys earned it. Hell. We all did."

"When will you be visiting us in Cape Town?"

"Not sure. Hadn't planned on it. Maybe after the flagship is running smoothly."

"Well, you can be sure all of us here are more than excited to tour you about *Gisela*, so you can see how she works first hand." Then he stepped closer to the screen. "Dale, my friend—you've created *history* here this night."

Dale looked up at the tech, smiling as the screen shut off. Turning away, Dale walked out of the room a proud man. "That's it, fellas. Let's go swing by the party. The computers can earn our pay."

Shutting down the lights, the men hurried out the room looking forward to mixing it up with the rich downstairs.

Butta'—lying in the vent, having watched the entire event transpire—cried.

Something she hadn't done in a long, *long* time. Not because she was any closer to her goals—but right in front of her, she bore witness to her father's goals. He was an unrealized *genius*, ironically recognized by a sadistic murderer. Leaving Butta' and Lingo the only two on Earth who knew her father; a simple black man who loved his family and had the greatest idea of the entire human existence.

Fade let her have her moment, not wanting to disturb what may be flowing behind all of her tears; all the years of frustration, hate, anger, sadness and loneliness.

No sooner than she started, she stopped. "I'm sorry."

"Don't be. Make *him* sorry."

Perhaps the first on point thing Fade had said to her since they'd met.

Yes, she agreed. Destiny waited fifty more stories up and time was against them. Fade crawled back to continue his climb upward. "We're gonna need to double time it. You ready?"

Butta', having gained her second wind, was ready to go. "Let's do this."

Corey A. Burkes

- BOOK ONE -
Big World

Corey A. Burkes

Opening Events

Present day. Las Vegas, Nevada – 8:36 pm
Rain—it didn't happen often in *Sin City*, but when it did, some would say it was a little depressing. The twenty-four hour, seven-day-a-week adult party came to a sudden and abrupt halt in order for the heavens to do their business on the man-populated desert.

City officials enjoyed storms like this. Not only did they add to the reservoir of water, pumped in from Lake Mead—it also cut down on the Los Angeles-type smog that formed over this ever expanding metropolis of *money*. For a change, the air was filtered free of alcohol, cigarettes and car exhaust—and people were off the streets.

Well ... not *everyone*.

Rain—it clears the land with a 'fresh start'. It also provided a unique *cover* when used properly. Dressed in black, matted down by the storm, *He* strolled past the grand entrance of the town's latest crown jewel hotel, *The Italiano*—an Italy themed adult resort and casino built in the heart of the strip. Green, white and red flags, soaked from the previous two hours of pounding rain and the smell of original *Sicilian* pasta, herbs and bread filled the air despite the weather.

He planned to double back once his job was done. There was nothing like a good Italian dinner after a murder.

Other than the main entrance, rear loading docks and employee entrance, the only other way inside was through the delivery door and *He* was prepared for that. *He* knocked on the door and the casino security opened it, eyeing *Him* as a known face.

One of the first laws of a true assassin was to become a *friendly* face weeks prior for easier access on the day of the *hit*. For a month and a half, every other day at this exact time, *He* delivered a package for a listed executive in the casino of little interest and security thought nothing of *Him*.

So on the day of the hit, *He* simply walked thru and prepared to locate his mark.

Penthouse Suite of The Italiano

Diandra Stein rubbed her forehead annoyed. She was sitting at the head of a table surrounded by stiff, grey old lawyers and accountants whom found more interest in the company numbers than her *painfully* sexy dress with revealing cleavage. They were prattling off law, figures, forecasts, projections and generally the boring stuff that made or broke an empire. An empire she now owned.

For god sakes, Diandra thought. *I just got back from my father's funeral.* Alas, the responsibilities of the newly appointed *Queen of Stein Industries* needed to carry on. Somewhere, *everywhere*—people still needed to be paid.

As bored as she was, she still heard four distinct sounds just outside the meeting room doors—two muzzled gunshots followed by two thuds crumbling to the floor.

By the time Diandra's mind registered the trouble she was in, the door creaked open eerily and a metal silencer peeked through. Two subtle *poofs* of air and the two bodyguards inside the room were finished cleanly. Before they fell, *He* was through the door—walking slowly and purposefully—pointing his gun at *eight* of the *nine* Stein Industry number crunchers; firing eight shots only.

One lawyer and Diandra remained.

The lawyer would need a fresh pair of underwear.

In public, Diandra was not a weak woman; staring down the unknown hit-man whom brought *His* gun around to her forehead. She invited *Him* to do something she had failed to succeed in herself—*six attempts* for over the past six years. Her father spent millions for the best psychologists and media damage control, preventing the heiress of the dynasty from being revealed as suicidal. It seemed, today, *He* would have what it took to end her life.

Finally, she would find some peace from her restless thoughts. She closed her eyes, waiting for the end …

… Which never came. Instead, *He* retracted his gun and inserted an envelope between her cleavage. *He* was *all* business. *He* had no interest in her body nor was *He* contracted to take her life. *His* task was to remove eight, *not nine*, administrators of their lives—and deliver an envelope.

Mission accomplished. *He* was very precise about his work.

Walking backwards, the dripping wet assassin silently left the room; gun pointed at Diandra's forehead until *He* disappeared. Diandra had been, quite literally, *brushed* with death. No security. No alarms. No talking …

Just rain. A flash of lightning lit up the room of the dead—followed by rolling thunder in the distance—accenting the mood.

The extra lawyer that joined the group as a *tag along assistant* would eventually quit his position at the firm and spend the rest of his life fishing with his two boys; enjoying and *appreciating* his spared life. As for Diandra, she wasn't that grateful. Aside from eventually calling the police, she opened the envelope given to her. She hoped there would be some *anthrax* inside to finish her off.

Nothing.

Just a small, white business card; without a sentence or a word on the *finest* paper money could buy and a singular letter stamped in the center in gold:

E

Corey A. Burkes

Corey A. Burkes

Closing Events

Six Years Ago ...

Yancey Duncan was a tired, exhausted man. He had just finished working what was called an '*iron*' shift—where he opened the retail giant he worked for and closed it; staying a few hours extra into the next morning to help the struggling third-shift crew get their act together. This was living in *New York*—you did what you had to do to pay the *bills*.

By the time he left work at four-thirty, he thought he might as well stay awake since he had to pick up his daughter in a little bit anyway. If he crashed now, he would be knocked out for the entire day. By now, he had all his mental tricks to keep sharp and focused down pat. If he stayed awake into the next day, after drinking two or three cups of coffee, his body would be *wired*—fully functional but in a *zombie* kind of fashion.

For some reason, his tricks weren't working as well as they use to, and his *schlep* across Long Island, down the LIE and into Queens seemed long. As if he wore an extra pound of weight on his shoulders that oppressed his emotions, making him feel out of character.

Regardless, there was no way he would miss seeing his two-year-old daughter. He hadn't missed a day—an hour or a *minute*—of his court appointed *visitation*.

To kill time, Yancey joined a gym not far from his daughter's home that kept him in great shape. The gym had a twenty-four hour schedule, so if he had a midnight urge to bench-press some of his aggressions, it was his option—*and a three-year contract*—to do so.

His *ex-wife* drove him to be there on a nightly basis.

His choices were to lift weights or lift her *lifeless* body over a bridge. While he never was a criminal or had a negative strike against him, Yancey could see why some ex-wives wound up getting shot in broad daylight. Some people just *drove* others to commit murder and Yancey admitted his she made him think it over.

Often— *very* often.

Instead, he wore out the punching bag and occasional sparring partner. He would almost want to *thank* his ex for the excellent health he was in.

As for his daughter, she always had a smile for *daddy* when he visited.

She was a little girl that would never *want* for anything. Yancey created a work schedule based on achieving *more* for the benefit of his first and only daughter—in a relationship that crashed and burned before it began.

Yancey regressed over past events very often; reflecting on all the destroyed plans that never became. Most importantly, putting his daughter into a single-parent household was *never* part of the equation. He didn't want her to have the same empty, soulless life he had—alone with one parent working so much, she barely saw him.

No matter the trouble between him and his ex, Yancey struggled to make the relationship work. Nonetheless, when someone didn't want to be there, who could truly make them stay?

Now he's paying *child support* and working multiple shifts to make his own ends meet. To be honest, he wasn't 100% certain if his ex was spending the money on his daughter.

When he started thinking down *that* road, Yancey forced himself to change the subject. That kind of paranoia only led to asking questions, which led to arguing—*again*.

All he wanted to do right was be happy with his daughter and maybe get a little shut eye after dropping her off at school.

These were the simple joys of a single, hardworking man.

Eating always helped him ease that knot in his stomach during stressful times. He *loved* to eat the best and healthiest of foods: apples, grapes, peaches, low-fat yogurts; anything and everything that would fill him up and still keep him fit.

He wished he could impress the same thinking upon his ex, whom had a *passion* for chips and sugary snacks that trickled down to their daughter. He gave up that battle a long time ago after he was accused of trying to *brainwash* their daughter. To spite him, she encouraged more of the foods Yancey steered away from; claiming the girl needed to '*live more*' and not be so '*uptight*' like her father.

Live more—at two-years-old.

Just thinking of past arguments made him stuff his face with more fruit.

He wondered why he wasted years of his time associating such a counter-productive, hateful woman. He was certain the feelings were mutual and their meetings were *frosty*, at best. In order to keep the peace, Yancey always brought a small bag of *Cool Ranch Nachos*, his daughter's favorite, to show that he was adhering to her request—even at *seven-thirty* in the morning.

The plan was to actually give it to her as an *afterschool* snack. Today, they would start with a good breakfast where they can have *daddy-daughter* time before he took her to daycare. Since today was Friday, he was able to keep her straight through the weekend.

That also meant he took her to daycare on *Monday* morning as well. His weekends were solely for his daughter and he wouldn't have it any other way. No matter how tired he was—he would always sleep while she was at daycare.

Outside of the home he *once* owned—which he freely gave up in order for his daughter to live comfortably—there was a sizeable amount of *black trash bags* lined up on the sidewalk. He couldn't remember if Friday was garbage day, so he ignored them and walked to the side door as normal with an expectation to see his daughter's happy face looking out the window for him.

But this morning she wasn't there.

Maybe she's still getting ready, he thought, checking the time.

As a matter of fact, not only was his daughter *not* waiting for him in the window, but the *blinds* were gone as well.

That nervous *knot* in his stomach started to twist and turn his guts like a tornado.

First, he rang the doorbell—and waited.

Then, he knocked on the door–and prayed.

When he started *banging* on the door, the knot in his stomach turned into a full-fledged *fist*.

As he had expected, his ex-wife wasn't answering her cell phone and the house phone was cut off. The first person he visited was his ex's god-parents and they said: *'We don't know where she is.'*

He will later discover they *lied*.

He then went to the daycare center. All they knew was his ex-wife gave them the last of their payment and pulled his daughter out of the school.

They said they would miss his little girl *terribly*.

Only one last person would know their whereabouts; the last person on earth he would want to speak to: his ex-wife's *sister*.

"*Paula, where's my daughter!*" He barked; an immediate, unpleasant greeting the moment she picked up the phone. If he and his ex-wife had an ugly past—the sister-in-law and he had a *hideous* communication problem.

"Don't be calling my phone *talking shit*, Yancey," her indignant, *I've-got-you-by-the-balls* remark turned his blood to acid. He could *spit fire* right now, but he had to hold back—for the sake of finding his daughter.

"*Please*," he adjusted. "Where did she take *my* daughter?"

"Why should I tell you?" She taunted.

Crack. That was his fist crushing his cell phone past its *suggested grip threshold*. He stopped himself before totally destroying the phone. He still needed information and she was playing games.

"*Negro*, you can't find her anyway." She said it in the most polite, *derogatory* tone. "It's over. Just pay your *child support* and move on. She doesn't want to see you again and she doesn't want you near her daughter ever."

The poor cell phone never had a chance. It skyrocketed across traffic after being crushed into a mangle mess of electronics, wires, plastic and busted keys.

Yancey started to hyperventilate. Only one thing in the world was of importance to him outside of his own life—and she was snatched away from him without a care.

Just pay your child support and move on! The sister-in-law's voice echoed through his skull. He prayed that she would just *die* already. A good dose of *cancer* or *black plague* would settle his score with her and he wouldn't have enough *piss* to spread on her grave either.

The churning in his stomach threatened to eat him from the inside out.

He had to settle down or he was going to end up getting *violently* sick. The fruit wasn't going to do it for him.

His daughter's nachos were just the ticket.

While he sat in his car eating, not sure what to do…
Munch, munch, munch!
…He thought about what legal rights he had…
Munch, munch, munch!
…Didn't he have to *find* her first to serve *any* court papers?
Munch, munch, munch!
How could she just take his … *munch* … daughter … *munch* … away from him?

… Munch … Munch …

Corey A. Burkes

Chapter 1

"... ***Munch!***" Gisela *'Butta'* Thompson screamed at the top of her lungs, snapping Yancey *'Munch'* Duncan out of his daydream. "Get your *head* into this!"

Present day. Cape Town— South Africa
Stein Diamond Facility – Sub-Basement Level 6
Security was attempting to eliminate the only two individuals in the world *stupid* enough to invade South Africa's most secure central depository for mined diamonds. Armed depository security, backed by the deadly SASFB (*South African Special Forces Brigade*), mobilized in professional harmony to lay down cover fire and suppress their advancement. Twenty combat trained soldiers on one end of a steel hallway—

—Butta' and Munch on the other, holed up in the smallest of alcoves across from each other to prevent getting shot. The only way out was behind the SASFB assault team and these men were not letting them go.

Butta' fired back at them with an *Armalite AR-18 assault rifle*, reached for another clip, slammed it in and kept the defensive measure in motion.

There was nothing like a sexy woman using a rifle with expert poise.

The SASFB were *not* impressed.

"*Did you get it*?" Butta' yelled at Munch, counting down the remaining clips she had in her backpack—not enough to fight a small war, to say the least.

Munch, the resident *geek* in Butta's crew, was pounding a ham finger at his jerry-rigged, over-clocked *iPhone* to wirelessly communicate with the doors behind the assault group to no avail. "They're locking me out of *all* systems. I told you *before* we got here—I don't know *Afrikaans*."

"Just *one* door, Munchie!" She pleaded, blasting at troops ahead of them. Combined with their armored vests and Kevlar thick ballistic tactical shields, the SASFB had little concern for Butta's feeble attack.

They inched themselves closer as opportunity allowed.

All Butta' needed was the door *behind* the assault team to open. In Munch's mind, they had no way of getting around the encroaching soldiers even if he were able to. He was *always* put to the task—no matter how hopeless the situation became.

That would be his fault for pulling miracles out of his hat from time to time.

Butta' chucked her empty clip, popped in her *last one* and gave more controlled bursts to keep the soldiers from gaining any more ground and reserving what she had left. She need not say anything else to her longtime friend; just a solemn glance in *severe* askance, because the end was nearing.

With a final swipe of his finger across his ultra-custom wireless networking app, he triggered the wireless feed circulating around the depository and connected to the entire compounds electrical door systems.

Each and every door in the seven floor depository retracted open. That included hatches, private entrances, secret entrances, garages and roof passages.

Last, but not least, the one and only door Butta' wanted, directly behind the SASFB attack force.

Through that door came *Poco Fuego*.

Fuego (*Fire* or *El Fuego* to the many Mexicans that knew *and feared* him) stood five-feet four inches with black hair, but that was where 'typical' ended.

A longtime friend and the '*muscle*' on Butta's speed dial of *friends-on-call*; some have called him a Mexican *Jet Li* ever.

Fuego leapt into action the moment the doors retracted, surprising the armed troops, who became overly confident with mere inches to their intended target. Before they could get their bearings, Fuego slipped under, around and over to the center of the troops and started shattering bones.

Fuego's speed had been clocked at knocking out six men in less than a minute. His frame made him look like a human *Tasmanian devil*. Between his martial art induced hissing and attack cries, he had put true fear into the SASFB team before they could figure out what was happening.

They would all need some sort of critical medical attention.

Two of them would never walk again.

When he was done, Fuego was the last man standing.

"¿Qué duró tantó para abrir la puerta?" *What took so long to open the door?* Fuego asked Munch.

"¿Por qué usted se separó de nosotros en el primer lugar?" *Why did you get separated from us in the first place?* Munch responded, in a huff. How dare this little man question him?

Deep down, Munch was jealous of Fuego for the great shape he was in in addition to his usual protective nature of *any* man around Butta'.

Like most men working with Butta', Fuego was devoted to her mission and someone she could trust explicitly.

Butta' scoured over the bodies—most of them still squirming in agony—picking up a new rifle, clips and anything else she could get her hands on to resupply.

Munch spied around and through the open door. "¿Sabes una formá mas rapida de volver a la superficie?" *Do you know a faster way back to the surface?*

Fuego scratched his head, biting the inside of his cheeks. "Exciste una gran cantidad de basurá viniendo detras de mi. La unicá manera de salir is por la rampa del sub-basement, lo pasé en camino aqui. ¿Usted consiguio el diamante?"

"What did he say?" Butta' asked.

"He said the way back is getting jammed with soldiers and he knows of a way through the underground garage."

Butta' thought about it. "That would lead back to the surface, alright. It's just a six floor drive up *through* soldiers trying to come *down*."

"So we're screwed," Munch resigned. "Is that what you're telling me?" He turned his back to Fuego. "No, nosotros no recibimos el diamante?"

Butta' didn't speak *any* other language, much less proper English, but like most people she had a healthy *Sesame Street*-level repertoire of key words and phrases. "What did you just tell him? What did you tell him we *didn't* do?"

Munch didn't want to answer her, grumbling his annoyance under his breath. "He asked me if we got what we came for and I said *no*."

"Don't be too sure." Butta' grabbed the most conscious soldier and put a gun to his head. "Where's the big diamond? The Stein Diandra?"

The Stein Diandra was the last, and largest, diamond created by the now defunct Gisela process; *920-carats* of pure, synthetic diamond that Butta' had chased after with obsessive ambition.

"We—*moved* it," his British accent broke apart between his coughing and shallow breathing. Broken collar bones and a collapsed lung would do it every time.

"Tell me something I *don't know*." Butta' shook him back into consciousness. "Where the *hell* is it now?"

The soldier gave her a bloody-smile and a painful laugh through his broken rib cage. "We knew you … were … coming. It's … on its way to … *Berlin*. Sorry to inconvenience you … *bitch*."

Cold killing was never part of Butta's *method of operandi*, so she released him, thinking over Plan B and spied something in the breast pocket of the soldiers vest: a matchbook cover.

Not just *any* matchbook cover, either. It was to an expensive hotel with *'penthouse suite, today'* written on the inside.

"Munchie?" Butta' swallowed hard. "Which hotel did we set Kasey and Trig up at again?"

Chapter 2

Cape Grace Hotel – Penthouse Suite.

The most expensive hotel on South Africa's Cape Town Victoria and Alfred Waterfront, *The Cape Grace*, sat before the picturesque Table Mountain. Yachts lined up against the privileged bay, underscoring the amount of money at play in this part of town.

The exclusiveness of the hotel's 121 rooms, rooftop luxury rooms or private penthouse suites were the top of the *top* locations to be spoiled at by teams of hotel staff dedicated to making a guest feel as if they were royalty.

Eighteen year old, Monique *'Trigger'* Bolland couldn't appreciate this setting quite yet. Her mind was still at the malls and public shopping centers where people her age were seen and dressed to *be* seen.

She had experienced more things than anyone her age, somehow still maintaining a youthful, carefree air about her. A thief by accident, she was a unique member of the '*haves*' by stealing from those who *have more*. For the time being, she was able to relax and wonder what life would have been if she had stayed on the straight and narrow.

Certainly, she would *never had* experience South Africa and stay at the most expensive hotel aside from the Sabi Sand Game Reserve (*a cool $2,000 a night!*).

On this bright and sunny afternoon, with nothing much to do, Trigger gazed over the terrace of her penthouse suite, overlooking the pool below. The weather was a comfortable eighty-six degrees with low humidity; only a few clouds and just a *spectacular* day with an invigorating cool breeze intermittently.

She shared the space with her partner-in-crime, Kasey McGuiness, who chose not to kick back in their own Jacuzzi; stretched out on the side of the main hotel pool instead.

Hmph, Trigger scoffed, frowning from behind her sunglasses. *It's been three hours, no word from Butta', Munch or that Mexican kung-fu guy and all Kasey wants to do is chill.*

One thing about Kasey: she *always* relaxed when the time allowed and found time to instruct Trigger in the *ways* of things as well. She seemed to have taken it upon herself to teach Trigger everything about being a classy, sexy woman no matter the place, time or crime.

Trigger and Kasey were the operation's *Plan C,* which consisted of *waiting* unless things went terribly wrong. *Waiting* was NOT Trigger's finest quality, as she paced about huffing and puffing with all the pleasures an *adult* could ask for at in such a lavish hotel. She was like a child with many toys and nothing to do.

What she did have, however, were things troubling her mind.

Trigger had an unopened envelope; a request by an organization she only heard whispers about between Butta' and Kasey and never *ever* openly in public.

One you never *asked* to be in—only invited.

It arrived by a special courier with exact orders to hand it to Trigger alone. Butta' wasn't there to see it nor was Kasey, already on poolside, soaking in the sun.

The back of the envelope had a blood-red wax seal imprinted on the back. It took her some of the afternoon, but after some extensive internet searching, she discovered the symbol on the seal was of the *Assassin's Guild.*

This was why she did not open the letter. She was honestly, and rightfully, scared.

Trigger planned to keep the letter her *little secret* until she would figure some things out. She knew what it would say and made a *big girl* decision not to open it until the mission was over; in order to stay focused and on point.

She looked at it one last time, feeling the *richness* of the envelope and the old custom use of wax to seal it. Having this envelope meant *someone* was taking her seriously.

She then looked down at Kasey sunbathing without a care in the world—tucking the letter in her back pocket.

The once blond, *now brunette*, Kasey McGuiness was well-financed with money in multiple banks, plenty of long-distance suitors and a *lucrative* job as the power-bodied swindler and tactical organizer. When she was given the word to sit back and unwind, the skimpiest bikini popped out and she went poolside to distract the local men.

Sunglasses on and reading a pocket-sized bible, Kasey carefully read through *Exodus* line-by-line, verse-by-verse. Her interest in the ancient text began after their experience in New York at the Stein Tower.

Something about looking into Daniel's eyes—after shoving a knife through his throat—disturbed her.

A huge feat for a woman that had taken many lives before in her tattered past. This last one completely unnerved her. It was as if she watched the fire being put out of his entire timeline—*extinguished*.

Maybe it was her age—or how he stared her down without uttering a word—but something in her was searching for answers.

Suddenly, *life* mattered.

The bible didn't help, but it was the only spiritual source she could find and pack along. The current books of early Judaism did little to settle her discomfort with all the death and mayhem that went on during those times. However, she was intrigued by the way God interacted with so many people; thus, forming questions about her place with the *almighty*.

Before she knew it, she was turning pages and writing notes in her own *private* bible study.

She even considered getting her hands on a *Qur'an* to start cross-referencing because she read somewhere the Islamic text confirmed and acknowledged things in the bible. Who would have thought, after years of willful debauchery, the *high priestess of decadence* would start searching for God?

She would never admit to understanding everything she was reading, but as each day that passed, she began to feel that void in her starting to fill with every page she turned.

Combined with a blissful state of sunbathed and mental relaxation, Kasey was a *martini* away from calling this day *perfect* when under a towel by her feet, her cell phone chirped.

Each of her friends, associates and suitors had special ringtones so she could decide if she wanted to answer it or not.

This was a particular chime she hadn't heard in a few months.

The phone itself seemed very far away in her soothed state of relaxation and she thought to let the caller go to voicemail. At the same time, something nagged at her. Maybe she should not be this *lazy* during a mission. But how could she *not* enjoy this.

Especially when she had the pool to herself.

She picked up the phone questioning that fact, looking about the empty pool area to find herself there alone.

"Hello?" She answered, yawning. "*Louie!* Longtime no hear. *Wasuupppp?*"

Louie did not sound like he was in the mood for playful banter. His voice sounded *gravely* concerned. "*Yo, Kase*! Tell me youse 'n Honey ain't in South Africa right now. Please tell me dat! Tell me dat, like, right *fuckin'* now!"

Kasey closed her bible, lifting her sunglasses off her face.

So much for relaxing.

Anchored Yacht 'Sariya-Anne' off the Coast

Louie Frazetta was an exceptional bodyguard from Chicago.

He performed freelance work as a gun-for-hire and, occasionally, as a private investigator for the ultra-rich and famous. His client list was long, protected and he was known throughout the industry as '*Mr. Right-On-Time*'.

The only reason he decided to work for people with money was *because* they were people with money. People with large amounts of disposable cash *never* stiffed him or balked at his rates and they rarely had a job that broke a sweat.

Louie currently was assigned to babysit the languorous son of a Pakistani diplomat. At seventeen, all the boy did was sit around on the family yacht, play video games, smoke weed and pick up girls at every port. On one hand, the boy *wasn't* an ass; probably one of the *coolest* jobs Louie had the pleasure to work with. On the other, the excessive amount of marijuana the boy smoked was offensive to him.

Right now, the boy was not his *prime* concern. He had Kasey on the line and his tone was very, *very* urgent.

"Youse n' Honey gotta get outta *dodge* like yer *ass* wuz 'bout ta get bit!"

"Why would we want to do that?" Kasey asked.

"Cause I gots me a friend out here. We wuz gonna meet up tonight 'n catch up— shoot the shit like back on da block. He just called me sayin' he's goin' need a rain check 'cause 'dey rollin' out *everybody* ta lock down da depository."

"Everybody?" Kasey sounded in a foul, *sickly* mood.

"*Everybody.* Dey know 'bout you and *Honey*, Kase. Dey lookin' to *body bag* each of youse."

There was a long pause on the other side of the line. "What else do they know?"

"Dey know youse 'n Trig' are stayin' at dat pricey joint by da bay in da penthouse digs. In fact, what time is it? *Shit*—Kase, where are ya now?"

"Where do you think?" She said dryly.

Louie turned down the radios he was monitoring from the bridge. "Youse gotta get da hell outta 'dere! Scumbags been settin' up a perimeter 'n movin' guests out da area of a—"

Kasey could be heard sighing pitifully. "Pool area, right?"

"Yeah! How're youse guys getting' outa da Cape?"

"To be determined."

"Are ya kiddin' me? Lookie here—I'm on a crusier called da *Sariya-Anne*, anchored off da coast north-west of Marine Drive. Ya got dat? *Marine Drive.* Hook up wit' Honey, get yer crew 'n get here as *fast* as ya can! We ain't leavin' port till ya do. Get me?"

"How much time do we have?"

"Who da hell knows. It depends on how long dey need ta move da guests out harm's way. It's *on* and poppin' when dey cut cell phones within a five-mile radius 'n— *Hello? Kase?*"

His cell phone went dead.

Cape Grace Hotel – Pool Area
"Louie?" Her phone was useless.

Kasey scanned the area with caution, pretending to be reading. What was once a full pool area, teaming with men vying to get a good look at her, dropped to a singular family of three rushing to get their things together.

The family's littlest one, maybe five-years-old, pointed across the pool just before being dragged out by her mother.

Kasey followed the direction of the child's pointed finger to see men in black tactical uniforms crouched low behind the glass awning of the pool. Men with sniper rifles trained at her from various points of the hotel balconies. On the opposite side of the pool, fifteen SASFB troops ganged the entrance, trying to keep hidden behind the décor of umbrellas and greenery.

She sat motionless where thick shrubbery behind her separated where she was from a pathway that led around the back end of the pool. The SASFB had taken position behind her and their radios could be heard reporting the approach of a *different* unit about to make contact in the penthouse to engage the *other* woman.

Also under her towel was her gun, which she gradually used her foot to maneuver closer to her hands.

It was a good thing she had her bible. All she could do was *pray* that the training she hammered into Trigger on how to evade professional SWAT teams actually *stuck*.

Today, Trigger was going to be put to the test.

Chapter 3

Cape Grace Hotel – Penthouse

The SASFB entered through the penthouse doors, two-man groups of six—silently reporting the all clear throughout the penthouse with fists and hand signals. Black masks accented the seriousness of their skill; punctuated with rifles intended to bring down anyone in their path.

They searched the dining room, bedrooms, lounge, all three terraces, bathrooms, cupboards and every available closet.

Nothing.

The penthouse was now full of baffled Special Forces soldiers. Where was the target?

That's when gunfire erupted outside.

Radios claimed they had made contact with the brown-haired woman by the pool; she had already taken out six of their men and they were attempting to pin her down.

While the soldiers in the penthouse rushed onto the terrace to either watch or assist their fellow men, above the foyer, Trigger removed the air vent grating she had hidden in and slid down silently to the floor—making her first mistake during evasion: She didn't wait until she was 100% positive the enemy had left the scene.

Two SASFB riflemen posted outside of the penthouse saw her immediately. Using her foot to slam the door, she shut herself inside, creating her second mistake of evasion: Never block your only escape route.

She locked the door, but she knew it wouldn't be long before the SASFB soldiers communicated what was going on.

So, she was going to have to be creative.

Carelessly, the SASFB soldiers left packs of tear gas and grenades within Trigger's reach. Just as the soldiers started blasting through the front door, calling attention to the others on the terrace, Trigger started pulling pins randomly and throwing everything she had toward the Terrace. Smoke started flying and so did the soldiers; each exclaiming the same thing: *Grenades!*

Trigger—no fool—jumped back up and took cover in the air conditioning vent.

Kasey was doing considerably well with her back against a stairwell and bullets chewing up the décor all around her. A number of dead bodies piled at her feet—stupid SASFB that thought they would be heroes—and served as a warning to those who didn't want to die by the hands of this woman. This put a severe dent in her *life-mattered*, spiritual quest for answers.

Boom! Boom! Boom! The gunfire came to an sudden stop. Something was going on above at the penthouse. Multiple explosions weakened the penthouse terrace, added by the weight of the SASFB standing on it and down it came—soldiers and all—in pancake fashion one terrace down to the other; wrecking one of the most expensive hotels in South Africa.

Mass destruction.

Undeniable evidence that Butta' and her crew are in town, for sure.

If this was Trigger's doing, Kasey hoped she survived it to congratulate her on a job well done.

This also gave Kasey the distraction she needed.

A SASFB soldier too close to Kasey and looking at the damage in awe would be her shield. She slipped around him, bending him awkwardly with a headlock with one arm while taking up his rifle with the other.

Avoiding the pool, Kasey came out shooting, clearing a path and deflecting potential death with the Kevlar plated soldier as her shield. It was only after a fatal shot to his head did the word go out for the rest of them to hold their fire.

Dumping the dead body, and drenched in blood not of her own, Kasey jumped over a hedge, scooped up another rifle and cleared more SASFB out of her way, making a dash for the parking lot. She didn't want to leave Trigger, but they had planning for times like these—basically called *CYA- Cover Your Ass.*

Trigger crawled through the vent to the next room, falling out to a room full of guests cowering from the ruckus.

Excusing herself, she peeked out the entrance to see the rest of the SASFB finally ganging into her room. Once the coast was clear, it was time to go.

But go where?

What was the plan again? If they were to get separated, meet where? When? Eighteen-year-old confusion was getting the better of her and Trigger started to panic.

Where was Butta' when she needed her?

Depository – Sub-Basement Garage Level 6

Butta', Munch and Fuego hid in the garage which was taken over by teams of the SASFB who made it clear the thieves would not be leaving alive.

Alarms were going off on every level and the intrepid threesome were stuck six floors below the surface attempting to either make their way up or find what they came here for.

"Still can't reach Trig or Kasey," Butta' complained, putting away her phone, breathing hard behind some crates. Across from their position, a six-story inclined ramp leading to daylight far up to the surface.

"Unless we're using landlines, we've got to get at least another five flights up for reception." Munch was out of breath, as usual. He would admit, he lost a significant amount of weight since he met Butta', but not enough for this kind of action.

Nervous eating put on just as much as he burned off, as well.

"Munchie, you and Fuego find some transport and start up the ramp in five minutes. Once you guys get a signal, get a hold of Kasey and Trig."

"And where do you think you're going?"

Butta' was tying her hair back to a stronger pony-tail; a clear indication that things were about to get dicey. "Get *my* diamond back."

Munch grabbed her by the arm; not a common act between them at all. Looking down at his hand on her, she then looked up at her old friend in askance. "Do you disagree?"

"At what point do we call this *finished*?"

"When it's over!"

"When *exactly* is this over?" He demanded.

She shook his hand free of her. "What's wrong with you?"

"We're in the middle of freakin' South Africa with, like, the whole damn militia mobilizing to put a cap up our asses and let's not forget the bounty we have on our heads. All this for one pointless rock! *Just* to satisfy a vendetta that was finished when you buried Stein days ago."

The cards were on the table in the least likely of places by the least likely of people. If it were any other person, she would never afford them an explanation for her obsession.

Was all this an obsession? She considered that ideal for the fastest of moments. *What if it was? Did her fanatical desires need to be clarified to anyone?*

Didn't she owe that much to the *only* family she has had?

She stared at Munch with a mix of feelings. One part *step the hell off*—one part *don't make me offend you* and another part *I thought you would understand me*—all wrapped up into one frustrated ball of conflicted fires.

In the end, all she could say was: "I didn't kill that man."

Fortunately, she had a reprieve from her divergence of the conscience.

Three men with German symbols on their uniform, guarded by eight SASFB soldiers waving their weapons from side to side defensively, arrived from a freight elevator carrying a rather large black satin cube.

"Gehen Sie! Gehen Sie!" *Go! Go!*—said a German-speaking driver, ushering the satin cube and the men guarding it, to the back of a military troop carrier.

Making sure her gun was cocked and loaded with new ammunition, Butta' grimaced at Munch, pointing at the truck. "I'm getting *my* diamond!"

She skirted around the troop carrier, hiding behind other vehicles to avoid detection and readied herself to cling to the vehicle. Fuego made a move to join her, stopped by Munch. Munch's hand would have been broken in sixteen places—and he knew this, backing off Fuego quickly.

" Ellá esta loca. Nada la parará?" Fuego asked.

"No estoy segura." *I'm not sure,* Munch replied.

Munch thought about Fuego's question: *Will nothing stop her?* He had no concrete answer to give him.

Corey A. Burkes

Chapter 4

Cape Grace Hotel - Stairwell

This was new for Trigger. Though she had been baptized into this *kind* of action before, this was the first time she had to do it alone. If she could only hook up with Kasey—provided she wasn't dead—then she can go back to letting the elders of the group lead her around.

She had the wits enough to know that getting far away from the hotel was paramount while all of the South African police were coming to this location from far and wide.

To her advantage, SASFB troops were making their way up the opposite side of the building and elevators, attempting to lock down the situation while dodging around nervous and screaming hotel guests. Trigger blended into the crowd, all the way out the side doors and into the parking lot where the panic scene ensued.

SASFB brought in massive SWAT vehicles, dumping soldiers by the hundreds. This was the problem with being the most *wanted* people on Earth: everyone wanted a piece of the bounty which Stein Industries recently sweetened to fifteen million-a-piece—*dead*.

Gunfire erupted in the center of the parking lot. A mini-war zone had taken place and all guns were trained on a nimble bombshell in a bikini making a mockery of the elite soldiers. Bodies were being left in Kasey's wake, but even she knew her time was running out.

The hardest loss, thus far, had to have been her bible. In the middle of an all-out assault, flanking to gun her down, her thoughts were on that little bible she picked up at the duty free shop.

When her gun jammed, that signaled the last of her escape run and her thoughts biblically were well placed. Just as she was wondering if God would truly forgive her—there was a response.

A car raced past her and plowed into approaching soldiers, scattering them.

A few would not survive the 90% burns they received.

Before they could regroup, another vehicle burst into flames; a *Molotov Cocktailed Ford F-350.*

Trigger finally figured out the last rule of evasion: leave the pursuers in confusion. She jammed the gas pedal to a number of vehicles, lit them on fire with sent them careening into anything that moved.

Once much of the troops were sufficiently held back from Kasey, Trigger skidded next to her on a hotel guest's candy-apple red Honda CBR600RR Super Bike; kicking dirt up on Kasey and her skimpy beach wear.

Kasey was *full* of gratitude. "Thanks! Say, you wouldn't happen to have something I could—?"

Trigger flopped a pair of slacks and tank top onto her lap. Not the most stylish outfit she could find, but this was an escape and *not* a fashion show.

By the time the police got around the wall of fire separating them, Trigger and Kasey were plowing through their numbers at top speed. Handling a motorcycle was one of Trigger's underserved joys. Her passion for a good, solid bike rivaled her impeccable aim; thus her choice of the 600cc liquid-cooled inline four-cylinder designed for racing was deliberate in order for them to not only escape the assault, but to literally *vanish* at top speed.

The way from the hotel was straight against the Victoria and Alfred Waterfront; cleared by the police and SASFB for their advancing troops. Trigger took full advantage of the lack of traffic and opened up the throttle; launching them into a relative *hyperspace*. Kasey had to hug close to Trigger in order to stay aboard the small passenger seating on the rear.

From far behind, the SASFB were already mobilizing to pursue; aided by two approaching Denel AH-2 Rooivalk Gunships—South African Air Force attack helicopters coming from the north.

Kasey *really* hoped Butta', Munch and Fuego fared better because this operation fell apart before it began.

Depository – Sub-Basement Garage Ramp

The Stein Depository was one of the last havens of the older Stein regime to be dismantled by joint international investigators. Employees had been dispersed; diamond vaults were cleared and confiscated. For the most part, the depository had a skeleton crew with paid assistance by the SASFB.

Butta' was aware of all of this. As improbable as it seemed to take a small crew into the vault—she wasn't stupid. The art of thievery was to sneak about when security was at its weakest.

If the depository was at maximum security, full of employed and trained security personnel, Butta's failed break-in would have been a fatal disaster.

Not that this was any better. Now, her situation was only a *hot mess*.

At the time Trigger was laying waste to the balconies of the Cape Grace Hotel, a German-driven troop cargo truck held the last Stein diamond and Butta' was holding onto the underneath, inches from the road, as it climbed the ramp to the surface.

A skateboarders dream, the ramp was built to allow major vehicles down to the sub-basement vaults without interference. At full operation, every quarter mile stationed armed soldiers and cameras. All of which were gone, with wires sticking out, cameras missing and trash tarnishing the once professionally equipped empire.

Butta' hoped her count of the men inside of the truck was right; eleven bodies to deal with, including the two in the drivers compartment.

She had been holding on for almost half the trip and her partners weren't in sight. Not to mention her *Plan C* were still unable to be contacted. For all she knew, Butta' may have been the last woman standing.

She decided she might as well go *all out* and finish this—as Munch would have wanted her to.

She was being sarcastic. Munch *really* would have told her to *release, let go* and *go home*.

Not.

Hand over hand, Butta' made her move from under the truck, along the side of the camouflaged cover and clung to the top. Fifty-five miles per hour wind whipped at her hair. A speck of daylight could be seen far ahead. They were almost out of the tunnel where *who knew what* waited for her out in the open.

So if she wanted that diamond, she needed to take it now.

She unsheathed a knife and closed her eyes, taking a few deep breaths. Preparing herself, she then stabbed it through the roof of the truck, slicing a thick gash wide open.

She followed that move by tossing a smoke grenade into the cargo hold and flipped herself to the top of the front cab before they started shooting holes up at her.

The troop carrier clouded with a thick grey smoke. All occupants in the cargo hold ganged to the rear opening to get air and made themselves easier targets. Butta' secured her hair again and hopped back across the roof of the truck. Feet first, she propelled herself into the truck, hard kicking a set of men gasping for air.

Now, the fight was on—and the timer had started counting. While holding her breath, Butta' had to do the following:

10-seconds ... Nine strong, strapping soldiers were doubled over and handicapped by the smoke canister. Visibility was *nil* and Butta' started throwing anyone in hands reach out of the back of the truck. Two were tossed and they would be in pain for the next few weeks. Seven more to go. Two more in the front cab driving this thing.

15-seconds ... Someone blindly found his arms around Butta's neck, making thing difficult for her. The soldier was barely able to breath, but he knew he caught the prize of the day and found the military endurance to gradually put Butta' in the infamous *sleeper-hold*. She didn't have the arm strength to free herself. Her lungs were burning for air.

30-seconds ... Using a body in front of her as leverage, she shoved the offending soldier, and herself, back against the truck's cloth wall. The already torn material widened from the top; throwing them both off the side of a moving vehicle.

Bang! She and the soldier landed on the roof of a jeep breaking their fall. The jeep was driven by Munch—shotgun by Fuego.

Even the wayward soldier was appreciative of the unexpected rescue, grinning gratefully at Fuego. Smiling back, Fuego reached over the jeeps window and gripped the soldier by the nose. The old saying, *where the head goes, the body follows*, was proven true as Fuego flicked the soldier off the vehicle, nose first.

Butta' slid between her partners, taking up anything she can get her hands on, shoving a .45 handgun in the rear of her pants.

"You got the diamond?" Munch already knew the answer before he asked.

"I will in a minute," she replied, taking up a nasty .50 caliber M2 machine gun and propped it on a pedestal on the rear of the jeep.

The driver of the truck had been keeping an extra eye on the side view mirror, witnessing everything. His mouth dropped when he saw Butta' setting up the weapon and he spun the wheel wildly.

The remaining men on the cargo truck lurched left, almost toppling out the rear. While the smoke was faded, it gave them a clear view of Butta'—locked and loaded.

Fifty caliber bullets were made for long range snipers to strike people, tanks and even jets with deadly accuracy since the early world wars. Strung together on long belts, the ammo tip-to-tip were five-inches in length, while the bullet itself is a little over two-inches.

A little over two-inches of death ripped through the cargo truck, shredding the covering and forced the soldiers to dive out of the truck to save their lives.

Static blared from the jeep's on-board radio with a great deal of conversation in German. Not a language Munch specialized in, but he could pick out a word or two. "Road block ahead! They got reinforcements!"

"Fuego!" Butta' pointed at the front cab of the truck and, without knowing a stitch of English, was on the move. He jumped across and made his way against the moving vehicle to attack the driver and passenger.

Meanwhile, Butta' went to work on the core of this reckless adventure, jumping across and landing into the cargo hold to find her prize. She thought the truck was cleared of soldiers. Instead, she found a 6'8 muscular soldier with a densely dark complexion, de-cloaking out a pile of body armor vests—tightly *footballing* the black velvet box under his arm.

"*Gekommen.*" He realized she may not have understood him, gesturing with his hands. "*Come.* Ya?"

"You gonna give it to me?" She asked.

He laughed at her.

In his mind, this dialogue would have been the prelude to a long sweaty night with this gorgeous woman.

Butta' made no pretense about the situation and whipped out her .45 to blast this huge man into an immediate death. He swatted the gun out of her hand, but not before catching a shot to his shoulder.

It still wasn't enough to stop him. He dropped the velvet box behind him and was all over her.

Fuego was having trouble getting into the front cab of the truck. No matter what they show in the movies, breaking a window with a fist—particularly military grade shatter-proof glass—wasn't easy or *recommended*. The most he could do is snatch at the unlocked passengers side door and struggle with the occupant to pull him out.

Both driver and the passenger were yelling in German. Fuego was growling back in Spanish. Very little was being accomplished in this mortal tug of war until the driver revealed his Heckler & Koch .45 Tactical handgun and tried to put a bead on Fuego from behind his partner.

Fuego purposely swung on the door; one hand on the passenger and a foot on his neck, avoiding the guns nozzle. Finally, the driver had to take a shot, firing twice. The first one missed entirely. The second put a hole through the back of his partners head, blowing skull, brain fragments and blood onto Fuego.

Very nasty—very unsettling, for both the driver and Fuego, but Fuego recovered faster. He swung himself into the truck feet first and literally power dived into the driver, bursting him out on the driver's side of the truck and into the path of Munch's jeep.

Munch and the Jeep pitched about over the body. Not far ahead, the exit to the tunnel and full squad of soldiers waiting to stop them with MP vehicles blocking their way.

"*¿A donde esta Buttá?*" *Where's Butta'?* Fuego yelled, driving poorly

"*Ella tiene problemas!* Stop the truck!" Munch pointed.

"*No!*" Butta' responded in a deadly wrestling match with the last soldier. "*Keep ... moving!*"

Fuego only had time to look back once, then ahead to the road block and made the decision for himself—flooring the accelerator.

Munch spun the wheel and lined himself up with the rear of the truck, helplessly watching a very large man beat up on his friend.

Trigger sped with breakneck speeds to avoid not one, *but two* military helicopters hot on their trail plus a fleet of SASFB Military Police vehicles with sirens blaring.

They were way over their heads this time. They didn't know the terrain, and to say the least, didn't know the status of their friends. Trigger took it upon herself to do whatever she could to lose her pursuers , even if it meant scaring the hell out of Kasey.

Trigger took them off the main road and toward what looked like shipping yards against the wharf. To get to the dry docked ships, she first had to be creative and get through the open entrance of a warehouse.

That ought to confuse the helicopters.

But not the police cars, hunting them down right after her. Workers within the warehouse jumped and ran out of the way while MP vehicles splintered crates and machinery. Wood and supplies went flying.

Trigger's bike deftly dodged around obstacles and out a back door with their pursuers relentless on them, crashing through the walls in order to catch up.

The chase continued past old ships no longer commissioned for the sea; long defunct cargo cruisers and broken shipping boats lined up against each other, waiting to be dismantled. Trigger throttled up and found another clearing to put more space between them and the SASFB, entering major roadway that flowed through Downtown Cape Town.

Full of mid-day traffic.

Thoom! Crash! Some other action was going on and it wasn't coming from behind, but further back near another building. So many ruckuses, the MP's had to stop and look, giving Trigger and Kasey a moment of amnesty from the chase.

A bullet riddled military cargo truck had busted through a blockade and sent soldiers in its way hundreds of feet in the air. The truck was closely followed by a jeep driven by a heavy, sweating and glasses wearing black man.

Trigger came to a dead stop.

"Munchie!" Trigger shrieked. He couldn't hear her if he tried. He was preoccupied with his own pursuit situation. Both vehicles roared past them and into the main road.

A familiar face was being flung about like a rag doll in the back of the truck, going toe-to-toe with someone twice her size.

"You see that?!" Kasey checked her handgun, cocking it.

"You'd better hang your *ass* on," Trigger replied. The 600cc rocket they sat on snapped back to life, crackling the air with its intensity. Trigger spun the motorcycle around—popped a wheelie—and bolted after her friends reaching speeds only for the fearless.

Fuego use to drive trucks like these throughout the mountains of Sierra Madre del Sur, in his birth home of Mexico; delivering workers to and from the hidden fields and to clandestine pickups to make ends meet for his family. Martial arts were the only sensible weapon he could study, as hand-to-hand combat was a necessity.

Driving this cargo truck without restrictions on speed and precarious cliffs to navigate was a change for the better. He opened it up and let the LDS-427 Turbo Multi-fuel flow at its top speed of *55-miles* per hour. At any speed, it was a 13,500 lb. vehicular weapon driven by a man desperate to escape two helicopters and half the fleet of South African police and Special Forces.

Followed by a jeep—chased by a motorcycle.

Butta' knew the soldier she was squaring off with was toying with her. If she were a man, he would have been trying to bash her head in viciously. He was far taller, stronger and muscular than she was. Without a weapon to balance the playing field, they were unevenly matched.

So, instead of trying to beat him at *his* winning game, Butta' tried to use the erratic motion of the vehicle against him in order to reach for the satin box at his feet. The truck lurched about and jerked left and right making it hard to gain the upper hand for either of them.

As beautiful and open-aired as Cape Town was, the people of South Africa were no strangers to traffic congestion in the second largest city in South Africa. Various major roads (with names N1, N2, N7, M3 and so forth) crisscross beneath the stretches of blue sky; thoroughfares to prime hubs and towns—and here came Fuego smashing through cars moving too slow and jumping onto road shoulders; uprooting trees and shrubbery dividing the highways.

South African motorists desperately gave a wide berth for the high speed pursuit. Some were too late and found themselves hugging the walls or skidding out of control into other oncoming traffic. The Department of Transportation would need approximately nine months to a year to clean up this mess.

The truck bounced both of its passengers up into the air and tossed them about haphazardly. Eventually, Butta' found herself on the floor and the velvet diamond box landing on her lap. The German muscle man fell to the opposite end of the truck, realizing he no longer had the diamond in his possession—scrambling to get to his feet desperately.

Butta' gripped the box like she was *Emmitt Smith* on the last quarter of the Super Bowl, gathered all her strength and then pulled herself up to the roof. It didn't matter where she went as long as she was out of reach of the German soldier.

He was already snatching at her legs. He conveniently ran a hand down her inner thigh for extra emphasis.

He had a job to do, but he was a man first.

Butta' kicked his jaw—offended by the unnecessary stroking—leaving a boot imprint across his face, but he still didn't let go of her.

Fuego spun the wheel and decided that it was time to get off the main highway and through an embankment that would take them into the main populace. He needed to shake some of the pursuers off; what better way than to test their nerves by chasing into where the people are.

Kasey and Trigger didn't expect that sudden turn and kept going straight. Far out into the distance, another 10 miles and into the ocean was where Louie told them to make their escape. Something only Kasey was aware of. "Trig! We got to catch up with them! We have an escape route and they're going the wrong way."

"An actual escape plan?!? That's new. Hang on."

A set of SASFB cars kept up the chase behind them, swerving out of the way when Trigger suddenly stopped and skidded sideways to change direction. High-speed, really close games of chicken were Trigger's specialty. While the pursuers were trying to save their own skins, Trigger already plotted her course around them—adjusting for probabilities—and bounded after her friends in a feat of motorcycle handling that will be remembered by South African Special Forces for decades to come.

The fact that the cycle was driven by a *Black woman* would add more to her legend.

Chapter 5

Munch was holding his own, keeping as close to the truck as possible. The helicopters above managed to keep pace with them, regardless of the path of destruction Fuego put them through. He only had a moment to glance back and see Trigger make that sharp turn off the highway. Not *too* concerned, he knew how well she could handle a bike, but this was a deadlier circumstance. Off in the distance, he was comforted by hearing the distinct crackle of the cycle engines attempting to catch up.

His primary concern was Butta' on the back of the truck. He tried his best to stay within range of the truck so she can make an escape, but only found himself dodging traffic and swerving out of the way of people.

Butta' fell back into the truck to duke it out with the larger soldier and just when things couldn't look any worse, Fuego took the truck into a 90-degree turn, lifting the truck onto two wheels and scaring pedestrians as their heads are skimmed by the roof of the truck. Back on track, the truck fell back onto all fours and off into the city.

Munch had a more capable jeep to handle such a turn, but the pursuing SASFB didn't; either slamming into the buildings, into people or swerving out of control helplessly. The *best of the best* had never had to conduct a high speed chase in tight urban environments.

There just wasn't any budgeted training for this kind of thing.

Right behind all of them came Trigger and Kasey; threading a tight needle into the turn, around busted and overturned cars and in pursuit of their friends. Above them, the twin helicopters tried to navigate the buildings and avoid crashing into themselves and architecture.

Fuego's plan to scrape off excess pursuit seemed to be working and he yearned for open environments. By the time he hit Adderley Street, he wagered that he would likely find more open land toward the ocean and pointed himself toward what looked like a town circle.

The local constables, not wishing to seem out of step in their own jurisdiction, picked up where the elite SASFB failed and were coming to cut his trajectory off with a small set of police cars blaring ahead.

Fuego bent into the town circle and zipped up Strand Road, tearing through narrow streets against the side of a major office building and around the rear toward a park.

Birds were chirping and lovers were walking peacefully hand-in-hand. The beautiful South African skies bathed the park with a warm embrace.

Then all hell broke loose.

Fuego and his truck busted through park benches and picnickers who found sudden abilities to get out of the way with single leaps. Munch kept up the rear, followed by Trigger and Kasey and finally a fleet of police and SASFB, reaching speeds uncommon for a *no vehicles allowed* Public Park.

The helicopters decided to take a more direct approach to the chase.

One of them found open air and flew around to the side of the truck and disregarded the safety of the South African populace.

The Rooivalk Gunships carry F2 20-milimeter weapons, or 'cannons', at the front and underbelly of the cockpit; each with a payload of 700 rounds. The lead helicopter's front weapon began its initial spin, and in an instant, 300 rounds lit up the street and parts of the truck mercilessly.

Fuego prayed the trucks cabin was as bullet proof as it needed to be, ducking anyway as death sliced up the air around him, blasting out windows and much of the cabin.

In the truck itself, the German soldier took to protecting himself behind three vests of Kevlar and Butta' did the same, dropping the diamond. The cloth housing the truck *liquefied* from the damage; leaving the truck wide open and bare. Tires blew out and Fuego drove on rims—refusing to be stopped.

Munch avoided getting struck, hitting the brakes to get under the helicopter. The second helicopter, not looking to be out done, flanked Fuego's truck and fired two Mokopa ZT-6 anti-tank guided missiles to finish the job.

Thankfully, Fuego saw this coming and swerved behind an oncoming bus in traffic. The bus vaporized into the loudest explosion this side of South Africa had ever heard.

The close explosion sent fragments like an oversized grenade, engulfing one of the two helicopters and it didn't have a chance. While one of the copters managed to lift higher, the other spun into the crowded streets and exploded on impact.

Fuego needed kept his damaged truck moving, digging the streets with the rubber-less rims. The only thing in front of him was the Cape Town Railway Station and a loaded parking lot.

People were going to be very late for work.

The South African Railway Station was as cross between grand Central Station and the vastness of an airport. It was the main hub in the middle of Cape Town and the first stop for those looking to travel to the rest of Africa. This is a very busy location of people and transportation coming and going twenty-four hours a day.

The smoking and bullet damaged truck crashed through the central entrance; people scattered with the least amount of expectation of any destruction in their commute.

The truck came to a halt a few feet past the wrecked entrance. Steam came from bullet holes in the engine and front cabin.

Fuego, a very happy Mexican, sat back and kissed a cross he had dangling around his neck—thanking the Lord for yet another day of life.

First out of the truck was the German soldier; velvet cube under his arm and a Sauer 38H pistol in the other. He pointed the nozzle into the truck, expecting Butta' to be right after him.

He was right.

She poked her head out to chase after him, dodging a bullet to the head.

Fuego kicked his way out of the front cabin and in one fluent move—struck the German soldier, knocking away his gun. Fuego landed in front of the big man and used every possible punch and kick he could to bring the soldier down, but his opponent's arms and chest were thick as tree trunks. It was like beating into an oak tree.

The soldier saw that the little Spanish man definitely had skills, and would likely start going for his knees if he couldn't use strength.

Needing a free hand, the soldier slid the velvet box behind him to defend his knees and legs from Fuego's lightning fast attack.

Just the time Butta' needed to jump out of the truck and make her move for the box—

—Scooped up by a Railway Station Officer who happened to be at the wrong place at the wrong time. Clearly unaware of the big deal behind the box, he prepared to blow his whistle and order the brawl to a stop when Butta' came up on him with a no nonsense expression, *pimp slapping* him coldly with the back of her hand.

He fell back—losing the box—

—Snatched by the German soldier who then used Butta' as a shield between him and Fuego who was putting his weight into the next punch. Panicking, Fuego redirected a blow meant for the soldier before it could hit Butta'. The air snapped next to Butta's head from the impact that *would have* finished her if he had connected.

The German soldier wanted no part of this confrontation anymore and ran into the station with the velvet box just as Munch, Trigger and Kasey rode into the station.

Munch honked the horn, pulling up to Butta' and Fuego. "Are you guys okay? We gotta get outta here! They're cutting off our backend!"

"He got the diamond," Butta' blurted out breathlessly, rummaging around the back of the jeep, loading up with two .45's in each hand and another in the back of her pants.

"Good! Let him have it!" Munch responded.

"We're not having *this* conversation right now." Butta' ensured the weapons had enough bullets—*locked and loaded*—and she ran after her intended target. "Fuego! Vaminous!"

That was just about all the Spanish she knew and needed. Fuego asked no questions and ran after her, ready to pick up the hunt.

"Butta'! We're gonna die up in here for your *stupid* ass diamond!" Munch yelled after her.

"*Not now!*" She yelled back, now in full tilt dash after the soldier.

Kasey jumped off Trigger's bike, shoring up her disheveled clothing. Being a passenger on a high speed chase can make one a mess and for Kasey, that just wouldn't do. "Munch! What the hell?"

"That's *your* friend. You talk to her cause she's out her damn mind."

Chapter 6

The soldier ran like his life depended on it—because it did.

He was not of the South African Special Forces Brigade. He wasn't a local cop. He was on assignment to bring the *Stein Diandra Diamond* from Point A to Point B. He had lost his backup, he had no connection with his country and the SASFB did not care if he was in the way or not.

He could be killed and it would not matter to anyone.

On his side was a *bargaining chip* that both kept him alive and kept the heat on him. One thing he was certain, the *hot chick* was relentless and he would not put it past her to be within striking range any minute now.

He navigated his way through a sea of distressed passengers who saw the action in the station and were doing everything they could to get out of the way. A train was heading out of the station right that instance; his perfect getaway without delay. Announcements for the departing Shosholoza Meyl (*a long distance train service*) to Johannesburg echoed above him. He would get onboard, utilize his official credentials and likely get a sleeper car to rest until he can arrive at the Johannesburg German Embassy—diamond in hand.

But as they say of *the best laid plans of mice and men*.

Butta' arrived onto the main boarding station with guns in hand, scaring the people out of her way. The visual was as frightening as it was strikingly sexy. Scarred and bruised—chest heaving and two black guns in both hands—Butta' was both feared *and* wanted.

The noise alerted the soldier just when his train pulled from the station; gathering up speed incrementally. He cursed his height and build, standing out like a sore thumb.

Fuego launched after him like an attack dog with Butta' bringing up the rear. The soldier had no interest in round two with the Mexican and ran for the back of the departing train. As tired as he was, he ran *thighs up* for the back of the train and snagged the rear of it as the passenger car caught its stride and sped into South African territory.

Fuego was already exhausted from the drive and fighting, stomped to a dead stop at the end of the platform—hands on his knees and out of breath. Today was a lot for the little man—

—But not for Butta', dashing past Fuego with a mission above and beyond a simple matter of catching a man or a train. She gathered deep amounts of energy and pursued the train off the platform and along the tracks; regardless of how far and fast the train was moving.

The soldier knew she was way out of range and smiled; waving at the beautiful, yet angry woman—entering the car with no further thoughts of her.

The idea that she came this far to lose the prize ate at her tremendously. Her only chance at redeeming this whole mission: another train was rolling and within reach, going the same direction as her pursuit.

Still in motion, Butta' ran against the side of the second train. Each car had sufficient space between them for just about anyone crazy enough to jump aboard. The history books were filled with people being crushed between the cars or falling to the tracks.

Climbing aboard, Butta' would only hope her suspicions were right about how trains operate leaving stations. Otherwise, this was going to be a free ride to inner Africa.

Back on the platform, another melee caught Fuego's attention. On the far end of the platform, closer to the entrance, people scattered from the gunshots.

His friends have finally arrived.

Munch had driven the jeep through the stations wide passageways, normally utilized by passengers or the stations sanitation or supply vehicles. The jeep tore up flooring and screeched onto the platform tossing people and baggage. While Fuego waved them down at the far end of the station, Trigger arrived shortly behind with another squad of police officers shooting at them.

Munch found open space to drive and put the pedal to the floor to catch up with Fuego. Both jeep and cycle raced top speed to the end of the platform, slowing just enough to put Fuego on the back. Trigger released the cycle over into the tracks so she can board the jeep as well.

That was where the chase by the police came to an end.

Someone radioed for the Rooivalk Gunships to resume aerial pursuit and they were more than happy to do so.

The Shosholoza Meyl line had a collection of trains: luxury-class, economy and sleepers. All of which were designed to travel along the Spoornet, the South African main line.

The soldier was fortunate to escape onto one of the luxury cars while Butta' was on the *sleeper train*; moving alongside each other.

While both trains picked up speed; carefully traversing the web of tracks and signal changes, Butta' watched like a hawk for the soldier in the train across from her. He was busily passing between passengers to camouflage himself. She squinted to keep track of the man, reminding herself that she may have to look into some sort of glasses sooner or later.

She stopped between cars, staring out to her target. Her plan was based on knowing all trains all over the world, when leaving a station at the same time, tended to swerve closer to each other just prior to departing to their destinations. As that reality came to pass, Butta' had about a six-foot leap to consider.

The trains were not moving as close as she needed them to be.

That was when she saw her friends.

Her *loyal* friends—chased by an attacking helicopter—dodging certain death while trying to keep up with the train.

All of this just for her and her obsessed plans.

Anyone else on this madcap adventure would have left her long ago. They risked their lives for the sake of her fixation of a diamond that she surmised was rightfully hers.

While the wind whipped at her hair during her pause, she watched the soldier, safe

between standing passengers, eyeing her cautiously to see what she planned to do.

Munch had steered the jeep under the gunship to avoid getting shot, but even the most militarized vehicle would eventually run out of gas. When the warning light came on, he couldn't help but laugh at the irony—that a dose of reality such as *low fuel* would be the perfect ending to a *bad day.*

Someone took two shots at the helicopter, bouncing off with no more than a scratch to the protective shell. The very fact that someone would shoot at the copter forced the pilot to realign his focus at a tall Black woman on the back of a train, waving her gun in the air.

The pilot turned the gunships payload away from the jeep and aimed for the rear of the train. For the sake of killing the one woman, the pilot was comfortable with a percentage of collateral loss of life if he pulled the trigger; maybe 20-30 deaths with another fifty or so wounded.

The problem was he took his eyes off the jeep and its passengers.

The vehicle still sported its M2 machine gun and Trigger performed very little targeting and let loose the weapon's .50 caliber bullets at all of the gunships sore points: the underbelly, the missile armament and the blades.

The helicopter lost control and tilted away from the train and into the station's train yards, slamming into parked passenger sleepers and cargo cars—a mass of flame and metal followed by a bright explosion.

Munch caught up to the train to let Butta' jump onto the hood, sitting in the rear next to Fuego. Trigger kneeled next to her big sister and kissed her cheek without saying much more.

No one had much to say for a mission that, essentially, *failed.*

"Um," Munch cleared the uncomfortable silence, "Kase? You mentioned something about a way out of Cape Town?"

Kasey was annoyed and in her own thoughts. "Hmm? Oh, yeah. Louie. He's on a yacht. North-west of the city."

"We'll need to dump the jeep." Munch looked at Butta' who was not in a talking mood. "We'll need to lie low a little so we can get out to sea."

Butta' held herself, sitting back in her seat.

Las Vegas, Nevada – 9:39am
At the exact time Kasey and Trigger started pursuing Munch and Fuego across the highways of South Africa on a very fast motorcycle, a taxi arrived in front of the Wynn Hotel's curved and shining casino glory.

Attendants moved swiftly to retrieve baggage from the cab, welcoming the guests to the Wynn with all smiles.

Inspector Ellen Cobart—born, raised and worked New York's inner streets for years, was not use to all this *'steppin' fetchin'*; finding she wasted less time by carrying her own bags, no matter how much the valets insisted. Plus, being from New York, she didn't trust anyone disappearing with her luggage anyway. She was unaccustomed to the Nevada heat and her armpits sweltered with wet patches and she desperately needed a shower.

Her partner, Detective Frank Tulley—no stranger to Vegas by any means—flew into the adult paradise already dressed for the weather and a pocket bloated with money for the occasion. If it weren't for his NYPD badge sticking out of his pants, he'd look like any of the other yokels about to lose their shirt—and love it. *"Vegas, baby*! Somebody point me to the tables. Let's get this party started!"

Ellen ignored Frank entirely in order to stay focused, approaching an ultra-eager hotel attendant. "We're guests of Diandra Stein."

"Everything has been taken care of for you. You must be Mrs. Ellen Cobart with your husband, Mr. Frank Cobart?"

"*NO!* We're not married. If we were, we'd be looking at a *divorce* right about now."

Frank stuck his tongue at her, digging in his pocket to tip the attendants carting his baggage. Ellen managed to pack all she needed into a stealthy rolling carry-on bag—avoiding extra baggage fee's—while her partner might as well have brought his entire closet in three different sets of luggage. *He's worse than a woman*, she thought.

"My apologies, Ms. Cobart. All preparations have been provided for you and your friend. If you would follow me, please, to your villa."

"*Villa?*" Frank heard that from the other side of the taxi. "We got a Wynn Villa?!?"

"What's this *Villa?*" Ellen asked. "We're only staying for a night."

The attendant smirked. "For any *one* moment at the Wynn, Ms. Stein would like you to stay in *style*. Please, this way."

Inspector Ellen—upgraded from detective to a special, international investigator—was never comfortable with people doing things for her. The posh and general *butt-wiping* that she and Frank received made her uptight. They came a long way by request of a *very* rich woman and Ellen just wanted to get on with the reason why they were there.

Particularly, when the woman that summed them, was the daughter of the man she watched *die*.

Well, '*watched*' was not the exact word term. More like '*heard*'. Not seeing things for her own eyes left a question mark hanging in Ellen's ever suspicious mind. However, in this case, she was good with the facts as they were and would swear on a stack of bibles that the bastard, Lingo Stein, was dead.

The bastard's daughter, Diandra Stein, heiress to the Stein family's crumbling fortune and caretaker of international scandal, had a lot thrown on her shoulders in a matter of days.

More weight than anyone on Earth would need to manage. One day, living the high life of sports cars, expensive purchases with the world in her palm—the next, the *scourge* of the diamond trade with people looking to collect—with an additional bonus of being the daughter of a *white supremacy* leader.

Sucked to be her, Ellen snorted, not feeling *too* bad. She did feel a little *something* for the poor rich girl. Over the phone, she seemed *genuinely* unaware of her father's racist dark side.

Ellen witnessed that dark side first hand and he paid the price for such unrepentant *hate*. Ellen's frame of mind, when being invited by *these* people for a meeting, was based on her experience with them. She was guarded and untrusting with a dash of sympathy.

Just a *dash*.

The Wynn Hotel Fairway Apartment on the mezzanine of the hotel separated the senses from the common distractions of a Las Vegas casino to a world of its own. Overlooking a beautiful green golf course of *fantasy* proportions, the two-bedroom, terrace with private pool, massage room, seventy-two inch plasma HDTV, one-level *mansion* of dark cherry wood floors at $2,000 a night screamed heaven the moment Ellen walked through the door.

As for her partner—

"Look at that TV! *Holy shit* on the *Sabbath*! *El!* We're watchin' the game front *f'n* center! *Oh my god!* We got a fridge up in here *too*!?!"

Ellen sighed tiredly, addressing the attendant. "Please forgive my friend. He just got off the boat from the country of *Bumscrew*. Technology is new to him."

The hotel attendant smiled and backed her way out the room as the other hotel staff completed dropping of the bags. "No worries. Welcome to the Wynn Hotel. All of your expenses are covered by Ms. Stein, including a fifty-thousand credit in our finest casino. Please enjoy."

Frank almost toppled over the coffee table, hyperventilating. "*50 G's*? I'm gonna need a sedative."

Ellen ignored him again. "Before you go, when is Ms. Stein available for a meeting?"

"Ms. Stein is expecting you for brunch at 10:30 in her Parlor Suite."

"10:30?" Frank walked back into the living room: pink, spotted and naked except for a towel around his lower section. "Think I got time to hit the sauna?"

The attendant hurried out leaving Ellen alone with little more than she wanted to see of her partner.

Wynn Hotel – Parlor Suite – 10:27am

Diandra Stein sat solemnly at a table by the terrace; the only person in her expensive suite. Her personal bodyguards were within range, if she needed, but in her personal space—she was alone.

Alone inside her heart and mind, as well

The most sought after and richest woman on the planet felt cold with miserable thoughts plaguing her. The room was a comfortable seventy-eight degrees and the Nevada weather outside blazed at an easy ninety-plus; but Diandra still felt emotionless.

She was unable to shake her fears and self-loathing. She felt ugly. She hated everything about herself. She constantly assumed people were laughing behind her back, or at the very least, talking about how *stupid* she must be. She had no one to talk to and thought no one wanted to hear her.

She hated her life—and after six attempts at ending it—she even felt she was a loser at that as well.

She missed her father.

He would know what to do with all these papers, lawyers, lawsuits, trial dates, business meetings, financial reports and banking responsibilities. He would have handled all this and make it go away.

She knew who to blame for all this; the one person who twisted her life around 360-degrees in one solitary evening.

As often as she wanted to cry, she was equally angry. Diandra was a ball of emotion that couldn't find a purpose or home; shifting gears emotionally by the minute. About the only thing she could reason with clarity was if it weren't for that *Gisela Thompson* bitch—

The door opened and her personal assistant, Marcy, entered while knocking. She was a mousey, nervous little girl that kept order for Diandra during her inner insanity. Marcy was the only one permitted to bear witness to her boss at her lowest.

"Ms. Stein? The detectives will be here in a few minutes for your ten-thirty."

"Thank you." She glanced at her assistant helplessly. "Marcy?"

"Yes, Ms. Stein?"

"Am I ugly?"

"Of course not, Ms. Stein."

"I feel ugly."

"You're one of the most beautiful women on Earth."

Diandra sighed. "I still *feel* ugly. You know?" She touched her chest, rubbing to feel the faintest heartbeat. "Like inside."

Marcy had some decisions to make. Rarely had Diandra quested for an opinion from her underling and, to keep her exceptionally well-paid job, Marcy reasoned she would need to say what Diandra wanted to hear. The difference this time was Diandra was appealing for a *real* answer; woman-to-woman. The look in her eyes said she wasn't seeking consultation from a lawyer or a high-paid 'yes' woman.

Diandra needed a *friend.*

"Ms. Stein," Marcy started with caution, "I am not certain how you feel inside, I'm sorry. However, when I get a little down, I found that doing something for others made me feel better. I mean, that's just me. I'm not married or have any kids. The holidays are the worst for me, but I take my free time and help people who have less than I do."

Diandra stared at Marcy thoughtfully. Marcy waited for the laugh and belittling that would likely follow after spewing such nonsense to rich people, lowering her head and preparing to leave.

Instead, Diandra stood up, staring outside of the terrace; out to the Golf Course behind the grand hotel. "Write a check. Issue it to ... I don't know ... to the Children's Cancer Fund of America. Do you know about them? I heard about them on TV the other day."

Marcy smiled, surprised at the response. "Yes, Ms. Stein."

"Make it for three ... no, *ten million* dollars. Give them my regards and thank them for their selfless work. Tell them, I can ... *am* ... learning from them."

"Yes, Ms. Stein."

"And Marcy, tell them I don't need any special favors, or wings devoted to my name or anything like that." Diandra took a deep breath and, for the first time in a while, felt a glimmer of purpose. "Just assure me they will do something wonderful for the children."

"Yes, Ms. Stein!" Marcy was so happy she wanted to bust. In her ear, she sported a communication piece to keep abreast of the goings-on with security and they were reporting the arrival of guests to their level. "Ms. Stein. The detectives have arrived."

"Fine. Give me five minutes to collect myself. Oh, and Marcy ... *thank you* ... good idea. Maybe it will help me ... with these *thoughts.*"

"I hope so, Ms. Stein," and she turned to walk away.

"Marcy," Diandra called to her. "It's okay to call me *Diandra*. Don't feel you have to be that formal with me. We've worked together for a while now and ..."

"Ms. Stein," Marcy wasn't ready to step out of her lane and she may not know it yet, but neither was Diandra. *Soon*, but not yet. "I'll bring in your guests in five minutes. Take your time."

Diandra nodded. Can't ask too much or seem too desperate for a friend so soon.

The seeds were planted, though. Even this small amount of time with Marcy cheered her up more than usual; knowing she had someone who she can talk to. *Really* talk to.

Right out of the elevator on the top floors of the Wynn—completely exclusive to Diandra Stein alone—Ellen and Frank were frisked by two burly thugs armed to the teeth with every weapon imaginably holstered or sheathed against their chest.

Flashing their badge did not matter so they let the procedure carry on. They were advised not to come up to the level with any sharp objects or firearms long before they arrived in Las Vegas and this was just to ensure continued security.

Once completed, Bodyguard #1 led the way down the corridor with Bodyguard #2 flanking them from behind. They were wide body men with expressionless features; tall and broad shoulders. Every twenty paces, they passed more security; eyeing them in passing.

No one was getting up to this floor without major confrontation in order to avoid previously security errors at *The Italiano*. No room service. No cleaning staff. No one. Diandra had dedicated and background checked chefs prepare food right in front of her—under armed guard of six men.

Then the chef would taste for poison.

Approaching the room, two new goons gave the detectives one last assuring frisk. For Ellen, that was one frisk too many and she started getting irritated.

"It's tighter up here than the clasp on your purse, huh El?" Frank laughed, getting a smirk out of the security team.

"Ain't nuthin' tighter than my wallet, Frankie."

"Shit, you got that right. HEY! Watch it, junior. You may be a freakin' mountain, but I'll spank ya like I was yer daddy if you touch the family jewels like that again!"

The guard nodded with respect to the elder Frank and stepped back and opened the door to Diandra's suite.

Diandra was watching a CNN International report about a daring attempted burglary in South Africa and following high speed chase that killed twenty-three bystanders by the incompetent hands of the South African Special Forces Brigade. She pointed at the screen the moment she saw Ellen. "Have you heard about this?"

Ellen eyed the screen for a moment and returned to gaping at that the expense of the Parlor Suite. "The South Africa mess? Yes. We heard about it on the way here."

"*She's* in South Africa?"

"So it seems."

"Why aren't *you* in South Africa?" It almost sounded like a demand.

Ellen paused to adjust her thoughts; checking her attitude for a moment to make sure she said the right things. Frank held his breath. If Ellen went off right now, he'd be out of a fifty thousand credit waiting for him in the casino downstairs. He cleared his throat to remind her of her manners. "Because we're here *with you*, Ms. Stein."

Frank exhaled.

Diandra smiled and shook her head. "Of course. I'm … *I'm sorry*. I didn't mean to come off like…"

"Like your *father*?" Ellen shot back.

Frank was concerned again.

"I am not my father."

"That remains to be seen." Ellen wasn't letting up. Frank knew this was going to be a short trip due to Ellen's mouth

"Inspector Cobart, whatever you may think of my father, he was *still* my father and *he* loved me. I wasn't aware of his hidden circles and I'm not about to beg for his forgiveness. You can find your way to trusting me on your own. I asked you here on business, not some closure program."

Well said, Ellen nodded. W*ell scripted,* she also thought. Ellen had been around the block a few times and met a lot of people. What she saw in front of her was a scared little girl putting up an amazingly rehearsed front.

"Three days ago, I was assaulted by an unknown gunman at The Italiano. He murdered a number of my staff and left this letter."

She handed Ellen plastic bag with the business card inside of it for forensics protection. Ellen took the evidence and immediately handed it over to Frank who proceeded to get to work on the find. "How long, Frank?"

"Give me about ten minutes," Frank took out his glasses and held the paper up to the window to get a better look.

"Is there anything else you can tell me about that day?" Ellen asked.

"He shot up the place and left. Today, the Stein Diamond Depository is hit. I believe she's involved in both instances."

"Was it Gisela that came in with a gun that day?"

"No, some man. She must have hired him."

"Why would you think that?"

"She has unfinished business with me and my father. Since I am what is left of my family, she wants to complete her revenge."

Ellen didn't believe a word of it. "Her beef was with your father."

"She killed my father. You were there."

"Yes," Ellen sat aside from her host, turning the TV off. "I saw Gisela and her partners leave. I also watched her come close to throwing your old man off the roof, but she didn't. Might I remind you that conclusive evidence has proven that your father's death was an *accident*—by his own security system."

Diandra gritted her teeth, losing a moment of composure. "If she wasn't there in the first place he would be alive today!"

Ellen let her fume and said nothing. There were so many holes in the woman's beliefs and she wouldn't get anywhere if she started rubbing Diandra the wrong way. If Butta' was looking to kill Diandra, it would have been done back at The Italiano. She wouldn't leave cryptic messages and run to South Africa for everyone to chase her. Ellen was sure of Butta' to know that she wasn't *that* random. Which reminded her— "Frank?"

"Done," he returned to the women after a lengthy inspection through the plastic, "No prints, *except* yours, Ms. Stein. The paper has a watermark on it. A little faint but I can read the letters TOC. That stands for *Terrance O'Clough*; an Irish paper maker. They don't make the crap you just slip into your copiers. They make paper for the *ultra-rich*. At $3200-a-ream, you just don't wipe your ass with this kind of stuff. Wanna know why?"

"I'm sure you want to tell us, Frankie."

"Damn right I will. Cause this here paper is lined with *gold* fibers."

Diandra was confounded. "No disrespect, Detective Tulley, but how do you know all this?"

"Frank is a well-spring of *worthless* information that comes in handy. He's my personal *Alex Trebek*. Ain't that right, boo-bee?"

"Aww shucks." Frank grinned, handing the plastic to Ellen. Ellen ran her finger on the impressed letter centered on the card. "What's with the letter-E?"

"Not sure," Frank scratched his head. "It was typed. I'm thinking with an Olympia Elite. They were made in the 30's. You know those big old *clank-clank-clank* old time typewriters? You can tell by the typeface and the grade of its strike. Like whoever did this, just took a finger and pressed 'E' with one hard strike. The gold ink looks new, though. They went all out to get this old typewriter and find the right ribbon for it. Custom obviously. Looks like real gold to me."

"So what does all of this mean to me?" Diandra asked.

Frank shrugged. "Somebody with *money* wants to tell you something."

Diandra turned to look out the terrace window with a mix of emotions. "I don't know why this is happening. The only suspect I have is Gisela Thompson and she has more motive than anyone to do this."

"No, she don't. She doesn't even have the means." Frank blurted, forgetting his place in matters. He'll miss that casino credit, but he was a cop first. "The papers too rich for her, plus her profile doesn't jive with dropping off mysterious messages."

"How can you be so sure, detective?" She asked, sounding a bit like her father.

"What my partner means is," Ellen helped, "the South African thing has *her* name written all over it. She's a thief not an assassin. She went there looking for something. If she wanted something from you, she'd come here and do the job *herself* before sending anyone to do it for her. You are not on her list of goals, but something out in Cape Town is. Obviously, she went there to get that diamond making machine."

"Well," Diandra said, "there is only one way to find out. You were tapped to investigate and hunt her down, so I am going to *increase* your expense account to make sure you have everything you need to get the job done."

"There's no need to—" Ellen stopped talking and watched Frank's attempt to wave her down; rubbing his fingers together with a *get more money* indication.

"Detectives. I trust you to find out who murdered my staff and sent me this letter. I think it was Gisela, so you'll have full access to investigate the South African Depository. Let nothing get in your way to bring her in so we can settle this. You will have unlimited resources at your command."

Ellen agreed. "In that case, we'll get over there right aw—" Frank cleared his throat quite loud—*quite obvious*—interrupting Ellen in mid-statement. "*Tomorrow*. Tomorrow morning we'll leave for South Africa. Probably won't catch a flight this late anyway."

Diandra raised an eyebrow at Ellen. "Catch a flight? What part of unlimited resources did you miss, Detective? A private jet will be available to you when you are ready to leave."

Frank hung over Ellen with the biggest of smiles. "First thing in the morning it is!"

In the elevator, Ellen remained silent with her thoughts while Frank pulled at his collar in a Rodney Dangerfield act; trying to get out of his tie. Now that the presentation was over, he wanted to get back to his *let-it-all-out* demeanor. "Damn ties."

"Frankie? Why do you have us here an extra day longer? We could just as soon be on our way. Yeah, I know. You wanna spend *Brittney's* money."

"Golly, *Officer Krupsy*. They *did* give you that detective's badge for a reason. El, they made you top brass and gave you a new title. I'm still New York blue and I'm just tagging along 'cause you asked me too. When will I ever get a free ride like this again? Donald Trump isn't exactly calling me over for tea, you know?"

"I need you with me, Frankie. I wouldn't do this without you."

He waved her off. "Aww, you don't need me."

"*Yes,* I do." She looked at him with dead seriousness.

"Nah, you don't. Come on. She's blowing cash up yer ass. You can get all of the intelligence you need to help you clean things up without so much as a fuss."

"It's not that easy for me to do things—*this* kind of thing—without my partner. You know exactly what I mean, *you putz.*"

"You're shining now, El. Don't let this *putz* hold you back from making that *cheese*. You're getting paid so lovely, I almost want to rob yer ass right here. Throw away my badge and just cold '*this is a stick up*'."

"Take some more personal time, then. We can go to Cape Town, follow the trail like we do and catch up to Butta' in a few days. Two weeks, tops. The chief can miss you for a couple of days."

"The chief wants my ass on a platter. Yours, too, to be honest. You broke up his number one team."

"I couldn't resist the offer. Besides, I was up there. I saw things, Frankie. That tower thing—" She trailed off, remembering 112-stories of terror.

"Yeah. You did good while I was tossing my gut out some cab. That's why you're making the big bucks. El, I couldn't afford to go even if I wanted to. I can't lose the time and I got bills piling up."

"What if *Ms. Chick* here pays you for your time? She's already talking about *money is no object*. What's your time worth for a couple of weeks tracking down a perp?"

The elevator door sprung open from the smoothest ride ever. Not-too-distant sounds of the casino played out in the background.

"You're not kidding." Frank looked at Ellen and gave it some thought. "Okay. What are we saying? Two weeks?"

"Tops," Ellen assured him. "Come on. I need you on this one."

"Alright. See if she'll flip me two-hundred thousand. That's a hundred-thou' a week. That's more than I get now till I go *ass-down*. She'll never do it."

Ellen flipped him an envelope from the folds of her jacket, taking Frank off guard. Opening it, he revealed a cashier's check with his name on it with breathtaking numbers across the front: $700,000.

"I had a chat with *Brittney* before we got here. I told her how valuable you were to me in this and future investigations. She understood and had some people talk to the chief already. You're all set. All you have to do is say *yes*, partner."

Frank was still gasping. "*Christ*, El. What the hell?"

"That's just the down payment for saying *yes*. Check number two comes when we bring Butta' back home. *Two-hundred thousand, Frankie?* Come on! You sold yourself short."

Catching his breath, Frank only had two words for his partner while looking at the check in his hands: "*Bank*, please."

Ellen patted Frank on the back and walked him into the casino. "We'll take care of that right away."

"So wait. How long have you had this check in your pocket? Are you holding out on me? Got any more *dough* in that magic coat of yours? *Come 'ere!*"

Playfully, Frank felt his partner up and frisked her body; something only this *one* man could ever do without asking.

Only with her partner did she genuinely *let-it-all out* laugh— trying to get away from his probing hands, running into the casino.

They were going to have a good time in Vegas today.

Tomorrow, the work began.

Chapter 7

Berlin, Germany – Robertson Technologies Euro Headquarters
"So in conclusion, the surgical possibilities would be *limitless*. With the FrG-20 Concentrated Emitter, we'll be able to have far greater precision and save lives within the most remote locations on the planet with its portability."

Professor Wyman Fowler, one of the few Black men of significant status working at Robertson Tech, spent the past three hours speaking in an empty auditorium with only the front row filled with silent guests. They were people with expressionless, glazed faces partially hidden in shadow. Maybe ten or so guests with their arms crossed; quiet with deadpan expressions. Wyman could only see the medals on their uniforms clearly.

American officers of considerable rank.

"Thank you, Professor." A voice said from the small gathering, and then the group went into a privately whispered meeting.

Wyman did not like this one bit. But then, ever since he was commissioned to work for the Robertson facility, he had many misgivings. He should have known if a global technology empire offered such a *handsome* annual salary—with a signing bonus to boggle the mind—he was not just here out of his love for science.

He was *owned* by the company.

With that kind of *white-collar slavery*; he was expected to dance to whatever tune they expected.

When he last checked, this was supposed to be a presentation to the medical community on his laser technology project. *Where were the lab coats and what in the hell were the military doing here?*

More shadowy grumbling in the dark while he waited patiently.

Wyman Fowler grew impatient, as he commonly did, while others spent time judging him and his work. A devoted scientist, Wyman spent his life seeking to develop just about anything people needed to live longer, healthier lives. Wyman purposely sought out every necessity in order to parent a much needed invention. From the smallest useful household appliance to major, life-changing/saving technologies, Wyman has successfully made a name for himself bouncing from one well-paying company to another doing the one thing he did best: create.

Unfortunately, for every one positive talent there was another *negative* trait and his was *criticism*. He *HATED* people passing judgment on the things he developed. All the hard work and sweat he spent putting things together was overwhelming; the *nerve* of people to question or shake their heads at him just because they couldn't see what he could. Regardless of the glasses he wore, in Wyman's mind, it wasn't *he* who had a vision problem.

This wouldn't be the first time a well-meaning, intended project was perverted into a Robertson tech *monster* for the sole purpose of revenue. Then it always brought him back to the reality that he served a company with a very specific clause in his contract: *all projects henceforth, planned, sketched, partially developed and/or fully operational are the sole ownership of Robertson Technologies.*

"Question, Professor Fowler." That came from the man in the center; a booming, commanding voice fit for the four-star General he was. General William Tucker stood, reading through the supplied companion sheets to the presentation. "When can one of these roll out for use?"

"*General Tucker!*" That was Lester Grumman's cue to skip down the aisle to get the General's attention. Lester was best described as Robertson Technologies resident concierge. The go-to guy for the people with the *money* and the people with the *merchandise*; always making sure both provider and client were happy. Lester was not on Wyman's favorite people list, considering him a corporate sellout who would find a price on anything he developed without an interest in the purpose.

Lester heaved, almost out of breath. He was a little man that was paid more than most people in the company for the relationships he managed. "To answer your question, allow me to show you this."

With a flick of his remote control, the lights dimmed and a silver screen lowered to start a movie, taking Wyman by surprise. Lester's grin was suspicious for a simple medical laser presentation; scaring Wyman to the bone. "What are you up to, Lester?"

"You'll see." Lester responded; buttons about to burst from his proud, puffed out chest.

Apparently, his company had been tooling around with his invention without his input. On the screen, a team of scientists Wyman didn't know rolled onto an unmarked field a larger version of his laser—fashioned into a military grade *cannon*.

"Bloody hell!" Wyman gasped.

"Sssh!" Lester kept Wyman at bay. "Watch."

The cannon was positioned to target a farm house measured by signs to be exactly 1.6 kilometers across the field. With a wave of various signals, all the men surrounding the cannon backed to a safe distance.

"What did you do to my laser?" Wyman whispered.

Lester sneered. "*Your* laser? Read you contract again."

Static interrupted the video and unusual lights shined around the weapon, concentrating into a ball of light at the center of the nozzle. The cannon started off with a gradually rising pitch whine and grew to a shriek as the energy ball grew larger. Just as the video was unable to maintain its visual much longer from the electromagnetic feedback, the cannon jerked back and repelled a thick beam of light across the field, carving an instant trench from the front of the cannon, a mile across the field and into the farm house—splintering the target into an explosion of wood, dirt and debris. The flare-up was wide. Wind and dust kicked back over the testers, showering the video screen.

The lights came back on and the military brass applauded.

Wyman stared at the screen in utter amazement. "I didn't build a *weapon*. I'm trying to *help* people! The FrG-20 was for surgical procedures. This is insane!"

"What are you talking about. Of course it will be helping people." Lester said indignantly. "The *good* guys. Now calm down and go get me some coffee."

Wyman grabbed Lester by the collar, lifting a fist. "I just about had enough of your mercenary ..."

"Gentlemen!" The General eyed both men, soaking in the malcontent between the two. "So talk to *me*, Professor. Forget the suit. Talk to *me*."

"General … *Sir!* This *abomination* isn't what I was commissioned to design."

Lester tried to speak, but was cut off with a raised finger by the General as his only warning. "Continue, Professor."

"The FrG-20 was made to *help* people. High intensity, portable and designed to perform operations in the worst conditions. I can't vouch for its usability in this reconfiguration. I didn't authorize it's perversion or give anybody the proper schematically data to enhance a handheld device into ten times its size. Even if I approved of this *science fiction*, I can't guarantee that it will even work!"

"But it *does* work, General. As you can see and Robertson stands by its products 100%!" Lester pointed out. "So, Professor we will be saving lives and it's a win-win."

"Saving lives by *killing* others to do it? That's what you call a win-win?"

"Only the *bad* people," the General winked. "Mr. Grumman, tell us about the diamond."

Lester excused himself from Wyman and returned to the projector to bring up a very detailed exploded view of the original FrG-20. The laser had a look similar to the x-ray at most dentists' offices; posted on the end of a fluid-head rotating arm, the computer graphic imagery of the laser twisted around and revealed, at the heart of the casing, a palm-sized diamond.

Lester produced a cheat-sheet from his jacket. He wasn't as elegant with technical breakdowns as Wyman and the Professor wasn't willing to assist. "The FrG-20 is an ultra-fine tuned solid-state laser. Starting at the gain medium where the source of optical gain is produced from the stimulated emissions, then the amplification process is enhanced by a series of reflective surfaces and a synthetic diamond of extraordinary rarity."

"How rare?" The General was intrigued.

"Real diamonds just don't have the molecular characteristics needed to amplify the intensity of the laser. We've tried and they just didn't produce the levels we were looking for. Then came the Stein diamond and the rest is history."

"Stein diamond?" The General questioned, then seemed to realize. "From that Stein Tower debacle just the other week? Out in New York?"

Lester nodded. "The same. The man was creating mega-diamonds from a remarkable machine we had no access to. Personally, I don't see why they made the man such a pariah. I've seen his diamonds. They are far better than the genuine in so many levels."

"Because their all *fools,* that's why!" Wyman was hot. "People would rather obtain their jewels from the blood of *workers* in mines than those made from a machine." Wyman would never keep his moral points of view to himself.

"The problem," Lester continued, "is the processes dependency on these synthetic diamond. Now that his diamond making machine is dismantled, the FrG-20 relies on our *two* remaining diamonds."

"Two diamonds? That's all there is?" The General seemed highly put off, glaring directly at Lester for answers.

"That's all there is."

"Where are they?"

Lester paced around the General. "We have one on the compound so the good Professor could continue his research. The other, well, it's on route from Cape Town even as we speak by special courier."

"Can we see the diamond you have here?"

"General, I'm sorry. Unfortunately, Robertson Technologies has been the victim to *numerous* attempted thefts and a host of security concerns."

The General huffed. "That's an *understatement.* Our intelligence is quite clear on the excessive interest in this laser by *other* international parties. I wonder exactly how secure your facility actually is."

"This is why we're speaking to the United States government *first.*"

"Because you have to. If this weapon falls into the wrong hands, we'll have a *big* problem."

"Once we settle on the price, we won't have that problem, now will we?" Lester saw visions of dollars dancing in his head.

The General paced the floor, deep in thought. "How about recreating that diamond machine? There are enough brains here to get that operational again."

Lester waved a finger. "The Gisela is—*was*—incredible. From the few glimpses I caught of the specs, and that was under *armed guard* mind you, the whole concept was so out of the box—Stein gave *NO ONE* the chance to examine how it worked. When he died, Gisela was shut down, broken down into pieces and scattered. In essence, he took it with him. I wouldn't even begin to wonder how that machine worked. Urban legend has it some Black man invented but considering how much of a racist Stein was …"

The General shook his head. "So if you *lose* those diamonds the laser won't work?"

"Now you know our security concerns. No diamonds, no laser. Still, the problems at Stein Industries won't affect our relations with the United States Military. You don't have to be concerned of negative association or lack of resources. Two diamonds are more than enough."

"That's good to hear," the General nodded. "Especially with how *close* Robertson and Stein were in bed together previously."

Lester gave a nervous laugh, pulling at his collar.

Wyman helped him out, albeit sarcastically. "Robertson Technology *gladly* accepts checks, cash, all major credit cards and American Express. We do not discriminate the color of *green*." He almost said it with spit. There was *nothing* like a discontent employee. "Stein's embarrassment is *all* of ours, too. Or have you forgotten the countless projects we've beta-tested for the man, currently confiscated by the feds?"

"Wyman, this is neither the time nor the place to discuss those details." Lester was sweating.

"Sure it is. Particularly when you consider I built *eighty percent* of what we've lost! I create a unique multi-computer method to prevent bank robberies, Robertson sells it to Stein and it changes into that horrific *freak show* of a security system. I develop a jet powered bird to find people lost in tragic instances like Katrina or the tsunami in Japan. Robertson sells it as a heat-seeking weapon. Shall I go on?"

Enough was enough for Lester; stamping a foot in front of Wyman to gain *some* control, gritting his teeth. "Fowler!"

"Its fine, Grumman. Professor Fowler is just the father protecting his babies. I can respect that. Unfortunately, I have to apologize. We *must* continue the trend." He handed Wyman a folded paper from the folds of his jacket

Lester made a move to read it first, but the General made it very clear that snatching things from his hands would lead to unfortunate results. Wyman open the paper and read the notice; for all of the paper's big words and extended sentences it boiled down to just one thing.

"This is a purchase order," Wyman gasped. "For two re-fit FrG-20's."

Lester clasped his hands together, smiling ear to ear. "Excellent choice, General. If you have any custom requirements, now is the best time to discuss them at length."

"What *medical* division is receiving the laser?" Wyman asked, already knowing the answer, but hoping for the best.

The General thought he would know better. "They don't send four-stars down here to talk *medical* supplies, son. Give it up, Professor. It's a weapon now."

"The hell I will! Lester! Don't allow this! *Please!*"

"We'll talk later, Wyman." Lester finalized.

The General put on his cap and closed this conversation with the Professor. "I suppose we're done here. Good day, Professor Fowler. Grumman."

While the General turned to face his companions to continue discussing the future, Wyman grabbed Lester and pulled him away from earshot. "You *damn* fool!"

"Get your hands off me. You need to remember that this is a *business* we're running here. Not a science fair. This presentation was just a formality and a little Q&A. Get with it, Wyman. We're freakin' *uber-retailers*, for Christ's sake."

"This is all insane. You're crazy!"

"You signed up for this, Wyman. How many times are you going to cry sour grapes every time your projects are purchased?"

"They are *not* being used for their original intention! This is a travesty how everything I build is raped for clandestine purposes and I won't have it anymore!"

"I just have two words for you, Wyman. *Con … Tract.* Know your place in the scheme of things and shut the hell up before we start reviewing your tenure with this company."

"*Please*, little man. Your bosses will fire you long before they get rid of their golden goose laying laser eggs. In fact, I don't even know why I'm talking to you. You go play with your toy soldiers. I'm going to talk to someone who can actually get things done."

"You're wasting your energy, Wyman. Man-to-man, seriously … keep your head down, do your job and collect your paycheck. There's no room for your indignation in the power moves around here."

Wyman snorted. "This transaction *will not* happen. I'm going right to the top and settle this with no *ands, ifs or buts.*"

Wyman pushed past Lester and stormed out of the auditorium.

Later…

The CEO of Robertson Technology resided in The United States, so all communication took place via satellite among the German office board of directors and governing officers of the sprawling corporate entity at the top floors.

With Wyman Fowler standing in a corner, grinding his teeth, the sixteen-member team of company *yes men* sat at an oval table staring at the screen to listen to CEO Malcolm Ford's breakdown to Wyman's complaint.

"… *AND* though we deeply respect your concerns in regards to how your creations are being redesigned, it's important for you to understand the level of interests we propagate throughout the world stage and the amount of help we've become to various causes not directly in line with your personal points of views.

"*IF* you take the time to see the bigger picture, you'll find your work has not been pushed forward into new directions in vain or limited purpose. You have to take into consideration the millions who have benefited from your re-purposed inventions for the greater good worldwide.

"***BUT***, if the matters of your conscience bothers you, I can only suggest you remove yourself from the business of where *our* products are utilized and refer to section seventeen, article nine, subtext twenty-seven of your contract with Robertson Technology in regards to property and rights ownership."

Wyman's wisdom tooth fell out from the unrelenting, angered grinding.

Back in his office, Wyman flopped into his leather chair defeated; staring at the walls hidden by drawings, sticky notes, graph papers and blueprints—an organized task to make sure not one ounce of actual wall could be revealed.

He was in a *surly* mood. Caught between a rock and a bottomless pit—Wyman might as well have asked for a clean pair of *shackles*.

When all felt lost or he was having a mental block, there was always that one person he could rely on to sooth his worried brow. She was on every speed dial he had immediate access to.

"Hi babe," his wife, Desiree, answered the phone. She never let the phone ring past the first when it came from his office. Especially if it was in the middle of the day, as it usually meant he was troubled. "What's happening? How did the presentation go?"

Wyman stood up to close the door to his office and locked it. "They're doing it again, Dez. They're selling the laser to the military and they're going to use it for anything *but* surgery. I can't take this anymore. I can't live like this anymore."

Desiree had seen and listened to, as the dutiful wife, Wyman's raging pent up anger on matters of work and internal politics many, *many* times. When he was like this, she made sure she chose her words carefully. "We've discussed finding other work."

"In this economy? I can't take a pay cut and no one is *ever* going to pay me like this place. I should have known they were waving that *golden carrot* at me for a reason and like the *ass* I am, I've been chasing after it ever since. I'm *so* stupid!"

"You're not stupid, baby. You did what was best for our family and we appreciate your sacrifice. We've gone over this before and if this is *really* bothering you, I completely support you if you want to quit and find something else."

"Who will hire the man that built Stein's murderous security system? Oh, that will look lovely on my resume. That and the latest combat laser weaponry used by the U.S. military killing millions? Desiree … *I'm a murderer*! I'm not supposed to *take* life. This isn't what I was born to do."

His tears were real and she could hear them through the phone. "Baby, I'm so sorry. Do you need me to come up there? I can have Pilar watch after Crystal and …"

"No," he wiped away tears, collecting himself. "How does that look having my wife come up here to kiss my skinned knee? Next you'll have me calling you 'mommy'."

"Only on Friday nights, dear," she joked.

He found a smile, laughing. "You got that right."

"Only you, Poindexter. My nerdy-daddy."

"I got your nerdy-daddy." Wyman looked about the office and found no reason to stay the remainder of the day; none that he would get an argument over, anyway. "Aww, hell. I'm coming home."

"Great! I got the *honey-doo* list waiting by the door. You can start by bringing home some bread and one of those foiled pans. I'm cooking a turkey tonight so try to find one that holds about 20lbs. "

Wives, he thought. Trigger happy to put their husbands to work the first chance they get. As Wyman listened to her rattle off his list of things he had to do, he pondered a few things: how his lack of freedom was worse than he thought. How crowded the local *hypermart Kaufland* must be by this time of the day and how he hated waiting on long lines. Finally, his lingering thoughts rested on one of the Stein diamond that rested in a container on his desk in front of him.

920-carats within arm's reach; plainly and openly.

Then everything became so clear. Freedom was a touch away.

"Dear," he interrupted her somewhere between ordering chocolate and the need to have the gutters cleaned around the house. "I'm coming home but I'll be a little delayed. I … I have an idea."

"Oh, okay. Call me when you're on your way." Translation: *I'll have more work for you by the time you walk out the door.*

Hanging up, he held one of the two remaining diamonds capable of allowing his laser to work. He glanced up at the inner office camera he had deactivated long ago in an epic battle with management to control a sense of privacy.

That decision would help him win the forthcoming war.

The diamond in his hand was scheduled to be returned to the vault this afternoon and was usually sealed in a box, signed off and delivered via inner-office security to go through a series of repeating security checks and confirmations as it left one set of hands to another.

Wyman called for his secretary. "Marg, can you send in the security detail?"

"Yes, sir. Security detail on way."

Wyman readied himself.

If any of what he was about to do failed, he would be in a world of trouble.

In order for his plan to work, all he had to do was open the window and let the brisk, Berlin air in. Papers fluttered about from the sudden gust of wind.

The ordinary method of returning the diamond back to the Robertson vaults for the day required security to personally come to his office with a black velvet box that would hold the diamond for transportation. In the box was a series of thick industrial rubber bands that created a sturdy shock-absorbing trap for the diamond; keeping it free of movement.

One stocky company security officer—issued with a standard Glock .45 pistol and a shiny badge on his chest—was the usual officer during these transactions and after about a thousand of these hand-off's, Wyman bet the bank that the procedure would become *relaxed.*

"Wie geht es ihnen?" *How are you?* Wyman asked the security guard, smiling nervously.

"Your German getting good, yah?" The security guard placed the velvet box on his desk, opening the top as he usually did, writing a few things on his clip board. "My English not so good."

"It's getting better. Say, would you be kind enough to close the window for me, please? My papers are flying everywhere."

As Wyman motioned with the diamond to place into the box, serving the security a visual that he made the *attempt*, the officer turned his back— just for that fleeting moment—to close the window. When he turned back to address the professor, the velvet box was sealed and security tape wrapped about the clasp. Tape, that when broken, clearly suggested a security breach.

Wyman signed off on pickup and the security guard skipped the most important step in the detail: *keep his eye on the diamond.*

Why should he have any cause to not trust the professor? They've worked together for a very long time and he even helped him with his son's illness. Accepting Wyman's signature, the compliant officer marched back to the vault to secure the velvet box for yet another day.

The diamond itself was smuggled into Wyman's jacket pocket in less than usual comfort as he left the Robertson compound to do his wife's bidding.

No one would follow him this evening, but he still sweated uncontrollably.

Inventor, professor, husband, father and thief, he grumbled.

Regardless of his fears, he managed to get the diamond out of the compound and back home without a problem.

The harder stuff was yet to come.

Chapter 8

Anchored Yacht 'Sariya-Anne' off the Coast of Cape Town, SA
Chakrapani '*Shabba*' Chinmayananda, age 17, barely noticed all the action going on around him when he and *Master Chief* did battle against the Covenant in far away galaxies all in the safety of his Xbox. Assisted by the effects of the marijuana he *constantly* smoked, the boy wouldn't notice World War III if it occurred under him.

Which was fine for Louie, who was running from one end of the deck to the other; up and down stairs and back and forth from the bridge of the yacht; without so much as a word to the poor little rich boy he was guarding.

It was only until Shabba fell to his doom off the side of Halo's rings did he take a breather and look up from his seventy-four inch plasma screen TV to check the time. Early evening and it would be another three months of doing exactly what he was doing right now: smoking, gaming and essentially working hard at doing nothing.

The feeling about him, weed or no, was not of the monotony of being a wealthy privileged son. He could go, do and have anything he wanted without second guessing his needs. He had the rare confusion of having *options*. So many options to do with his boring life of endless pleasure, his emotions cancelled themselves out and he ended up back in front of the screen—playing the latest game and rolling up more joints.

Much to the ire of his mother and father.

Speeches upon speeches of what their expectations' of him were and that he had been slow to aspire to. The typical Indian doctor wasn't for him and sitting in one spot to study gave him the hives.

Maybe he should have been a doctor. Weed cured his inability to study, but all the pretty colors interfered with the text in the book. When the pink rabbits joined him to offer tutelage on the human anatomy, he knew his time in a college was over.

He lazily glanced over to the windows looking out from his palace-level cabin to see Louie jetting back and forth, stomping along the deck. Looking at Louie expend so much energy doing who-knows-what made *himself* exhausted.

That man needs to get laid, Shabba thought. Rubbing his crotch, he proposed that the feeling was mutual and stood up, stretching. "Hey, Lou! How about me and you go to shore and get some *pootang?*"

Then he laughed to himself in a haze of smoke still streaming from his mouth. "Poo," he chuckled. *Who came up with that word? Disney? Man, I'm wasted.*

Louie ran past the window, ignoring the boy and disappeared somewhere into the yacht.

Bridge of the Sariya-Anne

Louie cut the lights to the yacht to stay under the cover of the darkness. Except for moonlight and the essential, eerie red glow of the bridge command panels, the yacht was almost invisible.

He peered out to the ocean with a pair of night vision goggles, scanning intently with sweat streaming down his brow. He managed to get the yacht's crew off the ship and put them all up in hotel space indefinitely; each with an expense account to survive on until further notice. Louie, as Shabba's nanny/bodyguard, had that kind of ability and did not have to ask for permission to do what he felt was necessary to protect the boy.

Tonight had nothing to do with Shabba and he would only hope the rich brat, attempting to sneak up on him, would mind his business. "Wadda ya want, Shab?"

Shabba laughed, slapping Louie on the back. "How do you do that? I can't sneak up on you for shit!"

"I'll give youse a hint: ya needs ta brush yer teeth, wash yer ass n' change yer clothes afta' ya smoke. Kid, I getta contact high a mile away from ya."

"If that's all it'll take, I'll catch you off guard one of these days."

"Not in yer lifetime," Louie maintained his search into the night without much deviation. "It'll take someone a whole lot more pro than youse."

"Where's the crew?" Shabba asked.

"Gave 'em the night off. Gonna have some guests. Is dat alright wit 'chu, or do I gotta give ya my full report?"

"Dude! Cool! Umm... *female* guests?"

Louie put down the goggles and looked at Shabba differently than usual. "Shab, I've gotta level wit 'cha. I got some friends comin' over 'n I need ya ta cover fer me. Is dis gonna be a problem or no?"

Shabba closed the distance between them and put his hands on Louie's shoulders. "Dude, I've got you covered. With all the crap you stashed for me? I'm with you. Right here, man," Shabba patted his heart. "Right here. I've got you. Whatever you need. You got some friends coming over—no problem by me. *Females* right?"

"Don't chu' worry 'bout nuthin', Shab. Just keep it on da low fer me."

Shabba allowed his brain to do a measure of thinking; concluding something completely different than what Louie was talking about. "Oh, so … it's *men*? Dude, I didn't know. No disrespect for your *preference* and all. I'll still cover for you *if* you roll *that* way." He gave a freaked-out, goose-bumped shiver. "But that kind of stuff *wigs* me out and I think I'll give you the space you need and go to shore for the night."

"Wot da hells wrong wit'cha? Yer not goin' no place. Youse is still my job, get me? When my peoples gets here, we're takin' a little trip 'n youse is comin' wit' me."

"Aww, dude. Lou. I don't know."

"I know! Dat's all ya needs ta know right now." He squinted into the night sea. "Dere here. Now would be a good time ta brush yer teeth, buddy." Louie ran off the bridge with Shabba shortly behind.

"Lou! Wait, man! My folks really got pissed when I took the yacht to Brazil that other time. I mean, we had a blast and all, but they took my AMEX away for twenty-four hours and that was living hell."

"Youse will survive, kid. 'Sides, dis time imma takin' her out. It won't be on ya."

Louie let down the side gates of the yacht and lowered a rolled ladder off the side. Everything had to happen in the pitch of dark, making Shabba uncomfortable; standing on the stairs a measure away from Louie's activities on the deck.

"I feel like I ought to say something." Shabba coughed. "I'm not saying I'm not *willing* to help you out, Lou. You're my boy and all. I don't know about taking the yacht out with people I don't know. They got pirates out there and—"

The first on deck was Butta', soaked and annoyed; followed by Kasey, Fuego and Trigger. Bringing up the rear, needing a little effort to climb up the ladder was Munch. Each of them tired—*exhausted*—and with a quiet aura of irritation hanging about them.

Louie, happy to see his old friends; closed up the boarding gate and rolled up the ladder. "Welcome 'board da Sariya-Anne, folks. Christ on a stick, *Honey*! It's been a dog's age."

Then quite suddenly, Shabba's vision widened, allowing more light into his brain to bear witness to three shimmering goddesses in the moonlight—soaking wet. It was an image from some of his most erotic pornography collection in real life.

Happy-happy—joy-joy.

"*Yeah!* Welcome aboard! Mi casa, su casa, *honey's*." Shabba grinned ear to ear, completely ignoring Munch and Fuego.

Butta' looked at Louie, cocking a brow and looking for an answer. He waved off the thought of Shabba. "Fergetabout da kid. I got all ya need downstairs. Kick back, all da booze, eats, change o' clothes, showers—*whateva*. It's yers. We can talk lata' afta' I get us outta dodge."

Trigger felt Shabba's gaze on her like a scanner running its beams over every inch of her body, trying to ignore him.

The shower was hot and it was followed by twenty minutes in the onboard sauna. Within the hour, the Sariya-Anne was moving out to open water and Butta' was far less tense than when she came aboard. Even though her body was refreshed, her mind still had some hard to remove grime.

There was always *something* on her mind.

Her friends were keeping a wide berth from each other since they arrived on the yacht. As close as *partners-in-crime* could be—every now and again they just needed to *stop* being under each other.

The yacht had enough space to get lost in and they took advantage of that to unwind in their own fashion.

How does Butta' relax? Studying maps and the next plan of action ahead.

Louie provided maps of Johannesburg, Germany and Berlin. She also had full access to the internet and, between sips of a caramel-mocha hot chocolate topped with whipped cream, she was back at work hunting; searching, reviewing and plotting.

Somewhere out there, *her* diamond was on the move, and depending on how fast this boat cruised, she expected to have what was hers within the next twenty-four hours.

With any miracles, she thought realistically. Fortunately, Butta' was the kind of person who made her own miracles, keeping a silent vigil at a constantly updating hand-held screen that flashed many technical details with three sets of numbers that constantly changed at the top.

"You're tracking the diamond," Kasey knocked, just outside of the cabin. Both women were dressed in only a towel, covering their chest and mid-section.

Butta' hiked up her constantly slipping towel and winked with an *I got this covered* expression. "You think I'd let that diamond get away *that* easy? You *must* be crazy."

"You little *shit*." Kasey snickered. "That whole *thing* in town *wasn't* easy—and let me tell you something," Kasey was careful on what she said next, slipping into the room, shutting the door behind her. "Trig can ride the *hell* out of a bike. Did you know that?"

"No. She talks about bikes here and there. Buying one and all that. Who knew?"

"You'd better watch her, girlie. She's a handful."

"Aren't we all," Butta' sighed.

"You got that right." Kasey moved some of Butta's charts out of the way and stretched out across the bed. "Munchie wants to talk to you."

"He can't come here and talk to me himself?"

"Maybe I'm using the wrong word. *Talk* is a little too soft. I don't know—let's try *discuss* something with you." She rolled over to stare at the ceiling; towel covering her chest, heaving over an hourglass physique.

Somewhere nearby, there was a muffled bump. Kasey immediately looked at Butta', who was already looking back at her, scowling, pointing to a closet across from them.

"So what does he want to discuss?" Butta' continued, wrapping her towel tighter, moving off the bed and armed herself with a pair of scissors under a pile of papers.

With her, Kasey sat up and reached for an empty holster slung over a chair. She passed silent facial expressions of annoyance at Butta' for not keeping weaponry at arm's reach. While hunting for anything that maybe used as a weapon, she eventually picked up a *hole-puncher* and gripped it tightly. "He's having trouble understanding what this whole thing is about anymore."

Butta' gestured to the closet—a double-door, wood slate design, like everything else on this yacht; excessively rich in detail. Both women crept to either side of the closet with their office supplies-for-weapons.

"Tell you what," Butta' smirked, "instead of talking tonight, how about you and I get naked and rub oil on each other. After that, we'll take out our *special toys*."

That was followed by another, more defined *bump* and *crash* from within the closet. Having had enough, Butta' snatched open the closet and dragged Shabba out by the ear, scissors under his neck. Harshly, he was thrown on the floor with Kasey landing on his chest, casting out a plume of marijuana from his mouth, causing her to cough as if she were gassed.

"Oh!" Shabba was embarrassed, waving away the fog. "Please excuse me."

"This is a limited conversation, boy," Butta' stated while getting dressed out of his visual range. "I'm going to use simple words so you can understand. The next time I see you sneaking around any of our rooms, you will be *killed*. I don't care who you or your rich parents are, I'm not the one. Are we clear?"

Kasey shoved her hole-puncher deep into his ribs for added effect. "Respond, boy. Nodding once will be a sufficient acknowledgement of your receipt of our threat, thank you very much."

Shabba, understanding the fear they put on him, nodded once as ordered. He didn't expect Kasey to be as strong as she was; lifting him up and out the room; gripped by his shirt, and thrown into the hall in front of Louie's feet as he was walking through the corridor.

Louie laughed. "Dis was gonna happen sooner or later. I see ya met da ladies."

"*Christ* Lou," Shabba said, trying to get on his feet, laughing at himself. "I think I'm in *love*."

Both Louie and Shabba laughed off the experience, giving the rich boy a swift kick in his pants to chase him away from the door. Not taking any chances, Louie knocked, respectfully, on Butta's cabin door.

"Ah, *Bruce Wayne*," Butta' smirked. "Out for a stroll in your *stately* manor? When you get a chance, please talk to your ward about peeping before he gets *popped*."

"Sorry." Louie said.

"What the hell's going on, Lou?" Kasey laughed. "You can't get a decent gig without being that druggie's sponsor?"

"He ain't no *druggie*, per se. He smokes a little weed—gets a little high. Ya know how it goes."

"Actually, I don't. And what do you mean *a little high*? You can slice him and he'll sprout grade-A."

"He's a good kid wit no direction 'n I get paid two-mil a year just ta make sure he's tucked in. I got command of a thirty-million dolla' yacht, all-a dere security, personnel 'n I don't have ta pay fer *shit*. Youse do da math."

"Those numbers add up to me!" Kasey coughed, fanning herself dramatically. "Jeez, Louie! You're getting *broke da fook off.* You wanna marry me?" Kasey laughed.

"Go 'head, Lou." Butta' said. "She comes with a few skeletons, though."

"Not I, young grasshopper," Kasey yawned in a fashion no man, especially Louie, would ignore. "I got lots of *Ying* for Louie's *Yang*."

"Ladies, please. Youse can't do dis ta me 'n expect me not ta walk funny. We're on da way ta da coordinates ya gave me, sweets. We should reach da *Bay o' Durban* by tomorrow afternoon 'n it's a couple 'o hour's trip ta Johannesburg from dere by land. We're runnin' roughly da same amount o' time between da Cape n' Johannesburg as da train is. 'Bout twenty-six hours give or take."

"So what's that? Tomorrow? Late evening? That won't work!" Butta' fumed.

"Oh!" Louie sounded offended. "I'm sorry, dere princess. Let me take dat time machine out 'o my ass fer ya."

Having checked her, Butta' replayed how she sounded, wishing it didn't come out the way it did. "I'm sorry."

"It's cool. I get it. Stressed out n' still runnin'." Louie knew Butta' enough to know her head and her mouth don't often connect very well at times of intense emotion. "Almost this entire cruise is on auto. Da most we have ta worry 'bout are da pirates, but god save dat bunch if they pick *this* boat." He said this with a confident, haughty laugh. "Just dispose o' the bodies fer me 'n we're good."

"How are you getting permission for this ride, Lou?" Kasey asked. "Will junior's parents *axe* you for this?"

"Kid's parents are neck deep in da South African social scene n' don't return ta da ship fer anotha' week. Don't ya worry yer pretty head 'bout da details. I'll explain everything later n' *Smokey* will cover fer me. Like it or not, ya know? I got shit on him. He'll be cool."

"Thank you," Butta' said, always appreciative, "but don't go losing a ten-figure salary over my crap. I can't replace your pay day."

"Nope! Ya can't." Louie assured her. "How're ya guys getting' along deese' days?"

He meant *financially*. Butta' couldn't respond as confidently as she would like. "We're getting by."

Kasey gave an unmistakable *harrumph*. The fine line between friend and enemy were best seen when pockets were fat or thin. These were lean days for her crew, but Butta' still had friends.

For now, at least.

"I could help youse guys out wit' some cash, if ya need." Louie was a true friend indeed when one was in need.

"We'll talk." Butta' did not shut down the offer as she would normally. "Our resident accountant could give you a better outlook of our —"

"*Dire straits*," Kasey snickered, already thumbing through an on-board Mormon release of the testaments.

Perfecting timing for Butta' to ask her a question that has been burning her for days now. "What's with you lately and the bible thing?"

"Huh?" Kasey asked. "Oh, this? I'm— looking for something."

"Oh, my sister," Butta' slipped on a pair of sandals and walked to the door. "If you're looking for salvation, you'd better hope God doesn't remember that time we were in Chicago the night of the Faberge Egg job." She said this, attempting to come off as if she were joking. Unfortunately, she couldn't mask the underlying emotions behind it; that emotion being, of all things, *envy*. Or maybe anger.

"Maybe," Kasey nodded. "But from what I'm reading, I just need to ask for forgiveness."

Butta' took offense; still riding that mix of emotions that she didn't understand why. "Don't think for a minute that asking for forgiveness is enough, Kase. Because here we are, still doing what we need to do."

Kasey shut the bible, sighed and looked at Butta' with a lengthy, thoughtful gaze. "Which will be the topic of our *next* conversation."

Butta', having known her friend for years, didn't know where this talk was going. While the world around her always seemed to change, the *hint* that things could be different between them was an uncomfortable thought.

"But not now," Butta' finished for her; her eyes burning into Kasey's mind, trying to read her.

"But not now," Kasey agreed, and returned to her reading.

Louie stood between the two women experiencing a moment of loud silence. As Butta' left the room and Kasey buried her thoughts into the bible, Louie followed the team's leader, shutting the door behind himself.

Kasey re-closed the bible and sat to watch her life replay in her mind; wondering where she was going next.

Butta' went looking for Munch, walking along the deck of the yacht, feeling the light breeze of the warm African night air.

While on the way, she needed to assess her emotions. Kasey's decision to find God was her own business, so why did it bother her so much? Honestly, if she really thought about it, it was likely because she had not found the aloof creator herself and lost faith many, *many* years ago.

Yeah, that was likely it. After years with her team—her *friends* trusting in her to guide them—who was this *God* to come into the mix and break up their act? Why should Kasey be so distracted by someone she could not *see* and … *and …*

Not put her faith in me? Butta' grinded her teeth to that most real of thought. Truth be told, she and God were at war. On one hand, who was she to tell Kasey to quit that *God stuff?* Then on the other, why was she so angry about it? This was not a life for the followers of God, but this was the only life she knew. As far as Butta' was concerned, God did not care about her.

If he did, he would not have let her family … *her father …*

"I know that look," Munch said from the background. Not necessarily sneaking up on her, but not making too many sudden moves either. "You're thinking about your family."

Butta' didn't realize she had stopped to stare at the full moon hovering over the crystal clear sky; staring thoughtfully. "You're my family now, Munchie."

"Thanks, baby girl. I feel the same. When we can't have blood family, we just make do with what we got."

"The difference is you *do* have family out there. I know how you feel about your daughter."

Munch walked over to the guard rail and exhaled. The sea was calm and the atmosphere was sensational. Any one deemed a fugitive should travel in such style. "There isn't a day that passes by."

"Munchie… I…" Butta's *conversation* with Kasey had affected her more than she expected; choking her words from the start. "I never thanked you—and the others—for all of this."

"No need for thanks. This is what friends do, right?"

Butta' covered her eyes. "*No*, this is a lot. I'm going crazy and taking all of you for this insane ride. I'm so sorry."

"Hey," Munch went to comfort her, "you don't have to…"

"No wait," she stopped him, sniffling. "Hear me out. You, Kasey, Trig… You're all…" She tried to compose herself unsuccessfully. "You're all I have. We're talking about family and you guys are it for me. This circle is my comfort. *YOU* are my everything on levels beyond just some man and woman connection. You're my brother and a father, so please understand, when you tell me something, I hear you. Everything you guys say… *moves me.* At the same time, I need to get this diamond at all costs. "

"I know."

"That *cost* makes me feel like I'm tearing us apart and I can't lose you. *None of you.* I'm out here chasing a rock to honor a dead family when the live one is dying. I know you're mad at me. You risked your lives for me and here we are at it again."

"So what do you want from me?" He asked. "You want me to tell you *I quit* and let you go your own way?"

"If you did, I'd understand."

"Then I'd be breaking up the family, wouldn't I? You know, Gisela, you never asked any of us *why* we're still riding with you. Why we want to be shot at by damn helicopters in the middle of Cape Town?" Munch laughed. "Who the hell *does* that?"

Butta' chuckled between the tears. "Oh my god. I bet they raised the bounty a notch on that one."

"It's like I said, we are all making do with the family we have. In our circle, there is love that we are looking for. We found it with each other. Trust, security… All of the essentials. I was going to get on you earlier about this whole thing. With Stein dead, I thought you found some closure. I thought chasing after this diamond was a waste of time. After we settled down and got my feet in that jet-stream massager followed by the sauna—Whoooo! Let's just say you could have locked me in a dungeon and I'd be cool with it."

Butta' laughed with him, hugging her teddy bear-like friend.

"See, baby girl. Where in the world can I associate myself daily with three attractive women since my own daughter? You ladies give me a chance to *take care* of you. I know it sounds silly and I know you ladies are grown and all…"

Butta' kissed Munch on the forehead. "You are the *greatest* father a woman can have."

Munch appreciated that. "You could call me *daddy*, if you wanted to. Trust me! I'll have no problem with that. So, when I happen to say, I don't know… '*Who's your daddy*', you can easily respond…"

Butta' laughed so hard she started tearing, interrupting his comedy. "Oh, *gawd*. Stop right there!"

McCarran International Airport, Las Vegas, NV

At the same time Butta' and her crew were boarding the Sariya-Anne; wet, disheveled and angry *prior* to sauna treatments and heart-to-heart conversations—Diandra Stein would have her fill of the *City of Sin*; having answered all the questions the local and federal officials required, it was time for her to leave.

Marcy sat next to her in the limo doing Marcy-things: scheduling, flight checking, security coordinating, phone answering and a multitude of details that Diandra need not be concerned with.

She only had the one task of trying to stay alive and that was *barely* manageable.

Eventually, the limousine arrived at the airport through a special entrance to park directly beside her private jet. Following them was an entourage of security in black vans in front and behind her limo. Upon arrival, they would go through the tedious task of securing the area before she boarded; average runt-thru time of twenty minutes after redundant checking every inch of the plane.

"I'll be back," Marcy commented, opening the door to the limo and shut it behind herself.

Diandra felt less stressed than usual. Maybe it was the fact that *she* orchestrated the hiring of Ellen and Frank on her own and gained a little bit of an *independent backbone* than she realized she would have.

Reexamining her steps, she truly felt she presented herself well; spoke with confidence to the detectives, stated her case and demands sufficiently. Enough of these grown-up decisions and maybe she would actually *feel* life was worth living.

As she was considering what else she could possibly get done, the limo door opened and it wasn't Marcy who sat across from her.

The woman was of Hispanic descent, professionally dressed with a pair of sunglasses on with a *devastatingly* phenomenal body for her age—roughly mid-thirties. She sported small mole on her forehead, accenting her no-nonsense, sexy allure as she smiled at Diandra without saying too much.

Diandra asked the obvious: "Who are you?"

"Ms. Stein. My condolences to you and your family for the loss of your father, Lingo Stein. He was a fierce competitor."

"My father *was* my family. Who the hell are you?"

"We're going to get to know each other very well over the next few days. I wanted to meet you personally as there will only be two times we'll ever speak face-to-face. This is number one. We're both busy women. Well, at least I am."

"How did you get past my security? If you don't—"

"If I don't, *what?* What are you going to do? Call for help? Hold on." The woman rolled down the window and held out her hand. Two of Diandra's own security personnel skipped over to give her a manila envelope and a business card. Thanking them, she lifted the window to resume their privacy. Diandra just barely managed to catch a glimpse of Marcy; not necessarily held back, but not permitted to get close to the limo.

The look of horror in her eyes.

"Who are you?" Diandra whispered, remembering the assassinations from earlier.

"I'm not here to kill you. No shootings. No mysterious letters with engraved typefaces. I'm just here to say *hello*."

"How do you know about the—?" Diandra sputtered.

"Ms. Stein, I know as much as I need to know. As it happens, the letter you received wasn't something I needed to know, so I can't help you with that yet. Right now, the only thing you need to be aware of is the time."

"The time?"

"That's right. It's Tuesday and you need to remember 10:15 am Friday morning. At *10:16*, I will own Stein Industries and all of its remaining holdings. 10:15 will be your last minute of the *free ride*. Use these days wisely and prepare for become a normal human being soon."

"You're insane," Diandra sneered. She could believe a lot of things, but the day someone else would take over her father's company, and to a greater extent *her money*, was ludicrous.

"That's fine," the woman shrugged, unconcerned. "This envelope covers, in detail, a play by play of what I have been doing while you were attempting suicide or hiring detectives to find meaningless people in South Africa. It concludes with what will happen on Friday through various Wall Street exchanges and corporate jargon that you should hand-off Marcy for proper definition. It gets quite technical. I could sum it up for you and say that this is an old fashion *hostile* takeover, but that cheapens the overall *umph* of it all. *The impact.* You know where I'm coming from? I don't believe in being *hostile*, in the violence kind of way. Let's call it a '*you have no choice handover.*'"

"And you assume I'll just let you do this?"

"Ms. Stein, please pay attention. I said you have *no choice*. Just before your team of attorney's were murdered right before your eyes, you were pretty much allowing them to run *you* anyway. To your father's credit, he let *no one* run him or his business. Something you haven't grasped yet. Maybe never will." She sat closer, reaching out to touch Diandra's hands. She pulled them back defensively. "It's okay to stop pretending to be bigger than you are, Ms. Stein. Your father had the heart for the big boy games and I'm afraid you're just not ready. You may never be."

"You're not taking anything. I swear to you, it's not going to happen. I don't even know who you are. Who the hell are you? Nobody! This is *my* company!"

The woman smiled at Diandra as a woman would smile to a five-year-old trying to make demands about what she wanted for dinner.

"Very well. It's been a pleasure. Please feel free to read through all the information enclosed in that envelope. Take particular note of the severance pay option I'm giving Marcy. She truly has been good to you and I couldn't see why she shouldn't leave the company well taken care of. I've even given you a *golden parachute*, as they say. You'll find it quite handsome. You'll still maintain your lifestyle, just on a *insey winsey* budget. Oh, and some advice. Call off the detectives from the Gisela Thompson pursuit."

"Why?!"

"Because I don't approve of it. You are spending *my* money." She said plainly, and opened the limo. Stepping out, she peeked back in once last time to rest the business card on her seat. "Ms. Stein— *ciao.*"

She closed the door, leaving Diandra to herself… *alone…* as usual. Moments later, the door reopened and Marcy rushed in frantic.

"Ms. Stein! What the hell?!? Who was that? Are you okay?"

Diandra didn't respond, taking up the business card. Everyone seemed to want to leave her something to read; disappearing into the ever growing mystery surrounding her.

The card merely had one name, embossed, in the center of the card:

Marigold

Corey A. Burkes

Chapter 9

Potsdam, Germany – Fowler Residence - Morning
Eight-year-old Crystal Fowler landed on her father's chest abruptly, waking Wyman out of a restless sleep. The bed sheets were in disarray from his consistent tossing and turning; damp from his sweat and his heart racing; dreaming about people after him… *shooting at him* … just about to *kill* him.

Looking into his daughter's face, Wyman realized he was safe at home where he belonged.

"You up yet?" She asked.

"Well I am *now*." He could never be put off by such an adorable, beautiful child. Especially since his dreams were haunting him. She was a breath of the freshest air and he gave her a big hug.

"*Eww!* Daddy! You *wet* the bed!"

"No I didn't, sweetheart. Daddy was just *hot*. I did a lot of sweating."

"Are you sick? I sweat in bed when I'm sick."

"Maybe I am."

She backed away from him with a wide-eyed expression. "You got the *cooties*?"

Now was Wyman's chance for revenge. "Yup! Come 'ere and let me give you some!"

Crystal's scream encouraged Wyman out of the bed and he gave chase around the large, master bedroom. Pillows were being thrown, tickles were being traded and laughter reigned supreme in the house that Fowler built.

That is, until mommy walked in to break things up as she usually did.

"What's going on up in here?" Desiree, the ruling matriarch, laid down the law as her eight-year-old daughter and forty-something husband usually didn't have better sense on a school day. "Why aren't you dressed, young lady?"

Crystal hopped off the bed from under her father and skirted out of the room. "Daddy's fault!"

"What? Come back here you!" Wyman cranked back a pillow to take aim until his wife blocked his path. "Oops."

"What's with you?"

"Sorry."

"Between the two of you, I'm gonna need therapy. She's going to miss the bus and *you're* going to be the one taking her to school this morning. Is that what you want? And don't give me any of that *you can't drive her to school cause you have some scientific Captain Kirk crap to pull out your ass or the world will burn in a pit of hellfire* cause I'm wise to your lies, Wyman."

"Do I really sound that way?"

"Do you ever listen to yourself? More drama than the soaps. Now look at this bed! What happened to you? Did you pee the bed? Nasty ass. I thought we said we weren't going to try that…"

"Look! You and Crystal are two in a pod. *No,* I didn't pee in the bed and NO we will *never* try that… *ahem…* in any other situation."

"Thank *fucking* god. So are you sick?"

Wyman flopped back on the bed, rubbing his face. "In a matter of ways, yes. Sick *and* tired."

"See that? Drama." Desiree took this as her moment to really listen to her husband and sit by his side. "I heard it in your voice last night. What happened?"

He thought for a moment, and then covered his head with a pillow, letting out a primal scream. He needed two pillows to muffle his anguish. Once through, he stared up at the ceiling.

"Feel better?" She asked.

"I've doomed us all."

"Okay, *comic book man.* Can you say that with any more theatrics? What's going on now?"

Wyman stared at his wife and smiled sheepishly. "Do you want the whole story or do you want it in a nutshell?"

"Nutshell. Crystal's bus is coming in twenty minutes."

"Fine. I built a portable laser that could help surgical procedures in remote countries and they turned it into a weapon of mass destruction. The only way for this laser to work is to use a diamond that cannot be duplicated anymore…"

He rolled over to the nightstand by the bed, digging through the books, papers and general junk he kept in there.

Desiree saw what was coming next. "Knowing my husband who waves a banner for every environmental cause on the planet, please don't tell me you…"

Wyman plopped a closed, velvet bag into her hands. The weight was mind-blowing.

Diamonds were *indeed* a woman's best friend. Even through the velvet sack, Desiree's mouth fell open. She felt the sheer weight and the possibilities of ownership. No matter how financially solvent her family was, in her hand was a diamond about the same size as her palm.

"*Jesus*," she whispered. "How many carats?"

"920."

"*Christ!*" Her heart pounded. She imagined it as a ring—one *huge-ass* rock on her finger that possibly, with a swipe of her hand, could cut the air and scratch the surface of every glass item in the room. She could use it to light her way in the middle of the night. Flaunt it at the women's club who loved to talk about their successful men and endless credit they *don't* own.

People would stop. People would stare.

She would love it.

"*Christ.*" She didn't even take it out of the bag yet.

Wyman didn't give her the chance to so, seeing her eyes light up too much as they already were. He took it back and gripped it with utter concern. "I'm in a middle of a mess. A *huge* mess."

Wyman wiped the sweat from his brow. All this was proof positive he wasn't' engineered to be a thief, let alone some moral cause terrorist. *Of course* they would realize the diamond was missing. *Of course* they would figure out he was the last person to have handled it. *Of course* they would prosecute to the full extent of the law.

The word *fugitive* crossed his mind like a hot brand; embedding its mark in his mind to welcome him to the fraternal order of men on the run.

Men whom eventually were caught and killed in a blaze of glory.

"Wow," Desiree thought, considered saying something else; unable to come up with the right words. "Wow."

"Des, I had to," he swallowed hard. He began to doubt his original wisdom on the matter—what his original *moral integrity* was about. Did he *really* have to take the diamond? What the hell was he thinking? "Or at least, I *think* I had to. I just couldn't let them do this to me anymore. Or to others. The world. I didn't want to be a contributor to power war games anymore. They were going to take what I made for the good of the people and change it to *decimate* whoever they saw fit."

"Fine." Desiree concluded, taking Wyman by surprise. Desiree tended to roll with a situation better than most people. This current lifestyle of international living and limo services was a 360-degree change from her earlier life of struggling for her next meal and working two or three jobs. In her own words, *you can't be disappointed about things if you just keep it moving.* "They were sticking it to you anyway and you made a quick decision to set your soul right. I'm good with that. I support your decision."

He *really* loved her right now.

"I'm not saying you didn't go cold *gangster* on a billion dollar corporation. Look at you! Rolled up in there and *taxed* their shit. That's MY nerdy baby! *We'll* get above this. I believe in what you're doing."

"I might as well have just thrown *everything* we worked for away. If—and that's a huge, big IF—I don't get arrested, I'll never be able to work in the science community again. What will we do?"

Desiree harrumphed. "Get another job elsewhere. Personally, I just about had it trying to rub elbows with these fake housewives who know damn well their husbands keep them quiet with an expense account. We were *just* talking about going back home to the states, too."

Home was New York for her. Roswell, Georgia for him. Going back to America was a constant dinner conversation that never got old. Especially when he vented about how much he hated his work and the lack of other Blacks to associate with.

What an opportune time to hasten travel plans.

"Here's my suggestion," she started to speak, getting up to close the door before their daughter or Pilar, the live-in nanny and cook, could hear. "Do they know it's missing or if you have it yet?"

"No. As far as I know, thank God, no. The phone would be ringing off the hook if…"

The phone rang.

Wyman and Desiree almost jumped out of their skin. A severe *flop-sweat* blanketed his body as his heart drummed away like a musician in concert. Desiree played it cool and answered the phone; hands shaking. "Hello?"

She paused to listen, keeping Wyman on edge until her body relaxed and she waved him down. "*Erica*, I'll have to call you back. I don't care what time it is in New York! Email me. I'm in the middle of something. Bye!"

"Your sister?" Wyman sighed.

"Bad timing. Look, they'll find out. No question about that. They're going to connect the dots and check you on this. If that's the case, make *them* ask you for the diamond back, but only if they find you. Don't go volunteering shit, you get me?"

"I don't understand. Find me? What do you mean?"

"First, let's get you to stop worrying about getting arrested and what not. You're doing something for the good of yourself and for others. These guys are looking to twist your inventions into military weapons. Maybe the world needs to know about it. You get my drift?"

It started to dawn on him. "Lift my *cause* on the matter. I *am* doing this for a reason."

"That's right you are. You're not just some petty thief walking off with their property to fence somewhere. You're making a *statement*. But don't be a *martyr*. Crystal and I love you and want you to be around to fix the garage door."

Wyman laughed. "I knew I was worthwhile around here for something. I love you both so much," he exhaled—finally.

"So we're going to play this *professionally* and get you in front of as many people as possible so they don't try something stupid. First bad move on their part, you'll let the press know about all of their secret crap and that'll be the end of Robertson."

"You're amazing," he whispered. "Thank you for understanding."

"Thick and thin, shine and shit, baby. You are my *husband* and we ride all things out together."

"Yeah… *Yeah*… I know you didn't sign up for this. I'm so sorry."

"Whatever babe," is all she said and he knew his wife had his back.

Then, out of nowhere, he remembered something vital.

"Oh my god! There's a *second* diamond!"

"I thought you said this couldn't be duplicated?"

"It can't! I mean, not anymore. They had two made and I was blind to their reasons why. Of course, why sell one when you can sell *two* laser weapons?"

"Do you have the other diamond?"

"No. It's being moved from South Africa—on its way to the facility even as we speak. *Oh god*! You know they're going to want to pair up the two when it arrives and the next thing you know, they'll be coming for me!"

"Mommy!" Crystal's voice came from behind the closed bedroom door.

"Coming baby!" Desiree stood up and approached the door. Better to open it up than listen to her bang on it insistently. "That's to be expected. They'll find out sooner than later, but make them work for it. Don't you have a Physics Conference this weekend?"

"Mommy? I'm done!" Crystal started knocking.

"In Prague, yes. I was going to skip that stuffy thing and take Crystal to the beach."

"Change of plans" She had to make it quick before opening the door. "We're taking a family trip and we're taking the diamond with us. If they want that thing, *make them* take it from you in front of a lot of people."

"But where will I hide the damn thing?"

By the time he put out his last word, Desiree opened the door for Crystal who stood there in her school uniform looking up at her parents suspiciously, nuzzling her brown teddy bear.

Both parents gaped back at her, making Crystal feel a little uneasy.

"What?" She questioned. "Am I in trouble?"

Stein Depository – South Africa - Morning

"They did all this?" Ellen asked, counting the bullet holes along the ceiling, walls and floors. The Stein Depository had seen better days.

Ellen and Frank silently walked the destroyed halls using a mental walkthrough pattern—following the path earlier charted by Butta' and company. Ghostly echoes of gunfire could still be heard if Ellen listened carefully.

The intrepid detectives, now under the Diandra Stein payroll, have traveled around the globe to pick up a half-baked crime scene investigation—relying on instinct and time tested deducing skills because the local law refused to help or share resources.

Stein security had all but disbanded as they shuttered the depository doors for good.

Whatever happened here—and where Butta' may be heading next—was told within the previous shoot out and escape.

"What did they take?" Frank asked the depository liaison, Michael Swosland. He was the last man on the totem pole and drew the smallest straw when officials were asked to 'volunteer' and address any last minute concerns for the detectives.

"Nothing." He said flatly.

"Nothing?" Frank pressed. "Then what was all this about?"

"Do you at *least* know what they came here for?" Ellen inquired, back tracking to the heart of the matter; twin double doors with all the signage removed. The faded, dusty remains of earlier text could still be read above the door: *Project Gisela.*

"So, she came to take Gisela?" Frank guessed aimlessly; mostly to annoy the liaison who wasn't being as helpful.

"Hardly," he grimaced. "Gisela is a one-ton stationary, complex machine. The woman thief would *not* be walking out with it."

"*Was*" Ellen sniffed the air. The whole compound smelled of gun smoke, beer and blood.

"Excuse me?" Michael asked.

"You said Gisela *is* a one-tone machine. It was dismantled," then she paused, "right?"

The man grunted an acknowledgement that really wasn't an answer at all. One of those 'I won't lie to you, but I won't say nothing either' grunts. Ellen would let that slide—for now. "*Anyway*, according to the report, they were discovered here. Is the vault and storage unit on this level?"

"*Was*" Michael smiled, triumphant with himself. "The storage unit *was* down that hall."

"Don't play games with her, *flat head*," Frank warned. "She'll give you a *titty-twist* you won't appreciate."

"Better listen to the man," Ellen smirked. "So, I'm thinking they either came all this way to destroy Gisela, found out it was too late... or came to take something else. Kind of like a *plan B*. What you got, Frank?"

"Vendetta mission. Rolled in with a small posse. Maybe to case the joint. I don't know about coming here to destroy something we all know they could just rebuild. It's rakin' leaves in the park on that idea."

"What is that term? Racking leaves in the park?" Michael asked, keeping a comfortable distance from the both of them.

"He means it was a *fruitless* effort." Ellen opened the double doors to the Gisela room and peaked into utter darkness. *This is where they made the biggest diamonds on Earth.* "Yeah, Frankie. That wasn't the goal. It had to be something else. Stein's dead. That score settled itself. How did the Gisela process work? Did it roll out anymore diamonds before they shut it down?"

"Gisela was *not* a conveyor belt, detective." Yes, he said it with *that* kind of attitude. "The process delivered one piece per operation."

"*What* and *when* was the last diamond produced?" She asked.

Michael thumbed through a clipboard he carried with him, detailing shipped inventory records. "The last and largest produced was the Stein Diandra. 920-carats and developed a little over a week ago."

"Let me see that thing." Frank lifted the clipboard out of Michael's hands and sorted through the information, noticing one very important fact Michael failed to mention. "It says here they made *two* of them. Where are they?"

"That's classified," he concluded. "I'm sorry."

"Classified?" Frank shook his head, looking at Ellen. "Get this guy."

Ellen started to get mad. "How can anything be classified when *your* boss told you we had complete transparency in this investigation?"

"The Stein administration had provisions in place that override those of the company founders at times of *ill-placed* commands. No offense, detectives, but I have orders higher than the owner herself by contract."

"So we're not going to know where any of these diamonds are or who ordered them?" Ellen was already dialing Diandra's direct phone number. Stalled investigations like this were *not* in Ellen's job description.

"Is the knowledge of any of that pertinent to the overall investigation?" Michael inquired.

"*Is the knowledge of any of that pertinent to the overall investigation?*" Frank mocked. "Shut yer trap, *apartheid boy*. You're dismissed. We'll take it from here."

Michael took back his clipboard and walked off, glad to be away from the Americans and their savage ways.

Ellen couldn't reach anyone on her cell phone and folded it away, deep in her usual thought. "Bet you a six-pack they came for one or both of those diamonds. The largest and last of them. I would. The whole *father's legacy* bit."

"But they got jammed up. By order of that *International House of Pancakes* you work for, they shut down Gisela and confiscated all his goods pending investigation. They blew it. No diamond. No Gisela. They're runnin' empty handed."

"Shoot up the place, escape and wreck half of South Africa in the process. Yep! Sounds good to me."

"Question is, did they get what their looking for?" Frank queried.

"If we say yes, then what? We're still at square one. However, if we say *no*—and they *didn't* get out of here with anything—that will help fill in some holes. Didn't we get reports that *she* was chasing someone else?"

"Crabby-ass local yokels won't help worth *shit*," Frank hated it when his peers didn't help one another during investigations. "Arrogant fuckers."

"We don't need them. We'll track the chase to the final point and see if we can score some traffic and security cams on the way. It's like we were back on the Bronx stroll. Hunts Point. Remember those days? Nobody heard or saw nothin', but there's a body in the middle of broad daylight, crowded street. We'll still get what we want."

"I'll bet your panties we will." Frank affirmed, lighting up a cigarette.

Chapter 10

The Yacht Sariya-Anne – Ocean outside of South Africa - Morning

Fuego's arms failed him on the 124th push-up and he collapsed on the deck; sucking in the morning African sea breeze. Out of all the adventures he had seen, this had to be the most laid back of them all.

Even with a complete, outfitted gym in the lower deck, the old-fashion *hands-to-floor* exercise would never go out of style. This morning, he worked out to watch the sunrise and appreciate being alive.

When that morning spectacle was over, he continued to watch the African day begin with his own deep and private thoughts. The world was beautiful and he watched it play out in front of him. He would never need a translator for the smile on his face.

Neither would Kasey—one of the few people in the world who could still sneak up on Fuego silently without him noticing. She sat at a table, sipping a cup of coffee; staring out into the horizon.

Fuego flinched unprepared, naturally getting to his feet in a fighters stance. "¿Porque usted siempre hace esó?" *Why do you always do that?*

"Porque a usted le encanta."*Because you love it,* Kasey responded. Maybe not the most perfect Spanish, but she could hold her own in a conversation. "¿A donde esta todó el mundó?" *Where is everybody?*

"Todavia durmiendo yo creó." *Still sleeping, I think.*

Everyone was still sleeping. Chasing through the South African streets could wear a body out. Whereas Kasey would normally be stretched out until the latter half of the afternoon—instead, she was still hung up on the thoughts of *what next*. She had seen the world three times over in her *many* professions. This was the first time she really asked herself: *Where do I go from here?*

Bible by her side, the only thing going through her head was just those two loaded words: *what's next?*

As she pondered the concept of getting a real, decent job; going back to school and, *god forbid*, paying taxes…

"You're up early, aren't you?" She asked Trigger, whom was approaching from behind purposely light footed in a vain attempt to catch Kasey off guard. It was very difficult to be *cat-like* while dragging a blanket wrapped around her body.

Kasey gawked at her young partner incredulously. "Where are you coming from?"

A guilty looking Trigger shrugged. "My room. Good morning."

"Good morning." Kasey sat up, suddenly much more intrigued. "Your room is *that* direction. Where did you sleep last night?"

"Well, I… I can't say I actually got *any* sleep."

"Oh, you didn't!" Kasey grimaced. "With the *pot head*?"

Trigger scurried closer to Kasey, looking over her shoulder to make sure no one heard. "Don't tell, Bee."

"That depends on how you answer the next few questions. What were you *thinking*?"

"Kase, come on. We're on the road all the time. I don't ever meet anyone. He's really cool and he's richer than a *mutha'!* So, I needed to let off a little steam, ya know?"

"Richer than *a mutha'*." Kasey snorted. "I guess that answers everything."

"For real. Between us girls, he ain't much, but it's been *a while* so anything felt good right about now."

Kasey's frown deepened and she turned to look out to the ocean, away from Trigger. "You don't know what *awhile* really is."

"Girl, go get you some!" Trigger encouraged.

"First," Kasey said sternly, "I don't feed into sexual needs that easy. Especially with any joker I meet for the first time. Second, there's a time and place for everything—and on the good ship lollipop—*it isn't*. Haven't I taught you *anything*?"

"What? How to be a prude?"

"How to be a *woman*. You think that weed smoking ass is going to care about you?"

"What if I don't care?"

Kasey stared at her for a moment, speechless. "Then I suppose I didn't teach you a *damn* thing at all."

Trigger pouted and backed away, pulling up her blanket. "I'm grown. I didn't ask for no teacher no way."

She marched off in the direction of her room, tripping over her blanket with immature grace.

Fuego sat up on the deck, looking up at Kasey. "Usted no puede ser su madré, ella necesita aprender ella mismá." *You can't be her mother. She'll need to learn for herself.*

She didn't even bother to translate it. "I don't want to be her mother. I'm just trying to save her some bad steps. Like the ones I made at her age."

That annoyed her to no end. Kasey needed to get on her feet and move about—do *anything*, but sit there and reflect on what she just saw of her *ex-protégé*.

"I'm going to see if she's up." Kasey of course referred to Butta' and left Fuego to his deck exercises.

Try as she might, she could not ignore Trigger's last request *not* to tell Butta' and that was the first thing she planned to do. On one hand, maybe it wasn't any of her business. Trigger is an adult, albeit a young one. She could make all the stupid decisions she wanted.

Then Kasey rethought. *Nah! Not on my watch.* She was Trigger's unspoken guardian in the world of vice and abuse. She wasn't going to let her only pupil go out like a *punk*; bedding any creep that came along.

Her semi-latent motherly instincts would not allow such self-destruction.

She was about to knock on Butta's cabin door when it flung open. Butta' was already dressed and with a *ready to go* expression in her eyes. "Mornin'. I was just coming to get you."

"Hey. Think we got time to talk about Trig?" Kasey asked.

"What do we have to talk about?" Butta' asked.

Followed closely by Trigger—a few paces away; dressed with her hands on her hips looking squarely at Kasey. "Yeah, Kasey. What do we have to talk about?"

The three women stared at one another in the moment of uncomfortable silence until Kasey decided to just go with what she had to say. "Hell if I care. We can do this right here and now."

"Is that so?" Trigger stepped closer; a clear threatening motion of closing the gap between them that Kasey picked up immediately, cocking an eyebrow at her. As if she was seeing Trigger for the very first time. Not as a friend—but as someone she would have to knock out.

"Tell me I'm misreading you, right now. Please tell me you're not stepping into my airspace as if you plan to rise up on me."

Butta' took a firm stance between the two, putting a hand on Triggers shoulder. "What the hell is this?"

"I don't know, ask her! I'm minding my own business. Maybe *she* needs to take a cue and get a clue."

This was Kasey's chance to let it all out, but the timing and anger in the air was wrong. She didn't want to start saying things out of emotion. Reluctantly, she backed down. "Forget it."

Butta', whom knew her longest friend better than anyone, looked into Kasey's eyes and the two transmitted a silent communication only trusted friendship could comprehend. They would get to the bottom of this later on—just not right now. "Alright. Wanna get Munchie and Fuego? It's time for a huddle."

"Sure." Kasey turned and walked the opposite direction from Trigger. By the time Butta' turned to look at her other partner, she was already gone.

Is this how a family comes to an end? Butta' thought.

Overnight, Butta' refitted her cabin into a war room. Print outs of awkward angled security camera photos of that German soldier she fought with through the streets of South Africa. Blow ups, slightly blurry, of his face just as he entered the train. Magnified shots of the box he tucked under his arm, circled in red, identified as the target.

Across the bed, a mock display of the Johannesburg train station and surrounding buildings made of cardboard, paper, bottles and string. Clearly, Butta's arts and crafts skills were put to the test.

Much to Louie's ire. It was cool to help a friend out, but how many times could he remind them all—this was *not* his boat. Whenever he felt like exploding, he remembered how this little crew of misfits came through for him on more than one occasion in their not too distant past. He owed them more than the mind could fathom.

Munch sat on one side of the room listening to a *Chris Botti* CD and a novel from the yacht's expensive library: *Too Many Lies by Daphine Glenn Robinson.* Both pieces of excellent works soothed his mind and soul. Nothing like smooth jazz and brilliant storytelling while waiting to hammer out details of the next heist.

Kasey and Fuego played a quick hand of *Spades* in one corner and Butta' was waiting for the last of three pages to arrive from an installed fax machine. She received the final, updated train schedule and passenger manifest. Once it rolled out, Butta' glanced over the papers and spied around the room for the missing component to her group.

"We'll just have to start ahead without Trig. Louie, we're still on course to arrive at Durban Harbor?"

"Yup. On auto. Clear seas ahead, capt'n. I'd say we could make da bay in 'bout two-three hours."

Butta' was eternally grateful. "Perfect. Thank you, Louie. Train schedule reports that there have been no delays and will arrive at six o'clock this evening. More than enough time for us to cross from Durban to Johannesburg with prepared vehicles also courtesy of Louie and his partners locally."

"Hey, I got peoples everywhere." He shrugged.

"Thank goodness for that. The plan is really cut and dry. Call it a variation of the *Spank and Shake* we did in London except this time we have our eyes on the prize." She held up a constantly beeping and number scrolling tracker. "Train arrives; we keep tabs via the tracker and maneuver him and the diamond into a boxed location so we can discretely jack him of the diamond. *Case closed.* Munchie, I'm going to need you to…"

In came Trigger, giggling, with Shabba holding on to her waist like two fun-loving couples accidently walking into a room.

Corey A. Burkes

Those in the room looked toward the rude intrusion and Trigger's laughter came to an abrupt halt. Louie cut his eyes at Shabba with a mix of disappointment and fury.

Munch closed the South Carolina native's novel, realizing an equally moving drama next to Mrs. Robinson's characters was about to play out right in front of him.

Which was nothing compared to the dead-on glare Trigger received from Butta'. "Glad you could make it."

"What?" She asked indignantly—with a tone as if *they* were inconveniencing *her*. "I'm here. What're ya'll lookin' at me for?"

Butta' nodded at Louie in the direction of Shabba who was just as ready to sit amongst the crew and get comfortable, already pulling out a rolled cigarette. "What? I can't hang with you guys? I got enough *spliff* to go around."

"Private meetin', boyo. Let's go take a walk."

Shabba was pulled out roughly; only because he refused to move peacefully. "Private meeting? Hell, this is *my* ship?"

"It's ya daddy's boat, partner. Out ya go." He turned back to Butta' as he left. "I'm sorry 'bout 'dis, suga'. Can ya manage while I keep 'dis clown busy?"

"You're the best, Lou." Butta' sighed.

Just as the door to the cabin closed, Butta' threw her papers at Trigger unceremoniously. "Trig, what the hell!?"

"Ya'll throwin' shit at me now? Wow!"

"This isn't a damn joy ride. We're out here on business."

"Yeah." Trigger huffed. "*Your* business. It's always *your* business and maybe I need a break."

"*Oh, shit.* You ungrateful little—" Kasey was annoyed *for* Butta', sitting up from her card game and about to say something—held off by Butta's hand.

"No, that's fine. You want out to mess around with that kid? I thought we were in this together"

"Together? Sister girl, this is *your* show. It's all about *Butta'* and I rode with you, maybe, as far as I think I want to."

"Where's all this coming from?" Butta' asked—a little hurt.

"I'll tell you where it's coming from." Kasey pointed out. "It's coming from a kid with deep pockets and *she's* just getting her *gold dig* on."

"You know what, Kasey?" Trigger reared around on her, prepared to fight. "You can go *screw* yourself. You're just a fuckin' high class *hoe* takin' dudes all over the world of their cheese with a big butt and a smile. You ain't got the right to say *shit* to me."

Kasey expressed faux concern, holding her rear end up to a mirror. "My butt is *big?*"

Fuego snickered. His limited knowledge of English covered, at the very least, some key words of the *female* anatomy.

Trigger was finished with Kasey and looked at Butta'. "If you don't mind, I'm thinking I'm gonna to sit this one out."

"Well, sorry, *sister girl.* You can't."

"What?" Trigger didn't expect opposition. This entire argument was out of their usual expectation.

"You heard me. You signed up for this. We work together and that's the end of it."

"Bullshit!" Trigger cursed.

"Watch your mouth!"

"You're *not* my mother. Why do you bitches keep holding me down like I'm your goddamn *step-child.*"

"Cause you got no sense!" Butta' pointed at her fiercely.

Trigger put a hand up, warning her. "Get your damn hands out my face. I'm not playin'."

Butta' did not back down. "How are you gonna come up here and sleep with that boy. You don't know his ass from a hole in the wall."

"That bitch told you?!?" Trigger pointed at Kasey.

"That's *one.*" Kasey counted. "I'm only giving you *three* since we go way back and all and you're feelin' yourself right now. We all make mistakes and I'm only giving you three. You're down by one, chicky. You'd better mind me." Kasey shook her head, looking to Butta' for help. A blazing fire in her eyes being held back by sheer waning will power. "Bee, *you* better advise her." Kasey could barely contain herself. "*Somebody* better wake her up. I'm telling you… *Maaaannnnn* ... um-um-um!"

"As if you're gonna do something." Trigger challenged, lifting her hands up at Kasey. "What the *fuck* you think you're gonna do?"

Butta' finally had to put a stop to this and put her hands on Trigger, slamming her against the wall. "What the hell's gotten into you?"

The unexpected jostling dislodged an envelope out of Trigger's jacket. *The invitation*; the same one she didn't open. Both women looked at the fallen envelope of fine yellow paper. Of note, at least to Butta', was the rear of the envelope; a wax stamp with a familiar symbol.

As Butta' squinted to cross reference the symbol in her mind, Trigger scooped it up and put it back in her pocket. Butta' backed off, glancing at Kasey, then Munch and Fuego—each looking at how unstable this little group had become.

"Okay." Butta' cleared her throat. "You have the right to do as you choose. You're an adult and I won't stop you. However, I'm asking you, *as a friend*, if you could help me out. Just this one last time."

"You shouldn't have to ask her for *shit*!" Kasey barked. "After all we've done for that unthankful son of a—"

"I *really* think I would like us to do this *last* job on a happier note." Butta' resigned.

"Last job?" Munch inquired. "You think so?"

Butta' looked at her old friend and nodded. "Last job. All of you stuck around with me so I can get at Stein and now that he's finished what more is there? This diamond—it's the last of my father's legacy. The largest diamond they ever made and, you're right Trig. This is *my* business. Not yours. All of you made a choice to help me and I—I realize I've taken all of you to the ends of the Earth and I'm sorry. I sincerely feel all of you are the best and only friends anyone could ever have. But this—" She waved her hand around at her friends, "*this* isn't what I want. The fighting. The yelling; none of this. I love you all, but I won't lose you over a diamond. It's just not that worth it."

The group simmered into their own thoughts; looking to the floor or at one another. Trigger leaned against the wall with her arms crossed.

"I'll do it. I'm sorry." After which, she slid against the wall and down to the floor, burying her head into her knees, sniffling and then crying.

Kasey and Butta' did more of their mutual, silent communication. Collectively, the group tended to handle situations *outside* of their inner circle well. For the first time, they had to deal with just each other; like a family that found they had to *talk* to each other when the TV suddenly stopped working.

Butta' sat next to her youngest friend and put an arm around her and the 'Trigger' she knew dug into her chest and let it all out; bawling emotionally.

"Yeah, this is our last job." Butta' confirmed.

"So this means I have to get gainful, fill out an application JOB?" Munch asked.

"Sure, Munchie. You can go back to working at Wal-Mart. What were you back then? Assistant Store Manager?" Kasey half-way joked.

Munch chuckled. "I'm going to go from million dollar heists, hanging from 112-story buildings and being chased around the *motherland* by flying gunships to re-stocking returned merchandise from the front desk and arguing with dumbass Support Managers named *Jorge*? Baby girl, there's no hope for me in the real world. I'd kill that guy if I went back there."

"What gets me," Kasey added, "is you remember those days with clarity. And who the hell is Jorge?"

"Just some asshole I had to work with during the overnights. He was cheating on his girlfriend with some chick that worked there and it was a hot mess." Munch shivered, remembering old crap. "I'm doing just fine now thank you."

"You sure?" Kasey laughed at him. "Do you need therapy?"

"Let's just say," he laughed with her. "I'd rather do what we did yesterday *any day* than go through another inventory at Wal-Mart *ever*. Hey, Trig! What are you going to do on the outside?"

Trigger sat up, wiped away some of her tears. "I don't know. Maybe—" Then she busted out giggling. "Maybe be a *cop*."

Their laughter carried its way up the yacht and to the pleased ears of Louie—who had hoped true friendships, like a ship piloted through raging storm, would eventually find their way home.

NATO Air Base Geilenkirchen - Geilenkirchen, Germany - Morning

By the time Fuego was on the deck of the Sariya-Anne, pushing out his 112th push-up, and Kasey was just waking up to take a walk onto the deck to sneak up on him, a large and hulking Boeing C-17A Globemaster III airlift cargo aircraft was being loaded with crates marked ROBERTSON TECHNOLOGY in the middle of an airfield in Germany.

General Tucker stood overseeing the operation, smoking a cigar he kept on hand when the time was right. That time was now— just coming off of a very expensive transaction that should put the United States ahead of the arms race by five years or so.

Lester Grumman joined the General, pulling up aside of him in the company Lexus with a small security detail; dressed in black and armed to the teeth with all sorts of nasty looking rifles and knives.

The General and his personnel group of officers looked at the ugly mob of angry men and grunted things amongst themselves.

"Good day, General Tucker." Lester greeted. "I trust you have everything in order?"

"Grumman." General Tucker nodded. "I also appreciate the extras. Thank you for the carbon fiber stealth material doo-hickey you included."

"Not at all, General. When the United States government pays as much as they have, you get something free with every of million."

"What's with the farewell committee?" The General didn't appreciate thugs in his presence—particularly when they were not U.S military.

"Sorry for the dramatics, General. As you know, we have security procedures we have to adhere to when it comes to the diamonds."

"Humph," the General smirked. "Speaking of which, here's intelligence from Langley."

The General handed over a folder with red letters across the front INTEL EYES ONLY. From the first page to the next, Lester's patented grin fell from a frown to dismal despair. "The Koreans?"

"*North* Koreans to be specific," the General corrected. "The Russians too. Your recent data thefts of the FrG-20 were traced to these countries and you need to particularly look at the following image on the next page."

Inside the folder was a black and white photo; an aerial shot from a conveniently passing satellite. It was an above view of a Korean made FrG-20 being rolled into a Korean hanger with hundreds of soldiers surrounding it.

Lester's stomach fell to his feet. "They *built* one? They actually have an FrG-20 built? This is a *disaster*!"

"Yes it is. To think that we actually had to *pay* for ours." The General and his officers chuckled. "God bless the American tax payers."

"How could you make jokes about this General? If the FrG-20 falls into the wrong hands, we could have an upset of global magnitude!" Lester was seriously concerned—if not for the world—he worried about his job.

"Forgive me if I'm wrong, Grumman. But according to you, these things don't work unless they have the diamond. As far as we're concerned, they have just a bunch of hardware taking up space. We're the only ones with the power source. I've got the receipts to prove it."

"That you do, General." Lester snapped his fingers and his detail brought out a velvet, security sealed box; flanking it with cocked weapons. "Here is one 920-carat diamond to power one of your weapons. The second one will arrive directly to you within the next 24-hours."

"We shall see." The General took the velvet box and immediately popped the security tape.

"I can assure you, General. The diamond's security is the least of—"

"No one can assure me of anything unless I see it with my own eyes, Grumman." With that, the General's conversation quieted while he peered into the box. Everyone hung there in the moment until the General handed the box back to Lester—an *empty* box. "Looks like your security problems are a lot larger than you thought."

Lester's body went cold while he stared into the empty velvet that was supposed to carry a diamond. As the General marched off to the awaiting cargo plane with his people, he didn't even care to say goodbye to Lester who was not in the mood to open his mouth anyway.

No—he did have one thing to say: "Where—is—*Fowler?!*"

Milano, Italy - Morning

Approximately one hour after Lester discovered the diamond was missing and all of Robertson Technology was being torn apart from the top down to find it and Wyman Fowler—Adian Crisp, the able and hard-bodied personal assistant to the elusive Marigold, pulled his XF-series Jaguar against the curb of the Caffè Letterario, an exquisite restaurant, bar and galleria.

Marigold was seated reading the morning paper and sipping an early cup of espresso. Seated in coordinated places around her were men dressed in black; either reading papers or talking amongst themselves until Adian arrived. All eyes locked on him carefully; each with a hand slid under their sport coats in preparation.

Adian came to an abrupt stop.

"If we can't trust my *only* personal assistant, who can we trust, gentlemen?" Marigold warned. Security was one thing, but to scare her assistant was another.

"Thank you, madam. I have news from our field in Germany."

"What news could possibly be coming out of Germany when all eyes are in Johannesburg right now?"

"The diamond at the Robertson Facility has been stolen, Madam."

"*What* diamond at the Robertson Facility?" Marigold was extremely interested. "I was under the impression there was only *one* and it was on route to Johannesburg."

"Apparently, there are *two* 920-carat diamonds; one in transit—the other stolen from their facility."

Marigold threw down her paper, revealing her frustration. "*Two diamonds*? Damn. That complicates everything."

"I'm sorry we didn't have intelligence about—"

"What are you apologizing for? Our intelligence was fine. The *opponent* is getting better at hiding things, that's all. My concern is if we're just finding *this* out, what else is there we don't know? Do we know who stole it?"

"Nothing confirmed yet. Robertson has just initiated a full investigation. I'm afraid we may have a new player in the mix."

"God forbid. There's only room for *two* in this game. I wager it was an inside job. Maybe a disgruntled employee jumping at an opportunity. Get as much information as you can on all the people who have access to touch that diamond. I'm almost positive you'll come up with a short list and on that list is the person we need to find."

"Yes, madam. Might take this opportunity to mention your *Russian* acquaintances have been expressing a great deal of impatience."

Marigold tapped her fingers on the table, thinking. *So many things, people and topics to juggle.* "They're going to find out there are two diamonds and our deal is going to go south. I need the Russians on my side for a little bit longer. We already lost the Koreans and see how that turned out. This is getting ugly, Adian. So this is what we're going to have to do. Continue to stall the Russians and tell them that my *associates* are about to recover the diamond in Johannesburg."

"Speaking of the North Koreans." Adian sputtered. He didn't want to continue passing out bad news.

Marigold looked at him balefully. "What now?"

"We've monitored their secret service, the Ministry for Protection of State Security, converging on Johannesburg. It doesn't look good."

Korean MPSS were the CIA, KGB, MI6 of North Korea.

But deadlier.

"Not good at all. My *associates* are going to be out gunned. Like it or not, Butta' and I are going to have to have a talk."

Corey A. Burkes

Chapter 11

Vokovická, Prague (Praha), Czech Republic - Morning

A cold chill went down Wyman Fowler's back.

It wasn't the common temperature this time of year around his Prague vacation home. It was a feeling of apprehension. That feeling of a storm brewing and it was happening directly over his head.

The Fowler summer home in Prague was for Wyman's mid-year conferences with the science community elite. He had the home built from the ground up based on his side-passion for architecture. Next to his wife and daughter, his homes here and in Germany were his pride and joy.

He had been so busy with work at the Robertson Facility, they have neglected the home for a couple of summers and the place was dusty and smelled stale. Even with Pilar in tow, there was a limit to the housework she would have to do. Her first task would be to orchestrate a cleaning crew to arrive and make the place livable.

Desiree sorted through the mail that never forwarded to their Germany address and Crystal ran about the floors of the two-story, eight bedroom mansion carelessly. If she wore out her welcome inside, there was plenty of space about the 2500- square meter (*25 acres*) with an in-ground pool and a 500-square meter basement, loaded with plasma screens, video games, pool tables. The treasures of making good money.

Wyman would throw it all away in a heartbeat if he had to choose between his conscience and a paycheck. Which is why he's in the predicament he's in now; wrestling with that age old conflict of the soul: *what's next?*

Instead of opening up the Prague house, he ought to be wondering how much he can get for it in this horrendous housing market. If he could get 4,432,000 Koruna (roughly $200,000 dollars) for the place, he'd be lucky. It will be a loss of almost $800,000, but worth it if he needed quick money to support his family while he was imprisoned.

Prison, Wyman grimaced. *How would that look to his science contemporaries?* He kept trying to tell himself all this was for a reason. He was doing this for a strong purpose, even though the *man* carrying the weight of this purpose was weakening every day.

He regarded Crystal's happy spirit and appreciated her blissfully, oblivious smile. Unaware of the hell he was about to bring down around her. This wasn't what he had in mind when he took on the duties of being a role model for her.

He wished he could run through the halls, too. Carefree.

"You have a fitting in two hours." Desiree broke his depressive chain of thoughts.

"For what?"

"Your tux, Wyman. Tomorrow's the dinner, remember? That's why we're here."

"Also because we're running, dear. Let's not forget that."

"Oh, I haven't forgotten anything. We're playing everything cool and making it inconvenient for them to find you, yes. But running? *Noooo*, we're *not* running. You want to know why most thieves get caught? Because they run. Dashing out and away. An easy target. We don't run, dear. We're doing our normal day to day thing. We're *vacationing* and you have a speech to give. I'm sure anyone with a halfway decent memory will track you down here soon enough."

"Then what? They take the diamond back and I'm carted off?"

"No. Then we tell them you're going to report everything to the press. Come on, Wyman. Where's your street cred? You need to start thinking leverage."

"I don't have any *street* cred. What I need to be asking is where did *you* get such a thug mentality? You're more *hood* than I expected for a woman prancing around Europe with a *Black* expense card."

"I'm a survivor, Wyman. Once I left Jamaica Queens with Crystal, it was going to be *do or die* and I *wasn't* going to be doing the *dying*. The same goes for you and this situation. Everything can be leveraged in our favor if we just think a little outside of the box. Besides, the world loves an underdog story. *Scientist builds mega killing machine; has a change of heart and wants to expose the tyrannical empire*. Sounds like front page news to me. You'll be heralded as a hero."

"*A* target. Robertson could make this ugly for all of us."

"I'm always up for a fight. Especially if it means keeping my family together. Wyman, listen to me. I love you and our family. I would go to the ends of the Earth to keep us together. Would I, *personally*, have stolen a priceless diamond to make an ethical statement? No, but I still love you and support you."

Wyman lowered his head and hugged his wife. "Thank you."

"You're welcome. Pilar is going to get the company over here to clean up the place. I'm taking Crystal with me to get my dress and you stop stressing the inevitable. No matter what happens, we'll get through it together."

Robertson Technology Facility – Berlin, Germany

All operations around the sprawling complex came to a hard stop. No further tests, productions or meetings were to be conducted during the massive sweep of the entire company. Everyone was scheduled for an interview with security and all lockers, drawers, closets, private stashes on the mighty campus were searched and meticulously investigated.

Regardless of the scale and depth of the internal *dragnet*, Lester Grumman knew only *one* man would have the diamond and this infernal procedure was just a waste of time. Even he was forced to reveal all of his personal effects and suffer questions about his time around the diamond.

The fact that Wyman Fowler wasn't anywhere to be found made it even clearer. He wasn't answering his phone calls. No one answered at his home. His family was gone as well. According to his security detail, the Fowler home looked like they shut down for the season.

Wyman was Robertson Technologies personal genius. He was the *last* suspect on the list after having won the company a multitude of contracts with his genius. The rush to question Wyman was too slow for Lester and he hated playing by the rules on this matter. Bottom line, he never really liked Fowler and his uncouth family anyway. He hoped Wyman did take the diamond so he could watch him burn.

Lester's office phone rang. Considering the private ID and the current mood around the facility—this call was miserably expected. Lester answered the phone with a heavy heart. "Hello?"

He listened intently and walked around his desk to sit in his chair. "Yes, this line is secure. Who are you?"

The voice on the opposite end was not very pleased over the state of things.

"I see. Yes, sir. We're conducting a thorough search even as we speak. No leaf will be left unturned." Lester responded.

He then listened to a lengthy bit of information he certainly didn't expect to hear. "That Black woman in the news? What's her name? *Gisela Thompson*? My best man is bringing the diamond to Johannesburg. There shouldn't be a problem even if she shows up to try again."

More dialogue from the phone. More information that disturbed Lester gravely. "I suppose that's fine if you feel you need to send a team there to assist in the recovery. I have my suspicions who *may* have taken the diamond here, but I don't think we'll need to go *that* far and—"

The voice interrupted Lester, forcing him to listen without saying another word.

That was when *He*, the assassin, stepped out of the corner shadow of the room, dressed in black with a black baseball cap lowered over his eyes. Either *He* was looking to the floor or right at Lester; Grumman couldn't tell. Nevertheless, Lester was in the company of someone who apparently dealt with the dark arts of murder. Hopefully, this would be the last time Lester would have to come within range of this mysterious assassin.

Lester was nervous, swallowing hard while trying to talk on the phone. "Yes—*He*—*He's* here. What do I need to give *Him*?"

The voice gave Lester a list of instructions and he hung up. Lester put down the phone and stared at the darkened individual.

"The man you want to question is Wyman Fowler. I'm to give you his address, picture and anything else you need to identify him by. I—I'm also to tell you he has a daughter. Eight years old. Your employer said you would know what to do if you find them."

He remained silent and waited for Lester; hands deep in his pockets. Lester wanted this person out of his office as soon as possible and reached into his file cabinet to pull out Wyman's personnel folder. Lester held onto the executive files for easy reach while regular employees stayed in human resources. Fowler's records of good deeds at Robertson created a fat, bulging folder of pictures and history—more than enough for *Him*.

He looked through the folder, taking a picture of Wyman and an address, leaving the rest and simply walked out. By the time Lester got up out of his seat, walked around the table to shut the door, *He* was gone.

Lester knew there was not going to be any *questioning* should *He* find Wyman. Suddenly, Lester felt something he never thought he would feel for Wyman Fowler: regret.

South African Railway Station – Late Afternoon

Frank stood outside the security office that was a yard from the main entrance to the railway station, which was currently under re-construction from previous calamity.

From behind the door, muffled arguing voices could be heard between Ellen and at least three of the railway's security personnel. They were on the hunt for any information and clues that would lead them in Butta's direction.

Absolutely no one from downtown Cape Town to the city limits wanted to help two American police officers.

The last part of Butta's pursuit ended here, causing millions in damage to the infrastructure. The local security and police swear that they are handling this with top people, but Ellen knew better. No one wanted help from outsiders after such an embarrassing, citywide chase, ending with the perpetrator—*a woman*—escaping right under their noses.

Adding further insult, Ellen arrived making demands.

Frank sat this one out while she did the arguing, admiring the once beautiful archway that lead into the station—now protected by yellow tape and diverting passengers around to a side entrance.

They still haven't removed the truck, carefully guarded by seven South African police officers. Shot up with holes and the star of news reports throughout Africa. Officials and passengers took pictures of the army truck that tore up the streets.

Just as Frank thought to approach the truck and poke around, Ellen barged out of the security office with a series of folders under her arm, marching toward the way out. "Let's go."

Frank kept a wary eye at the security officers yelling something in the Zulu toward them. From the look of their expressions, it likely wasn't good will tidings.

"Are we out of here?" Frank asked.

"Very much so. Don't stop for anyone. Just keep looking straight."

"What'd you take?"

"Pricks weren't giving me anything. Even with their busted ass English, they were trying to give me the *out of jurisdiction* crap and how they had no video of what happened. Then I saw on the table this folder and sticking out was this."

She pulled out a black and white, security image of the German soldier on the run with the velvet box tucked under his arm. On the back, a phone number.

"No cameras, *my ass*. Look at this. This isn't a South African country code. Thirty-nine … zero-two," Frank thought over it deeply, mind rattling off thousands of points of reference. "It's Italy. Some city in Italy. A phone number? No … it's on the back … people jot numbers on the back of pictures when they're …"

"*Faxing* them, right." Ellen moved out toward the parking lot of the railway station and into the passenger side of the rental car they were using. Frank drove; making sure no one else was following them. "Each and every picture in this folder are shots of Butta', her peoples and that big guy with the box. They were faxed to that number. I put the screws to them and wanted to know who they were faxing to. They didn't like my interrogation."

"Oh boy," Frank started the ignition. "They're lucky."

"Who you tellin'? I thought we'd get more *lip* from security after I took this thing. Looks like their leaving us alone."

"You just bold-faced took a folder of security images of the suspects and they're not coming after us?" Frank drove off into the streets, setting the road GPS for their hotel with a free hand. "Sounds like an internal clamp down. Somebody inside doesn't want too many people to know about this special folder. If you're walking out with it, they can't make a fuss without alerting the wrong people. Maybe this folder wasn't supposed to exist?"

"That's what I was thinking. If the local cops were really looking into this, they would have had this folder already. Instead, they're slinging crap about security cameras not working. They also said that one of them cold killed a South African cop. Point blank to the head."

"Who? In Butta's crew?"

"That's what they said. I smell a cover up. Who the hell is in Italy that would want pictures of Butta'?"

"Looks like we're going to Italy to find out. Thank god the rich chicks' pockets are deep."

"*No.* Butta's chasing this guy with the box. So we follow *the box.*" Ellen looked really close at one of the pictures while Frank navigated the city streets. "So we're going to *Germany.*"

The soldier with the black box had unique symbols blazed on his front and side arm of his uniform. It took her a great deal of squinting and comparing between three different pictures, but Ellen just made out the words: ROBERTSON, BERLIN, SECURITY TASKFORCE.

Corey A. Burkes

Chapter 12

Johannesburg, South Africa – Park station – 7:57pm
The rain was good cover for Butta' while she stood outside the train station, next to a frequented newspaper stand, attempting to down play her curves with a dowdy, baggy outfit.

It was hard to dress discretely being as sexy as this woman. Her curves would naturally deform clothing to match each slope.

Men still checked her out regardless of how unkempt she made herself; shrouded with a poncho to protect her from the storm. *God must be in my favor tonight*, she pondered.

Provided God even cared about her at all. Why would anyone with such ominous power ever want to put her through all this? It were questions of this nature that put her at odds with her spirituality.

At least Kasey found God, she frowned. *Everybody seemed to find what they wanted. Humph—even Trigger.*

Trigger. That was another story. She couldn't contain her and Butta' knew this. The whole '*coming of age*' thing was expected long ago and she knew the clock was running out on how long they would *play* sisters.

Something was eating at Butta' terribly about that whole, *mini-confrontation-thing*. She knew everyone was uptight lately being dragged around the planet. Still, Trigger's reaction was critical. *What was with that envelope that fell out of her pocket?*

The emblem on the wax; she saw it before. Although she didn't quite see the full thing, the glimpse brought to mind a tattered, forgotten memory.

Her cell phone vibrated.

No number listed in the caller ID; it could be any one of her partners as they all carried non-listed, prepaid phones.

"What's going on?" Butta' answered, expecting it to be Kasey with a report from her position.

But it wasn't Kasey.

"Hello, *Gisela*," the female voice said.

Butta' paused. Only the very loved—or the *very* dead— called her by her government name. "Who is this?"

"For the time being you may call me *Marigold*. We don't have too much time to talk, Gee-Gee. Not the time I was hoping for."

Gee-Gee?!? This woman was going above and beyond herself. For a split second, Butta' felt that little *nickname* sounded as if she was called that before. "I'm going to hang up if you don't start yappin'."

"You are in Johannesburg. You are waiting for the eight o'clock train to arrive. On it is the last leg of a very long journey for you: your father's *diamond*."

"Who the hell are—?"

"I want to help you."

"Help me?"

"Truth be told, I've been helping you since you arrived in New York to deal with Lingo Stein. You think you got out of Riker's all on your own with some *itching powder*? One day I'll give you the full picture. Not tonight, though. The game has changed and it's more important than ever that you get that diamond when it gets off the train."

"That was the original plan. When I get that diamond, I'm doing it for me."

"So you think. We'll argue over the particulars *if* you survive the night. Right now, I want to draw your attention to the black sedan across the street at about thirty feet from your position at the newspaper stand."

Sure enough, the mysterious woman pointed out such a vehicle across the road from Butta'; rain bouncing off its shiny black exterior. The window rolled down and an Asian man tossed out a finished cigarette, reclosing the window.

Butta's stomach started to turn. "Are they your people?"

"Hardly." Marigold's voice sounded annoyed. "Let's just say they are playing for the other team. Also take note of the three men taking cover a few yards to your left at the corner. The two on the roof to the right, above the bank and the covered jeep parking down the block."

For each and every person she pointed out, there were Asian men protecting themselves from the rain or attempting to blend into the evening. Butta' felt like she was in the middle of an impending nightmare.

"Who are those people?" She whispered.

"They came to take the diamond and, I can assure you, you do not have the skill or firepower to stop them if you tried. They're of the North Korean MPSS. North Korean secret service."

Damn, Butta' swallowed. "Thanks. This would have been ugly. Why are you trying to help me?"

"Gee-Gee, I'm trying to help *me*. Turns out you and I have the same goals and, what's more, I've helped you for so long, I think it's time for a little pay back."

"I don't even know your *Wizard of Oz*-ass. Until you come from behind the curtain and talk to me face-to-face, this conversation is just a friendly head's up by a stranger."

"Well then, let me give you another heads up. The North Koreans don't know you're in the area, but are aware you could be. Otherwise, you'd be dead already. The train is arriving even as we speak and they're going to move on the diamond swiftly. Are you still tracking it?"

"How in the *hell* did you know about—?"

"Sorry, I can't talk anymore. I've helped you out the best I could and even provided you with a little extra, shall we say, *cover*. We'll talk when you bring the diamond to Italy."

"Italy? But—?"

Marigold already disconnected.

Butta' stared down at the phone incredulously with a mix of apprehension and a dash of horror. The sound of the arriving train could be heard in the distant train yard and the locals were rushing into the station, either to pick up loved ones or catch their ride out.

Regardless of her advice, Butta's original plan of action had to be activated. No sooner did she get her mind back into the current situation, her phone rang again and she became a little concerned of the men posted all around her. She turned her back from the street and spoke into the receiver carefully. "Yeah?"

It was Munch. "Are we ready to roll? The train's here."

"Wait a minute, Munchie. We're not alone here. The place is crawling with professionals."

"How do you know?"

That was a tough one. How did she explain a random phone call? What if it was all a lie? They all came too far to turn back. Could she trust this Marigold person?

Decisions— decisions.

"No time, Munchie. Keep to the plan, but be *easy*. You can't miss them. They're Korean men and they're going to move on the diamond at the same time."

"What are you going to do?"

"The hell if I know. Just stick to the plan."

Butta' closed her little cell phone and stepped back into the sidewalk, not particularly paying attention and almost ran into a young man carrying a black box. What caught Butta' off guard was the box almost looked like the one she was chasing earlier. Square, velvet and drenched from the rain. Dismissing it as coincidental, she put the hood of her poncho over her head and ran for the entrance of the station.

Park Station – Boarding Platform

The train came to a halt after a twenty-six hour ride across the plains of Africa; hissing majestically into the terminal. After coming to a full stop, the doors opened and the platform unloaded hundreds of people from the multi-car train.

Barely seen, yet the tallest of the people, the German Soldier carefully peeked about, observing his surroundings and marched with the people heading to the exit. The velvet black box snuggled under his arm.

Six people *behind* him, Kasey slid into the flow of pedestrians, wearing a head wrap to cover her face and carrying two large articles of luggage in either hand.

Six people in *front* of the soldier, Fuego kept a watchful, low-profile eye with a baseball cap and jacket to cover his features.

To the soldiers *left*, with eight people between them, Munch kept his hands buried into his jacket pocket and followed the target as he made his way from the platform to the halls that led to the central station. Between the three of them, they kept the soldier in a moving visual perimeter.

What they did not see were the six MPSS agents that circled them all; creating a shrinking ring about them the closer the soldier approached the center of the station.

Butta' entered the station, choosing to keep her hood over her head and moved to the corner so she can get a better view of all the people coming from the terminals. In a blink of an eye, the vast station was crowded with a multitude of cultures and people arriving from the train.

For Butta' to see her target, she had to *first* see the people she knew. Once she saw Fuego or Munch, she knew the target was between them. If she saw Kasey, then she knew the target got by her and that would not do.

The good news: she saw Fuego, who nodded at her from a moderate distance. The bad news: she saw another man carrying what looked like a velvet box and got a little confused when it was not the soldier.

She did see a set of Asian men moving rapidly beside Munch.

Butta' moved forward to intercept the space between Fuego and Munch so she can lock onto the soldier. The place was so crowded with people coming and going—adding to the fact that more and more people were walking about them with the *same velvet box*— she could hardly keep up with the soldier who was also being jostled by passing residents of Johannesburg.

The soldier was about twenty paces from the door when the six MPSS men formed a neat enclosure around the soldier and the assault began.

Three of them grabbed his arms before he could make a fuss. One of them stuck a needle into his neck, removing the fight out of him before it began. The soldier collapsed into the men's arms and never saw it coming. One other rushed to make a path between them and the door and the last pushed the velvet box from between his limp arms and …

… Into Butta's awaiting hands.

The element of surprise was on her side and she elbowed the unsuspecting agent in the jaw, laying him out.

People screamed—Butta' ran—shoving people out of her way.

The MPSS holding the soldier dropped him to realign on the new target—the velvet box in Butta's hands. Unfortunately, velvet boxes were suddenly floating about in many people's hands.

So many to choose from, Kasey picked one up and swore she had the right one.

"Got it!"

Munch pointed toward the direction Butta' was running. "No! *No, no, no!* She got it! *Fuego!*"

Fuego doubled back, skidding to a stop over the unconscious German Soldier. He missed his chance at a round two. Removing his cap and jacket, he launched after Munch and Kasey who were pursuing the Korean secret service.

One of the spies dove through the air and tackled Butta' to the floor. The velvet box slide across the floor and bounced against a mountain of *more* black boxes—a fine brick-laid design that reached halfway up the side wall; picked and slowly reduced in size as people walked by, taking a box in passing. A huge sign hung over the tower of boxes written in Zulu: *Mahhala.*

Meaning *free, gratis—without charge.*

The tackling agent paused to long in his search for the right box, giving Butta' enough time to recover and push him aside, taking up the first box she found.

Not taking any chances, she popped it open—

No diamond.

Smash! Two of the North Korean agents pounced on her with fists and feet flying with native martial arts styles—*Kuk Sool Won* and traditional *Taekwondo*—way too much for Butta' to manage on her own.

On the other hand, she had Fuego.

Lucky for Fuego as he finally had worthy opponents.

The deadly dance between the Mexican and Koreans was a sight to see of incredible skill and timing.

Fuego gave Butta', Kasey and Munch the time they needed to search box after box for the diamond without luck. In a crazy life-sized version of *concentration*, Butta', her team and a few scattered MPSS agents picked up boxes, tossed boxes and repeated the steps.

"*Oh shit!*" Butta' exclaimed. "What the hell is wrong with me?"

She removed the tracking device from behind her and let the expensive little device do the work for her—waving the handheld tool over the boxes until the readout directed her away from the mess altogether.

While all the *professionals* fought and struggled to find the right box, it was a passerby of Johannesburg; with her four children, that stumbled across the right one.

The mother lifted the velvet box out of her littlest one's hands to look inside and almost caught a heart attack from the contents.

Her fleeting moment of joy vanished when a series of automatic rifles lowered on her and her family, clicking and locking in place by a small army of seven MPSS Korean agents.

Everyone came to an abrupt, breath held stop.

Munch had one of the smaller MPSS's in a headlock trying to pry a box out of his hands. Fuego was on the floor with two MPSS; one foot in a jaw and a knee in the other's eye. Kasey was on the back of an MPSS pounding his head with a box and Butta' had her tracking device pointed right at the frightened woman.

The scene was frozen like a perverse *Norman Rockwell* painting.

Sirens were heard approaching from the distance. A taller, trench-coated member of the MPSS group pushed past his armed men and looked around at the melee with his hands on his hips, directing his attention to Butta'.

"Gisela Thompson?" He asked with a thick Korean accent.

"Maybe." Butta' responded.

He smiled at her warmly. "Well played. Now, you work for me."

Butta' looked to Munch and Kasey, who both shrugged at her just as bemused. "Come again?"

He snapped his fingers, pointing to the innocent woman in the middle of the floor and his people stripped her of the velvet box—thus taking the diamond.

Butta's heart sank.

What she failed to notice was the men that surrounded Fuego had injected something into his neck during the break. He collapsed and was dragged from the station.

"No!" Kasey saw this and attacked the nearest Korean spy viciously. Munch tossed a box into one of the spies and swiped his gun. All rifles re-trained themselves Butta's crew; effectively stopping the fight again before it began.

The Korean MPSS team left with Fuego and backed out of the station with rifles at the ready. The tall leader among them smiled at Butta' and stepped back from her. "You work for me now. We have that one. Bring me the *other* diamond."

Butta' grinded her teeth. "*What* other diamond?"

"You go to Berlin. Find other diamond. Bring it to People's Republic or we kill friend. Three days."

He walked out briskly and Butta' followed keeping a good measure of distance between herself and the rifles still pointed at her. With a million and one questions, for some reason, Butta' only managed to call out one: "What *other* diamond?"

The MPSS leader laughed as he stepped into the rain, jumping into one of six cars that pulled up aside of the station. Butta' stopped outside fists clenched and hair matted down over her shoulders and back. Down the block, Johannesburg's finest were approaching ever closer. "What *other* diamond!?" She screamed.

Munch and Kasey pulled Butta' back into the station, away from the cops that would surely want to apprehend them for indefinite questioning.

They easily evaded the Johannesburg Metropolitan Police and started a safe three-mile hike in the opposite direction to their car.

With yet another mission failed—and a teammate abducted, conversation was in short supply on their trek back to their ride.

Trigger waited in their parked vehicle hidden in bushes for the past four hours with instructions to show up at the station if signaled. Without word from any of them, she thought either the worst happened or they were on their way back via the low road.

Sneaking without detection and that sort of thing takes time.

This gave Trigger the moment she needed to read the letter that has haunted her for days:

You are cordially invited to accept compensated

> *employment for selected targets as deemed through*
> *communication by the Guild of Executioners.*
> *Significant recompense will be deposited to a private Swiss*
> *Account and assigned to you upon agreeing to this invitation.*
> *(678) 453-8102*
> *This number lasts seven days only.*
> *You are welcome to disregard this offer.*
> *It will not be offered again.*

She laughed at the simplicity of an ominous proposal. *Offered to be an assassin in a neat little invite. What if someone else found the letter? God help them*, she thought.

Trigger was young minded. She never took in the gravity of such a recommend and simply saw dollar signs. *Significant recompense sounded liked a lot of dough*—and there was only one way to find out.

She dialed the numbers through her cell phone.

It took some time for the connection to be made. Long distance calls from Africa tended to need extra time to connect properly. Finally, after two rings, someone picked up. "Monique Bolland?"

The voice was British accented; a female and she waited for a response. Trigger nervously attempted to open her mouth, but no words came out.

Trees and twigs snapped outside and from behind the car she was parked in, causing her to panic. She snapped her cell phone shut, folding her letter into her pocket just as Munch entered the passenger seat next to her, shortly followed by Butta' and Kasey—all three joyless, silent and down one teammate.

Now wasn't the time, Trigger thought, sinking into the driver's seat.

"We're heading back to Louie, Trig," Munch grumbled.

"What happened out there?"

"Same story. Different train station." Kasey remarked.

"Where's Fuego?" Trigger noticed they were shy one of the members. "Oh no! Did he —"

"*No*. He's alive. They took him and holding him hostage." Munch relayed.

"Hostage? Who's *they*?" Trigger was almost glad she didn't go down to the station with them.

Butta's phone started ringing. Up until this moment, her mind was separated from her body, the time and the location. She was looking out the window from the back seat, letting the phone ring.

"Are you going to answer that?" Kasey asked.

Butta' looked at her. Her eyes filled with loss and defeat. She never lost a partner before; especially those who were as dedicated to her as Fuego.

Taking out her phone, the caller ID registered a private number. Butta' grimaced with a mix of anguish and furor, answering it. "What the *fuck* happened back there?"

"You're asking me?" Marigold didn't sound too happy herself. "I *told* you to get the diamond!"

"I don't even know who the hell you are! I don't take orders from you!"

"Well I guess you'll have to now if you want to get your friend back."

"Damn right I'm getting Fuego back! Where are you?"

"*Everywhere*. The game has gotten ugly as hell. The Koreans have the diamond and they are leveraging *you* to get the other one. Why *should* they expend extra resources and man power to steal the duplicate of what they already have? You've *fucked* us all, Gee-Gee and you're going to have to—"

Butta' hung up on her in mid-tirade, looking up at her partners who were silently awaiting answers.

"Do any of you know or heard of a chick named *Marigold*?"

Everyone shook their heads bewildered.

Butta's phone rang again.

"We're in something real thick. It's no longer about me, Trig. I don't think it *ever* had anything to do with me. *This* right here—it's something *bigger*."

"You think?" Kasey huffed. "A team of killer Chinese guys showing up and crazy copies of that velvet box. We ain't in Kennesaw anymore."

"They're Koreans." Munch corrected, explaining the details to Trigger. "Once we— hell, *if* we find this second diamond in Berlin, we need to get it back to North Korea in order to save Fuego. We have three days."

"Three days?" Trigger coughed. "That's impossible. Did any of you know there was a second diamond? Is it just like the one we're looking for?"

"No and *yes*." Butta' thought on the hopelessness of the situation and how much she owed it to Fuego to save him. "We're just too damn out gunned, cash short and tapped out of resources."

Her phone continued to ring. Thinking rapidly on her choices, Butta' answered her cell and listened.

"Finished having your *pity party*?" Marigold fumed.

"What do you want?"

"I want you to tell me what I need to hear, Gee-Gee."

Butta' bit her lip, extremely annoyed. This mysterious woman thought she knew her. Even down to a nickname she barely remembered. She *did* warn her of the Koreans and that multi-box trick was brilliant while it lasted.

She had nothing and Fuego was out there held hostage.

"I *need* your help." Butta' relented.

"I *know* you do." Marigold gloated. "Get back to the yacht and head to Germany. From this point forward, you will do exactly as I say to the *letter*. I will speak only to you, at all times, and if you fail to follow my instructions precisely, your friend will die; either the Russians or the Koreans will get the last diamond and the world will be at risk of an *extensive* shift in the balance of power. Welcome to the real world, Gee-Gee. No pressure, though."

No pressure. Butta' felt the weight of the universe resting on her and all she could possibly remember was her desire to get a memento of her father's legacy. "What was that about *Russians?*" She asked.

"Oh!" Marigold paused. "I didn't tell you?"

Chapter 13

New York City – Stein Tower – Friday morning 10:16am
All hell had broken loose in the world of Diandra Stein. As predicted, there was nothing she could do about it.

The New York Stock Exchange opened promptly 9:30am Eastern Standard Time. A little over forty-five minutes later, Diandra sat in her father's office with hundreds of men and women running in and out; paperwork flying and phones installed by the multitude ringing off the hook.

With the mountain of complex shareholding acquisitions and market rules upon her, Stein Industries was being aggressively taken over by more than half of its stock, thus giving controlling interest to an unknown financier.

While her pack of aids struggled to figure out exactly who that financier was—Diandra knew.

"We're losing everything. Our close shareholders are vanishing and selling off their majority bids!" Marcy was in tears.

"I thought we had dual-class stock? We were supposed to be protected from this sort of thing." Diandra poised the questioned; not 100% sure what the terms meant.

"That was up until your father passed. The company is contractually obligated to turn the overwhelming control he had in dual-class to a regular *single* class, opening Stein Industries up to this madness. We should have prepared for this."

Diandra *did* see this coming, was told this was coming, did not have the business mind to protect herself from it and she powerlessly watched her father's empire shift gears. All around her, professionals that knew what they were doing in math, finances, incredibly large amounts of money and the skillful arts of playing the stock market sweated out how to save a sinking ship.

One young man, tie undone, sleeves rolled up and with a cordless phone under one ear, an ear piece in another and piles of papers in his hand approached Diandra in a manner he would never have done on calmer, professional days.

"Ms. Stein! *Money*! Where can we find *more money*?"

Diandra stammered, looking at the young man with a blank expression. Her father knew many people with money. Those people didn't know her.

Marcy jumped at the young man like a guard dog. "Excuse *you. That's your* job to—"

"I'm *not* talking to you!" He retorted, shutting her up swiftly. "Diandra! You are *losing* your father's company right here, *right now*. We need to know where you can get more money to challenge the purchases of these stocks. What can you liquidate? Who can you borrow from? Anybody—anywhere. I need an answer or we're finished."

"I— I don't know." She said, almost in tears.

"Not good enough! We need a *white knight* to step in and turn this around. Maybe another company. Someone Stein Industries can rely on. Our *poison pill* tactics aren't working. There's isn't even a *crown jewel* we can use. *Nothing*. Whoever is after us is looking for blood and taking it!"

Somehow, Diandra found the ability to just come up with one solution. Desperate, just one name came to mind. "Robertson Tech. They've worked with us in the past. My father was close with them."

"Right," is all he said and turned away to make more calls.

This was zero hour and anything could happen in the next ten minutes, let alone 24-hours.

"The nerve of that boy," Marcy frowned. "I'll have him removed."

"No, we won't." Diandra countered. "He's saving your job, or haven't you noticed?"

"Your father would never have—"

"I'm *not* my father." That was the point of this whole mess. Too many things were happening around her because she let the ghost of her father run the company when, in fact, she was supposed to be in control.

Finding the strength, she willfully decided to get her head into this game.

Provided there was a game left for her to play.
God willing.

Suddenly, there was a cheering in the group of men and women on the far side of the room and the pace suddenly picked up with smiles on their face. The defiant young man from earlier ran up to Marcy and hugged her. "Robertson Tech is buying in! They're going to help us and buy Stein Industries right from under those bastards! Thank you, Ms. Stein!"

"No, thank you. What is your name?" She asked.

He didn't expect a regular conversation from her. "I'm Sam. Sam Jestickowiz from accounting. The Junior exec pool, ma'am."

"Thank you Sam. I need men who will tell me what I need to hear. Enjoy your new vice-president position. Pay increase effective immediately. I will be calling on you for your advice in the future more often."

Sam almost fell over. Her father would have *never* promoted someone from the lower ranks. As Diandra thought more on what she would do next, blocking out Marcy's *what her father wouldn't do* prattle, Diandra spirit woke up.

She *was not* her father.

Milano, Italy – 3:20pm

"*What the fuck!*" Marigold screamed, throwing over her office table.

Everyone around her—men and women dressed in business suits preparing to pop open champagne and Adian, her faithful assistant, stopped what they were doing.

Marigold was not a pleasant person when angered.

She was on the phone, storming about the office; kicking over the stationary and desk material that was sprawled along the floor. "Who the hell bailed her out? *Please* don't tell me Robertson. Those mother fuckers ain't got a *pot* to *piss* in."

She stopped to listen on the other end. "Well, where in the hell did they get the cash? *Fuck it*! It doesn't matter. Drop the pursuit. They win."

Instead of hanging up the phone, it went flying across the room and through the *closed* window with a *crash*. Glass shards went out of her office some thirty stories above the busy Milano streets.

Then the room waited for her next explosion of anger.

When nothing happened, Adian stepped closer to his boss with caution.

"Madam? Might I remind you about the Russians?"

She raised her hand, silencing him. "Thinking."

She motioned around the mess on the floor, looking out the hole in the window, pointing at her people to pick up the table.

Marigold spoke, but made sure her face and body were turned away from the others, looking out to city, whispering to Adian. "Everything is going according to plan, Adian."

He kept his voice low, facing the window. "Yes, madam. With your secret controlling stake in Robertson effectively made you the owner of Stein Industries. For less, might I add."

"*Excellent*. We keep the charade going until we finish this business with the missing diamond. Let Diandra Stein believe she's in control, find both diamonds and sell one to the Americans and the other to the Russians as planned."

"What about the North Koreans?"

"*Fuck them*. Let them have the Mexican, but we *will* get that diamond back. I trust Butta' to accomplish that mission, if nothing else. She'll cross the widest sea for a friend. I love her, but she's a *fool*. Once she's working for *C.R.E.A.M,* she'll figure out how the world works and get in line."

"Yes, madam. Provided she joins us."

Marigold cut him a look and chose not to respond to that comment. "We're still being monitored?" She asked.

Adian nodded, gesturing subtly to corners of the room, a lamp and a table not far from them. "Audio. No video feeds. We're still tracing the source, but the technology is groundbreaking."

"Don't bother wasting time. We both know who it is and I need that person to keep thinking I'm pissed and losing the game. We're almost there, buddy. Let's just keep up the appearances of failure."

"Yes, madam."

"Oh, and get in touch with *Sam Jestickowiz*. Tell him I said *good job*." She ended, turning around and faced her people—yelling and barking orders in light of the recent *alleged* failed bid for Stein Industries.

She was always a player in the game.

Perhaps the most devious of them all.

Yacht Sariya-Anne – South Atlantic Sea – 4:30pm
With time against them, there was no way on Earth Butta' and her crew were going to make it to Germany via yacht in under three days. As hard as Louie pushed the Sariya-Anne, she couldn't turn around and get past Angola before a helicopter was needed to take them the rest of the way.

As usual, Louie made a few calls and over the horizon, a brilliant multi-passenger HH-65 Dolphin, commonly used for Coast Guard rescue, flew in to pick up Butta', Trigger, Kasey and Munch.

There was space on the rear of the yacht for a small craft helicopter pickup, but they would need to be airlifted due to the blade span and weight. That concerned Munch, the heaviest of them.

Trigger and Kasey spent time reassuring him while Butta' and Louie waited for the approaching transport. Shabba was requested to keep his distance during this transition and he, reluctantly, agreed.

"Are youse guys gonna be good?" Louie asked.

"We're survivors."

"Yeah. I got 'dat. We'll steer 'round to Germany n' catch up with ya inna few days. All packed up?"

"As best as we could." She responded.

"Tough break on ya partna'. Da Spanish guy."

"Fuego." Butta' sighed. In her heart of hearts, she planned to get him back. How? She did not know and just the fact that she lost him troubled her.

"Yeah, him." Louie sniffed. "Anything ya need, ya know how ta reach me."

"You know," she thought aloud, "you're certainly right where I need you lately. What gives?"

"Dat's what friends are for, right?"

"Don't give me that. What brought you to South Africa in the first place, Louie?"

Louie looked at her and noticed the change in tone. "I told ya. Da owners have —"

"Yeah. That's what you told me." She cut him off purposely. "Now tell me the *truth*. The coincidence of you being here, transporting us around, giving us the funds and access we need is too easy."

"It is what it is, babe."

"Don't play me, Lou. Who is Marigold?"

Louie stared at her. "She talked to ya?"

"I knew it. Lou, who the hell is that bitch?"

Louie looked at the others, pulling Butta' out of ear-shot. "Honey, you're in da middle of a lotta *shit*. I can give ya da bad news and da worse news. What ya want first?"

"The *good* news."

"There ain't any, so pick ya choice."

"She knew all about the yacht, where we are, what we are doing. Someone is keeping tabs on us for her."

"Dat would be me. Marigold is lookin' out fer ya best interests."

"Why? I don't know her."

"I dunno. She just told me ta be out here n' ready ta help out."

"What about the owners of this boat?"

"She took care of 'em. Dey won't be askin' no questions. Wot ya gotta understand is, da world moves n' shakes by just two people. Mari' is one of 'em."

"If she is *that* big, why haven't I heard about her?"

The helicopter approached. The blades were loud and cutting off their ability to hear each other.

Louie shouted above the noise. "Ya never see da puppet master."

That's true, she thought. Not that she enjoyed the idea of being *pulled by strings*.

"Ya want my advice?" Louie whispered closer to her. "Listen ta what she says n' ya life will get straight."

"And what if I don't?"

"'Den 'tings *won't* be cool. Ya ETA ta German town is 'bout three hours. Mari' will have da 411 n' details ready for ya when ya land."

"I hate this, Lou. I have no control over anything. A bunch of Koreans telling me I work for them. Some mystery chick making demands. Can't you give me anything?"

"She only gives ya wot ya need ta know 'n I don't need ta know anythin' more 'den what I just told ya."

"Did you know there was a second diamond? Where am I going to find it?" Many, *many* questions plagued her.

"Just get ta da *krauts* n' let her tell ya what ta do."

"That doesn't help me one bit."

Butta' walked toward the heli-deck where Kasey was already being raised onto the helicopter with a harness.

"Oh yeah!" Louie called out to her. "She said ya need ta watch yer back. She got da word dat one of yer crew jus' got signed up wit' da odda' side."

Butta' looked at Louie as if blindsided. She looked at Trigger first. That would explain a few things. Kasey? Munchie? She could not *fathom* that kind of treachery from those two, but stranger things have happened.

She only had but a handful of friends. The very thought of needing to watch out for one of them was …

… *Scary.*

Early Butta': Worldwide Cover

Butta': Worldwide Promotional Poster

Samantha Murdock as Butta'

Doris Morgado as Marigold

Christina Boykin as Crystal

Kida Davis as Trigger

Roxzane T. Mims as Ellen Cobart

Christina Boykin and Haji Abdull

Christina Boykin as Crystal

Samantha Murdock and Author Corey A. Burkes

Actress and Model Doris Morgado

Left to right/top to bottom: **Kida Davis, Kandiss Lewis,
Doris Morgado, Samantha Murdock, Christina Boykin and
Roxzane T. Mims**

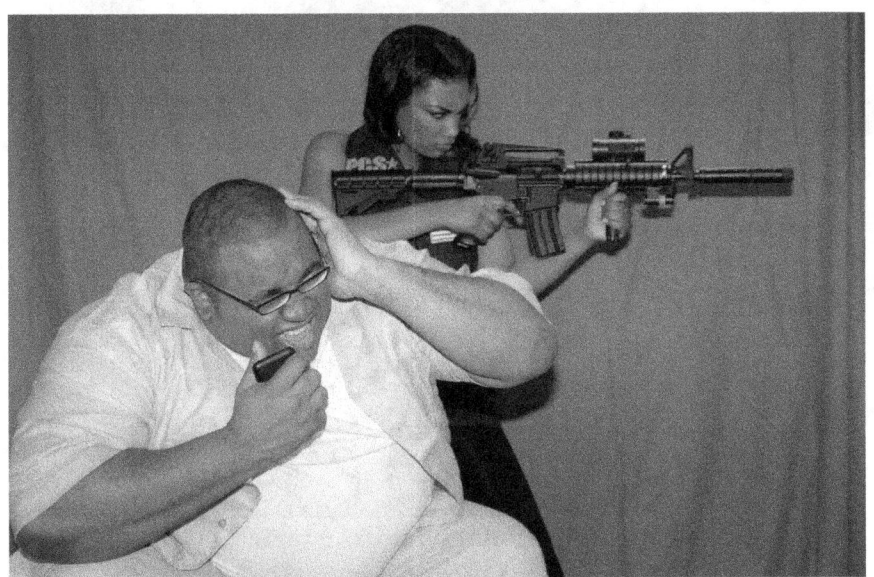

Haji Abdull and Samantha Murdock
Raiding Stein Depository. Pre-effects.

Actress and Model Kandiss Marie Lewis

Actress and Model Christina Boykin

Corey A. Burkes

Model and Entrepreneur Samantha Murdock

Model Samantha Murdock

Christina Boykin and Kida Davis as Crystal and Trigger
(pre-effects – Notice Guitar Hero guitar in BG)

Post-effects. Promotional image for calendar

Early sample of potential Butta': Worldwide calendar

Actress Roxzane T. Mims

Model Kida Davis

Actor and Artist Haji Khalid Abdullah

Model Kida Davis

Samantha Murdock as Butta'

Kida Davis as Trigger

Christina Boykin as Crystal Fowler

Nefertiti (Butta')
and Author Corey A. Burkes
Photography: Kim Davis MysTiQ Photography
Skyelight Literature © 2009

Samantha Murdock as Butta' and Author Corey A. Burkes

Kandiss Marie Lewis as Kasey

T-Shirt for Butta': Worldwide

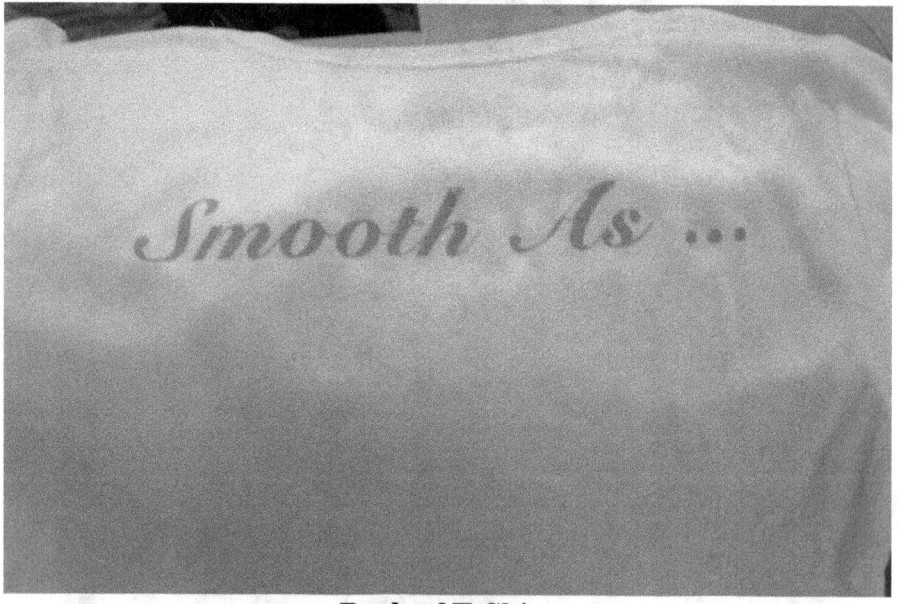

Back of T-Shirt

Butta', Munch, Kasey and Ellen

Corey A. Burkes

- BOOK TWO -
Small World

Corey A. Burkes

Chapter 14

Vokovická, Prague (Praha), Czech Republic – 6:02pm
The invitation welcomed the esteemed physics community to the *14th Annual Black Tie Gala and Honoring* ceremonies. Keynote speaker: Wyman Fowler.

The event took place every year in the Czech Republic; a convenient spot for Europe's greatest minds to convene, eat, get drunk and bask in their own glory. Normally, this was a trip paid by Robertson Tech. This year, Wyman prayed his *greatest* prayer that they totally forgot he was on the lineup.

Dressed in his Hart Schaffner Marx 'Capital Collection' Gold Trumpeter Tuxedo, tailored to fit him perfectly, he waited at the bottom of the stairs for his wife with her jacket in his hand. A horn blew outside and he took a peek through nearby blinds to make sure it was just the limo driver and not the police.

Wyman was scared and paranoid like never before. He was going to start sweating on his very expensive tailored suit and ruin it.

"Honey, let's go!" He called out to her. Late for an affair and the impatient husband was a global man and wife phenomena.

Desiree stepped lively down the stairs, still attaching an earring. She looked stunning in a Nicole Miller off the shoulder gown in all black and silver.

The effect worked on her husband. He forgot his worries and fell speechless.

"Mission accomplished." She smirked.

"You're damn right *accomplished*. You look fantastic." He gawked.

"You look like a Black *James Bond*. All *Goldeneye'd* and err'thang. You got a *License to Kill*, baby?"

He hugged his wife close and kissed her. "As long as you got my *Octopussy*."

"Oh, I got your—."

There was a clearing of the throat at the top of the stairs. Faithful Pilar reminded the two that Crystal, in her little pink PJ's and teddy bear in hand, was still up and listening to her parents playful back and forth, which was getting raunchier by the moment.

Wyman stared at his daughter sadly for a moment. "Diamonds are forever, they say."

Desiree pulled at Wyman toward the door. "Let's not think of those things. Tonight, let's show them how the rich Black elite work it."

Easier said than done, Wyman waved back at his daughter and left the house. Desiree looked back one last time, putting on her coat. "You know the drill, baby."

"Listen to Pilar. Brush my teeth and stay in bed." Crystal bemoaned the painful ritual.

"That's my girl. Pilar, I've got my phone. We'll be at the Prague Hilton. It's only fifteen minutes from here. Wyman is leaving his phone home so call me on my cell if you need anything, okay?"

Crystal leaned over the banister, looking down to her mommy. "When are you coming home?"

"It'll be really late, sweetheart. By the time you wake up in the morning, I'll have breakfast ready for you."

"Promise me you'll kiss me when you come home." She begged.

"I *never* missed a night kissing you, baby." Desiree closed the door behind her, locking it.

That was last time Desiree will see her daughter for a lot longer than she expected.

Outside, the limo driver opened the door for Wyman and his wife. This was all a part of the *good life* that they were enjoying.

How long would it last? For all of his magnificent intelligence, he did not know. So he took his wife's advice and planned to just live in the moment, for as long as that moment would last.

Which would not be for much longer.

Nauen, Germany – Hotel Stadt Nauen – 6:03pm During the time Wyman peeked out of the window to assure himself that it was the limo that arrived, Butta' and her crew arrived at the *Hotel Stadt Nauen*, a quaint, out of the way hotel in the middle of a subtle street. With only four double rooms and eight single rooms, this was definitely *not* four-star residential living—way beneath Kasey's level of quality—but very comfortable for the price.

Which was *free*.

Accommodations handled by the mysterious Marigold—their new benefactor—or taskmaster. Depending on whose point of view.

They were all given one room; a double with low-lying beds and a window that overlooked the street from the second floor.

The bed creaked the moment Munch sat on it. "I'll be sleeping in the chair, thank you."

"I don't think we'll be doing much sleeping, Munchie." Butta' suggested.

"So what *are* we doing?"

"Beats me. We just got to wait for a—"

As if on cue, Butta's phone rang and she immediately picked it up. "Okay, we're here. What now?"

"In your room," Marigold reported, "in the closet space, are your supplies for the evening."

Butta' gestured for the nearest closet and Trigger went for it immediately. Inside was a briefcase with a series of expensive looking wires and electronics, Deutsche Mark's in stacks of 200 DM's, fake ID's and common thievery tools of the trade that Butta' was familiar with.

"We got it."

Marigold was pleased. "Good. The goal tonight is information. The target is at the Robertson Technology Facility in Berlin."

"Why?"

"Someone in that facility took the second diamond. Once you get that information we move onto the next steps."

Robertson Technology. They were the clowns that built Stein's torture chamber called a security vault. It all made sense to Butta' now. The barest wisp of Stein still haunted her no matter where she went.

"Do you have any influence inside the facility?" Butta' asked.

Marigold paused; an unusual amount of time given how *exacting* she has been with her commands, making Butta' wonder if she finally stumped her.

"No. You're on your own the moment you get in there. The diamond is rare, except for the one you let the Korean's take, so I'm certain the one who took the duplicate is someone on a very small list of handlers. I just can't get into their administration manifest without revealing myself. Security in there is tight as hell. Regardless, you are to get into the facility, ask questions and come back to the hotel."

"I can't go in there. I have to be on their most wanted list just beneath Bin Laden and Obama already took care of that."

"I never said you were going in yourself. This is a job for Kasey."

Butta' looked at Kasey sorrowfully. Kasey was looking through the briefcase, pulling out an ID with her picture on it. "It's my picture! *Diandra Stein??*"

"She doesn't look like Diandra Stein!" Butta' protested.

"Do you know how many people actually seen *Diandra Stein?*" Marigold asked and then answered. "A handful. She was Stein's greatest treasure and he kept her unseen by the public eye. She has never been photographed in public. Robertson Technology recently bailed her out from an unsuccessful corporate raid. Kasey is to get into the facility as Diandra Stein and thank them personally, doing what she does best. Shaking her ass, showing some tits and what not."

Butta' thought this plan was risky. "Can we arrange some other plan? That sounds crazy … uncertain. What if some joker in there actually *seen* the woman?"

"Then Kasey will need to do what she does even *better*, won't she?" Marigold said sharply. She was not trying to hear anything less than compliance.

What choice did Butta' have? "What do the rest of us do?"

"Stand by at the hotel and monitor Kasey's transmissions with the supplied devices. They will likely be monitoring any and all communication. The software enclosed will scramble and encode your transmissions but they are very good at Robertson."

"I'm sure."

"Your resident geek—the big on—*Yancey*, is it? He'll work that out for you."

"You certainly know a lot about us."

"That's my job. Now go do yours."

"One second." She covered the mouth piece. "Guys, she gave me the rundown. Kasey, you'll be doing exactly what you think."

"Then I'd better take a shower and get my *Stein* on." She then disappeared into the bathroom.

"Thanks, Kase."

"It's for Fuego."

Butta' walked to the room door and stepped outside while Munch and Trigger tried to figure out the items in the briefcase. Closing the door behind her, Butta' stood in the hall running a hand through her hair. "Louie told me something."

"I certainly hope not." Marigold made it sound like a threat.

"Who do I have to watch for?"

"Oh, that." Marigold remembered. "I've gotten a tip about a young lady being invited to be an assassin. It's a privilege. I'm sure it's not you. You're too sloppy."

Instantly, Butta' remembered where she saw that symbol on Trigger's fallen envelope. *The Guild of Executioners*. While Butta' was a paid *Thieves Guild* member, an *executioner* was different. Far worse. Far deadlier. The kind of mind set to do that *wet work* was *darker* than anything she would ever get in to. "Trig. *No*."

"Well, it wouldn't be Kasey. If I were a betting woman, I would have had my money on Kasey. The way you were hampering Monique's killer instinct, I would have never thought they'd notice her."

"She's just a girl, *damn you*. That's not a life for her!"

"Correction," Marigold stated. "She is a *woman*. You've sheltered her long enough while you've attempted to be the parent you lost. Wake up. Those days are over."

Butta' caught a chill. "You don't know anything about what I lost."

"You'd be surprised what I know. Nevertheless, I've got plans for you, *Gee-Gee*. The *dynamics* of your little team are going to change. You'll find, when it's time to personally evolve, some friends and loved ones will either stick with you or some won't. Change you think necessary divides your true friends from those who aren't. Be prepared for change; it has to happen in order for you to move forward."

"Why do you insist in calling me *Gee-Gee?!?*"

Marigold thought a moment and then said only ten-words. "Because that's what your father use to call you."

Butta' was left with dead air as Marigold hung up, leaving her mind was reeling.

How did she know?

Radisson Blu Hotel Berlin – Berlin, Germany – 7:00pm

About forty-five minutes from Butta's hotel in Nauen, Germany, Ellen and Frank were checked into a Radisson just off a major interstate. They arrived four in the morning and, after the incredible amount of international flying, the jet lag finally caught up with them both and they slept in the whole day.

Frank, already cleaned up, shaved and with a new suit, courtesy of Stein Industries and Diandra's flowing credit, and sat in the hotel's bar sipping on a light drink. He planned for the harder stuff when tonight's Q&A was completed.

All of this traveling has been fantastic. He had never been to Germany before nor South Africa. Up until now, he could barely remember getting past New Jersey. Inhaling deeply, he took in the beautiful people of the country, smiling at a passing blonde who said something in German to her friend and giggled.

She could have said something derogatory for all he knew, but she returned the greeting and Frank was good with that. He had Ellen to thank for taking him along on this whirlwind experience. For a man that has dealt with other people's miseries; when hunting down bad guys was a way of life, this excursion to the four corners of the Earth was *exhilarating*. Taking another sip of his drink, he nodded his head feeling genuinely good. The world was *huge*. Why did he think the New York grime was the center of everything?

For a glimmer of a moment, the seeds of a mind expanding thought sprouted in his consciousness. Not influenced by drink.

Influenced by the *new*.

He liked it.

He liked it *a lot*. Like a child going on a cross country road trip with his family, he practically got excited when he asked Ellen *where to next?*

He knew this much. When he returned home, his *vision* would never be the same again. He started thinking about the kids he would arrest off the streets; some punk who thought the world was *everything* between one corner and the next. He could share what was on his heart right now and make that kid see *and feel* what he did.

The proof that there was *so* much more out there.

"What's with you?" Ellen snapped his attention back to the bar. She, too, freshened up and felt like a new woman. "You had this smile on your face. It wasn't sarcastic, for a change."

"Yeah, I guess I did." He responded dreamingly.

"What's on your mind?"

"I'm thinkin'. I'm thinkin' of callin' Cora."

Cora Tulley Mancuso was Frank's only and estranged daughter. They had a falling out after she got married for the third time and lots of other family strife. Things were said. Feelings were hurt. People stopped talking.

They haven't spoken in eight years.

Ellen knew not to bring it up. It was a subject that she understood as taboo. Everyone knew he loved his daughter, but as the song went *words got in the way*.

Ellen and Frank stared at each other silently. They were like the perfect married couple and she felt him like no other friend or person ever would.

He went back to his drink. "Yeah. When we get back, ya know?"

Ellen sat next to her partner and took a load off. "I know."

No rush to get over to the Robertson Facility. They had an appointment with Mister Lester Grumman and they had another thirty minutes with the facility just down the road. Ellen ordered a drink and simply let her BFF continue thinking, watching him smile.

Corey A. Burkes

Chapter 15

Berlin, Germany – Robertson Technologies Euro HQ – 7:45pm
A limousine rounded the front of the exquisite Robertson fountain
and parked at the front entrance. Lester Grumman walked out of the
doors, pushing his hair back and beamed all of his teeth to his most
gracious guest.

The limo driver came about and opened the passenger door for a
pair of luscious legs owned by none other than…

"Ms. Diandra Stein!" Lester bowed, taking her hand to help her
out of the back seat. "A pleasure meeting you."

Kasey nodded looking down at the little man with a touch of
apprehension. "Mr. Grumman. Thank you for meeting me at this late
hour."

"By all means. After all, we're partners now. Even more than ever
before and a whole lot stronger. Come! I have a small banquet
prepared in your honor."

"My, you certainly roll out the red carpet." Kasey blushed.

"Only for our most honored clients. Allow me to take this
moment to extend my condolences for the loss of your father."

"Hmm?" Kasey blurted out, almost forgetting who she was. It
was actually a lot deeper than just *pretending* to be someone. She
had to remember, for the time being, she *was* Diandra Stein; heiress
who just lost her father. "Oh, yes. Thank you. As you can imagine,
my head has been in a cloud."

"I'm sure. I would be too." Lester started walking his guest to the
inside of the facility. "With that incredibly last minute stock issue,
well, I'm just glad that we have such a great relationship that we can
help when we can."

Interesting, Kasey thought. "Yes. That was really something.
What was your opinion of those events?"

Lester grandly ushered her into the cavernous lobby and on
toward the elevators past security that didn't raise a fuss at all.

"I admit I do not know the intricate details. As Facility Administrator this flagship complex, my communiqué with the Boards of Directors and CEO are limited. Nasty business I can tell you that. Hostile takeovers are troublesome to say the least." He then waived off the entire conversation. "Bah! That was then—this is *now*. I'm certain Robertson will engineer something to prevent future attempts and we will continue to progress as partners as we always have."

The elevator doors opened and the entered…

…Just as Ellen and Frank arrived in their rental, parking directly behind Kasey's limousine.

"Why aren't we drivin' around in a ride like that?" Frank asked, pointing at the shining black limousine.

"You just want to juice that rich chick for all she got, don't you?"

"Don't *you*?"

"You got a point there." She laughed.

Ellen's phone rang. "Speaking of the devil." She answered the phone and paused before walking into the building. "Hello, Ms. Stein."

New York City – Stein Tower - 2:45pm

Diandra stood in her office while construction men and painters milled about, taking down old pictures that were hung by her father and replacing them with different artwork.

"Hello, Detective. I was just checking on your progress. How was your investigation in South Africa?"

One of the workers brought to her a very large, rolled up Nazi party flag with a repaired tear down the center. Diandra didn't even want to touch it.

"*Burn* that damn thing."

Berlin, Germany – Robertson Technologies Euro HQ – 7:47pm

"So far so good, Ms. Stein. We have leads that Gisela Thompson was, or is, on route to Germany and the Robertson Technology facility. Since your company and Robertson worked so closely in the past, we suspect she's in pursuit of something the facility has on site. Possibly created by the Gisela diamond making process."

"I wouldn't doubt that at all," Diandra responded. Ellen was surprised to hear such a tone of confidence from her. She wasn't *trying* to speak like an adult. She was actually presenting her conversation to Ellen with authority. Ellen liked that; the rich girl is finding her voice. "Robertson and Stein Industry shared the same bed for years. She's likely after the last of the diamonds named after me."

"Right. We found out there were two of them."

"If you're at the Robertson Facility, then you're going to want to meet with the facility administrator. I think his name is Grumman."

"Yep. We have an eight o'clock, our time, with him."

"Never met him, but then, I never met anyone so that doesn't say much. All that is about to change. I understand he's an excellent host. Robertson recently helped Stein Industries out in a little situation recently. They will give you all the information you need. Any troubles, don't hesitate to call me."

"Will do. Thank you, Ms. Stein." Ellen hung up her phone.

"What's her deal?" Frank asked.

"Nothin'. She's just checking in."

"We still got our expense account, right? She didn't cut us off, did she?"

Ellen playfully shoved her partner. "She actually called to say she got the *hots* for you and wants to put you in her will *provided* she has your baby. In fact, she wanted about six kids out of you and she was too shy to ask."

Frank laughed so hard he almost cried. "Done *and* done! First thing we do is take down the *Stein* logo and call it *'Tulley Industries'*."

Ellen shook her head, opening the door. "Sounds like a friggin' *pizza* conglomerate."

They entered the lobby and were immediately greeted by security. "How can we help you this evening?"

"Inspector Ellen Cobart. This is my partner Detective Frank Tulley." Each flipped out their badges with the usual smooth timing. "We have an appointment with Mr. Lester Grumman."

"Ah!" The security officer checked his electronic records. "Yes. He is here for your eight o'clock meeting. You just missed him. He escorted Madam Stein to the upper levels, but I'm sure he'll be right back."

Ellen and Frank stared at the man speechless, and then looked back at the limo.

"Madam *Stein*?" Ellen asked.

"Of course. Ms. Diandra Stein."

Milano, Italy -Milan Malpensa Airport – 7:50pm

As Marigold prepared to board her private jet, walking inside a circle of her assigned bodyguards, Adian ran from a driven BMW with a paper in his hand. "Madam Marigold!"

"What is it, Adian? Jet fuel costs way too much for delays."

"Madam Marigold!" He huffed out of breath. "We've been compromised!"

He handed her the paper and she read it quickly. "I thought you said the detectives were still in Cape Town?"

"Yes Ma'am. Our sources in place were breeched and we were sent erroneous information. The detectives tracked everything back to the Robertson facility. They're at the location in Berlin even as we speak."

Marigold did not waste any time and made one phone call.

Nauen, Germany – Hotel Stadt Nauen

Butta' sat on the bed with one-side of a pair of headphones in her ear while brainlessly watching TV; flicking station after station. The headphones were attached to the briefcase where Munch, also with a pair on his ears, listened to Kasey's conversation with Lester Grumman. He adjusted the audio for clarity through the very technically advanced system of electronics.

Trigger laid stretched out across the bed at Butta's feet, bopping her head to some music through her IPod. Every now and then, Butta' would look at Trigger and wonder when her *supposed* friend would open up to her about the whole *Guild of Executioners* thing and...

Her phone rang.

Trigger was closer to it, saw the private number on the face and tossed it to Butta'. She caught it and flipped it open. "Hello?"

Butta's face disfigured with confusion. "What the hell?!? Kasey's gonna get caught out there! You know—you're really a piece of work! I thought you had this whole thing under control. Where's all that *I'm everywhere* big talk now? You didn't even see this coming! I swear to *god*, I'm going to *choke* you when I see you."

Milano, Italy -Milan Malpensa Airport

Butta' hung up on Marigold.

Adian looked to his boss in askance. "What did she say?"

"She's going to *choke* me." She chuckled. "Come on. Let's go."

"Aren't we going to help them?" He asked.

"I'm training her. I'm allowing her to follow through on her own and think out of the box by herself. I can't *coddle* my protégé all the time, can I? That was her failure with *Monique*."

Nauen, Germany – Hotel Stadt Nauen

"Get Kasey! Tell her Ellen and Frank are there—at the facility!" Butta' barked.

"Here?" Munch questioned. "In Berlin? Now? That's not good at all." He turned back to the controls and tried to reach out to Kasey as fast as he could.

Berlin, Germany – Robertson Technologies Euro HQ

Kasey was led to an executive conference room full of food and three chefs awaiting for their guest. The room smelled delicious and, given the time, Kasey would easily get her *grub on*.

Unfortunately, she heard Munch trying to reach out to her in her micro-ear piece. Full of static and faint as could be, she thought she heard one or two key words of great interest: DETECTIVES ... EL ... OUT

Kasey ignored 80% of Lester's yak to focus on what she needed to do. Either Munch was saying DETECTIVES GET THE HELL OUT or DETECTIVES YELL OUT-something.

So she concluded it had to be bad news if he was trying to call her in the middle of an operation which was, on average, a tactical no-no.

Kasey had conducted this sort of game before and very little shook her from her appointed directive. She also knew that any good mission *never* went according to plan. The ones that succeed were those that didn't quake under pressure and sudden shifts in tactics.

Kasey *never* quaked—and sat to enjoy a wonderfully prepared meal. As long as her host was not suspecting anything, her portion of the mission was moving smoothly.

Lester's phone jingled in his pocket between serving Kasey a plate of steaming butter roasted shrimp. "Excuse me, Ms. Stein. I have to take this."

Food stuffed in her mouth, Kasey waived to him gleefully. "It's alright. Do what you gotta do."

Lester walked off to the side of the room to answer his call. "Yes, hello? Oh! I almost forgot. So much going on today. Extend my apologies and tell them I'll be down in fifteen minutes."

Turning off the phone, he returned to Kasey who was dining on some delicious strips of duck delicately wrapped with bacon. Whatever was going on, she was in heaven.

"I'm sorry, Ms. Stein. I have a number of meetings going on today that were previously arranged. But, I like to believe I can multitask and I will tend to them in a moment. Is the dinner to your liking?"

"Far exceeded them, thank you." She was swooning from how *juicy* and filling the lobster tails were. She washed down her meal with a bottle of the finest and most expensive wine on the market; a Bordeaux 1787 Chateau Lafite.

This was what being a guest was all about. Lester was the consummate host.

"If you don't mind, while you continue to dine, I'll tend to another meeting. I shouldn't be long. Help yourself to anything. Our home is yours, Ms. Stein."

"Well, thank you. Oh! Before you go, the reason I came is to discuss a little situation that occurred here a few days ago. I was hoping we can get to the bottom of it *together*." She said '*together*' in an attempt to sound sexy and create an intimacy for them to talk privately. But it was difficult to express seduction with shrimp scampi and a second entrée of Peking Duck consistently entering her mouth. *Man this food was good!*

Lester was not fazed by her womanly wiles; needing to tend to his other obligations. "I see you heard about that? Well, unfortunately, no administration is free of theft. I suppose that's why the detectives from New York are here."

Kasey started coughing and hacking.

The nearby chefs ran to her attention, patting her back. Lester stopped his exit only to ensure that he was not going to be left with a dead heiress on his watch. "Ms. Stein! Are you okay?"

No. "I'm fine. Just —wine —went down the wrong pipe. I'm sorry. You said *detectives*?"

"Two from New York. They're on the hunt for one of the last treasures of your father's legacy. I assure you, Ms. Stein. No need to worry. We *will* get to the bottom of this affair."

He left Kasey alone to be catered, but quite suddenly, she wasn't the least bit hungry anymore.

Time to get to work.

Getting the attention of one of chef's, she stood up, straightening her dress (suddenly a little tighter around the stomach area). "Do you know where the bathroom is?"

Ellen and Frank stood patrolman-silent; hands in their pockets staring at the elevators.

Waiting.

This, of course, was very unsettling to the security officers holding their breath—waiting for anything to happen. The stern expressions on the detective's faces said trouble was about to happen.

The still in the air was immediately broken the moment the elevator *dinged* and out came Lester, smiling and with open arms. "Good evening, friends. Welcome to the Robertson Techno—"

He was cut off in mid-sentence by both Ellen and Frank; both speaking as if by one person: *"**Stein**? **Where**?"*

Chapter 16

Robertson Technology Facility – Lester Grumman's Office
Kasey ducked out from the conference room to look for the bathroom with her real intention of checking around for Lester's office. Cameras were everywhere; security with dogs marched about hall. She casually marched about freely since, according to Lester, everyone was one big happy family. If that was the case, security should be very permissive of her wanderings.

All the same, Kasey needed to work fast. Lester's office was the larger of the executive offices with his named chiseled into a stone plaque; a room separated by a large secretarial space.

But what was she looking for? Definitely an inside job. Kasey was well aware of most of the major crooks on the planet and, before she left the hotel, verified through the some friends in the *Thieves Guild* that no one major pinched it. Quite frankly, it would have taken someone of Butta's level to have pulled off the theft in such a tight security environment.

What she was looking for was a manifest of people who had access to the diamond. At 920-carats, that sort of information *had* to be on the top of Lester's desk somewhere.

Many security reports rested on the top of his desk referencing to enhancements needed to securing the transfer of the diamond from the vault to level 80 accesses *only* in the future.

Level 80 access. That was a pretty high number. What happened that they needed to *improve* it for the future? How many people have such a high numbered security clearance?

Lester's badge rested on the desk by the lamp; a happy little man in his picture, cheesing after the news that he was given an incredible bonus.

Shoot, I would cheese too. Of particular interest to Kasey was the security clearance under his title: Level 80.

There had to be just one, *maybe* two, other people with that kind of clearance. Kasey shifted through the papers and files currently resting on the desk and sat back when she could not find anything worth gleaning.

Thinking over what she *should* be looking for, one very thick folder, loaded with information caught her in box on the corner of the desk.

She opened the manila folder of *Wyman Fowler*.

Apparently the company golden boy, she thought. He was designer of the Stein security vault and a host of inconsequential inventions that made the company millions in military and science contracts. Most importantly, he was in possession of level 80 clearance. A *very* golden boy.

What really stood out to Kasey was how this Fowler engineered a revolutionary surgical laser through the unique properties of a Stein Industrial 920-carat diamond. Additionally, the last person on the diamonds handling list was a security guard currently being held for questioning, not before being signed off by…

"Fowler," Kasey murmured. Even if he did not have it, he was the man they needed to see. The security guard? The cops had him and he was just a transporter. Wyman Fowler was the only person she had to. At first, Kasey swiped up his home address and any pictures of Wyman through available newspaper clippings, then decided … *fuck it*. She would take the whole folder.

Dinner was *fabulous* and it was time to go.

Ellen, Frank and Lester marched into the conference room to find the chef's talking amongst themselves, but no Diandra.

"Where is Ms. Stein?" Lester asked.

"She went to the ladies room, sir." One replied.

"That's fine. We'll just wait here and—"

Ellen pulled out her gun. The room, except for Frank, gasped. "Frankie, take care of things here. Grumman, do you have a vault or some place that you lock up expensive crap?"

"Wha—? Well, I— I— suppose in the vault room downstairs, sub-basement two. What's going on?"

"You stay put with Frank. Call downstairs, tell them I'm coming and give me full clearance to everything. Tell them don't give me any shit or I'm cappin' a fool. If *she* comes back here and don't look kosher, lock her ass down, Frankie."

"Gotcha, El."

Ellen ran out of the room and back to the elevators. Lester was confused and highly concerned for the safety of his facility and especially Ms. Stein.

As for Frank…

"Peking Duck?!? Lobster tails?!? Buddy, you got some beer?" He sat down and immediately tied a napkin around his neck, picking up a fork and knife.

"Beer?" Lester shrugged. "Well, after all—this *is* Germany."

Hosting is where he excelled and felt normal being.

Kasey left the office with much more apprehension than when she arrived. She now had a folder that she did not walk in with. People could start asking questions she would not have answers for.

She had no intention of leaving the same way she arrived. That alone doubled her anxiety. If the detectives were from New York, she might even know them. Worst case scenario, they may even know the *real* Diandra. Kasey could not risk walking into anybody.

But she did anyway.

Down the hall, Ellen was waiting for the elevator to arrive. No matter how silent Kasey tended to walk, Ellen had years of harden peripheral vision that caught her the moment she rounded the corner.

Both women looked at each other. Kasey grinned helplessly.

"*You*." Ellen remembered. "At the tower. Where's Butta'?"

"Not far."

Ellen took a step forward.

Kasey took a step backwards.

Kasey kept her eyes on the gun Ellen did not put away.

"Don't make this a problem. Just tell me where Butta' is so we can try to work something out."

"I wish it were that easy," Kasey said, taking another step backwards, getting ready to make a dash.

"What's that you got there?" Ellen noticed the folder.

"Stuff."

"What kind of stuff?"

"Look, I can't stay and chat, officer. We need to get this information back so we can save a friend. So, why don't you just let me walk and take care of our business?"

"I can't let you just walk, or did you forget that you and your *funky bunch* are the most wanted clan on the planet? I can *cap* you right here and still collect a mill' for my troubles."

"But you're not, so I'm walking away." Kasey stepped back again, and just as Ellen raised her gun threateningly, Kasey spun and made a run for it.

Naturally, Kasey was right and Ellen didn't shoot—angry at herself for not being *that* kind of cop. She doubled back to the conference room, pushing open the door to see Frank chowing down over some grilled steak and talking to Lester about the Oktoberfest.

"Am I interrupting?" Ellen glared at Frank.

"Nope." Frank looked at his partner and already knew the deal, taking off his napkin, wiping his mouth and following after her and down the hall.

Ellen yelled back before disappearing after Kasey. "Grumman! Sound the alarm. Lock this place down. Tell everyone to find and capture *Diandra Stein*!"

Soon after Kasey bolted away from Ellen, the alarm shrieked throughout the facility. All of the decorated, ornament windows sealed magnetically and two-inch radius titanium bars lowered to shield the facility.

Kasey was running top speed toward a window in the middle of the hall, but missed getting through when the bars lowered almost jamming her fingers. Fortunately, the bars were not closing in unison and she made a last ditch sprint for one more window, scooping up a standing metal cigarette ashtray and wedged it between the sill and the bars.

Crunch! The bars were too much for the tray, but paused for the half-second Kasey needed to slide herself under the bars and out of the window just as the bars crushed the ashtray.

Ellen rounded the corner just in time to see Kasey's dress get caught.

Outside, two stories up and on the south side of the building where the employees parked their cars, Kasey ripped off the remaining part of her dress and attempted to hold on to the ledge with one hand, and with the other, continue to hold the folder. She looked up at Ellen banging on the window and bars from the inside.

It wouldn't be long before security found her in this predicament. The good news: she was outside and radio communication was clear and static-free.

"Kasey! Hold tight. We see you!" Said Butta's. A welcome and most appreciated voice at this moment in time came through her earpiece.

Munch drove a little *Smart Car fortwo*, which he barely fit in, with Butta' hanging out the sunroof and Trigger in the passenger seat. Security and police sirens were approaching. Munch slid the micro car against the side of the building under Kasey.

The lithe super-thief leapt from ledge to ledge, shimmied across to a tree, down its branches and got into what available space she could behind Trigger and next to Butta'.

"You guys are better than having a *husband*. Right on time and you never *come* early. Thanks *so* much." She said this very relieved.

Munch smiled. "Till death do we part, as it seems."

Butta' pointed at the police arriving right behind them. "I have no plans on *dying* tonight, thank you very much. Munch, floor it!"

The Smart car spun out, found its traction and tore through the parking lot. After a minor amount of dodging, Butta' and her people evaded the pursuit and disappeared into the night. Their ability to escape authority had never been in question.

It was their *respect* for authority that had Ellen gritting her teeth.

She watched the action from above and behind the barred window of the facility as the little car out maneuver the German police; cars crashing into each other with *Keystone Cop* grace. Ellen sighed miserably when the Smart car busted out of the facility grounds and toward the major highways heading East.

Lester walked up to Ellen patting his forehead of sweat. "Who was that? That certainly wasn't Ms. Stein! Was it?"

"Of course not. That was a thief; a *known* thief. She's in a set of four with the ringleader the reason we came here."

Frank was still picking food from out of his teeth. "Did she get anything?"

"Some folder." She said.

Lester was frantic. "Shouldn't you be chasing after them too?"

Ellen disagreed. "They're *gone*, Grumman. For now. These people are very good at what they do. What we're going to spend evening figuring out is what they took from you."

"The *entire* evening, detective?" Lester had plans of his own, checking his watch. From the look on Ellen's face, he knew those plans were cancelled.

"So where are we going?" Munch asked, still driving at a high speed to keep any pursuit at a distance.

Butta' searched through the folder with help from Kasey and Trigger; each holding a batch of information.

"I got an address here!" Kasey pointed out. "Trig, put it in the GPS."

"Okay." She replied. "What's dude's name?"

"*Wyman Fowler*. He's originally from Georgia; specializes in physics and electrical engineering. Says he's married with a child. Anything on their names?"

"Nope," Kasey shrugged. "Nothing in my pile."

"I suppose it doesn't matter if he has a family or not." Butta' concluded, tying back her hair. "If we're going to find that diamond, looks like he's the best shot we got so far."

Butta's phone rang; probably the most calls that thing ever received since she bought it.

"What?" She answered.

"Status, Gee-Gee." Marigold demanded.

"Stop calling me that."

Marigold exhaled loudly. "Where are we, Gisela? Is that better?"

Grrrr. This woman was getting under her last nerve. "We got Kasey and we're on our way to the next location."

"Did she get a name? Who are we after?"

"Someone named Fowler. *Wyman* Fowler of Potsdam, Germany. It could be a long shot, but he can at least tell us what happened to the diamond or where to get it."

"At least we have a name. I'll take it from here."

"Okay. So check back with us in—what? Munchie?"

Munch looked at the GPS, adjusting it from arrival in *distance* to arrival in *time*. "About forty minutes."

"You heard that?" Butta' asked Marigold.

"Yes, but standby. Do not engage the target until I give you feedback." Marigold ordered.

"Yeah," Butta' snorted, *"whatever*. Call us back later."

"Don't play with me, Gee-Gee. You'd better stay in line on this one. There are others that—"

Butta' closed the phone, hanging up on Marigold again. She started getting comfortable being able to do that. *Nobody runs me,* she thought.

"What did she say?" Kasey asked, taking off her Diandra costume.

"Nothing worthwhile."

Robertson Technology Facility – Lester Grumman's Office – Hour's Later…

"They took Wyman Fowler's personnel records!" Lester pounded his desk. He sat back and felt his heart beating. He was sweating and had to undo his tie before his neck burst a vessel. "I knew he had something to do with this. They took it to cover his tracks. This is gotten out of control."

Ellen was looking through other files when she noticed Lester's overly-dramatic appearance. She looked at Frank—who looked at her—acknowledging his crazed demeanor.

"Mr. Grumman. Would you like some water?" She asked.

"Please," he gasped, "thank you."

Ellen nodded to Frank to get the pitcher on the far end of the room near the bar. She stepped closer and looked at Lester in the eye. This man was in a terrible state of mind. "What's the problem, Mr. Grumman?"

"That *poor man.* I never wanted things to go this far. Never. *Ever!*"

"What do you mean *this* far? Talk to me, Grumman."

Frank handed him the water and Lester swallowed it practically whole; resting back breathing heavy.

"Detectives. You have to help that man. *Please.* Before it's too late. We can forgive the theft of the diamond. Really, it's just a piece of rock and it's insured. But—"

"But what? Help him from what?" Frank asked, very concerned.

"Wyman and his family are in danger. There are people—*god-like* people who control almost everything."

"Don't give me any of that *illuminati* bullshit, Grumman. Tell us what you know!"

"One of them did not appreciate the diamond being stolen from our facility. It's my fault. He wanted to know who I thought had it. Wyman and I had a difference of opinion about how the diamond should be used."

"El. *Hitler-boy* out in Apartheid. The two diamonds on his manifest."

Ellen nodded, agreeing with her partner. "Two diamonds. One there. One here. Butta' went for one. Dude here—."

Frank added to her thought. "—Takes the other. Everyone's flippin' wigs. Now there are two most wanted people on the list."

"Do you detectives think—?" Lester attempted to interject a thought.

"Shaddap!" Frank shoved him back into his seat. "*Ass-cheeks* and her crew get to Africa. Lookin' for the diamond. Big ta-do. It's her daddy's invention. It's the last diamond. She's going for broke and callin' it hers."

"Either they got it or they didn't." Ellen finished. "Don't matter. They find out there's a duplicate and come here to find it. Guess what? It ain't here. The blonde sneak in, fuckin' with this one's head—."

She pointed at Grumman.

"—Pulls the lead professors files and they're on their way to have a sit down with him."

Ellen crossed her arms and marched around the office with her mind clicking away to put the pieces together. "Butta' is on some bullshit if all this is about some diamonds. I thought she was smarter than that. Everybody knows Stein wronged her. She thinks I'm trying to arrest her. I'm trying to save her ass from stein's leftovers. Fuck Diandra Stein. I was up there in that tower. I saw and heard everything!"

"You see that, El?" Frank pointed out. "You mad and that wasn't even your family that got killed by that guy. You wanna think these diamonds ain't shit enough to tear up South Africa and raid a tech facility but the bad guy is dead and his company is in possession of the largest diamonds on Earth. What the hell would you do? Seriously."

"You don't let that slide. You can't. But check it. There are some new players on the board. People who want those diamonds for some shit." Now, she looked at Grumman wanting answers. "What are the diamonds for, Grumman? Who wants them?"

"I don't know who the caller is. He told me he was part of the board of directors and wanted to know who took the second diamond. I told him all I knew. The diamonds were purchased by the United States Military as part of a package weapons deal."

"The military must be looking for him."

Lester shook his head. "No —*not* the Americans. That's not who called here."

"Then who?" Ellen demanded.

"I don't know who. But whomever it is, they sent someone to get *rid* of the problem."

"Someone put a hit on Fowler!" Ellen said to Frank grimly, and then turned back to Lester. "Because of your differences, you didn't call the man to warn him, didn't you?"

Lester stammered. "No—I'm so sorry —I didn't think it would get this bad. I only wanted to—"

"Shut up!" Ellen handed him the phone; practically shoving it in his chest. "Call the man—*now!*"

Lester, fearing Ellen's wrath, sat up to flip through his rolodex and picked out Wyman's name and dialed the number. After a number of rings, the answering machine picked up—no answer.

"Any other numbers on that card?"

"His cell, but he never answers it. Even when he wasn't so *in demand* right now."

Frank took the card from his hand and started walking to the door with Ellen. He immediately started calling the emergency number listed on the card.

Ellen pointed back at Lester. "We'll call his wife and start on our way to his house. You call the local fuzz and tell them to meet us over there!"

Prague, Czech Republic - Casino de Prague Le Hilton

Hilton's magnificent congress hall fit 1500 in a stadium fit for kings and queens. The center seats were replaced with draped, candle lit tables for dignitaries of various degrees.

This was a glamorous black tie affair that acknowledged great minds for the work they did all over the world. This event gathered some of the most intelligent men and women in the science community.

In the middle of the sea of well-dressed potentates, Wyman sat with his lovely wife at their dinner table while an announcer spoke highly of Wyman's accomplishments over the years. By his conclusion, the spotlight struck Wyman and he stood to an applauding audience. As keynote speaker, he approached the podium to a thunderous series of claps.

While her husband walked on to begin the evenings events, Desiree's phone rang in her purse. She looked at it—a 212 number from *New York*—and she didn't recognize it.

This would be an entirely different story—with a different ending— if she answered the phone. Instead, since it wasn't an emergency from Pilar, she let the caller go to voicemail.

Chapter 17

Potsdam, Germany – Fowler Residence
"*You have arrived.*" The GPS announced, signaling Munch to park the *Smart car* on the road a few paces from Wyman Fowler's home.

Butta', Kasey, Trigger and Munch stared at the expensive home cautiously. Apparently, the family was home: lights were on, a TV flickered in what was a second floor bedroom and there seemed to be movement in the kitchen.

"How are we going to play this?" Trigger asked.

"Above the belt, for now." Butta' tapped Trigger on the back so she could open the door to let her out. That little *Smart car* may have been their means of escape, but it was cramped beyond belief. She stretched in the moonlight; a shimmering, shapely sight of curves from top to bottom.

No one was there to witness it.

The whole area was quiet as a mouse and that stillness bothered Butta'. She stood there looking at the house and wondered to herself what she *really* should do next.

Trigger closed the door as Kasey was about to step out, almost catching her hand. "Hey!"

"Oops." Trigger shrugged with flippant carelessness. "Sorry."

Kasey glared at her and simply said, "That's *two*."

Butta' was so caught into the moment of how to handle approaching the home; she didn't notice the *thing* between her friends. It was becoming a toe-to-toe that was getting worse by the day.

"Let's just go." Trigger bounced forward. Butta' followed, albeit hesitantly. Trigger led the way, steadily walking toward the front door.

Butta' had the faintest thought of how nice it would have been to hear from Marigold for advice right about now—when her phone rang, playing it's familiar tone she set specifically for private numbers.

Trigger was about five feet from the front door.

Butta flipped open the phone. "Your ears must be burning 'cause I—"

"*Where are you?*" Marigold jumped in.

Trigger stepped up to the front of the door, not noticing she tripped an invisible, infrared beam.

"In front of Fowler's house right now." Butta' said. "Why?"

Trigger looked back at Butta' once, then decided to make an executive decision and ring the bell.

Her finger lowered to the ornate button on the side of the door.

Marigold shrieked. "Get the *hell* out of there! *Now!* Now, NOW *NOW*!"

Trigger pressed the doorbell.

Quite suddenly, she was jerked by the arm by Butta'—literally sailing backwards as Butta' grabbed and ran top speed from the house.

She only made five steps before the house exploded, splintering into pieces and lighting up the exclusive neighborhood. A small mushroom cloud of flame and smoke temporarily blotted out the moon.

Butta' and Trigger rolled into the road, thrown from the blast.

Alive to tell the tale.

Munch and Kasey rushed to their aid, watching the house, and whatever was left of it, crumble upon itself.

"Are you okay? Are you hurt?" Munch checked his friends for any damage.

Butta' bled from her arm and a nasty cut across her waist and Trigger's jacket was burning. Kasey rolled her about to get the fire out, helping her to her feet.

All the while, Trigger was laughing. "That was *crazy!*"

"Gee-Gee!" Marigold could be heard from over the phone in Butta's hand. "Gisela! Talk to me! What happened?!? Are you okay?"

"We're good," she coughed. "Who has a hit on him?"

Marigold sounded relieved. "How'd you tell? I don't know who wants him dead, but I have an excellent imagination. The game is changing every minute, Gee-Gee. You've got to watch each and every step, get me?"

"I get you." Butta' sighed.

"You okay?" Marigold asked again.

Butta' held her head, catching her breath before sitting up. "We can't be here for long and the trail's gone cold if that guys dead." More and more she was terribly concerned for Fuego's life as *time kept on slipping.*

"He *isn't* dead. Once we had a name to look for, I can find him anywhere. Get yourselves over to Berlin Tegel Airport; I will have a private jet waiting to take you to Prague. I'll have another hotel and a plan waiting for you when you get there. Wyman Fowler is giving a speech at a physics conference. He owns a summer home there with his family. Obviously, you're not the only one looking for him."

"Obviously." Butta' coughed.

"My people with in the Guild suggest that a recent contract set an exceptionally evil bastard on his tail and *he's* not looking to leave any witnesses or angry little children to grow up and avenge the ones they lost, are we clear?"

No one on Earth could ever understand more. Turning to face her crew, Butta' relayed everything to them and left the Smart car to find some other means of transportation.

Twenty-minutes later, Ellen, Frank and the whole Potsdam Polizei (police) and Feuerwehr (fire brigade) were shifting through the wreckage of Wyman's once glorious home.

A lot of the German language went back and forth between the officers—none of which Ellen and Frank could understand.

"I got the impression they didn't find no bodies." Frank coughed. The smell of burning wood and brick was miserable.

"Nope," Ellen thought. "And I got the impression we're forever late to the party."

"You think the chick with the nice ass is trying to kill that guy?"

"*No*, Frankie. Of course not." Ellen kicked some of the debris out of her way. "And her name is *Gisela*. Butta' if you're forgettin'."

Frank raised his hands, not wishing to annoy Ellen, who was trying to connect the dots to the situation. For as street smart they both were, this was a tough case to crack. "Now what?"

"Between you and me, I'm just about out of ideas. I know this much—Butta' is not an assassin."

"Not countin' Stein."

"She didn't kill that man. She had a chance and didn't do it. *Stein* killed Stein."

"So where do we go now?"

Just as she was about to consider going back to New York, Ellen's phone rang.

A private number.

"Hello?" She queried. "Who is this?"

"Hello, Detective. Time is limited and you have to listen carefully. You and your partner are in the wrong place; all of the action is taking place in Prague. I can use you both to level the playing field and, if you hurry, you can reach Butta', her friends *and* rescue Wyman Fowler before things get worse. My records of you prove that you are a wise woman and I also know your standing in the middle of a posh neighborhood not sure where to go from here. Instead of watching a burning house, I have prepared transportation for your trip to Prague at a nearby airport. Keep your phone on at all times and I will give you instructions when you arrive. I know you have *one* question."

Ellen signaled Frank and walked back to their rental. "You got that right. Who the hell is this?"

"Welcome to the war, Detective. You may call me *Marigold*."

Vokovická, Prague (Praha), Czech Republic – 9:15pm

While Butta' and her friends were boarding an awaiting private plane to Prague, *He* staked outside the summer Prague home of Wyman Fowler, looking about the mansion; careful not to enter sooner than he had to.

He kept a detonator response device in his pocket, and about forty-minutes ago, the red light informed him the Germany home was a burning pile of bricks and wood. If, for any reason, *He* missed killing his target while in Prague, *He* liked to make sure his work still carried on when *He* wasn't there.

Rule #3 in the game of assassination: tie up all loose ends. The only problem with leaving explosives was an assassin could not guarantee the target was actually taken out.

In Prague, his target was not home—but his child was; under the protective guidance of a nanny or babysitter.

She would have to be the first to go.

Then the little girl.

No witnesses. That's rule #1.

Every now and again, it crossed his mind: *Why am I killing this man and his family?* Such thoughts were quickly dismissed and buried. The longer he lingered on wondering why, *He* would start to care for his victims. What kind of a killer would *He* be if *He* couldn't put a bullet into an eight-year-old girl's head and claim a paycheck?

Rule #8: Never know why. To this date, *He* never asked or received information on why he had to kill someone and *He* preferred it that way.

He checked the time and gave himself another thirty minutes before circumventing the house alarm to do his dirty work.

Butta's flight from Germany to Prague was an *exact* hour.

Chapter 18

Ruzyně Airport - Prague (Praha), Czech Republic – 10:15pm
Prague is the capital city of the Czech Republic, an enclosed country with Germany, Austria, Poland and Slovakia surrounding its borders. What was once called *Czechoslovakia*, in 1993 the country split to become the Czech Republic and the Slovak Republic. This central European country has a rich history of culture, change, ownership and tradition.

Also this country often was the hotbed of international intrigue and the perfect democratic breeding ground for spies and counter-intelligence to convene in the center of all European affairs.

Butta's private jet arrived in Prague with a host of plans, photos and weaponry waiting for them in a van. Three other jet black town cars were also parked nearby.

While in flight to Prague, Marigold laid out the battle plan for them all and expected Butta' to follow every step carefully as timing was crucial:

Munch was tailored into a suit during the entire trip. He wore a sharp looking *Brioni* tuxedo that made the large man feel like a million dollars. He was also given a wad of cash; credit cards already printed with his name and activated with an unlimited spending account. A haircut, shave and use of the onboard shower as well. The personnel onboard even did his finger nails.

This kind of treatment was usually reserved for the ladies in his circle. Now he understood why they clamored for spa days. It looked like he'll be visiting the *Hibiscus Day Spa* back in Brooklyn when he returned to the states.

His job was to confront Wyman Fowler directly, who was at the conference, and convince him to where the diamond would be.

Sending the women would not work because he was reportedly a dedicated family man and his wife would be with him, cancelling the T&A approach.

Munch had to approach him geek-to-geek.

Kasey would be monitoring his conversations from van in the hotel's parking lot and acting as Munch's *eye in the sky* by tapping into the security cameras.

Trigger would be on her first solo mission. Encouraged by Marigold—argued by Butta'—until she had to relent in order to accomplish her own mission that Trigger could not go on.

Trigger was assigned to scope out the Fowler home and stop the assassin if he arrived there. She was already warned that the assassin may already be there and the house may be rigged for explosives also.

Butta' spent more time than usual giving Trigger all of the possible things to be careful of like a mother would, sending her child off to the corner store for the first time.

Trigger claimed to be ready.

Butta' wished she weren't, but even she could not deny that hunger in Trigger's eye to be more active. Butta's final words on the matter were short: "We all must leave the nest and fly."

As for Butta', Marigold assigned her to a special mission that required her to go to a location between Wyman's home and the conference; outside Prague Castle off of Thunovská Street.

Kasey took Munch and drove off to the hotel, taking Butta' with them to drop her off at her destination. Trigger took one of the town cars and drove to the Fowler residence with a personally selected German-made Walther TPH Taschen-Pistole (*Pocket Pistol*) Hammer. The small, agile weapon came with a 6.35mm caliber chamber, so only the most surgical of users could actually make use of the weapon of its size.

Trigger was a master marksman and could do more damage with this light weight gun than most people could do with a rocket launcher.

Butta' gave her long time friend and protégé a lasting hug before they parted ways, watching Trigger drive off in the direction her GPS pointed her to.

"What are you feeling?" Munch asked Butta', brushing off his sensationally fitting suit of lint.

"Loss." Butta' sighed.

"We're losing her?" He asked rhetorically. He knew the deal.

"That we are." Kasey concluded and drove her partners to the next location.

10:35pm …
Twenty minutes later, same airport, another private jet arrived.

Ellen and Frank deplaned following instructions from a highly secretive voice over Ellen's phone.

Frank questioned the logic of all this. "What makes you trust this broad?"

"'Cause we have *absolutely* nothing else. She's promising to lead us to Butta' and all the other loose ends."

"Just seems like we're going places a little blind, that's all."

"I hear ya, Frankie. I just know you got my back no matter what."

"No matter what, partner." Frank took out a cigarette and propped it in his mouth as they walked toward two awaiting town cars. The driver of the first car stepped forward and smiled to Frank.

"Mr. Frank Tulley?" He greeted.

"That's me, pal."

"You will come this way. Madam Ellen Cobart? You will take the other vehicle."

The two detectives looked at each other and refused to budge.

"Not in this life time, bud." Frank said, lighting his cigarette. "We don't break up the act."

"Your benefactor *insists*." He said this looking directly at Ellen.

Prague, Czech Republic - Casino de Prague Le Hilton – 10:36pm
The physics meeting was wrapping up and the majority of people who have attended scattered toward the core of the festivities: the hotel casino.

Gambling wasn't on Wyman's mind and he looked forward to getting home as soon as he could. At the same time, he felt secure standing in the middle of thousands of people; a sense of stealth and faux comfort.

Least he not forget he was a wanted man.

He was not aware *how* wanted.

At his table there were a group of men, with their wives, chatting away about their expensive lifestyles and how much money they had and their hundreds of acres in different parts of the world; totally against Wyman's grain.

A bearded, Russian administrator directly to his left was talking about something; constantly attempting to get Wyman's attention and opinion on various topics, but Wyman couldn't concentrate on a word he had to say. Plus his accent was thick as the vodka that vapored from his breath.

Desiree disappeared into the ladies room while he sat at their table snacking on what was left of his dessert; cheesecake smothered with strawberries and a chocolate cream. When she returned, he intended to tell her it was time to go. He was not feeling comfortable at all.

Maybe I'll just give it back, he thought. If he did it early enough, they might even forgive him. He knew he was not suited for this kind of *paranoia*. His conscience chewed at him constantly and that was worse than being arrested.

"What's on your mind, dear?" Desiree returned, searching through her purse for things.

"What do you think?"

"I'm trying not to. I want to have a good time. You should try to also."

"That's easy for you to say."

"Even easier to *do*. Tell you what—we're done here. Let's go to the—"

"What? Casino?" He interrupted. "Des, I want to go *home*."

"Wyman, no. We have all night. Let's enjoy it while it lasts."

While it lasts was the key. He looked at his wife's sweet face and relented to her pleas. "Fine." He sighed. "Where's the bathroom?"

"Through doors and right." Said the Russian, whom Wyman didn't expect was listening. *How much else did he hear?*

"Thank you." Wyman responded, standing up and putting his napkin on the chair. On his way to the bathroom, he glanced back at his wife for a final look of assurance, which she gave with a warm smile.

Desiree sat and nodded to one of the wives across from her at the table while the Russian leaned close to her.

"That is a good man, your husband, yes?" The Russian smiled to Desiree.

"Yes, he is. A good man *and* father."

"Hello." Said a voice from behind Desiree. "Is this the table of Mister Wyman Fowler?"

The Russian looked up to welcome the person with a handshake. "Yes! Come, sit. No assigned seating. Enjoy ! Drink! What country are you from?"

Munch sat next to Desiree, moving the napkin out of Wyman's seat and onto the table. "The United States. Oh! Was this seat taken? I'm sorry."

Desiree looked up from her purse to lock eyes on Munch. "No, no. My husband and I were—"

Time stood still.

No one breathed.

The music seemed to have come to abrupt stop in their ears as time went into a full reverse.

Two people from two different ends of the Earth found themselves suffering a form of vertigo; falling from an extremely emotional height.

Munch's mouth dropped open in a slow, disbelievingly wide expression of incredulity. Desiree's eyes practically dilated to the size of dinner plates.

But it will be Munch delivering the first words between them; from a question imprinted—chiseled and tattooed—across his heart…

"Where—*is*—*my daughter?*"

Vokovická, Prague (Praha), Czech Republic – 10:45pm

Earlier on, little Crystal Fowler acted on a voice in her head that her mother called a *conscience*. Her mommy said it was God's way of speaking to us; kind of like a telephone call. *In order for the call from God to work, we have to wash behind our ears and listen.* She went on to say *the less we listen, the less we'll hear our conscience and it's important to always listen.*

Crystal's conscience woke her out of a dream about her daddy just in time for her to hear a *thud* somewhere downstairs.

Maybe her parents came home.

Slipping on her pink robe and slippers, she grabbed her teddy bear and stepped across the room. She long since mastered how to get around without creaking on the floors. Wyman would call her his *little ninja.*

The lights were off throughout the house. Not even the TV was on downstairs or in Pilar's room.

Crystal stepped to the top of the stairs, letting her ears guide her; gripping her bear in a choke hold.

Still nothing.

She parted her lips and inhaled, preparing to call out for her caregiver when she saw Pilar downstairs being thrown from one end of the wide foyer into the wall—*screaming*.

Crystal covered her mouth, gasping. Pilar slumped about on the floor having had the wind knocked out of her. Still, she got to her feet and ran for the kitchen.

Crystal watched after her without saying a word, noticing the dark shadow of *Him* walking after his prey—carrying a knife poised for the kill.

The little girl's conscience said something about hiding and she rarely challenged a message from God.

Outside the house, Trigger was overwhelmed by the aura of *death*. It was a feeling that, even in her youth, she was getting accustomed to and sensitive to its presence.

Like a cross between the old folks home or a funeral parlor. A feeling of a life concluding with no tomorrow. She didn't know where or when, but the feeling was distinctive. Just as long as it was not going to be *her* life, she kept to the plan of action.

Her original orders were to wait outside the house and see who shows up. With the entire house pitch black, no lights and the front door wide open, Trigger could not see any reason to stick to the plan anymore.

She carefully avoided the front door and snuck around to the back, finding a window by the bushes to push open and slid her slim body through. She had a few years to go before reaching Butta's physique.

Inside, the *feeling of mayhem* persisted even worse. She couldn't tell if she was too late or not. Everything was just too quiet.

Wait! Trigger heard something. Something small. Like a creaking of wood suppressed by a carefully placed foot. She dodged silently into the shadow of the living room, hiding behind drapes to survey the house with her ears and keep from being seen. She wouldn't make the same mistake she did at the German house. *Time to step up my game*, Trigger affirmed, gun at the ready.

She waited a few minutes to listen for the noise again.

Nothing.

What she *saw*, however, was nonetheless chilling.

A woman of Hispanic lineage crawled along the floor, clawing at the hardwood; bleeding from her head, mouth, arms and a knife stuck from her back. She dragged a trail of blood from the kitchen with her. The further she dragged herself, the more she started to whimper and cry out.

Trigger, seeing this from a reasonably safe location, had decisions to make—none of them meant securing her own safety and she optioned to stay right where she was. Her instincts kicked in and told her to stay put just a little longer.

He stepped behind the dying woman like a ghost and kneeled behind her, applying his knee and body weight into the knife protruding from her back, sinking it through her spine, severing it heartlessly.

The knife impaled her into the wood floor, making her release a final dying screech…

… Causing a very frightened eight-year-old girl to come out of her hiding place at the top of the stairs and witness the brutality she would never forget again.

Crystal screamed, drawing *His* attention.

He stood, pulling out the knife from the dead au pair and brandished it toward his next, littlest victim.

That would not do for Trigger, who pushed past the drapes like a phantom, *almost* catching *Him* off guard as she came out shooting.

He found a worthy opponent.

Prague, Czech Republic - Outside Prague Castle – 10:47pm

Prague Castle was the home of the Czech Republic Crown Jewels and listed as *the* world's biggest castle. The thief in Butta' thought about returning back here one day to see about those jewels, and then thought against it. With so much on her plate right now, defying the Thieves Guild and conducting an unsanctioned theft would compound her troubles.

Why the hell am I standing out here? She wasn't informed *why* she was standing on the corner of cobblestoned streets like some Czech hooker. Such was the way this Marigold communicated with her. Do this, do that and show up where ever she told her to.

Why am I listening to this chick again? Because she hinted at knowing her family; a sore subject that was a hole in her life just waiting to be filled by anyone who can shed some light in that area.

That was what had her out in the Central European cold air waiting. Sooner or later, she would be able to connect the dots about her family and if it was through a mystery woman, so be it.

A car pulled up against the curb; a black, shiny town cars with tinted glass. Butta' recognized it as one of the town cars from the airport when she arrived. The tint was so thick, all Butta' could see is her own reflection in the rear passenger window.

It rolled down to reveal the occupant.

"This Marigold seems to have an interesting sense of humor." Ellen remarked, smirking at the baffled Butta', who stepped back from the car not sure whether to run or *really* run.

"Get in the car, Gisela. I'm not here to bring you in. We got to put our head together and figure out who the *fuck* this Marigold character is."

Chapter 19

Prague, Czech Republic - Casino de Prague Le Hilton – 10:55pm
"*How did you find me?!?*" Desiree growled; teeth grinding to the bone.

She looked Munch up and down with utter disgust; like a *thing* from the past that she remember slicing, dicing, killing multiple times and then burying only to see it rise from the dead.

Munch, himself, was at a loss for words, repeating the only ones that mattered to him. "Desiree… *Why?* Why did you take Crystal away from me? *How could you*? Where is she?"

"You listen to me, Yancy, and listen good! You will *never* see *my* daughter as long as I am breathing. I don't know how you found your way to this side of the Earth, but you're going to see yourself back and forget me, forget Crystal and most of all, *get out the fuck of my life*!"

The words were harsh and spat with venom; tainting any mission he came there for. In fact, he totally shut down—unable to respond or fight back.

"I see you know each other, yes?" Asked the Russian, chuckling. He was very interested in the sudden drama between them.

"*No!*" Desiree lied. "He's no one. He'll forever be a *nobody*. He's a mistake in my life I thought was gone for good. Like shit on a shoe, you can wipe it all day but it keeps coming back and smellin'."

"I refuse to believe," Munch muttered humbly, trying his hardest to maintain control, "that the universe is so cruel that I was to travel around the world only to have my heart broken. I am sorry that you and I fell apart as we did. It wasn't even my intention to find you at all but now that I have, I beg you, Desiree. *Please*. I just want to see *my* daughter."

"The *hell* you will! *My* daughter doesn't need to know about your *fat ass*. Look at you! You're a goddamn *loser*. I don't surround myself with pointless *fuck ups* that can't get more out of his life. Her *real* father and I are her role models and she will grow up to be a *leader*. Not some poor, hopeless excuse of a man that—*oh, wait*. Are you still working for Wal-Mart?

"Are you still letting people walk all over you? Look at you? Fat as all hell. Still a nervous eater? Probably ate the entire *damn* food aisle at the store. Why in the hell would I want *my* daughter to witness the self-destruction of a *clown*? That's right—I said it! A *clown*. Have you looked at yourself in the mirror, lately? I'm so fucking sorry I met you, but I suppose your *sperm donation* was just served. Crystal is a beautiful child and she has *nothing* of you in her. *Nothing!*"

Munch looked down into his lap, unable to keep eye contact with the vicious woman, rocking back and forth, wincing at every thrown remark, and whispering the same thing: "*Please*. I just want to see my daughter. She's my daughter. I want to see my daughter."

"She's *NOT* your daughter! Can't you get that through your *fat head*! She has a *real* father that makes *real* money and is far smarter than you will ever dream to be. You are *dead* to her. She doesn't even know you exist!"

A tear rolled down his eye as he gathered the strength to look up at Desiree. "She loved me."

"Love you?? Shit, she *doesn't* love you. She doesn't even know who the *fuck* you are! As far as I'm concerned, she *never* will!"

Vokovická, Prague (Praha), Czech Republic – 10:58pm
What goes through the mind of an assassin during a gunfight?

Primarily, they are counting: counting how many bullets the opponent *should* have left. Counting the time between the moment the opponent pulls the trigger, to the moment the hammer strikes the bullet's primer, igniting the propellant in the casing, sending the bullet out through the barrel.

The perfect assassin would also be counting how many spiraled grooves are within the particular weapon the opponent was using; counting how long it took from the release of the bullet through the barrel to get to its target.

Most of all, determining how long the assassin needed take to get out of the way.

Superior assassins even accounted for wind, air, mass of target, distance, height and weight of the shooter and, in some cases, where they are on the planet, as a bullet will not necessarily travel the same way in two different air spaces due to gravity and temperature. Even the weather plays a role in knowing what to expect.

It's all those thoughts that made Trigger one of the best, natural marksmen on Earth—with her opponent, a trained killer, her equal.

Trigger rolled across the floor shooting at *Him* without taking an eye off the target—but somehow, he still got out of the way; dodging her attack while slipping out a Heckler & Koch MP7 submachine gun from under his coat.

In half dive, *He* let the gun rip holes through the walls and floors, shredding anything unlucky enough to be in the way. Trigger made sure she was not in his line of fire and skirted up the stairs; rapidly followed by his shower of bullets. She bounded up the steps and slammed into Crystal, taking them both, and her teddy bear, across the upstairs floor.

While still sliding across the hardwood, Trigger reversed herself and caught *Him* by surprise as he attempted to capitalize on their disorientation and get up the stairs after them. Now was one of those times she regretted having such a small gauge weapon to fight with and had to make every shot count.

Clearly, the Black girl was much more than *He* expected.

What *He* thought would be random pot shots from her little pee-shooter of a gun, turned out to be near misses to his eyes and face; deadly weak spots to *His* head, should any of the small gauge bullets hit their mark. She had to be something of a *great shot* to pull that off in motion. For the first time, *He* was little concerned. Yet again, *He* dodged her attack, needing to jump back down to the first floor, busting through the banister, grunting.

She hurt *Him*. That was rare also.

Trigger scooped up Crystal and rushed into a bedroom, slamming the door. Poor Crystal was crying hysterically.

"I wish I can tell you it's going to be okay." Trigger warned; locking the door and rushing about to scour the area with her weapon extended in front of her. With a free hand, she opened her cell phone and started dialing. "We're in a lot of trouble."

"I want my mommy!" Crystal shrieked.

"Ssssh!" She closed the phone, grabbed Crystal and got down low in front of the room's entertainment center on the far end of the master bedroom—holding her breath.

From across the room, the bedroom door was kicked open, followed by feet walking in, stalking *His* prey.

Trigger held her breath and looked at the situation for what it was: dismal.

Her weapon was only good if the target would sit still. He's sporting a multi-round machine gun and knew how to use it.

Time to get a little physical.

She gestured for the little girl to stay as far back as possible. Trigger listened carefully to triangulate where her attacker would be, put down the gun and counted to three, rolling across the floor under his line of fire.

By the time he realized she came low instead of straight on, she had one leg between his and a foot under his weapon to keep it from lowering into her. With all of her strength, she toppled *Him* to the floor, reaching out for the machine gun as it lit up the room. Bullets tore up the walls, TV and the floor nearest to Crystal by inches.

Trigger began her struggle; a brawl where the loser would not just walk away bleeding. The loser would not walk away at all.

They struggled for the weapon. Each trying to point the nozzle at the other. *He* couldn't believe he was wasting this much time fighting this woman, pulling out a blade from a sheath and swiped the air for her neck.

She blocked his blow with the machine gun, catching the blade in the trigger, thus also slicing into his hand. *He* howled in pain; allowing her to pull at the knife and swat the gun away from them.

Now the two struggled for ownership of a Ka-Bar Black Fighting knife with a serrated edge. Trigger had to dig deep for the strength she *needed* in order to survive this tug of war. Her life depended on the final outcome, and this man had strength and experience with close hand-to-hand combat on his side.

Trigger had leverage and street-sense on hers. If the streets of *do-or-die-Bed-Sty* taught her anything, it was there were *no rules to a fight*. She shoved a foot hard and relentlessly into his groin, taking 50% of the fight out of him.

Any man will claim, if they had to choose between a kick in the groin or a knife in the gut—the knife wound *would* heal.

Struggling over both the knife and the *family jewels* were too much for *Him*, so he bodily threw her off and over him. She took the knife with her and she recovered quickly, stabbing and swinging the knife at him without talent or coordination.

She was young and inexperienced but skill with a gun. *He* watched her swing at him wildly, forcing him back. What she did not know was he was allowing her to think she had the upper hand when, in truth, he was waiting for her to wear herself out.

Exhausted from the attack without connecting with the target, Trigger lost timing; completely out of breath. *He* grabbed her arm, disarmed her and twisted her into a head lock with the knife now in his possession.

He planned to finish this by slicing open her throat and cutting open her chest—a gruesome conclusion for the inconvenienced time spent.

As he readied the knife for the final blow to gut Trigger like a fish, the bedroom door burst open again.

Enter Detective Frank Tulley—taking *no* prisoners—gun extended directly at *His* head.

"What the *fuck* we have here?" Frank smiled. "Put the kid down, pal. Come dance with a grown ass man."

He threw the knife at Frank. It flipped through the air at lightning speed and stuck into Franks shoulder. Frank, no slouch from years on New York City streets, took time-honed shots at *Him* with one hand.

He let go of Trigger and ran for the window, dodging and rolling from the shots; but this wasn't an inexperienced woman with a low caliber weapon. Frank was an trained adult that did not waste his shots. Even with a wounded arm, Frank squeezed the trigger of his Glock Model 22 with .40 caliber rounds and blasted *Him* just as he attempted to get out the window. Once the first bullet struck and went through *His* chest, all Frank had to do was finish him.

His body crashed through the second story window, riddled with bullet holes and a final one to the back of his head.

This was the death of a master assassin by New York's finest.

For emphasis, Frank blew the smoke out the nozzle of his gun, spun the weapon around his finger and holstered it—winking at Trigger. "World class out this *beeatch*!"

"Oh my god! Thank you!" Trigger was very surprised. "How did you—?"

Removing the knife, Frank wrapped up his arm with a pillow case. He's been stabbed before. "We're just pawns in someone else's game, sweetheart. Grab the little girl. We're blowing this camp."

Lights from a car shined across the window and the walls. Someone just pulled up in front of the house.

"You got a ride with you?"

Frank looked seriously concerned. "Yeah. But I told him to hang back." He reloaded his weapon, getting ready for the next round of action. "That sounded like *two* cars."

Crystal could not stop crying, holding onto her only sensible form of normalcy—her brown teddy bear. She had a vice-like grip on the toy, refusing to let it go.

Frank took the lead. "You two follow behind me. Don't say nuthin' to nobody and get ready to run if we need to, get me?"

Trigger nodded, as did Crystal; tramping about in her pink robe and PJ's. Frank marched out carefully to the hallway and down the stairs. For all he knew, this could be the local cavalry coming to save the day. There certainly was enough gun fire to alert the neighbors, even if they were acres apart from one another.

Outside, there were two black vans with their engines running, parked outside the front door. A team of tall men in trench coats milled about in front of the lights, effectively hiding their faces.

Opening the front door wider, Frank had to put his hands over his eyes in order to see who the men were. He used another hand to wave Trigger and Crystal back toward the house. "I'm a cop." Frank called out. "Detective Frank Tulley. Who are you guys?"

One of the men said something indiscernible in *Russian*, directing it at Frank. Frank stepped forward, pulling out his badge. "I'm a cop. Police."

The first bullet ripped his left knee in half, dropping him to the ground hard. Frank screamed in agony; Trigger covered Crystal's eyes and pulled them both into the house.

"You grimy bastards! I'm a *goddamn* —" Frank attempted to fire back, but the second bullet pierced his throat with such impact, it tossed his entire body backwards and to the ground.

He choked, unable to speak. Blood filling his lungs.

Two of the Russian men approached the incapacitated Frank Tulley, said more things in Russian and then had the nerve to laugh. One of them was smoking and dropped the lit cigarette onto Frank's chest, stamping it out with a foot.

Frank growled in pain and received a number of life ending bullets to the chest.

Trigger had to cover her mouth to prevent screaming. These things would be seen in the movies or would be heard about in the news. Regardless, the world becomes an uglier place when someone is actually witnessed getting killed.

Monique 'Trigger' Bolland was baptized into this world and, through this visual, became a changed woman.

Another man appeared from behind Trigger and Crystal, pushing them outside. He stripped Trigger of her gun and phone, but let the little girl keep the bear. Anyone would children would know it's best to keep the littlest one quiet.

Trigger maintained her hand over Crystal's eyes. She did not have to see Frank this way. She didn't want to see it either. *That could've been me.*

They were led into the gathering of other men who all had something to say in Russian. One of them got close to Crystal, patting her on the head.

He laughed and pointed for both the little girl and Trigger to get in the back of a van. All the men boarded the vehicles and pulled away from the house, leaving Frank; barely alive and fading fast—reaching for his cell phone.

Fingerprints in blood pressing redial.

Corey A. Burkes

Chapter 20

Prague, Czech Republic - Outside Prague Castle – 11:00pm
Ellen caught a chill she could not explain. The car was warm with all the vents blasting so she could not understand where it came from.

It was a deeper cold than she ever felt before.

Butta' sat next to her, looking out the window with not much to say to Ellen. Though they fought side by side at one point in time, Ellen worked for people who had made it their business to find, capture and possibly kill her. "You know, before I got here, *Marigold* told me I was going to meet with someone who she wanted on her team and that person would help me with my problem. All I am to tell you is you'll be paid lovely for your work."

Ellen didn't know how to respond. "Who is Marigold?"

"You think I know?"

"She dragged you out here to talk to me."

"She dragged you too." Butta' retorted.

"What problem do you have? What the hell's going on around here? What kind of work is she offering? Why me?"

Butta' shook her head, thinking she was sent on a *fool's mission* when her phone rang.

Ellen's phone as well. "Hello?"

She could barely hear anything on the opposite end, but it didn't matter. The number came from Frank's phone.

"Frankie?" Ellen shuddered. She couldn't hear anything except a faint whisper. "*El —*"

As for Butta'... "Kasey?"

"You got to get back here. Like now!" Kasey rushed. "Munch is being torn down by some crazy *bitch*. He's no good to the mission anymore. You got to get in there and pull him out."

Ellen reached across the seats to the driver, pulling at his neck; the look of anger, fear and desperation in her eyes. "Do you know where my partner was going? *Tell me right now!*"

"Yes, madam. I can take you there."

"Do it! *Now!*"

"Are we taking your guest?" He asked.

Butta' was already out of the car, closing the door. "I'll pass. I've got work of my own to do."

Ellen ignored her, yelling at the driver. "Go! *Go, go, GO!*"

The driver sped down the street in one direction; Butta' ran in the opposite toward a major intersection in order to hail a taxi, all the while listening to Kasey breakdown the situation with Munch. She replayed a recording for her to listen on the way to her destination.

This woman, Desiree, ripped into Munch emotionally. Anyone who cared to know about Munch knew how much he loved his little girl.

How small could the world possibly be? The issue with coming to Munch's rescue was they still needed to come out of this evening with results. Butta' could not rush the scene in her street clothes at a black tie affair without screwing up the overall plan.

As her taxi parked up against the hotel grand entrance, she spied a woman dressed in a shimmering black Tadashi sapphire chiffon V-neck ruffle gown.

She didn't have Butta's hips and her dress would be a snug fit.

It would have to do.

The Russian administrator clapped his hands and laughed from the entertainment: the complete and utter *destruction* of a man *without* raising a finger.

While the others at the table felt embarrassed for Munch and left for the evening, the Russian remained and literally kicked back to continue enjoying the show. His cell phone chirped, providing the only break in his concentration on the Munch/Desiree battle—of which she won by a landslide.

Munch was not confrontational like most people. He never liked to argue or put up a back and forth fight. He had to especially be careful because one wrong word could lose his chance at seeing his daughter.

To people like Desiree, this came across as weakness—and she *detested* weakness.

"Where's Wyman?" She stood up; clearly finished with her work on Munch. "It's time to go. See what you did, you *fat fuck*? There you go ruining a perfectly enjoyable evening. Everywhere you go you leave a trail of failure. Can't you get it through that disgusting pea brain that a girl like Crystal can only be a woman *without* you? Don't ever try to find us. You're dismissed."

"Not so fast."

Munch responded to that voice as if the heavens opened up for him. Looking up from his hands, he smiled at the one and only woman capable of his rescue.

"I'm sorry I'm late, honey." Butta' kissed Munch on the cheek. She fit the dressed like a tight glove; a magnificent gown that accented her curve. Men salivated from one end of the event to the other.

The woman Butta' *jacked* the dress from didn't put up much of a fight after receiving all the money she had in her pocket: over 201,000 Czech Koruna's (about $10,000 USD).

Big gains for undressing earlier than expected.

"They had trouble parking our Rolls. All is well. I'm here now. Did I miss anything?"

Finally, Desiree had a loss for words, looking at Butta' with a mix of emotions. She could not connect this devastatingly attractive woman with the likes of Munch.

"Who's this? Your psychiatrist?" Desiree sharpened her claws. "Only woman that'll want to spend time with you has to be your mental care provider or a couple of cans short herself."

"*No*," Butta' said politely. "Mun—*Yancey* and I have been together for three years. We're quite happy and he treats me well. So I advise you to mind your manners. You don't know me, miss. You don't want to."

"Excuse you? You and him?" She laughed. "Honey, you apparently don't know what a *man* is."

"Once again, you don't know a thing about me and what I know, and most certainly, you don't know a thing about Yancey. If you keep coming out of your face like that—"

"*Yancey.*" Desiree huffed. "Even the name sounds *gay*."

"I'm being very patient with you, miss." Butta' warned. "You watch your *goddamn* mouth. He is one of the greatest men on this planet. Loyal and giving. So, what's this I hear you are not going to let him see his daughter? I have a problem with that."

"Bitch, fuck your problem. He's a *nobody*! I don't know what he's done to disillusion your skanky ass—maybe you're damn near high on some shit. But he ain't gonna get near my daughter and you can bank that statement."

Butta's blood was boiling, turning her chocolate skin tone to a shade of purple.

She smiled and attempted to defuse her rage by taking a drink out the closest glass she could reach for. "Wow. Miss, you need to ease back. Nothing I'm telling you is an option. You don't have a choice. You are gonna let my man see his daughter or—"

"Or what?" Desiree's *Jamaica-Queens* was showing. Gone were the pomp and circumstance of the European black tie affair. "What the *fuck* do you plan to do? Any *whore* with this *pig* can't be worth the *shit* she's dressed in."

"Bitch," Butta' cracked her knuckles, "I will *hurt* you. So sit your hot mess, fake ass down before I break my foot off up in your 'rass and lose a good boot. Ain't no PhD in this joint gonna surgically remove that when I'm done."

Desiree stood up, taking off her earrings. "Oooooh. Well, now. Look at this. She's got more *balls* than you do, *Nancy.* I don't give a fuck about you or this asshole. *Fuck you!*"

Butta' stood up, forgetting the mission. This was personal. "Fuck me? Bitch, we don't even have to take this shit outside."

Desiree was already removing the rest of her jewelry. "After I stomp your neck," Desiree pointed at Munch, "I'm coming for you too, fat boy. For fucking up my life."

Desiree motioned to throw the first punch, caught by Wyman who pulled her away from Butta', kicking and swinging her arms to engage the fight. "Desiree! What the hell!?!"

"Bitch, you don't know!" She growled. "You just don't *fuckin'* know!"

Butta' held her arms open, stepping toward Desiree. "You see me going anywhere? I'm right here, you *sloppy transvestite.*"

Wyman had to grab his wife by the shoulders. "What the hell's this? Desiree! Get a hold of yourself!"

The Russian stood up and clapped his hands with the same energy someone may applaud a Tony Award winning show. "Bravo! Bravo!"

Surrounding him, a number of tall men dressed in black approached with hands deep in their pockets.

The Russian administrator was laughing, completely enjoying himself, stepping over to Wyman. "You missed good show, Professor Fowler. Now you arrive just in time. Always a pleasure to witness fight of emotions. Fights with fists? *Eh*, you see every time. The fight of heart—mental crushing of man by woman. *That* show worth paying for."

"Well, I'm sorry to interrupt your fun, sir. I'm taking my wife home—"

"You go nowhere, yes?" the Russian responded, still smiling.

The men came in close, making sure Butta' didn't leave the group. Each carried a rifle discretely under their jackets.

"As you see, Professor Wyman Fowler. The show has only just begun."

Kasey was in a frenzy.

She was monitoring everything from her parked van and the high tech cameras that tapped into the hotel. She heard, and from awkward distant camera angels, *saw* everything.

Butta', Munch, Desiree and Wyman were being carefully ushered out of the dining area and into the lobby toward two awaiting black vans.

Arming herself, Kasey realized the time for diplomacy was over and she dashed out of the back of her van, running to the front of the hotel.

Unfortunately, she arrived too late, pushing past people with a raised gun, chasing after the vans on foot.

She thought she would do better by cutting across the hotel's fountain, shooting at the vans from the middle of the water where she had a better shot at the driver.

The vans picked up speed and sped into the night, leaving Kasey furious…

… And *arrested*.

Prague police surrounded her with guns drawn. She had no choice but to drop her weapon, defeated.

Vokovická, Prague (Praha), Czech Republic

Ellen's ride came to a stop in front of Wyman Fowler's home and the message was clear before she arrived: she wasn't going to like what she was going to see.

Her partner laid on the ground covered with blood. The devastation Ellen was going through was monumental. Frank was already gone; the guilt in her churned into flashes of rage and despair.

She fell by Frank's side, finding it hard to breathe.

Her driver rushed out, saw the chaos and made an immediate phone call requesting police assistance and an ambulance.

Naturally, the ambulance was, as Frank would have put it, *raking leaves in the park.*

Chapter 21

Marigold's Private Jet – Currently In-Flight
The mistress of the game sat back in her chair, blown away at how her intricate web of maneuvering fell apart in one evening.

Adian stood in front of her, giving Marigold the breakdown of events from Butta' and the Russians to Frank's untimely death and Kasey's apprehension by Prague authorities.

So when Adian saw Marigold smiling, he knew there was more up her sleeve than she admitted.

"What?" He asked.

"All except *one* thing is going according to plan. The Russians have gone *way* too far. They've not only agitated the situation, they've *aggravated* me. Now I want everything *plus* both diamonds. The deal is off."

"I can assume we now proceeding to Plan Z?"

"No, Adian. We're still at *Plan Y*. Let's hold our last card for as long as we can. Have the pilot turn us back to Milan. We have to setup our war room. Get me a location on Louie; I'll need him to be ready for his next assignment."

"Yes, madam."

"And when you get a chance, find out where they are holding Kasey McGuiness and get her gear ready for a trip to North Korea."

"Yes, madam."

"In fact, make sure you pack enough gear for *two*. Kasey's taking a partner."

Prague, Czech Republic - Praha 1 Police Station
Most foreigners were brought, willingly or kicking and screaming, to Praha 1 Police Station as they tended to have ready access to interpreters.

Ellen was shuttled in to give her report to the local detectives. Prague had a very low crime rate except for pickpockets and minor pilfering from parked cars or unwatched handbags.

Considering it was late and the weekend, finding an English interpreter was in short supply. It was just as well; Ellen didn't feel like talking to anyone anyway.

She just sat in the hallway; empty and cold. She could, without a shadow of a doubt—swear and testify to a court of law on a stack of bibles—that she *loved* Frank Tulley. A kind of love reserved for two platonic halves of the same coin.

She would say *god bless you* before he sneezed. He would know how to calm her down when she would want to shoot up the place.

Only Frank.

No more.

When she cried, they were genuine tears she had not shed for anyone since the passing of her grandmother; a woman she missed so dearly, words just could not describe.

Many people were speaking to her in their native Czech and babbling in such broken English, they gave her more of a headache than being helpful. So she shut them out to mourn inwardly, as she always did—privately.

What did catch her eye was *someone* unexpected.

Pushed in by a troop of heavily-armed men, *Kasey McGuiness*, locked eye to eye with Ellen as they passed her to secure their catch of the evening. Both women looked at each other; each with a distraught expression, with a dash of '*this is a small world*' astonishment.

Ellen couldn't stop staring after her—the most unlikely last source of familiar a strange land … in an even *stranger* time.

Thanks to Kasey—Ellen felt a lot less alone.

Russian Military Transport Ilyushin Il-76 – In Flight

The Ilyushin Il-76 strategic airlifter was designed to carry Russian military up to forty tons through the harshest weather. These days, this particular model performs commercial transportation for the right price, but still imposing nonetheless.

Tonight, one of these enormous birds carried far less in weight, but still crossed into some of the most overwhelmingly difficult climates on Earth—just above Siberia.

Any Russian worth their weight in *pelmeni* (*a superb and delicious form of dumpling*) would be familiar to this climate and preparedly dressed for it. As the interior of the plane dropped to a low, *teeth chattering* three degrees, the occupants who were *not* Russian received a crash course in how to *be* one.

Those occupants were: Wyman Fowler, Butta', Crystal, Trigger, Desiree and Munch. Each tied, blindfolded and gagged; seated on the cold metal floor of the plane's hold, with only the sound of four jet engines to keep them aware of their predicament.

Intermixed with the occasional Russian conversations whispered in the darkness, Wyman could hear Crystal whimpering; sobbing endlessly. She would go quiet from time to time—perhaps falling asleep—then start up again.

Wyman Fowler hated himself for this; fully aware that he brought this upon his family. The worst part was, he didn't know the status of anyone in his group and couldn't call out to Crystal or Desiree to comfort them.

Who was there to comfort *him*?

However, there was good news. While all hope seemed dim in the mind of a man not commonly abducted and flown into the unknown—he was in the company of people with experience in this sort of adventure.

As long as they were still alive, this was just an inconvenient diversion from the original plan of action.

Butta' and Munch were still alive and tied back to back—with more than enough time to communicate through a form of Morse code between each other; tapping each other's arms and keeping each other warm.

During their four hour flight, they devised a new plan only they could understand.

East Hampton, New York – Georgica Pond

When in New York, and looking to relax, Diandra Stein stayed at her Hampton home, away from prying eyes. Her estate nestled comfortably between Steven Spielberg's summer home and not far from Grey Gardens.

The thirty-two room Stein mansion was patrolled by fifty on-guard, secret service trained security officers. Always in her direct company was Marcy.

The two sat in the day room, silently reading. Diandra, above all, had much to think about. She was rescued from a catastrophe and did not want to play victim again.

She was aware that the world was playing a bigger game around her than she could imagine and tonight, she had to make decisions: was she going to be a *player* or be *played*?

"Marcy?" She called.

Her attendant had a small handgun by her side and looked up at her boss. "Yes, ma'am."

"I want to move some money. A lot of money."

"Oh?"

"But I want to keep it quiet—*very quiet*. Can you help me facilitate that?"

"How much are you thinking of moving? Where and what accounts?" She asked.

Diandra thought for a minute and then looked around her room. "We had this place swept, correct?"

"Security checked it three times over for explosives and other things. But if you're asking if they checked it for listening devices—"

"Right." Diandra sat up. "That's what I'm asking. Did they?"

Marcy checked a bunch of papers sticking out of her Filofax. "I don't have any information on that."

"Then we're not going to talk here about this. Don't bring it up again until I do. First thing in the morning, we need to work on some things, okay?"

Now, she had Marcy scared, checking under the lamp near her side for hidden wires.

That's when there was a ruckus outside the door. People were milling about, shouting and running. Marcy stood up, dropping her gun to the floor ineptly. Diandra scooped it up and, affirming her mental change, stood prepared to use it if anyone came through the door.

Marcy looked at Diandra and caught a glimpse of *Lingo Stein* in her posture and the way she handled the weapon.

The door burst open and Security Officer Robins came in, talking into his sleeve; ducking when he saw Diandra pointing a weapon at him. "Don't shoot! It's me!"

"What's happening?" Diandra demanded.

"Three of our men dead; shot outside the perimeter of the estate. We're locking down the entire location until the police come in to assist."

Marcy watched Diandra squint at Robins, wondering what her boss could possibly be thinking.

Diandra approached Robins and ripped off an envelope that was loosely taped to his back.

Both he and Marcy were in a state of shock; but not Diandra.

She was a Stein. She *would* survive.

Opening the envelope, she pulled out yet another piece of paper of the finest quality. Dead center of the parchment, a single typed letter similar to the first:

V

Yes, she thought. *I need to be a player.*

"Marcy, tomorrow—we have work to do."

Corey A. Burkes

Chapter 22

Prague, Czech Republic - Praha 1 Police Station

Kasey sat in an enclosed interrogation room with her hands cuffed behind her in the chair. Caught, but still sexy, she took the peaceful moment to retrace what went wrong, what would happen next and, of course, how she would escape.

For the time being, she would let the Czech police rotate her through the system. Their current tactic was to let her cool her heels and get nervous. All it did was give her time to pick the lock on her handcuffs with a paperclip she scored on the way into the room.

At the point where Kasey considered catching a couple of winks of sleep, the door opened and the local detective strolled in with another woman; both holding coffee and a clipboard.

"*'Alo!*" Said the detective.

"He says *hello*." The interpreter followed.

Kasey looked at them both and rolled her eyes.

"*Proč byli tebe stříleni dnes večer? Jaký is tvůj dobré jméno?*"

"He wants to know why you were shooting tonight and what is your name?"

The door opened again and another man rushed in, whispering something to the detective. What followed next was a whole lot of yelling in Czech between the two. Judging from the tone, it seemed as if the man told the detective he had to do something the other did not want to. All the while, pointing at Kasey numerous times and looked to the interpreter for assistance.

She said a few words, shaking her head at both the men, and gestured to Kasey with a shrug. She stood up and left the room saying a few things in Czech.

The man waved his hands in front of the detective, saying a great deal of *something* and marched out.

The detective was left alone and stared down Kasey.

She stared back at him knowing very little of what just happened, but she could tell he was angry. Like someone above him snatched his case away. Walking back to the door, he kicked over the chairs then turned back around.

"*Tebe got pryč tato čas čubka,*" he said angrily, and then tossed the handcuff key on the table in front of her. She didn't understand what he said, but she was certain it was nasty.

In response, she held up her already released hands, giving him the globally understood middle finger.

He didn't like that at all; walking out and slamming the door.

After a heartbeat, the door reopened.

"You!" Kasey gasped.

"Me." Ellen greeted. "Here's your phone call." Ellen tossed Kasey her cell phone, already open and connected to a call. "Don't waste my *anytime* minutes."

Kasey wasn't sure how to react, taking the phone and looking at the private caller ID. "Who is this?"

"Hello, Christian? Did you get baptized yet?" Marigold joked.

"I should have known." Kasey sighed. "What did I do to get a phone call from the omnipotent Marigold?"

"Come now, dear. I'm not *that* powerful. Yet. By the way, I thought we had a deal? You were supposed to keep Butta' from killing Stein. You know this whole thing is your fault, don't you?"

Kasey huffed. "*Bitch,* please. She didn't kill Stein and what's happening right now is because your reach is about a *foot long* at best. I can get a Subway sandwich longer than your influence."

Marigold decided to let that one slide. "Humph. Just testing you, Kase. How is the world's deadliest female soldier?"

"Getting a little tired of your games, but thanks for asking. I know you're aware of the status, so cut to the chase and tell me how're we're playing this. We need to rescue Butta' and the rest of them from the Russians."

Marigold laughed again. "In due time. First, you and your new buddy have to take a trip and go on a *Mexican* run for me."

Kasey already knew what she meant. "I see. By way of North Korea?"

"Damn *I love it* when we're on the same page. You're free from your Prague lockdown. Outside the station, a car will be waiting for you and Ellen to take you both to the airport where a special plane will be waiting to take you to P'yongyang."

"The capital of North Korea? Ain't gonna happen."

"Sure it will, or have you forgotten, you have one more day to get your *karate-man* back. What was his name again?"

"Fuego!" Kasey frowned.

"Well, dear. I've got a plan, and you're running out of time. Take Detective Ellen with you and I'll brief you on the way."

Kasey looked at Ellen who was dying to get some answers.

"What does she know already?"

"Only what I told her. That the North Koreans were responsible for the death of her partner. I think she'll be a very *willing* participant in your new assignment."

"Her partner is—?" Kasey paused on that thought. "Is that true?"

"Does it have to be? The Russians did it but I need someone to ride with you ready to kill. Look at her. Ellen wants to kill somebody. Get on it Kase."

Kasey closed the phone and looked at Ellen who had a fire in her eyes that could have burned the entire room. "I'm sorry about your partner."

"Thank you. I understand we're taking a little trip?" She snarled; clearly looking to get a great deal of payback.

Norilsk, Russia - Castle Zapolyarny

Above the Arctic Circle rested the second largest city that far to the north and, previously, one of the most notorious *gulags* ever to have existed.

Norilsk is now home to some 200,000 residents and is severely polluted by smelting and mining plants—the local industry—for nickel and a host of other money-generating deposits.

There were also, scattered about Russia, abandoned castles and mansions from an earlier, richer age when tsar's ruled the region. For the right purpose, ghost castles such as *Zapolyarny*, overlooked gigantic mining operations; hiding dirty deeds.

The weather was minus thirty-two degrees Celsius. They say spit can freeze before it struck the ground.

Munch had no spit to test that theory and Wyman Fowler had no tears.

Both men sat, tied in chairs, without winter coats or protective gear and only a small fire to keep them warm.

With all that they have gone through, Munch decided not to dwell on their quandary and admired the architecture. They seemed to be inside an old castle's dining hall. It was stripped of royalty portraits and was a gutted, cold and foreboding chamber.

"Magnificent." Munch gawked in tourist fashion.

"What was that?" Wyman questioned, snapping out of a trance.

"I was just commenting on the architecture."

Surprisingly, Wyman chuckled. "You know, I was thinking about that myself. Not the sort of thing you want to talk about when you're being held captive. I didn't know what you may have thought of me."

"I would have thought you were a man of *vast* tastes in a time of crisis." Munch smirked.

Wyman had to agree, smiling back. "Yes. Under any other time, these ruins would be a *fantastic* tour. Simply breathtaking. I'm thinking Shchusev. 19th century."

Munch looked at the arches and what was left of the shapes and styles of the castle, shaking his head. "More like *Boitzov.*"

"Oh! Boitzov! I'm sorry. The French inspired molding."

"Sorry? What do you have to be sorry about? You had the right century. Look at the grace of his portals."

"Sensational." Wyman sighed, momentarily forgetting where he was. "Wyman Fowler, by the way."

"A pleasure. Yancey Duncan. I'd shake your hand, but—"

The two, tied up men, laughed.

"So how did you get caught up in all this, Yancey?"

"Well, this is what comes from wanting to get *your* autograph, I suppose."

"You're not serious," Wyman shuddered.

Munch laughed. "No, no. I'm joking. But I am familiar with your work."

"Oh really? The media makes more of it than it really is."

"*Love is but the discovery of ourselves in others, and the delight in the recognition.*" Munch quoted from off the top of his head.

"Who said that? I know who said that!" Wyman thought. "Alexander Smith?"

"Correct."

"And he *reads* poetry as well? Old Scottish poetry, at that! All this time I thought I was the only *Black man* interested in the classics. Mr. Duncan, you are a man of many talents. Here's a quote that I really believes drives home. Perhaps you know this one. Its Smith. *A man's real possession is his memory. In nothing else is he rich, in nothing else he is poor.*"

Munch sighed, thinking of Crystal. "No truer words could have ever been uttered from the mouth of man."

"True indeed." Wyman looked over to Munch inquiringly. "Say, Mr. Duncan? Do you play chess?"

"Yancey is fine. Friends call me *Munch*. Don't ask. If you happen to have a chess set on you—"

Their conversation was interrupted by three men marching in from the shadows. Of the three, the smaller one was the Russian administrator from the dinner, *Maksim Sidorov*. He pulled up a seat in front of Wyman and Munch, sitting and smiling.

The fire casting an eerie glow on his beady eyes, teeth and beard. "You like accommodations, yes?"

"No!" Both Wyman and Munch said at the same time.

Maksim ignored them. "Ancient Russian mansion. Bigger ones near Moscow. This one a little drafty."

Which, of course, was an u*nderstatement*. Through holes in the walls, ceilings and floors at random places, snow piled in spots closer to the outer walls.

"So. We talk of diamond." Maksim abruptly changed subject.

"I don't know what you're talking about." Wyman shivered; both cold and scared.

"Professor Wyman Fowler. Genius and creator of the FrG-20 Laser Cannon weapon. You know what I am speaking, comrade."

Wyman took great offense. "I did not build *any* weapon! If you know anything about me, I designed a surgical laser."

Maksim waved him off. "Yes, yes, yes. Facility take idea and turn to super weapon. No big deal. You take it personal, now you here in Russia. Very commendable. Now, it is time to hand over diamond."

Wyman was amazed at how much this man knew. Maksim laughed a hearty, Russian maniacal laugh. Each bellow bounced from wall to wall and echoed into Wyman and Munch's core.

"I was KGB. Information easy. Now, I sell weapons in black market. Make good money. You should try, yes?"

"Are you kidding me?" Wyman gaped at the ludicrous concept.

"Eh. Not for everybody. Look, my latest product. Up for sale next week."

He proudly gestured to the far side of the chamber where two men were pushing in a massive FrG-20 laser cannon with the words *Robertson* blazed against the side.

"Sixty million American dollars from friends in Afghanistan."

"Terrorists." Munch whispered.

"*Freedom fighters.*" Then Maksim had to snicker. "Who we kidding. Terrorists to be sure. But *cares who*. They pay cash. Problem is—no diamond, laser no work. You got diamond."

Wyman saw where this was going and got colder than the room's lowered temperature. Maksim leaned closer with a terribly evil grin.

"I remind you of wife and little girl, comrade. Like I said. Information *easy*."

Munch felt sick. Now wasn't the time to debate or bring up the soap opera-level drama of whose daughter was who. Crystal's life was being threatened. What could he do but hope Wyman would do the right thing.

Give up the diamond? Effectively releasing a deadly weapon to global terrorists and their bargaining chip? Or deny them and watch his family die.

Who would want to be Wyman Fowler right about now?

Not many people at all.

Classified U.S. Military Aircraft – 20 km above North Korea

This plane did *not* exist. Its current position *wasn't* where flying into North Korea and its passengers *weren't* aboard it.

Regardless, at the same time Munch took notice of the Castle décor, Ellen was dressed in a specialized pressure suit in the hold of this unspeakable airplane, undergoing an accelerated course on HALO (*high altitude, low opening*) jumps by two United States Naval SEALS's who were not mincing words on how a terrible her death would be if she did not pay close attention.

They went over how to prevent blacking out, when to pull the cord, what to count, what not to do, what she *absolutely* had to do and what she wanted to watch out for.

"I suppose all this was to scare me, right? Good job."

The SEAL's chuckled, but didn't deny the seriousness of her plans, and continued to give her the breakdown from decompression sickness to hypoxia which all was a direct path to death even before she would hit the ground.

In the *slim* chance that she should survive the fall and parachute into the enemy territory as coordinated, there was the second opportunity to die in the hands of the North Korean's who don't take kindly to paratroopers landing in their backyard unannounced. Thus, this trip was being disavowed and if she were to disappear, there was nothing that the U.S could do about it.

All Ellen could think about: *For Frankie.*

Kasey, dressed in the same version of the pressure suit, didn't need the HALO drill beat into her. She stood hanging onto straps attached to the wall, meditating while inhaling her oxygen.

Once completed, the SEAL's patted Ellen on the back and went about their business, leaving Ellen to speak with Kasey. "You seem quite calm about all this?"

"After the sixth HALO, it's a breeze."

"I was wondering why they didn't give you the doomsday report. I didn't know you were military."

Kasey glanced up at her from a broken meditative state. "This is my unit taking us to the insertion point."

Ellen regarded Kasey in a whole different light. No longer was she *just* the buxom thief on the run.

"Well," Kasey also added, "my old unit anyway. ST-6"

"I'm sorry. I'm not following."

"Naval Special Warfare tier-one special missions and counter-terrorism unit. SEAL Team six."

"*Get out*, G.I. Jane! All this time I thought you were just the tits and ass crook of the team. Well, you worked for the government, so not a big change in your resume."

"Wah-wah." Kasey snickered sarcastically. "Why are you doing this, Detective?"

"Son of a bitches killed my partner, that's why."

"So what? Take on all of North Korea? I'm going in for someone and something specific who may or may not be alive. I'm really sorry for your loss, but let's be realistic. Unless NYPD has super trooper training I don't know about, you're just a cop."

"So you think I can't ride with you on this? Frank was more just a partner, you know."

"Were you lovers?"

"No. Just a friend. A *good* friend. I can say my *only* friend. *How* many friends you got?"

"Roger that. Butta' and Munch, for certain." Notice she left out *Trigger*. "Fuego. He's why I'm doing it and on the way, pick up a diamond. But, once again, I have a 50% chance of my friend being alive."

"So what's your point?"

"Don't get me wrong. I don't mind the company, but I just want it clear that this may be a one way trip for us both."

Ellen saw that as a possibility. She was prepared to die. Not before taking a bunch of them with her.

"Who the hell is Marigold?" Ellen asked.

"A pain in the *ass*. She hired me awhile back to *look* after ole' girl."

"Gisela."

Kasey nodded. "The whole thing is a mess and I'd rather not get you involved. You being Johnny Law and all."

"I don't see no cops in here."

Kasey smiled at her new partner. "Five by five. If you didn't know, the world is broken up into two powers: movers and shakers. Marigold is the *shaker*."

"Who's the *mover*?"

"That would be her opponent, whomever that maybe. It's all about big money, high priced shakedowns, conspiracies, assassinations and global takeovers."

"Is there room for peace on Earth in all that?"

"*Shit*, we wish. Peace is *not* profitable. Remember that, detective. Those four words will give you the answer to everything."

"I hear that."

Kasey's expression changed after her last statement. "You know, I quit the military—some time ago—cause I had issues with the stuff I was doing. I thought it was all behind me —until recently. Funny, how the more you try to get out of the crab basket—"

The shift in tone confused Ellen. "I'm not your priest, *chicky*. If you're looking for absolution—"

"Never mind." Kasey quickly reversed her feelings on the matter and looked away. For a moment, she was missing her bible.

They shared a silent, inward thought; letting the instant marinate into their consciousness. A red light above Kasey started flashing. Then, the plane felt like it dipped in a downward motion.

"What's that?" Ellen jumped.

"Two minute warning. We're lowering down at the bare minimum height to make the jump. We're in North Korean airspace."

The SEAL's reappeared helping both women switch from the oxygen they've been breathing on the plane to the ones they carried in their tanks. Both women's suits also sported specialized helmets that were solid black; but inside had the latest in high-tech HUD systems straight out of science fiction.

Unexpectedly, they also started strapping Ellen to the front of Kasey.

"What? I'm not getting my own chute?" Ellen questioned.

"How many regular skydives have you accomplished?"

"Good point." It was bad enough that Ellen never did a parachute free fall *in her life* let alone one from the *stratosphere*. Kasey would take her down tandem, and after that, the second chance to die would be upon them.

"All you really need to do is *not* go ballistic, breathe and let me do the work. Are we clear?" Kasey's military background pouring out in every word.

"Clear." Ellen affirmed.

"Remember the mission. From the moment we jump, to the moment we enter the drop zone, I will not be speaking to you so don't look to me for answers. Follow my hand signals, keep lock and loaded and keep up. I guarantee it's going to get ugly at some point, so leave your *human rights bullshit* on the plane. We get in, extract the target and fight our way out, you dig?"

"Right. Hit and run. Gotcha." Ellen was much more ready than Kasey would ever likely want to know. As far as she was concerned, Ellen blamed all of North Korea for Frank's death.

The rear of the plane opened, dropping the temperature to even lower levels than Ellen expected. Kasey was strapped and harnessed to her and both women marched to the sloping end of the cargo hold.

The sky around them showed nothing more than wide evening space; stars above and a sea of dense clouds. Reality smacked Ellen in the face as did the bone chilling cold. Her breathing started to pick up a rapid pace.

Knowing this, Kasey reassured her. "I've got faith in you, detective. I trust your police experience will see us through Part-B of this caper. I promise you. I'll see us through Part-A."

With no further words spoken, Kasey launched them both out of the plane at ten miles above the Earth's surface—just above regular commercial flights typically venture.

The feeling was nothing short of exhilarating.

Both women plummeted through the clouds at speeds exceeding 127-mph, as noted inside Ellen's helmet. If it weren't for her pressure suit, helmet and oxygen, at such heights, speed and temperature, death would have been slow and agonizing as her body would be depleted of air.

All before Ellen was a rush of clouds, engulfing them like a quickly moving chamber of gas that seemed to go on forever. She passed so much time in its bliss; she had to remember they were dropping like *rocks*.

Then it happened. The clouds parted, giving way to the planet Earth.

She saw *everything*.

Far off mountains, hundreds of roads, valleys, the sea, little moving dots of lights and, majestically, the moon shining down on them; lighting their way to a thriving metropolis far below. It was awe inspiring.

It was scary.

It was deathly frightening.

It was sensational and a once in a lifetime moment.

All Ellen could do was think of Frank and something he said: *Life was good.*

Meanwhile, Kasey was counting and making sure she was pitching and rolling their bodies in the right angle to avoid radar detection. Their lack of metal assisted a great deal in the stealth dive; in addition to the cover of darkness, but all it would take is one vigilant North Korean soldier on his game to question the smallest of blips streaking toward their primary military base.

The goal for Kasey was to maneuver them as close to P'yongyang as possible in order to enter the military insertion point, but still far enough not to be seen. The Korea Bay snaked between the main land creating various rivers. It was the largest chunk of bay waters that Kasey shot for and timing was everything.

Off by an inch, they'll parachute over land and into the awaiting hands of American-hating North Koreans.

Off by a mile and she'll land them in severely dense and compacted fishing routes and they would surely hit some poor Koreans boat.

Which is why she did not speak to Ellen—she needed to concentrate for the sake of their lives, Fuego's and just about everyone else's.

Kasey checked her altimeter and she was right over the patch of water she planned for. She snatched at the cord and her parachute caught big air—a black tarp sturdy enough for the both of them. The sudden break in speed was jarring to both women, but they lived. Surviving a stunt best left for the movies.

At about fifty feet above the waters, Kasey first released Ellen, and then she released herself from the parachute, letting it flutter away. The ladies went under the Korea Bay for a moment, and then found their way back to the surface, removing their helmets and letting them sink into the murky waters.

Kasey guided Ellen by flashing a red filtered flashlight in her direction and they swam for land.

The North Korean landscape off the bay was as quiet as Kasey's earlier satellite reconnaissance suggested. Curfews prevented *legal* fishermen to boat at this hour—leaving those needing to work under the cover of night to mind their business. If they saw two darkly clad shapes emerging from waters to the shoreline, they weren't in a position to report it.

Keeping low, Kasey pulled out a map and an electronic tracker that beeped east toward P'yongyang. Ellen looked about the evening landscape to insure no one was around or approaching. "Are we safe?"

"As safe as two female American spies, about to attack the capital of a militant Communist country—*single-handed*—can be. Why do you ask?"

"Cute. What's that thing?"

"A map." Kasey smirked.

"Don't mess with me, Kasey."

"Sorry. I'm a smart ass when I'm nervous. It's a tracker set to Fuego's frequency."

"You can track your friend? Good. That makes the job easier."

"Yeah. This whole thing is easy." Kasey rolled her eyes. "You got one too, by the way."

"Me? Where'd you slip it?"

"*Dorothy's* in your boots. It's a high frequency signal only turned on when you click your heels together."

"*Dorothy*. That's appropriate."

"Fuego got one and according to this, he's still alive. If you stray off plan or get captured for any reason, click your heels and I'll find you."

"Let's hope it doesn't get to that. All your partners have this *Dorothy*?"

Kasey stowed away the map and tracker; assured of their direction, pulling a mask over her face. "Each one of us."

Chapter 23

Norilsk, Russia - Castle Zapolyarny

In what can only be called a dungeon—set in the recesses of the ancient Russian castle—Butta' hung, by her tied hands, from a hook about a good fifteen feet from the surface. Holes in the walls and ceilings around her allowed moon light to shine through the cracks and there she was—the shapely, sexy female with flawless curves hanging in slivers of moonlight; gently turning and swaying depending on how much she fidgeted…

…Clicking her heels.

Why Butta' was up in this predicament was lying dead on the ground. One of the Russian thugs that underestimated Butta' carelessly got too close and she concluded his lifespan. Maksim decided it was better to leave her hanging than to start having a body count. She might prove worthwhile to him sooner or later.

Desiree sat on the cold ground next to the dead body, shivering. Maksim must have thought he was being smart by putting the two *venomous* women together in the same place. Maybe they would finish each other off on their own.

"So cold." Desiree complained. Her teeth chattering.

"You sure are." Butta' responded. She couldn't resist the timing on that one.

"We're going to die here and you're still on that *shit?*" Desiree gathered herself as best as she could against the wall, holding herself. The Russians didn't have to secure her too much; the cold would lock her down for them. She wasn't as much of a threat as the one with the sexy body.

Butta' wasn't fairing any better, but in order not to lose feeling in her arms, she forced herself to occasionally perform hanging crunches to flex her muscles and keep the blood flowing. "It's that *shit*—is why we're here in the first place. If you weren't such a *bitch*, we'd be alright."

"You don't know a damn thing about me." Desiree defended.

"That's alright by me."

Desiree chuckled. "What the hell do you see in that fat tub of lard?"

"When I get down from this, I'm gonna clock you good."

"You're not getting down from shit. You're delusional."

"Your ex saved my life so many times, I can't even count. He's too good for the kind of woman you are and you don't even see it. You're not *trying* to see the good man he is."

"Saved your life? Are we talking about the same *Yancey Duncan*? The man *I know* can barely save his *own* life let alone someone else's. He's always in debt. He was always needing to work two or three jobs and never amounted to anything."

"What's a *man* to you? Someone who can pay *your* bills?" Butta' frowned.

"What the fuck you think?" She spat.

"Figures."

"Damn right! Any man that can handle his money is someone smart and capable of handling everything else. Wyman is *everything* I was looking for. Yancey was a mindless detour. A mistake."

"There are a lot of wealthy, financially smart rapists, child molesters and murderers in the world." Butta' knew of—*and buried*— a few of them.

"Not my Wyman."

"Maybe not." Butta' struggled, putting her hands in the right position around the hook, rubbing some of the skin off her wrists from the tight ropes. "But did you ever stop to think that Yancey was prepared to *die* working for you and his daughter?"

"MY daughter. What good is a dead man who can work fifty jobs when I can have one *live* man with one *great* job? Yancey is a child. He could never amount to more than an assistant manager and I wanted more. Crystal *deserved* more."

Butta' took three strong breaths and lifted her legs forward; applying years of climbing and crawling to use. Her waist and stomach muscles burned from the strain—an incredible, gymnast positioning of her legs and body in a straight L-shape with her arms still strung in an upward position.

But the energy it took to do something she had not done in a long while was too great and she dropped her legs, swinging her entire body about in the air. She exhaled, exhausted and sought to gain her second wind.

At least, she was warmer now.

Desiree looked up at Butta' with her mouth opened. Evidently, this woman was more than meets the eye. Desiree would *never* have been able to accomplish an inch of that move. "What the hell are you up to?"

"Here's what you don't know about the man you gave up on. He thinks about his daughter every day. *Every single day*. Not everyone on this planet got it together to have one job and a fat paycheck, but in my book, that don't mean a damn thing to me compared to how he treats me."

"That easy for you to say. You got a damn body to kill for and you got men dropping cash at your feet! You don't have to work a goddamn day in your life."

"I'm not about money."

"I am. This is reality, baby. Love doesn't pay the mortgage."

"You keep thinking that way and you'll lose good, honest men for it."

"I've *got* a good and honest man!"

"Does he know who Crystal's father really is?"

"He knows what he needs to know." Desiree snorted, not wishing to get further into that.

"So you're lying to him. You're lying to an honest man about *another* honest man."

Desiree found the strength to get to her feet—anger bringing the warmth she needed to her body. "Yancey is **NOT** honest!"

"How you figure?"

"He told me he'd take care of us and all we did was live paycheck to paycheck. Get paid Friday, broke by Saturday morning. We never caught up!"

"I bet you helped the family by getting a good job yourself?"

"Work? Why the hell should I? He's the man of the house. He should have known his place and took care of me! I never had to work a day in my life and I never will."

Butta' readied her palms again, burning off another layer of skin in the process—but she knew all too well, a little pain meant nothing compared to *a lot* of death. Additionally, when attempting to do this kind of maneuver, 70% of her success is mental—and keeping Desiree talking infuriated Butta' to the point of resolved determination to get off this hook one way or another.

Just the kind of internal fire she needed to accomplish an incredible feat of leg control that Desiree would never forget.

Butta' lifted her legs again after a count of three; slowly raising her thighs and legs up to waist level, then extending them straight out—a move commonly performed by Olympic-class gymnasts on the rings.

Her hands and arms shook from the raw energy it took to then raise her legs further up—past her chest— past her head—until finally, she was upside-down, feet clinging to the rope above her.

Careful to secure her legs around the rope, she lifted her hands over the hook, freeing herself. Making sure her head was clear of the hook, she let herself go, landing on her feet and expending the energy into a roll across the floor, in order not to damage her back and knees.

Desiree stared at Butta' with absolute terror.

"You see," Butta' stood panting; chest heaving in the moonlight, "Munch is *1000%* family to me. I take it *very* personal when gold diggers like you cross him. When we're through here tonight, he *will* get his daughter back."

"You'd have to kill me first." Remarkably, Desiree held her position, waiting for whatever came next.

"Have it your way."

Butta' knocked Desiree out with one slashing motion of her tied hands. Not dead, but she would have a good headache. Butta' considered how easy it would be to kill her right now and blame the Russians.

Then a little girl would be sad for the rest of her life.

How familiar was *that* story?

Butta' searched the dead Russian for anything sharp and found a small knife which was good enough for these desperate times. She also found her cell phone.

Perfect. Time to start finding her folks and turning tables. As for Desiree, she would come back for her later.

Much later.

North Korea, P'yongyang Military Base – P'yongyang Airfield

A 7,000 foot runway off Downtown P'yongyang had been established here since the Korean War in the early 50's. Travel to the DPRK (Democratic People's Republic of Korea) to see such sites were never easy then and are still difficult today. Only guided tours with heavy restrictions were allowed and solo exploration of North Korea was forbidden.

Military installations are of extreme secrecy and off limits to everyone.

Thus, Ellen looked at this undercover stealth mission as a quasi-honor. She was probably one in a handful of people who had seen a place that would be punishable by slow torture and/or death.

There was still an opportunity for that to happen to her. Every step she took could be her last.

Kasey remained silent for the past two and a half hours; stopping to drink from their portable water, keeping an eye on the tracker, adjusting to coordinates on the map, and throwing hand signals to Ellen when it was time to keep low.

Ellen appreciated Kasey's professionalism. They managed to negotiate a strong measure of the Korean countryside undetected while bypassing everything from land mines, roving patrols and troops of soldiers. This whole country was in a constant *army* state of mind.

Kasey kept them both hidden in tall weeds situated beside the airstrip. Their location was loaded with APP M-57 antipersonnel blast mines, capable of turning their bodies into fine pieces of meat. Kasey reasoned landmine zones are the least frequented and least likely to be suspect of enemy traffic, allowing them to get as close as possible to the North Korean base.

Her trickery to evade landmines was time consuming but kept them alive. Ellen concluded, after all her NYPD work was said and done, she would rather take the straight-forward route and kick some doors in over all this sneaking around. She never knew how much she treasured a straight fight until she was wading through mine-infested territory for hours.

Silently, Kasey stared out to the constantly moving airfield and military compound, searching for weaknesses and patterns in the incoming flights and troops, finding nothing of use except a parked piece of aircraft refueling on the furthest end of the strip against a hanger. "That's our ticket home." She whispered.

"I was wondering when we were going to get around to discussing exit strategy." Ellen muffled a yawn.

"I tend to think through an exit *after* we've been in the pot a little while."

"We're not just in the pot. We're damn near *cooking*!"

"No, sweetie. The real deal is about to kick off. You haven't seen nothing yet. The good news is our flight home is being fueling up even as we speak. How nice of them."

She referred to the Sukhoi Su-30MKK fighter jet which sported two seats; one for the pilot and one for a co-pilot to handle excess details during long missions. Hence the term '*long missions*'; meaning it can fly long distances between refueling. It was a long way back to anywhere *American-friendly* and that did *not* mean South Korea.

By its side and dwarfed by its shadow, an Airbus 380; a superjumbo aircraft with a double-deck, wide body and deemed the largest passenger plane in the world—was also being refueled.

That one had more than enough space for their escape if the fighter became inaccessible. That would be the last resort.

"Okay. This is where we're going to part ways for a little bit?" Kasey said.

"What?" Ellen choked. "I'm not a *sneaky chick* like you! I'll get busted 'rounding a bend!"

"Detective Ellen Cobart, you'd better *not* get caught." With that, Kasey handed her the tracker. "You find Fuego. You can't miss him. Mexican with black hair. Short guy with a lot of muscles. Hopefully he's not drugged 'cause he'll help you in a pinch. Meet me over at that hanger by that jet in, say—an hour."

"What are you looking for? The other diamond is out here, isn't it?"

"They don't call you *detective* for nothing. I have a contact I need to hook up with."

"How can I reach you? We don't have any radios."

Kasey checked her weapon for the final time. "Don't worry about finding me. You'll hear a lot of gunshots, a bunch of sirens, yelling and a whole lot of running around. After that, it's time to go."

Yacht Sariya-Anne – Off the Coast of Finland

Louie pushed the micro-cruise ship engines to its limit in order to reach this point within the time allot by Marigold. He was not in the business of failing her requests, especially when it had to do with his friends.

However, the Finnish waters were bone cold and he, nor the Sariya-Anne was prepared for this kind of weather and he hoped to bring the yacht back in one piece. Surely, Marigold would compensate all parties concerned should anything befall the owner's craft.

Shabba, had been off his self-medicated high for days now. He ran out of marijuana just after their guests left for parts unknown. With a clear head, he didn't know what do with himself. For instance, he spent some of his time reading old college textbooks, found out cleaning the yacht was actually enjoyable and he discovered CNN through the yacht's satellite.

On the other hand, this annoyed Louie to no end.

Every ten minutes, Shabba showed up with an interesting tidbit of information he never heard of and sought genuine conversation.

Louie almost … just *almost* … wished Shabba got back to his smoking habit.

"Hey Louie!" Shabba returned to the deck. "Did you ever hear of this place called *Darfur*? It's incredible that over four hundred and fifty thousand people have been killed. Four hundred and fifty thousand! How can we, as humans, have allowed this to happen?"

Louie concentrated on steering the ship, trying not to show his irritation. "Dat's really cool dere, Shab. *Real cool* dat ya takin' an interest in da world—"

"The Sudanese government is a monster! They're clearly funding the *Janjaweed* and promoting genocide. People are *starving* because of this conflict."

Louie sighed, readjusting the blanket he wore to protect from the bitter cold. Yes, the yacht was well heated, but he chose to save as much power for the trip home as possible.

The radar blipped.

"Shab, hold dat thought. We got more guests."

"Who?" Shabba got excited. "Is it—?"

"No, ya hard up clown. She's not coming back no time soon. Dis is somethin' different."

On cue, his phone rang. A private number.

"Ms. Marigold. Always on time."

"As well as you, Louie. My contacts are nearby and they tell me you're at the coordinates. You made great time."

"Am I ever going to say no to you?" He smiled.

"I don't expect you to. So this is the deal—my contacts are going to drop off a package and then you have to keep heading North."

"Dat would put us 'n *Rusky* waters. We got clearance?"

"I'm afraid not."

"Figures."

"Don't worry Louie. If all goes well, this will be a snatch, grab and run. And I do mean *run*, if you get my drift."

"Ok." Louie frowned. He mainly worried about the yacht. "I'll need ta refuel. Maybe winterize da boat or somethin'. Furda'nort' is da Arctic Sea. She's a fine cruiser but she's been takin' a beatin'."

"Louie," he could hear her smiling over the phone, "what's my name?"

Shabba looked out the bridge windows, eyes widening. He waved for Louie's attention which was unnecessary. He already saw the Iowa Class United States Battleship pulling up against the side.

"Are they here to get us?" Shabba feared, thankful he ran out of pot. "Are they gonna drug test me?"

Louie stepped outside and watched the naval vessel unload sailors, preparing to row the short distance between them, while a huge crane on the deck of the battleship was getting ready to transport a large crate.

"What's that?" Shabba asked.

"I dunno."

Corey A. Burkes

Waving from the deck of the battleship, General Tucker used a loudspeaker to call out to Louie. "Ahoy! Prepare to be boarded and accept a package from a *mutual* friend."

"What is it?" Louie yelled.

"It's classified!" The General responded. "Just bring it back to us in one piece. My men will set it up on your deck. When you're finished, you never saw us, we never gave it to you and this meeting never happened. Are we clear, Mr. Louis Frazetta of South Chicago with social security number 432-54-0365, blood type A?"

Yeah, it was *clear*.

Corey A. Burkes

Chapter 24

North Korea, P'yongyang Military Base
Rank and files of the People's Army soldiers goose-stepped about the military base while others drove tanks and smaller jeeps to destinations unknown.

A Korean officer decorated in the colors that ranked him as a *Sangwi*, comparatively to a Captain, saluted a group of higher ranking men on route to some barracks. Upon turning a corner, a pair of hands reached out and grabbed him by the mouth and head; a knife prepared to slice him like a fish from the throat down.

The voice behind him said something in broken Korean.

"*Youth movement*?" The Captain was confused. "If you're going to be a spy, you need to work on your *Korean*."

Kasey let him go, stepping out of the shadows, sheathing her knife. "I was going for '*don't move*'."

The Captain pulled Kasey with him into an empty, nearby office. Once clear, he removed his cap and sat with the lights off.

"Amazing that you made it this far."

"There's still another leg of this race to go. What's going on, Dae-Hyun?"

"Chillin'. A little of this. A little of that. You know the score. When Marigold gave me the call, I thought we were going to war. When she told me *you* were coming *personally*, I just knew the *shit* already hit the fan."

"Things don't change, Dee. Same fight, different players."

"Marigold is looking to wrap up her half of the battle. I heard she just bought Stein's camp."

"Did she? That's bold. Wasn't she just cutting a deal with your people over here?" She asked.

"No, that deal fell through. She was pissed. N.K. top brass didn't appreciate a woman running things and took it upon themselves to get the diamond. Which they did."

"I know. I was there. Speaking of which." She reminded.

"Oh, yes. Here." He handed her a crudely drawn map of the compound. "I don't know where they're keeping your friend."

"It's okay. I got someone else on that."

"Is it Marigold's new partner she keeps talking about?" He asked.

"No," Kasey shook her head, "not *her*—someone else. Where's *this* location?"

He traced his finger over the drawing and guided Kasey to a location in the middle of the base. "We're here. Changing of the guard is going on even as we speak, so lie low for about thirty minutes."

"I haven't got thirty minutes."

"Fine. Just so you know, they've already installed the diamond into the laser canon located here. They have a rotating shift of eight guards and they plan to test it tomorrow."

"I'm only here for the diamond. Are there any vents? Any access points I can use?"

"None. It's a sealed location. One way in. One way out. It's our most secured compound."

Kasey thought on the matter quickly, looking up at her contact with that old look in her eye. That *look* which worried Dae-Hyun tremendously.

"What are you thinking?"

She smiled devilishly. "I'm thinking that's a nice uniform and I think I can fit it."

North Korea, P'yongyang Military Base – Lower Level

Elsewhere in compound, Ellen carefully used the shadows to her advantage; pacing herself and restraining impetuous urges to rush in—which would be a grievous mistake.

Fortunately, much of the direction she needed to get to wasn't secured with badges she had to swipe or checkpoints she would have to circumvent. The tracker was leading her through office space for military paperwork. At this late hour, anyone with a drone-like position was home. Only the occasional soldier walking his beat casually interrupted her approach.

Once she was certain the coast was clear, she let the tracker zero in on a room down the hall. Silently, she checked to see if it was locked, and of course, it was.

All the same, she heard voices within; muffled sounds of the Korean language. Definitely one or maybe *three* people.

Without doubt, the sounds of a fist hitting the flesh of another followed by those same men cheering.

Ellen twisted the silencer on her gun and tucked her years of officers training in her back pocket. What she was about to do was against everything she originally stood for. Gun at the ready, she knocked on the door.

Someone asked something in Korean. The beating inside went silent and at least one footstep approached the door.

Ellen rolled her eyes and responded. *"General Tso."*

The voices laughed, completely oblivious that anyone would be a threat and one of the men opened the door, receiving a bullet to the head.

Ellen, well-trained on urban combat entry, would have long since demanded people to get on the ground and start the arresting process. Tonight, she wasn't in New York, and any one of these bastards was responsible for the death of her partner.

At least from her perception.

Head and chest shots from Ellen's pistol dropped the three Koreans in the room. Fuego was handcuffed to a chair and bleeding from the face with puffy eyes and what may have been a broken nose. Still, he was alert and twisted his head toward Ellen after she shut the door.

"¿Quien eres?" *Who are you?* He asked.

"Sorry, buddy. My Spanish isn't what it should to be. Neither is my *Spanglish*. Umm, Kasey, Butta'—Friends. *Amigos*."

That perked him up. *Way up.* Ellen un-cuffed him with a generic key she always kept handy and helped him to his feet. A little wobbly, Fuego had to shake off a day of being worked over. Then he went and freaked Ellen out by snapping his nose back into place with a creepy, wet *snap*.

"*Christ.* Are you okay? Uh— ¿Está … usted … *okay*?"

Fuego was bent over trying to let the pain subside, raising a thumb up, stretching and cracking his neck—ready for the fight.

"Good." Ellen searched the dead bodies looking for extra weapons and handed Fuego a gun, knife and some extra clips. "Cause it's time to go."

Norilsk, Russia - Castle Zapolyarny

Crystal was dragged in screaming at the top of her lungs, still clinging tightly to her brown teddy bear. The Russians showed a small amount of courtesy by keeping her warm with a blanket.

With each cry, she called out to her father and it pained Munch to the core.

In Munch's mind, nothing good could come of the following events with the way they were pulling his little girl into the room. Wyman was already agitated; trying to free himself to no avail. He did not have the skill nor the brawn to release himself from the chair, tied with thick knots.

Munch, however, had been working on his tied hands since they arrived and tapping his heels together to activate Dorothy's signal. As painful as it has been, rubbing his wrists raw, he needed to keep twisting his hands about in a method that he affectionately called a *Kasey Move*—a series of defensive/offensive escape maneuvers that the secretive bombshell would teach their little crew whenever the free time or mood struck her. In the middle of a bright and sunny day, she would just come out of nowhere with one of her patented: *Say, if you ever want to know how to escape from a chair, tied up, and use the chair to toe-tag your opponent, just let me know.*

Maksim came in behind Crystal and warmed his hands by the fire. "It's cold, yes?"

"Let go of my daughter, damn you!" Wyman snapped.

"Give me diamond or she dies. Right here. After her, your wife. After your wife, all your friends. My patience finished and I missing *America's Got Talent*. Reception not so good in gulag."

The thug holding Crystal shoved the barrel of his gun to the back of her head and pulled back the hammer. Munch went cold, and that took a lot for him in his girth.

"Okay!" Wyman relented; angry and crying at the same time. "Okay. Please. Just don't hurt her."

Munch knew the game: who said any of them would actually leave this place alive regardless? He feverously worked on repositioning his hands to grab hold of the back frame of the chair.

"Good!" Maksim clapped. "Excellent! Now we all go home. Where is diamond?"

Wyman gestured to his little girl. "Crystal—*baby*—it's okay. Daddy's here. Give the man your teddy bear."

The thug snatched the bear out of Crystal's hands and she cried even more, tearfully running to Wyman and sobbing in his chest. Munch's heart sank for his little girl; watching the touching moment between her and the only father she knew. Between grabbing the chair and working his hands, he wondered if it was even smart at all to break this relationship up and create confusion.

He loved his daughter enough to let her go if he had to.

Besides that, Wyman was a good man.

The Russian thug patted down the teddy bear, feeling something in its chest and flicked open a switchblade. With one rip, he produced a black satin bag and in it…

"The diamond!" Maksim almost swooned. "Hide in plain sight! Very crafty, Comrade Fowler. Thank you. Now, we say goodbye."

Maksim then gave his partner a nod.

From his tied position, Wyman realized where all this was going. He buried his head into his daughter's hair and kissed her. "I love you so much."

Munch heard that and believed it.

The Russian wasted no time; repositioning his gun at Wyman and prepared to pull the trigger. Instead, Munch made his move and threw his body forward and to the side, literally tossing the chair at the Russian with a significant amount of force that sent the big fellow and his gun careening into the fire.

His screams echoed throughout the castle.

Munch, on his knees, spun about and purposely toppled Wyman and Crystal over to the floor so they wouldn't be in the line of fire of Maksim, whom already had a gun out and started firing.

But he was on the other side of the fire, spread about due to the burning Russian, and his aim was unclear; missing his shots while making his way to the exit.

Munch, with his hands still tied to his back, slid for the gun dropped on the edge of the fire ambers. The metal was steaming hot and it cooked his hands; searing them terribly. He let out a raging, painful yell but kept hold of the gun to shoot Maksim twice in such an awkward position; once in the arm and once in the leg.

Maksim fell, dropping the diamond and rolled to get out of the way. He squirmed out of the area, yelling in Russian for immediate backup.

Crystal was already trying to untie her father, whom doubled around to help Munch as fast as he could. Munch's hands were covered with third degree burns and blistering horribly.

"You poor man!" Wyman sympathized. "You saved us."

Munch took the gun and cooled it off in a corner of snow; burying his hands deep for what little comfort he could get from the cold. "No time. Get the diamond. They're going to be back any—"

"Got it!" Crystal ran between them, holding up the expensive rock cheerfully.

Munch looked down to the little girl, full of pride. "What a little trooper."

Wyman hugged her close. "That's my baby."

Machine gun fire from four Russian men interrupted them.

They separated: Munch and Crystal in one direction—Wyman in another. Munch protected his little girl behind a column, firing back regardless of the pain. Wyman had no weapon, but he was closer to another exit—into the halls of the castle, using another column for protection.

"Crystal!" He called out. "No!"

In the middle of all the action, a knife gleamed across the room like a silver laser, striking one of the machine gun toting Russians square in the eye. Before his dead body could hit the floor, Butta' slid under him, scooping up his machine gun, and spat a blaze of bullets at the opposing attackers.

Maksim and his men took cover while Butta' backed up next to Wyman to protect him.

The Russians didn't give up, shooting from one end of the room to kill anyone they can get a lock on. Butta' looked over to Munch from across the floor, keeping her head down. She knew Munch would be out of bullets soon enough and had to get instructions to him without the Russians knowing. What's a woman who had no radio and little knowledge of diverse languages to do?

"Munch!" She called out. "Listen—*Aketay ethay irlgay andway indfay Iggertray.*"

Munch squinted at her for a moment, confused, then caught on between firing the last of his bullets. *Take the girl and find Trigger. Pig Latin* was one of the first *designer* languages most kids ever played with.

"*I'llway ogay ackbay orfay ishay ifeway*" Butta' yelled out. *I'll go back for his wife.*

Munch nodded—and oddly enough, so did Crystal, covering her ears from all the gunfire. "Okayway." She responded. A real trooper, indeed.

"Go!" Butta' yelled, giving cover fire for Munch to scoop Crystal up and run into another darkened hall. Once he and the little girl were clear, Butta' shoved Wyman out their side of the room, making good their escape for the moment.

Maksim sealed up his wounds the best he could with a cloth to stop the bleeding. He was definitely a very angry *Bolshevik*; limping about and sought retribution. "Get diamond! No one leaves here breathing! Kill them all!"

Norilsk, Russia - Castle Zapolyarny – King's Chamber

All this time, Trigger was tied up on the floor in what was a vast bedroom for the tsar. No heat, no warmer clothing—just the rug she lied on with her legs tied and her hands tied behind her back securely. She had not been able to release herself or get in a better position for the past few hours and the bitter cold left her drowsy.

That sleepy feeling people suffered shortly before hyperthermia.

The only thing keeping her conscious was her need to keep tapping her heels for Dorothy to work and all the sudden noise vibrating through the castle: a little girl crying, men screaming, gunfire and people dying.

Sounds like she was about to be rescued.

The other thing keeping her warm was her anger. She tapped her heels for what seemed like eternity. No one came.

The people dying part gave her bursts of erotic energy that couldn't quite be explained. It was one of those things where she never knew her reaction until she tried it.

She also thought of her place in the world. The *what's* next scenario of her life. The invitation to do this fulltime. Taking lives and getting paid royally was a dream unfathomed. She never spent her time thinking of killing people, as most people didn't. Sure, the idea crossed the mind and people toy with the concept: *I would kill that person for what they did.* But only a small percentage of people *premeditatedly* prepare themselves to actually do it. The majority of murders are unplanned or accidental; a byproduct of fight gone awry, rage or act of passion.

But to wake up every day, get a list of people that need to stop living and receive a paycheck per confirmed kill…

For Trigger, the thought was *hot* and it turned her on from her lips down between her legs.

By the time her mind sluggishly thought about how sick she must be to get off on people dying, five burly Russian men marched in with black jackets and approached her menacingly.

Suddenly, time returned to normal for Trigger—while also a sense of resolved calm bathed her. *This is it*, she thought, letting her body drift.

She stopped thinking, she stopped worrying and most of all, she stopped being Monique Bolland; the trendy 'round the way teenager. Between the cold and her semi-consciousness, she let go and became her instinctive namesake…

… *Trigger.*

The look on her face was expressionless as she swept her legs under the first Russian, sending him off his feet. The others with him laughed at his stupidity as one other picked up the girl from her tied back while another put a gun to her head. The one holding her said something in his native language in the line of *wait, let me get out of the way first.*

Trigger used her legs to kick her feet deep into the gunman's groin.

His child bearing days were over.

She continued to twist her body out of the grip of the one holding her and his hands got tangled in her ropes. While he struggled to free himself, he flung her about, cursing in Russian. Trigger used his erratic thrashing to strike and kick the other men in range until he made the final mistake of trying to slam her against the wall.

Trigger poised her legs against the wall and shoved out, throwing both she and her captor backwards. On the way down, using all of her strength, she made sure to poise her weight and back into his head.

The crash of his head into the ground left a dent in the stone and cracking a portion of his skull. He will slowly die from brain injuries in another hour or two.

Trigger rolled backwards throwing her arms under her and now, still tied, had her hands in the front and digging into the jacket of the fallen Russian she just crushed.

The others rushed her but they were too late. She didn't even remove the gun from the holster and fired four shots each; one with flawless accuracy to each head.

The King's chamber went silent with just Trigger scurrying back against the wall getting a sudden rush of adrenalin that made her smile with a psychopathic edge.

She just killed five men, saving her own life in the process. No help from anyone. No one came to answer her call. From this day forward, she swore not to need anyone ever again.

In her mind, this was so much better than sex. To think, someone was willing to pay her for this. As she untied herself, she noticed one of the men had a cell phone.

No, she was not going to call Butta'.

Corey A. Burkes

Chapter 25

Norilsk, Russia - Castle Zapolyarny

Munch and Crystal survived well because the castle was big, dank and full of holes; a crumbling ruin only preserved through time by the Siberian winters.

When they were able to find a good hiding spot, Munch rested in the dark with Crystal across from him shivering.

"Come close. I'm a little warmer." He offered.

Crystal looked at Munch warily, and slid next to him, leaning her head on his stomach. He stroked her hair and a flood of memories rushed through him. The days he carried her from little baby bath and cradled her. He would be tired after working three different jobs and that was the time he looked forward to most.

He looked at the diamond everyone sought after and believed, in his heart of hearts, it could never replace the child comforting herself on him.

"I want my mommy." She whimpered.

"I'll take you to her. I promise."

"Do you know my mommy?" She asked.

"Yes."

"Can you help her and daddy too?"

"I'll try."

"Thank you."

"You're very welcome. Do—do you know what my name?"

She shook her head.

"My name is Yancey. What's your name?"

"Crystal."

"Nice to meet you Crystal."

"Know all fifty states! Wanna hear me say them?"

Amazing how her little mind averted the dangers of frostbite, certain death and the darkened castle to want to impress Munch with her knowledge; the most important thing on her mind at this very moment.

Munch smiled at her and yearned for such a simple way of life once more; to be proud of something he had long since taken for granted. He *badly* wanted to say *yes*, but that would draw attention.

"Tell you what?" He whispered. "Can you name all of the midwestern states? Can you whisper it to me as quiet as you can?"

Oh, she couldn't wait.

Inhaling, she started to name the states. Munch listened to every name and savored each one. He had his daughter back in the worst and coldest location on Earth with deadly, angry Russians looking to kill them—but he had his daughter back.

He would take the good when and where he could get it.

Something caught his attention.

A room down the hall from his position; it sounded like footsteps and a females voice speaking. Munch waited for Crystal to finish and smiled ear to ear, giving her a soft applause.

"Yayyyy!" He whispered. "I'm so proud of you."

Crystal smiled. "Did you know I like science, too?"

"Darling, you are so smart. Do me a favor and stay here for a minute."

"You're leaving? Don't go!" She was getting loud.

Munch did all he could to ignore that nagging feeling that he was abandoning her—*again*. The first time was not a fault of his own, and at least this time he's in control of how far she will be from him.

"Don't worry. I'm not going far. How are you with your numbers? Will you count to thirty for me?"

She nodded.

"I'll be back by the time you get to twenty-nine. Deal?"

She loved playing games, and began her count. Munch counted with her and stepped toward the room a few paces away from Crystal's hiding spot.

Munch peeked into what was a royal bedroom. Lying about the floor were five dead Russians and Trigger, standing in the middle of the carnage on a cell phone, unaware of Munch behind.

"This is Monique Bolland." She paused, listening to what the voice had to say, and then she responded with two words only. "I accept."

More conversation unheard by Munch from the opposite side of the phone. Trigger's back was to him while she listened intently. "When's my first job?"

Something else was said to Trigger and then she hung up, tossing the phone. Munch could not make head or tails over who she was calling and decided it was time to reveal himself. But he needed to do it carefully. Trigger was not seasoned like Butta' or Kasey. Sneaking up on her could get himself killed.

The rocks under his feet and the unstable wall shifted on him, surprising both he and Trigger.

Her gun was swift and unapologetic as it appeared in her hand, turned and fired at Munch without seeing who it might be. Munch dodged backwards, expecting that to be her first reaction. The bullet bounced off the wall where his head would have been a millisecond ago.

"Trig! Hold your fire. It's me!"

"Munchie?" Said the newest assassin; reverting back to her semi-innocence—holstering her gun and hugging her long time friend.

But Munch couldn't take his eyes off the corpses. "You did all this?"

"Huh? Oh, no big deal. Where's the rest of the crew?"

"Scattered. Butta's on the move. I don't think Kasey's with us."

"No loss there." She mumbled.

"What was that?" Munch questioned.

"I said she's *probably out there*. You know? Looking for us. Let's get moving. I'm tired of this place."

"Yeah —right. We got my dau— I mean, the little girl with us." Munch knew he heard something else out of Trigger and kept it to himself. All that mattered now was getting Crystal and the others out of dodge.

North Korea, P'yongyang Military Base – Security Zone

In the absolute center of the base was a perfect square building. 152-meters high, wide and long; made of brick and steel, with no windows or ventilation ports. Two guards protected the only entrance in; a simple rollup wide door for wheeling in vehicles or other things with mass. A total of eight guards; two on every side, surrounded the encasement which was also protected by a high fence—barb and electrically wired.

Cameras were in every corner, motioning to and fro. Sniper perches were a short distance away, in clear view of the roll up doors.

A walk in the park, Kasey thought, trembling ever so slightly. Sucking what could be her last breath, she marched toward the secured zone with papers and folders under her arm—dressed in the Captain's uniform, walking like she had severe business to take care of. She kept her Captain's hat low with dark glasses on.

The Korean guards saluted the assumed Captain.

Kasey, gloves and all, saluted back, handing over papers without saying a word.

One of the guards asked something in Korean.

According to her contact, this was the word she was supposed to look for *permission* or the *request for authorization* before she handed the next *forged* set of papers.

The guard looked over everything and marched them back to his partner. They silently said a few things, running their hands a long their rifles.

Kasey started to sweat, making up possible scenarios if this did not pull off. After a longer than expected conversation with his partner, the Korean guard returned to Kasey and withdrew his gun.

Kasey's heart skipped but she held her ground as the guard handed her the paperwork—*and* the gun—into her possession.

Not what she expected.

He said something she wouldn't understand in a million years and the doors to the secured location rolled up.

Showtime.

The doors had not rolled half way up before a loud and ear-piercing shriek echoed the base. The alarms were going off and three Korean soldiers were running toward Kasey's position, yelling something that was universally understood as *stop!*

Kasey threw off her cap *Frisbee-like* into one of the guards and shot down the one closer to her. She ducked into the security hanger and shot the first man that came too close. Within a minute, the entire security zone was surrounded by hundreds *upon* hundreds of North Korean soldiers; all pointing rifles, machine guns, tanks and everything in her direction. Spot lights lowered around the box attempting to shine light on the inside.

Kasey hid as far back as she could, using the box's lack of windows as protection. Only one way in and one way out.

No one entered without expecting to get shot.

Wasn't I just relaxing by the side of a pool, reading my bible? She chuckled to herself. *How time goes by so quickly.*

The box was spacious and used primarily as a storage facility. No weapons, no vehicles. *Nothing.* She was trapped inside and it would only be a matter of time before…

Wait. There was *one* weapon she had at her disposal.

The FrG-20, loaded with its diamond, sat ready for action.

Outside, the huge gang of soldiers parted to allow the same North Korean from the Johannesburg train station through. The tall man of the MPSS that made demands on Butta' earlier.

In a choke hold, he pulled out Dae-Hyun, stripped down to his underwear.

Kasey cursed herself for not getting him further out of the compound.

"Step out or we kill him." The MPSS officer yelled at Kasey.

Kasey didn't answer or make any moves. She could shoot that man but the distance was great, she was sweating and she was not the marksman Trigger was.

Dae-Hyun cried out his loyalty to the People's Army and wanted to know why he was being treated this way. The MPSS officer slapped him once and put a gun to his head yelling *Conspirator* in Korean.

Kasey closed her eyes and prayed for an answer—which came with a shot to Dae-Hyun's head. She worked with that man for years. An acquaintance, to be sure—still he was reliable.

She felt like she had this man murdered.

She would answer both her own prayer and the Koreans demand at the same time.

The tall Korean kicked the body and spat on it, raising his arms up into the dark hold of the box—waiting for Kasey's next move. "No way out for you. Come out and we talk."

His response: a ball of light forming in the middle of the hanger, backed by a slow grinding noise, growing to a loud roar.

The MPSS officer blanched and dove for cover.

A wide beam of light ripped through the exit of the box and cut a swath nine feet wide through the soldiers and their vehicles. Ground, people and metal were disintegrated with *negative zero* chance of survival. The beam shot out as far as a mile away—through tanks and explosive materials in its path. A trench of flame burned in a straight line across the base.

Even Ellen and Fuego almost got hit by the blast.

She just managed to pull Fuego out of the way when the laser beam fried the land next to them, taking out two unlucky soldiers that got in the way.

The North Korean military base was burning.

Kasey was turning the cannon about for a second shot—this time with more of a sweeping motion. As the cannon revved up for another blast, Kasey turned the entire machine from right to left. While in motion, the laser tore through the box, through hundreds of scattering soldiers, wrecking with cataclysmic damage to everything in its path.

I gotta get me one of these for Christmas! Kasey's thoughts were broken when soldiers took a chance and raided what was left of the box, shooting at her from all angles. She jumped for safety behind the cannon and ran, shooting behind her. So much was going on around the base with dead and wounded attempting to be treated amid random explosions and fireballs; Kasey's escape was easier under the cover of confusion.

The MPSS officer, dirty and bleeding, watched her run and made his way for the laser cannon, scheming to extract the same hell back on her. He pushed the cannon to point at her direction and started the firing sequence.

The cannon blew up with him on it.

The explosion lit up the compound as the cannon wiped out another batch of soldiers.

Kasey shoved the *real* diamond between her cleavage, an impossibly snug but secure fit, and ran with determined focus toward the airstrip. *The old switcherooo never gets old*, she thought.

At the location prearranged, Kasey turned a corner and was met by Fuego, giving her the biggest hug.

Kasey kissed the little fellow, hugging him back. "Pará esó son los amigos." *That's what friends are for.*

"Are you okay?" Ellen asked of Kasey, noticing her change in outfit.

"I think I need to take this in a little in the back. But do you like the color?"

"You must be nervous."

An explosion happened not far from them, making them flinch. "How'd you tell? Let's see about our ride."

Norilsk, Russia - Castle Zapolyarny

Desiree was already awake and leaning against the wall, protecting herself from the cold when Butta' came through with her gun.

By now, Desiree didn't know what to expect from Butta' and cowed from her advances. Only until Wyman came in behind her did she feel relieved; practically knocking him off his feet, as the two embraced.

"Baby!" She cried. "What the hell is going on?"

"It's not over yet. Are you okay? We're getting out of here."

"Where's Crystal? Have you seen our baby?"

"She's in good hands. I trust the man she's with. Once we get connected, we're all getting out of here."

"Right." Butta' confirmed, checking the tracker. She switched between Munch and Trigger's signals and it showed they were together. "Stay close, don't say anything and do as I say. I don't know how many more of them are out there."

"Right." Wyman nodded. "You people are amazing. How can I ever repay you?"

Butta' looked at Desiree and then at Wyman, making sure Desiree understood her next few words. "The truth will do."

She left them with that thought, entering the hallway and checked around. As the two followed her, Wyman was left with questions. "What did she mean by that?"

Desiree couldn't answer.

Norilsk, Russia - Castle Zapolyarny – Court Yard

Munch, Trigger and Crystal arrived in the court yard of the castle and, essentially, the best possible way out as the Russians' parked their vehicles here: two jeeps and two snowmobiles.

With all the excitement inside, Munch halfway expected someone to be guarding the escape route. Buried in the snow was an old shovel and he took it up defensively while approaching the court yard.

"I'm going to check for keys."

"Probably not in there." Trigger remarked.

"I know. Stay here with Crystal and cover me if anyone comes out."

Trigger nodded and checked the ammo in her gun, ready to go.

Munch stepped out to the middle of the court yard and opened one of the doors. As expected, no keys—so he had to hotwire it.

Gun fire shattered the silence, tic-tacking across the hood of the jeep. Munch ducked down and around the jeep to get out of the way.

Crystal screamed, concerned for Munch's safety and leapt out of Trigger's grasp, running for the center of the court yard. Trigger made a motion to stop her, but machine gun fire chewed at the ground by her feet, forcing her back.

"Crystal! Wait!" Munch called. "Get back!"

He grabbed her and held her tight behind the other side of the jeep. Two gunmen were at windows above the court yard and Maksim marched out with one of the last few thugs he had alive. "You! Come out. Bring diamond."

"Trig!" Munch called out.

"Don't nobody move!" Trigger warned, hiding behind a wall. She had trouble keeping track of the two in the windows and the two on the ground. She was good—but even this tested her skill when her loved ones were in the way.

"You can't us kill all. Someone die here before you get first shot. Big man! You come to me. Bring diamond."

Munch banged his head onto the back of the jeep; mad and caught in the middle. Opening his eyes, he looked up to see Butta', Wyman and Desiree sneaking about in the shadows directly across from him.

Waving Butta' off, he pointed back at the two in the window and Trigger across the yard. "I'm coming out."

"Good!" Maksim growled. "You come now! Bring diamond."

Munch handed Crystal the diamond, kissing her head and whispered for her to stay put no matter what and to cover her ears. Standing, he walked with his hands up around the jeep and in front of Maksim and dropped the shovel in front of him.

Butta' checked her weapon and looked up at the two in the window. Wyman pulled at her troubled. "What's he doing?"

"Giving me time to get into position. This is gonna be close. Stay here." She signaled Trigger with hand signs that said to move out discretely.

"Where is diamond?" Maksim pressed.

"I ate it." Munch joked. Maksim didn't think it was funny and ordered his thug to smash the butt of his rifle into Munch's gut.

Munch crumbled to the floor on one knee.

"Now you see how we do things in Russia, yes?" Maksim walked to the nearest jeep and took out a long, thick linked chain—used for anchoring a medium sized boat.

Without saying another word, he reared back and beat Munch with the chain across his back one time. Munch roared from his soul as the incredible amount of pain sent shock waves through his back and skull.

"Now you talk. Where is diamond? Little girl has it, no?"

Munch was delirious, yet had the sense of mind to keep Maksim's anger directed at him. "*Bitch* ... It's ... it's ... up my ass."

"Up his ass." Maksim looked to the thug, completely frustrated by the evening's events. "Up your ass? I will kill you and take diamond from girl. Tell friend not to shoot and tell little girl to come out here."

"Trigger," Munch gasped, "you shoot ... anyone of these ... *fuckers* ... if they move on her." He glared at Maksim. "Leave my ... *daughter* alone."

"Daughter?" Maksim was genuinely surprised.

As was Wyman, looking back at Desiree, who sat back in the shadows, shaking her head. "I ... I didn't want to—"

Maksim laughed evilly. "It all makes clear now."

Laughing hysterically, he beat Munch twice in a row. Munch fell out on the ground, blood trickling down from his back.

"The devoted father, yes?" Maksim laughed. "She visit you in hell soon, I think." He reared back to pummel Munch's head.

The first window gunman never saw it coming as three holes appeared out of his chest.

As he fell out dead, Butta' replaced him from behind, shooting down Maksim with six shots to the chest and the thug next to him. Trigger rolled out to the yard and fired two shots: one at the second window gunman and a third—an unseen sniper sitting in the bushes. The shot went through his scope, right through his eye, blowing out the back of his head.

Just as Maksim collapsed, Munch found his remaining energy to take up the shovel and swing for his neck—a clean, single blow decapitation.

Maksim's head would be lost in the snow until the following season.

Desiree ran out to scoop up her daughter, kissing her passionately and shielding her from the blood bath. Wyman eyed her in passing and rushed to Munch's side; now a pained and bleeding mass on the court ground.

"Dear god!" He gasped. "The sacrifice. Now I see why."

Butta' jumped down to the surface. With Trigger and Wyman's help, they managed to get Munch to his feet. He was not himself—unable to properly get his balance and bleeding everywhere.

Out of all their adventures, this had to be the roughest on him ever.

"Munchie." Butta' said, choked up. "Oh god—Munchie."

"I'm ... I'm okay ... I'll ... live. Is ... everyone okay? Crystal?"

"We're fine, old man." Wyman helped Munch up. "Your... *daughter*... she's saved and well. Thanks to you. Thanks to all of you."

"Wyman—" Desiree started.

"No!" Wyman snapped. "How could you?!? You told me Crystal's father was dead. You told me—Lies! All these lies. Strung out on drugs? Good for nothing?"

"What does it matter, honey?" She pleaded. "That was an old life. It's just us now. We're all that matters. Just us."

"What the hell's wrong with you? This man saved our lives! He saved Crystal and risked his own life—his *health* to secure our escape. This isn't the man you lied to me about. Not by a long shot."

"He's not." Butta' added. "Trig, see if any of these jeeps can move. Munch is the next best thing to a father that I can remember. Way more than a friend. I would die for him, no questions asked. All he wanted—all he *ever* wanted— was to see his daughter, but she was taken from him."

"Taken?" Wyman was appalled. "You took this man's child from him?"

"She's *MY* child!" Desiree struck back. "Not his! I raised her!"

"You ran with his daughter to Georgia, met me and started everything over as if nothing happened. I believed your lies about a man that had shown nothing but valor and honor at the most perilous moment in our lives." He kneeled down to put Munch's arm around his shoulder to help him walk. "I don't give a damn what you say, Desiree. He *will* know his daughter and— and I would be honored to call him a *friend*."

Munch smiled weakly getting into the jeep, shaking his hand.

Two helicopters were heard above them followed by lights shining down searching the court yard. They were yelling something in Russian. Outside the court yard, cars could be seen coming down the road.

"Uninvited company!" Trigger got into the jeep and starting the engine. "Lots of company!"

Butta', Munch and Wyman got into one jeep while Trigger drove the other with Crystal and Desiree. Butta' took the lead and both jeeps sped out of the yard with the helicopters in pursuit. Finding the best possible road, the chase was on around the castle and away from the old mine.

Just as the weather turned for the worst.

The escaping jeeps pushed past the oncoming fleet of Russian Federation vehicles and raced into the core of the city.

Butta' punched numbers into her cell phone while driving. Only one person could possibly get her out of this jam.

Marigold's Private Jet – Currently In-Flight

Marigold wasn't in the habit of waiting. Unfortunately, she had little choice with so many operations happening at once and not getting any communication from her pawns.

Adian sat across from her reading the latest edition of the New York Times, minding his business and appreciating the rare moment of silence—which broke, soon enough, when her cell phone rang.

"Who?" She answered. "*Gee-Gee*! You're alive! How did you get this number?"

"Munch is a genius! No thanks to you and your *corny ass*!" Butta' seemed very testy.

"We're gonna have to talk about you calling me like this. That's not how things work. Nevertheless, what's the situation?"

"Where's Kasey?"

"How would I know? Maybe she ditched you. You know you can never trust a girl who changes her hair color."

"Look, shut up! We're on the move; we got the diamond, Wyman Fowler and his family."

Marigold twirled her finger in the air and pointed at Adian.

"Perfect! I've been tracking you and those fancy heels of yours within a ten mile radius of Norilsk, Russia."

"You're tracking me? Why didn't you rescue us? How did you know the frequency?"

"Never mind all that. Kasey gave me your heel code and I don't have the people to spare. I knew you'd make it. I've got your evac all setup. Head north toward the *Reka Enisey*."

"The what?"

"It's like a gulf. A big river that leads directly to the Siberian Sea. Whatever you do, don't stop till you get there."

"Fine. Do me a favor and locate Kasey, too."

"Yeah," Marigold twisted her hair with a tease, "I'll get right on it."

She hung up the phone and looked to Adian with a big smile. "We got the first diamond. Everything is looking up."

"What of Kasey McGuiness in North Korea?" He asked.

Marigold thought on it for a moment then shrugged. "She's a smart girl. She'll either make it or not. Either way, we got *one* diamond. Two would be a bonus, and most importantly, we taught the North Koreans a lesson for fucking with *C.R.E.A.M.* Overall, minimal collateral damage—I'd say this has been a good couple of days. Call Louie and tell him to get ready for his pickup."

Corey A. Burkes

Chapter 26

North Korea, P'yongyang Military Base – Airfield
Aboard the Airbus, the flight crew consisted of twenty flight attendants, two captains and two co-pilots. Their purpose for being in North Korea will never be known and their destination is never revealed until they are in the air. So, when they found themselves in the middle of a war zone, they weren't surprised to be the last to know.

Classic North Korean secrecy. A soldier only came aboard once to tell them to seal all portals, hatches and cargo holds then vanished into the light show of fire and bright white beams surrounding the base. No further explanations or warnings.

Obediently, the crew followed instructions, waited and watched. Outside their craft, the Sukhoi Su-30MKK fighter jet was left unattended as Kasey would have hoped for. The Airbus flight crew watched helplessly as Ellen and Fuego boarded the rear second seat. Fuego sitting on Ellen's lap and Kasey jumped into the front.

"So, you *can* fly this thing, right?" Ellen asked, strapping herself and the heavy little man just behind Kasey's head.

"Kinda late in the game to be asking me now, don't ya think?"

"Don't we need some sort of clearance to take off from this place?"

"Can you speak Korean?" Kasey grunted back.

"No!"

"Then we don't need no stinkin' clearance."

The immensity of controls, buttons, and knobs, Korean-language on all the dials, switches, levers and digital displays made Ellen's head swim. "Holy shit."

"Yeah." Kasey strapped herself in and started pushing buttons and flipping switches. Engine turbines started to windup outside. "If you think this is crazy, you should try setting up my nephews *Nintendo*. Just don't touch nothin'. Fuego! Rompelé los dedos si ella tóca algo."

Fuego laughed and kissed Ellen on the side of her head. Ellen didn't quite like the tone of his laugh or what Kasey said.

Military fighter aircraft came in a variety of sizes and types. This particular Russian design favored the U.S F-15E Strike Eagle by McDonnell Douglas. Outside of general body design, that was about all the similarities there were as the controls were in a foreign language and Kasey spent unnecessary time guess-working the controls.

That time could have been better spent getting them off the ground. Instead, North Korean troops zeroed in on their position and rushed the fighter. One thing that stayed consistent on all fighters was the location of the onboard guns. With just a flip of a switch and press of the throttle buttons, 30mm ammo decimated the assault before it began.

"Okay. It's time to go." Kasey had the cockpits closed and the jet engines prepared to move them toward the runway. "Welcome aboard Kasey Airlines. Your seat can be used as a floating support device, which will be pointless if we are shot out of the sky and not over water. Also, I'd like to advise those sitting by the emergency exits that you do have a responsibility to guide your fellow passengers off the plane in case of an emergency, which we are currently in right now. Please stow all cellphones and non-approved electrical devices."

Ellen rolled her eyes. "I hope there's an in-flight movie."

"Sorry, ma'am." Kasey moved the jet toward the runway, picking up speed, shooting at more jeeps and soldiers. "You're not in *first class*."

Kasey gunned the throttle forward and the twin Saturn AL-31 turbofans kicked the fighter forward. Under a minute, the jet was airborne and Kasey's passengers suffered from the gravitational force pressed against them. Ellen hollered as they rose into the heavens. Fuego gripped the straps protecting them to no avail—as the second seat was not designed for two passengers—making their ride very uncomfortable. Fuego pressed additional weight into Ellen's chest.

But they were alive.

How many people could say they assaulted a *world power*, took what they came for and made off with one of their fighter jets?

As far as North Korea was concerned, no one ever would.

Two LCD screens in front of Ellen showed a menagerie of codes and blips that absolutely meant nothing to her. She was still recovering from the liftoff and wondered if she would ever see her stomach again—left back on the runway.

"Ooof," Ellen belched. "Where are we headed?"

"North West." She said this while reading the tracker used to find Butta's signal.

"My geography is a little rusty, but isn't China in that direction? We'll get blown like a cheap hooker flyin' over there."

"Ha! You said *cheap hooker*. China is straight west from here. We're going up to—"

Alarms beeped within the cabin, tearing Kasey's attention from the conversation back to her forward controls. Ellen held onto Fuego so hard, she practically punctured him with her nails. "What the hell is that?"

"Oh nothing. Just some *missiles*. Hang on a sec. I gotta see about keeping us alive."

"What—?" Ellen genuinely felt uncontrollable fear. All this high adventure was not found in the streets of New York— or in her job description.

"We're missile locked. Look—you two share only one oxygen mask. You're gonna get sick. You're gonna black out. I can guarantee it. That might be the best thing for you cause you're not gonna wanna witness what I'm 'bout to do."

After her warning, Kasey took her occupants into a blender maneuver that instantly had Ellen vomiting onto Fuego and poor Fuego losing his bladder on Ellen. None of which mattered because both passengers passed out the moment Kasey pushed the jet to its limits.

The jet toppled and dove through the clouds by Kasey's agile hand, chased relentlessly by surface-to-air missiles. She had to pull out all of her tricks to evade destruction; a smorgasbord of stunts that may look fabulous to the spectator—but to the passengers, it squeezed and compressed their innards harshly: tail-slides, loops, barrel rolls and a whole variety of acrobatic tricks to stay ahead of the missiles. After deploying counter-measure flares to redirect and destroy the missiles, Kasey was home free and away from the North Korean attack.

Drenched with sweat, Kasey removed her air mask and hoped her passengers weren't dead. She looked back as best she could and saw the two leaning back; groaning and a god awful mess.

Alive.

Kasey thanked God and pointed her craft due North to…

Norilsk, Russia – Reka Enisey

The wide body of water that led directly from the Siberian Sea served as a supply for the industries and miners of this part of the country. Tankers use the Reka Enisey as a vital part of their transportation route. Without it, production would have grinded to a halt.

The Sariya-Anne crept her way through the inlet under the cloak of night as silent as she could. As important as these waters were to the Russian financial stability, Louie was almost certain they were being monitored to protect it from people like them—wayward travelers that had no business in one of Earth's coldest civilized region.

Louie piloted the yacht to coordinates he received from Marigold no less than an hour ago, and proceeded to shut down all engines once he reached his appointed location. Shabba, scared witless, sat in the dark as close as he could to Louie, with a blanket covering him.

"Ya might wanna get yerself anudda' blanket, Shab. I shut her down til ferdda' notice."

"What the hell are we doing out here?" Shabba shivered.

"Followin' orders."

"Whose orders?"

Louie really didn't want to get into it with him. "Tell ya wot? Youse stop askin' questions and I'll make sure ya get all da weed youse been missin'."

"I don't give a damn about the doobage."

"Ya say dat now."

"We're in the middle of Russian transatlantic waters. They'll kill us and then send an accidentally sank letter to my folks two years later *after* they torture us."

"Youse been watchin' too much TV, sport. Ya really need ta lay off dose video games, too."

"I'm serious!"

"I know ya are. The Russians won't—" He spied along the shore a series of fast moving headlights and decided this conversation was over immediately. "Stay here, go below or help. It's up to youse!"

"What? Okay. I'll help. What do you —?"

Louie pushed past him and ran out to the deck of the yacht, taking up a lantern, turning it on and waving it out for the headlights to see. There was a set of four headlights, evenly spaced chased by ten sets of headlights further back and two beams of floodlights shining from above.

The first set of headlights veered in their direction along the shore.

"Ten cars—two 'copters." Louie sucked his teeth. "Imma take da speed boat out ta get 'em. Ya wanna help, smokey? Youse pull da lever on dat thingy when I signal ya."

"On that thing?!?" He pointed to machinery attached to the front deck of the yacht. "I'm not touching that thing!"

"'Den ya don't wanna help, damn it!" Louie got in a speedboat attached to the side of the yacht, cuting the ropes and hitting the water abruptly. He had nothing more to say to Shabba, turning on the engines and breaking waves to reach the action on land.

Shabba watched, shivering from a mixture of cold and fright, glancing at the crazy jumble of mechanics that the military attached to his parents yacht.

On shore, with the mountains of Russia to their right, an expanse of water to their left and the Russian government on their tail, Butta' and Trigger pushed the meaning of *all-terrain* past the jeeps breaking point.

Butta' spied the waving lantern a few miles back and did not know how to react to it. Was it friend or foe? Only Marigold could answer that—

"Pick up... *pick up*... !" Butta' cursed, waiting for the phone to ring through once, twice, three times before Marigold finally answered. "Am I interrupting your goddamn bath? Stay by the damn phone!"

"Who in the *hell* are you talking to, Gee-Gee? I don't think I like your tone!" Marigold remarked. "Especially since we didn't discuss how you got my—"

"I don't give a damn what you don't like. Where the hell are we?"

"Calm down. That's your ride home waiting for you. Louie is *always* on time."

"That's Louie?!? Here?!? Now?!?!" Butta' was so relieved to know a trusted friend was within reach. If only they could get to him with the pursuit so close.

"When are you going to start trusting me?" Marigold asked sarcastically.

"When I wrap my hands around your neck!" Butta' retorted.

"You'll have to come to New York for that." Marigold laughed. "When you do, all your questions will be answered. Don't forget to bring the diamond."

Butta' hung up and felt like a new chapter in her life had started writing itself.

Her phone rang one more time.

Again, another private number.

"What did you forget to tell me this time?" Butta' shouted.

South Beach, Florida
A drink in both hands and dressed like a beach bum, *Fade Barrows* had his cell phone crutched between his ear and shoulder while dancing about to some *meringue*. Party-goers were behind him; champagne was flowing, bottles popping and everyone was as sexy as they could be.

"Hey baby cheeks!" Fade acted the fool and very drunk. "What's poppin'? Wassup?!? You were supposed ta holla at 'cha boy and— Hello? Hello? Butta'?"

Norilsk, Russia – Reka Enisey
She did *not* have time for that man right now and snapped her phone shut before he could get any further.

Haven't heard from that fool for days and now he's going to call me? If it weren't for the private calls she expected from Marigold, she would never answer an unknown number again.

She steered the jeep closer to the waters; driving past abandoned refineries and a mix of old and new roads that interconnected poorly in the underfunded industrial country.

Louie's moderately sized *cigarette boat* sliced the waters at speeds surpassing the jeeps themselves. The Russians turned their attention on Louie, firing as best they could at the fast traveling boat without a hit. Louie pointed ahead to Butta' and vanished forward to an array of piers ahead of them.

"Alright." Butta' looked to Munch, keeping her head low from the gunfire. "We get to the pier, I'll hold them off. You get Munchie in the boat."

"I will," Wyman assured her. "I'm in your debt."

"You sure are." Butta' mumbled.

"Be ... *nice* ..." Munch gasped. He wasn't doing well at all. Butta' glanced at her friend sorrowfully; blood matting down his back and the jeep's seat.

Louie let the boat coast to the front of the pier which extended about 750-feet from the shoreline and some old industrial warehouses. Butta' and her crew plowed into the warehouse, over debris and onto the pier itself without regard for whether or not the pier could support both jeeps weight—which, of course, they couldn't.

Both jeeps made it as far as they could before their tires crumbled through the rotting wood and the front end of Trigger's ride fell completely forward with its rear sticking out in a forty-five-degree angle, shaking up Desiree and Crystal.

"What? You don't like my parking? Get the hell out!" Trigger blasted, climbing to the backseat of the jeep and kicking out the side doors. She helped Desiree and Crystal out just as the jeep completely fell into the waters.

This made the pier unstable and the entire clan ran for the end to get into Louie's boat. Butta' and Wyman helped Munch, both feeling terrible they had to manhandle him in order to survive the crumbling pier and avoid getting shot at. Butta' clenched her teeth and shot back at the pursuing Russians back on the shore.

The Russians would not dare attempt crossing the pier in its damaged condition and tried to get at them from the 750-foot expanse, letting the helicopters take over.

Floodlights from two directions focused on the end of the pier and chased after Louie. He flipped the boat into gear and throttled his passengers back toward the Sariya-Anne like a rocket on water.

These types of speedboats were favored by smugglers and the Coast Guard for their stealth and inability to be monitored by radar. At 2100 horsepower engines, topping 135 knots (155.5 mph), the helicopters struggled to keep up, regardless of the boats extra weight of more than the usual amount of passengers. Infrared imaging onboard Louie's control panels guided him securely past debris floating in the water as they rocketed back to the yacht.

The helicopters, twin Soviet Mi-8's loaded with 55mm S-5 missiles and seven passengers each, battered down on the escaping boat mercilessly. Missiles exploded around the boat, tossing and lifting it from the water. Louie had to cut his speed and compensate for the weight and close call explosions before they capsize; as the faster they went, the higher the boat lifted from the water.

As a result, they were easier targets.

He did not want to chance piloting back to the Sariya-Anne; one missile and that would be the last of Shabba. He turned the boat away from the yacht and drew the helicopters pursuit away.

Far ahead, not for another few hundred miles, the open Siberian Sea awaited them and their *go-fast* boat was not designed for that kind of torture.

The missiles were getting closer.

The helicopter pilots were boxing Louie in with timed, patterned shots. Any one of them about to clip him any minute.

A rocket streaked into the fray, followed by an explosion of one of the helicopters. The remaining helicopter veered off hard to the left, just missed by a low flying military fighter jet with speeds that far exceeded Louie's boat and the helicopter combined.

The helicopter banked and let out one of its rockets aimlessly at the fighter that out maneuvered it in speed and fire power. By the time the helicopter leveled off to gather its bearings—it was already too late.

Kasey lowered from the moonlight in a landing maneuver into the gulf and released her Kh-59T short-range air-to-surface missiles at the helicopter. There was no escape for the crew—the ball of flame created a momentary flash of daylight across the land. The remains crashed into the cold, deep waters.

Kasey's fighter—well spent of fuel and armament—splashed down between Louie's speedboat and the Sariya-Anne—steaming while it floated on the waters surface.

Kasey popped open the hatches and stood waving to her friends.

"Fashionably late?" Butta' cheered, almost wanting to cry. It was so good to see her friends again. "Look at what I go." Butta' held up one of the diamonds.

Kasey reached between her bra and revealed the second diamond—hugging a groggy and worse for wear Ellen and Fuego. "There was traffic on I-75—Lockheed Martin was just off the exit so," she patted the fighter's metal hull, "I had this crazy idea."

Louie transported the rest of them back to the Sariya-Anne where Shabba waited anxiously. "You didn't signal me."

"Like ya were gonna to do anything. Go sit down someplace, boy. I got 'dis." Louie pushed past him and ran for the bridge. "Honey! Help me out. Get ready ta pull da lever on dat thing up front when I start da engines."

"What is it?" She didn't hesitate, but still wanted to know what she was getting herself into.

"Courtesy of da U.S. government n' Robertson Tech." And he disappeared up to the bridge, flicking on lights and starting the yachts engines.

Kasey checked over the machinery wrapped all around the front end of the yacht and studied it carefully.

"What is this?" Butta' asked again.

"Well," Kasey sighed, "if I didn't know better, I'd swear it was a—"

"Now!" Louie called out, and Butta' did as she was told, pulling the lever.

The machinery before her and Kasey came to life, churning and rumbling. Carbon-fiber plates along the sides, cosmetic additions applied by the military, retracted further plates and extended throughout the length of the yacht. The heavy mechanics on the front bow unfolded and continued the encasing process until the entire yacht was covered by a newly shaped metal shielding that likened the final result to the navel's stealth boat configurations.

Undetectable by radar and black as the night itself.

Louie set the craft on autopilot and charted a course back to the Siberian Sea which eventually connected to the Atlantic Ocean and onward home. "We'll need ta stay unda' cova' till we're at least get outta Finland. We're gonna take it slow n' steady till 'den. We should get ta New York in 'bout two days after 'dat."

"You're a life saver, Lou." Butta' kissed him.

"Aww shucks, honey. Jus' doin' my part for 'da cause. Ya betta go check on yer pals."

Munch was lying on his chest, on the bed, in the master bedroom cabin. Kasey field dressed his wounds with Ellen; emptying the yachts first aid supplies. Burns were on his hands and his back was torn apart near to the bone. He bit into a towel, screaming in pain as the women worked to heal him.

Kasey looked to Butta' furiously. "I hope you took care of the *bastard* that —"

"Yeah." Butta' confirmed. "You best believe it."

Ellen and Butta' acknowledged each other. She decided to let Kasey and Ellen do their thing and help Munch recover, stepping into the yachts hall where Wyman sat on the floor with his hands over his eyes.

"How is he?" He asked.

"They're doing what they can. He'll be in pain but survive. How are you?"

"Shattered."

Butta' could relate to that feeling. The sudden realization that everything she thought she knew—suddenly wasn't.

Fortunately for her, she was a living testimony to a common fact of life: *Tomorrow will be another day.*

A similar term: *It is what it is.*

Everyone came to that realization in different ways.

Wyman would need to do so on his own.

Leaving the man to figure out his thoughts, she went to check on Fuego who was being wrapped up by Trigger and Shabba in another room. They did a fair job wrapping up his chest and patching up his face.

"Gracias." Fuego smiled to Butta' with astounding gratitude. He followed it with a small amount English. "Thank … you."

"Don't mention it."

"John." He replied, pointing at his chest. "Mi nombre es *John.*"

"John." She liked that name. It fit him—considering she only knew him by his nickname all this time. "Umm … me … llamo Gisela."

"Es un placer trabajar con usted, Giselá." He gave a small bow and kissed her hand.

Butta' did not need a translation, leaving the room while he received the temporary medical attention he needed.

It seemed like everyone finally found the time to calm down and tend to their wounds, giving Butta' time to just step away from everyone and assess everything that occurred over the past couple of days.

She sat on the first available bed she could find and that was the last thing she remembered.

By the time some of the others found her, Butta' was *knocked out*—a severely hard sleep and did not wake up until the Sariya-Anne was about to dock in New York.

Corey A. Burkes

Conclusion

Four Days Later... New York City – Canyon of Heroes
Not since 9/11, lower Manhattan was silenced.

Thousands of police officers lined either side of the street while slowly moving motorcycles led a horse drawn hearse.

Tens of thousands of mourners gathered on the sidewalks to bear witness to the *sending off* one of New York's most decorated and favorite sons: Detective Franklin Jonathan Tulley.

Directly behind his glass encased coffin walked his daughter, Cora, her mother and a few relatives; all in black—all grieving. While the city lost a cop, *they* lost a father, brother and ex-husband.

The woman that was closer to him than *anyone* walked behind the immediate family alone—dressed in full parade regalia.

Inspector Ellen Cobart was the saddest of them all. In her line of duty, she did not make friends easily and when she did, the trust came even later. She trusted Frank with her life. He had saved her many times.

She trusted him to be her friend. He had *never* failed that trust. Now she had no one.

If she had *anyone* else to call a friend or even had a sea of people who could comfort her, no one replaced her partner in her heart.

She looked at Frank's daughter feeling sad that he did not have the chance to settle things with her. Ellen would tell her when she delivered Frank's part of Diandra's money.

Diandra extended her condolences and hoped the money would wrap up any loose ends for Frank's family for years to come. To her credit, what she gave the Tulley family came close to a *king's ransom*.

As for Ellen's loose ends, Prague forensics' eventually responded to her with results of the bullets that killed Frank. Though people often procured their weapons from anywhere, she took notice that these particular bullets were from an AKS-74U, which were specifically *Russian* made, not *North Korean*.

So what did this mean for Ellen?

After she buried her *heart*, she intended to ask Marigold why she misdirected her to North Korea and not after the Russians. She had an appointment to meet with this woman in a few days. She was told all of her questions will be answered at that time.

Not today though.

Today would be spent privately drinking in honor of her friend.

New York City – Stein Tower ... Later That Afternoon

Diandra made unannounced visits to her office to avoid reporters and people trying to take photos of her. Sometimes in the morning, sometimes in the afternoon. She was the *queen* of Stein Industries. She could make her own schedule.

On this particular day, she arrived at Stein Tower with Marcy in tow; an ordinary day, protected by her usual team of bodyguards. She arrived to the office floor without incident and entered her office and greeted by...

"I don't recall making an appointment with you for an interview. Let me check my schedule." Marigold said, thumbing through her digital calendar on her iPad.

"What?" Diandra gasped. "You again!"

Marigold started writing some notes, holding up a finger in a gesture for Diandra to *hold that thought*. Then she pointed to the door.

The bodyguards turned and left the room, surprising both her and Marcy.

"Where are you going? Someone call the police." Marcy yelled.

"Excuse me?" Marigold stopped writing to address Marcy. "Who are you again? Never mind, I just need to speak to Ms. Stein. You may go."

"I will not!" Marcy exclaimed, pulling out her cell phone.

No bars, no reception.

"Your use of company cell phone privileges has been cut off. Waste of expenses. If you want to work for this company, prepare to have your own cell plan. I hear MetroPCS is very good. Terrible customer service. The WORST! But by far, the cheapest I would recommend. Please get out."

Marigold pressed a button under Diandra's desk and two of the guards that brought them up there, re-entered the room.

"Please escort—*what's your name again*? Why do I keep forgetting? Mark? Maddie? No—Marcy! There you go! Escort her off the premises. Ms. Stein and I need to chat."

Marcy put up a momentary fight, dragged out by two men way bigger than her.

"So," Marigold sighed, "what brings you up to *my* office? Human Resources is downstairs. If you have an updated resume, we might have space for you in the mailroom. Please bring two proofs of identification like a passport, birth certificate—"

"What the hell are you talking about?" Diandra demanded.

"You are here for a *job*, aren't you?"

"You're mad!"

"No, I'm the *boss*. You know? *Imma bawse!*" She said with classic *Rick Ross* inflection. "As in, I *own* Stein Industries. Lock, stock and *Gisela*. Thanks for getting rid of the Nazi paraphernalia."

"I don't believe you."

"You don't need to. I don't have to prove myself to no one, and this is that *second* meeting I told you we were going to have. Recently, you sought the help of Robertson Technologies during your unprecedented hostile takeover bid. Did you ever stop to wonder who your friends were? Or who actually owned Robertson Technologies?"

"You do?" Diandra shivered.

"You catch on quick. I'll have to remember that." Marigold joked. "Not! You are done here and all assets attached to Stein Industries effectively belong to *C.R.E.A.M.* That means all homes, including that sweet one up in the Hamptons. All accounts and including the one you recently attempted to storage a little private cash in. Sorry, dear. Nice idea to hide money, but next time don't use the domestic banks. For god's sake! Haven't heard of a Swiss bank account? Jesus! Get yourself another handler. That *Maddie … Mookie* — whatever her name is you hang out with—will steer you wrong."

Diandra looked desperate and defeated. "You can't do this! I'll have nothing! No one."

Marigold simply looked at her after a moment of thought. "Yes. That's about right."

She pressed the button again and two more bodyguards marched in. "We aren't going to have the same scene we had with that other one, are we?"

Diandra was hyperventilating. She tried to dial from her phone. Deactivated.

In one swoop, everything her father built was gone with no safety nets this time.

The men that she thought she could trust flexed by her side; not willing to touch her unless Marigold gave the word—and for Marigold's part, she gave Diandra time to let the situation sink in.

It sank like a rock.

Diandra twirled on her heels and walked out while the guards followed behind her. Marigold started laughing maniacally. "All your personal things can be found in the loading dock. If you want some advice and you don't want to work for me, I hear they're hiring at *McDonalds*. I suggest you apply and work it for a couple of months. Build up some respectability and you'll go places. Like *Kanye West* said, *you got ambition baby! Look at your eyes! Today you'll wash the dishes—tomorrow the fries!*"

Diandra would never remove Marigold's mocking laughter from her head.

Ever.

Outside Stein Tower, Marcy waited. Not in or beside the limo they came in.

She just waited on the sidewalk not knowing what to do.

When she saw Diandra, she let out all of her emotions. "Ms. Stein —what's happening?"

Diandra was still speechless.

The world was suddenly big and strange to her. She had absolutely *no money*, no one to turn to and, effective immediately, *homeless*.

She just stood there while Marcy called out to her; a faint echo, fading further and further away as New York pedestrians pushed and knocked into the once *super* heiress who did not even know who she was.

There was a smaller voice trying to be heard in her head. The voice said the only thing she had left to depend on: *She was a Stein. She would survive.*

She had to.

New York City – Mount Sinai Hospital - Evening

It was evening in New York City.

On Madison Avenue and 100th street, at the top most level of the most prestigious hospital in the city, the finest care ever given to one person was provided to Yancey Duncan.

No expense spared; every cost paid and managed. His room was filled with flowers, roses and balloons wishing him well and hoping he would get better soon.

Loved? Munch was *adored* and *blessed.*

Wyman walked into the room with Crystal by his side to see Yancey's core friends: Butta', Kasey and Trigger—surrounding him.

Imagine three of the sexiest, smartest and ruthless women pampering *one man*?

He had seen these ladies *get to work* and he would never want to be on the receiving end of their fury; praying that he would not make any false moves and thankful Crystal was with him and *not* Desiree.

He cleared his throat to announce himself and the ladies clamored about Crystal, welcoming her into fold.

After a minute, they filed out of the room to leave Munch and Crystal alone. Wyman kissed his little girl's forehead. "I — I explained as much as I could to her."

Munch nervously rubbed his hands together. "I don't know what to say."

"You can start by talking to *your* daughter. I'll be outside."

Wyman walked out leaving Crystal staring at Munch timidly.

In her hands was a picture she drew for him and some flowers she handpicked.

"Hi." Munch waved.

She lowered her head, ashamed. "My flowers aren't as nice as those other ones you got."

"Baby, yours are the best in the whole wide world."

"Really?" She stepped closer. "I drew you a picture. Wanna see it?"

"Sure!" Munch sat up, painfully. "I want to see everything you do."

She unfolded the paper and showed it to Munch: a picture of a bunch of lines and stick figure people with a rainbow of colors. "That's mommy, my two daddies—the big one is you. See? That's Ms. Monique, Ms. Kasey and that's Gee-Gee."

"Gee-Gee?"

"Um-hmm. I *like* her. She bought me some ice cream and she wants to take me to get my nails done. When you feel better, do you want to come?" She asked.

"Can I get my nails done, too?"

Crystal laughed. "No! Daddy's don't get their nails done. Only girls!"

Daddy.

Munch held back his tears and tickled his little girl—soaking in her sunshine.

If life would to ever fail him, he swore to remember this moment for the rest of his life.

Wyman felt good about this *reconnection*, stepping back to give the father and daughter privacy, shutting the door.

Now to other matters.

Desiree stood a fair distance away from Wyman and the ladies surrounding him—each glaring at Desiree menacingly. She dared not to approach or say anything to the group. She, too, witnessed what their small band could do.

Trigger openly stated time and time again she could take care of her if it was an agreed decision and Kasey offered to hide her body.

Another rare showing of *unity* between the two women.

Desiree had much to fear. Butta' was not saying to finish this woman that offended their best friend, but she wasn't protecting her either.

The only thing between Desiree's thin line dividing life or death was Crystal's ultimate sorrow if her mother wound up missing.

Wyman had to step in when Butta' *suggested* that *she* eventually came to terms with the loss of her parents.

Sorta.

"It's not her fault." Wyman said. "Don't be mad at her."

"Is this that *forgiving* part of the story? I saw this coming and I'm sorry," Butta' harrumphed, "I refuse to read past that part. I promise you I won't kill her or even give the order to have it done. For Crystal's sake, she needs her mother. Just so all parties understand how close they were to needing a casket."

"She did what she thought was best at the time. Maybe her priorities weren't the greatest, but we all make mistakes."

"True." Kasey chimed in. "But don't we acknowledge our mistakes and work to set things right? The way I hear it, to this very moment, she still doesn't want to have anything to do with Munchie. She has full custody. She could refuse him from seeing his own daughter. That wouldn't be right."

"I'll work on her." Wyman said.

"No," Trigger clenched a fist, "*I'll* work on her."

Desiree heard some of that and flinched backwards, preparing herself to either fight or flee.

A group of nurses passed by in the hall, forcing Butta' and Wyman to shift out of the way. Nothing unusual about this in a hospital, except when they cleared and went about their duties, Trigger was left with an envelope on her lap that fell there from between the unknown selection of RN's.

An envelope very much like the first she received days earlier.

Surprised, she quickly tucked it away out of sight of Butta'.

But not Kasey.

She seen the subtle transaction out her peripheral vision and played coy.

"No... *no*." Wyman needed to defuse this right away. "We have to ease into this. Lots of ignorance, pain and suffering went on already. Yancey has rights as her father and, as far as I'm concerned, I will see to it that they are honored and then more. Like it or not, she will have to swallow her pride and let this happen."

"Or what?" Trigger asked.

Wyman was not sure of that answer. He looked at Desiree from a distance and knew their relationship was going to change.

"I don't know." He shrugged. "Let's just start with the *truth*." He winked at Butta'.

He walked away toward his wife to begin the long and winding road to whatever may come—a conversation of honesty and all cards revealed that both of them needed to talk about.

"Well," Butta' stretched, "I'm off."

"Where too?" Kasey attempted to step closer to Butta' to reveal what she saw with Trigger, but Butta' was quickly making her way toward the elevators.

"Stein Tower."

"Stein Tower? Are you kidding me?"

"Wish I were. Marigold overthrew the evil empire and I've been summoned by the Queen. She promised me all sorts of wondrous information as long as I bring the diamonds with me. Damn, diamonds. I'm just about done with these things. Kase, I love and miss my father a lot. I see, now, what I feel for him inside of me can't be replaced by whatever trinkets he left behind. The friendship I have in you guys can't be replaced either. I'm sorry for this whole thing. I really am. "

Kasey followed until Butta' entered the elevator and pressed the down button.

"Look, when you get there—when you speak to her, she's gonna tell you some stuff that you're not going to be ready to hear."

The doors started to close and Butta' looked at her friend queerly. "How do you know? I don't even know that woman."

"Whatever she says—it's *true*." Kasey finalized just as the doors closed and Butta' was gone.

And so was Trigger.

Kasey turned on her tracker, noticing Trig still wore her boots with *Dorothy* embedded in them.

55th Street and 12th Avenue – Cruise Terminal and Docks - Evening
Stripped back down to its original design, the Sariya-Anne spent the past few days replenishing and professionally cleaned before the trip back to Europe and return to Shabba's parents.

Corey A. Burkes

After the previous adventure, Louie wanted to get back to dry land for a stretch of time and go on vacation where no one needed a passport.

Some quiet place in New Jersey would do.

He inhaled the evening Manhattan air, watching the crew that spent the day cleaning the boat pack up and leave for the night.

Left alone on the deck, apprehension suddenly engulfed him.

These were time sharpened early warnings; gut feelings that body guarding had instilled in him. He could not tell *who* or *where* the threat was coming from, but he knew for certain that there was a problem.

He turned to look for Shabba.

Instead, he found someone else behind him.

"*Christ!* You scared the hell out of—"

The silencer *poof* came in three distinct shots.

Louie fell dead to the deck—bleeding on the polished wood.

The assailant shot him an additional three *more* times to make sure.

Shabba walked up from the lower hold with a thick medical book in his hands. He had just enough time to see Louie's lifeless form when the attacker turned on him.

Out of all the last words Shabba could have said in this lifetime, he only produced one: "*Why*—?"

The shots sent holes through the book he attempted to use as a shield, into Shabba's thin frame and he died instantly.

Shreds of medical book paper fluttered down about his body as the assassin fired three more shots completing the mission.

Forty-five minutes later, after following an unusually zigzagged pattern around New York, Kasey arrived to find the Sariya-Anne in flames; burning with all the local fire departments shooting water at it and pulling the remains of the yacht away from the dock.

Kasey stood there in awe, dropping the tracker that led her to this spot.

Trigger's beacon disconnected and resting on the pier.

A message. She wanted me to find her.

They never found *whole* bodies and what pieces they did find were burned beyond recognition.

Police final reports would conclude that the deaths of Louie and Shabba were accidental.

New York City – Stein Tower – Same Evening

Butta' arrived at her destination, walking through the front doors when not too long ago she had to sneak through a sewer. Security did not stop her when not too long ago security in this very building attempted to shoot and kill her and her friends. She boarded the elevator and pressed for the top floor, when not too long ago, this trip would never have happened.

Time and life had changed dramatically.

The level that was once Stein's residential quarters, where Kasey and Trigger fought the once mighty Lingo Stein and ended in a great explosion, had now become Marigold's lavish personal office.

Butta' would never feel comfortable being here. Marigold sat behind her table, typing things in her iPad.

"Start talking." Butta' ordered.

"Look at you! Ordering me around now." Marigold said, typing. "You must be feeling yourself something serious!"

Adian entered the room behind Butta' carrying an empty tray. Butta' looked at him and then placed the two diamonds in her possession on the tray.

"And that concludes the greatest adventure of this decade." She cocked a brow at Butta'. "The beautiful orphan has sought and accomplished her vendetta. Came to terms with letting go of the past and is embracing the here and now. Who knows what the future will hold for our young heroine, but unless she trims some of that *gray* showing up on her scalp, she'll get a new nickname of *Skunk-Girl* in three months hence."

"Very poetic." Butta' said, checking a mirror to confirm the hair follicles Marigold pointed out. "Damn. So soon?"

"We're not getting any younger, Gee-Gee. It was bound to happen." Marigold stood up and gestured for Adian to take the diamonds away. "Tell General Tucker he has my gratitude and he now has his diamonds. Let's give him the *eBay treatment*. Tell him the price just tripled due to shipping and handling. The US Government will pay. They *always* pay."

"That's it?" Butta' snarled. "All that crap for just a *payday*."

"Really, Gee-Gee. Is there truly *anything* else more than that? Come on. Think about it"

"Whatever. So I'm here. I came for answers."

"Don't you like the new *digs*?" Marigold gestured around the office. "Courtesy of Stein Industrial. Feels good being able to walk in here without *sneaking in*, doesn't it? You, of all people, should have fond memories of this place. You should check out the upper vault room. They really did a good job cleaning up all the blood. Almost as if he's never been there and—"

"Look, I've seen it. Who in the *hell* are you? Why do you keep calling me *Gee-Gee*? Why were you helping me? Do I know you?"

"Sure you do. For god's sake, is this any way to treat *family*?"

Butta's mental brakes came to a halt. "Fam—? What are you saying?"

"Gee-Gee—I'm your *auntie*." Marigold took a swig of wine from a nearby glass. "Your father's younger sister."

Butta' stared back at Marigold feeling her chest get heavy and the blood rushing from her head. The room started to spin. "Huh?"

"What?" Marigold paused. "Kasey didn't tell you?"

Butta' was enveloped by darkness and she collapsed on the fine carpeting.

Adian made a move to help her, but Marigold laughed loudly and waved him off.

"Leave her. She's been through enough for one, well, lifetime I suppose. I've got a dinner date and I'll ease her into her new reality in the morning after my meeting with Ellen." Marigold kneeled down beside the beautiful woman and moved her hair from her eyes, using a leather coat to cover her body.

"*My niece.* " She said proudly. "This was a reunion that took a long time to make. The king is dead; long live the *Queen*—and her *princess*."

"Madam Marigold?" Adian said. "I received confirmation that the *Gisela device* has been successfully reconstituted in our classified location. They are ready to produce diamonds at your command."

Marigold stood just as her body guard team entered to escort her from the building.

"Took them long enough. You can't get good scientists anymore, these days. Damn, I'm good. Did I set this whole thing up from the start or what? *Welp*, like they say on *Facebook*. Let's get this party started!"

<u>Epilogue</u>

A peek into ten years from now …

Corey A. Burkes

Ten Years Later ...
Late spring - Massachusetts Institute of Technology (MIT)

The graduation ceremony began on the calmest and clearest day of the year. During the previous week, rain storms threatened to move the event indoors, but as it turned out, they whisked away the clouds and left a perfect late spring/early summer breeze at a comfortable seventy-eight degrees.

A sea of graduates sat wearing black with caps, while an equally mass of proud parents and relatives sat in a half moon shaped gathering behind them; hushed while the graduate with the highest honors, *summa cum laude*, eighteen-year-old *Crystal Duncan Fowler*, addressed the people with a commanding, leader's voice that reached for miles from her microphone.

"I want to conclude by expressing my deepest appreciation to the professors and faculty of this great institution, to which my education would not have been complete. Finally, it needs to be said that I am the most fortunate daughter in the world to be blessed to have two fathers. To my *dad*, Professor Wyman Fowler, I love you. I thank you for your encouragement through all of these years and your support to always explore the depth of science. Your belief in me established who I am and you showed me the road, I alone, had to walk, with you right by my side.

"To my—*father,* by no means do I take anything away from one or the other and I say this with no prejudice or favoritism—but to my father," she started to cry, "Yancey Duncan. You have saved my life. I would not be here without you on multiple levels. I owe my life to you and nothing I say is strong enough to convey how much *I love you*. You have been my rock; a precise role model to what a *real man* has to be for me to even take a passing glance. You are my *knight in shining armor*. You are my hero." She completely broke down with tears down her cheeks. "*My daddy*."

The crowd joined her in tears as she left the podium, ran past her classmates and fell into Munch's arms.

Ten years older and wheelchair bound for the remainder of his life, Yancey cried in his daughters arms. Wyman Fowler, next to them, stood and applauded—followed by the entire audience—standing to honor this loving moment.

Later on, by the end of the festivities, Crystal pushed Yancey toward the parking lot with her second father by their side; all laughing and talking about the parties she planned to attend through the week.

A limo pulled up beside them and the driver hopped out to come around and opened the back door.

"*Auntie Gee-Gee!*" Crystal exclaimed.

Gisela stepped out of the car, sporting a pair of glasses and professionally dressed. A lock of gray hair down the front of her forehead with her ageless killer body; just a tad filled out in places with a sexy, *grown* flavor. "Sorry I missed your graduation."

"Cause you *suck!*" Crystal said playfully.

Wyman tapped her on the back of the head. "Goodness, girl. Show some respect. Mind your manners."

"Sorry."

Gisela sighed. "She's right. I do suck. I had more than enough time to arrange my schedule and here I am."

"Just got back from Washington?" Yancey asked.

"Yes. This time tomorrow, the *Times Agency* will go live and I start recruiting. Kind of like what I did for Marigold back in the days." She looked over at Crystal. "Ever think about your future, Crystal?"

"*Oh no!*" Wyman shook his head. "She's not going to be running around the planet getting shot at. I won't have it. *Not my daughter!*"

"I second that." Yancey nodded.

"I'd **LOVE** to! How do I sign up?" Crystal was ready to go.

"There's that." Wyman resigned. "No changing her mind now. If you'll excuse us, I want to take Crystal over to meet someone."

He dragged her away from Gisela and Yancey, much to her chagrin. "But *Auntie* just got here!"

"You'll have plenty of time to hang with your auntie. Gisela, we'll talk soon. Come on, Crystal, before they leave."

"But I don't wanna go—!"

No matter how smart or older Crystal became, they still heard that cute little eight-year-old from years back.

"How time just flies on by." Yancey sighed.

"That it does. How was the ceremony?"

"Very emotional. I wished you made it. I wished —*all* of us were here."

Gisela brooded momentarily and silence fell between them uneasily.

"I'd like to think that they are." She nodded, standing behind Yancey. "Yes—I'd like to think so."

She pushed her closest friend to his parked vehicle as they took the time to regress over the old days under the waning dusk sun.

But those old days **have not** been told *yet*—and there are *ten more* stories left. This peek into the future is over. We now return you to our regularly scheduled adventures in …

Published by
DesktopEpics Entertainment

Corey A. Burkes

How This Book Was Written

I am celebrating.

Not because I won some windfall of cash or sold my 100,000th novel (which I have not). I'm celebrating a personal victory that is setting the tone for the rest of my life because, quite frankly, it was *touch and go* last year 2011. I wasn't sure where the hell I was going with this so-called '*writing career*' and a fifty page resume of previous employments. Name it; I probably worked there for about a month or so.

I am not particularly *proud* of my scattered work history, and I touch on this topic more in the *How This Book Was Written* section of **Sleight of Death** (forthcoming), but I do look at the many jobs I've been at as my testimony that I have lived to only do one thing and one thing only with some level of quality: develop and write stories.

Now, it's all well and good to believe what you *think* you were born to do and not have a *dime* to show for it if you are living in your own personal world without a family to care for. *Trust me.* If you wish to be the pariah of your family and those around you who have only worked ONE job for FIFTY years and cannot understand how you can walk away from a decent paying job 'just like that', then by all means! Keep reciting how you were born to be *whatever* you think you were born to do and life suddenly becomes a very lonely road to walk.

Then comes the spouting of the '*believe in yourself*' material. How you must stay focused and stay driven to your goal in order to, one day, prove everyone wrong that you did know what you were talking about when no one believed but you.

Gather all the cute 'Facebook' friendly quotes to acquire as many LIKES as possible for some sort of inspirational '*never give up*' line. *Don't ever stop!* Keep your dreams alive!

Meanwhile, your children are hungry.

Meanwhile, you are standing in the middle of a work place listening to some *asshole* manager curse at you because he or she thinks she can get away with it—and you suck it in because you need to pay that rent or mortgage; or pay your bills and still go to school and get that degree because the job you are at won't pay you more unless you have that paper and it's a job you don't even want to be at because it has *nothing* to do with what really moves you.

The boss is still cursing at you. Belittling you in front of others.

Never give up.

Work multiple long hours and come home tired and still need to study for school but you are still expected to write your novel or create your art; digging deep for energy that just isn't there and find the way to go to work and smile without killing your boss.

Never give up.

But you do. You quit and people want to wonder *how you could?*

They don't see what you see.

They don't see the reviews you get and the *heart* you put behind your work—that's not making any money—but it *moves* you so much that you don't care. You and you alone know your work is on a path of infancy that promises to grow to adulthood eventually.

Maybe not before the mortgage is due, but you can't give up.

But you also can't stay awake.

You work very hard to prove to yourself and others that your ideas work so you're staying up around the clock. Pushing yourself.

People are quick to lose faith in people who don't stay at a regular job long enough. No matter how much of your art is fantastic; all most people see is how much of a *paycheck* you are bringing in. You can tell yourself that your art doesn't revolve around money exclusively all you want but the people around you may think differently.

We tend to *constantly* surround ourselves with people who think with the opposite side of the brain than we do. Chances are, you are an artist in a relationship with a person of logic that can't understand art, least of all, leaving a well-paying job just because it's stifling your creativity.

When your art doesn't produce *any* results or, say, you lose inspiration—that could be the most troubling of them all and while you suffer your own personal crisis of creativity, you're not working or miserable at the job you are at and people around you keep wondering why you are not happy.

Because you are *dying* and nobody seems to truly care or notice the signs.

Hey Fellow Drone. Why can't you eat your gruel like the rest of us? Awww, poor baby. You say being a drone is killing you? Well, this is life. You are born to die at the job you work at and have no further aspirations than to one day win the lottery and ONLY then will you reach nirvana. Otherwise, only the lucky few can be the next Steven Spielberg or Stephen King. Sorry, you can neither be. So pay your taxes, shut up and get to work on time to work among your fellow drones and to complain about Mondays, joke about Hump days and drink on Friday nights, rake your lawn on Saturday and lie at Church on Sunday. Come back to the slave mill on Monday and repeat eating your gruel.

There.

In a nutshell, I just gave you the past 10 years or so. My decision to *reject* that pattern of life has put me at odds with … oh, say *everyone*. While in my mind, I ask "Why can't I have the same support that successful artists get from their families?" The response I get is, "You're not living in reality. Now shut up and let's watch some reality show where people struggle to win ONE prize in order to prove we are right that being a star is far and few between!"

I never wanted to be a *star*.

I do want to be gainfully employed doing the one thing I do best and I see that day coming.

Which brings me back to why I am celebrating.

You see, in 2009, I did not think this book would see the light of day.

I was ready to edit and release Butta': Worldwide in 2009/2010. I pulled together all of the models and photography. I spent a lot of money designing this whole image of the Butta' universe for promotional purposes and, just like that, Skyelight Literature—the original publisher of Butta'—folded.

To be honest, it had to fold.

The company was too small and I was doing more of the work alone than I could in the framework that Skyelight was designed.

One of the biggest problems with Skyelight was I felt I had to answer to others in order to get things done. Naturally, since Skyelight wasn't 100% mine even though the flagship book was. So, if I had an idea, it was based around the 'group' of us that work in and around Skyelight. Unfortunately, the bulk of the work was on me and my ideas designed around 2-3 man teams were too much for me alone and I had to stop.

When I stopped, so did Skyelight.

Anyone who knows me knows I am NOT a team player.

I hate working in teams. Hate putting *our heads together* on a project and lord knows I do NOT do writers pools and that sort of thing. Between you and me, I think the most asinine thing in the world is a bunch of people around a table writing ONE script. People shouting out ideas and trying to form something with multi voices trying to outbid one another. You won't catch me in that environment and you won't catch me adding my voice to a group project of any kind.

Why? Because it's a waste of time to me. Just give me my task and leave me the hell alone. It's not about being a control freak, per se. I am actually very good at *following* a leader (i.e. give me my task). I am very good at being a leader as well and I know what the goals need to be. To that end, in a leadership position, I don't want to hear anybody's excess yack—you want me to lead, then shut the fuck up and do what I'm telling you so we can get to the goal.

Not in *those* many words, of course.

The thinking is, if I have to work as hard as I am doing, then I don't need to answer to anyone but my own instruction—and I will come up with ideas that are manageable to a ONE person operation.

So, after a few years of dismal depression and not sure where or how Butta' would continue, it seems technology and the publishing industry evolved around me. I would even go as far as to say it evolved FOR me.

Back in 2007 to 2009, self-publishing your book was an expensive venture. Unbeknownst to me at the time, it was rapidly changing into a compact easier process. In 2007, people were still thinking an eBook was a PDF. The Kindle was just hitting the stores and the idea of reading a full book on the screen was just creeping into the consciousness.

Print on Demand (POD) was rapidly catching fire with Lulu.com, Iunverse.com and a few others. Even still, the average cost to print one book through these sources varied from $9.00 to $99 per book. I remember my first book printed with 48hourbooks.com and it cost me about $100 for one book. Looked great at the time.

Then I printed the same book with Lulu.com for $12.00 and there was no difference in quality.

Got it in three days or so too.

That was 2007/2008.

Now, this very book you are holding cost less to print than I could have ever imagined, allowing me to mark the price down to something that beats the price of most other publishers for the same amount of pages and genre. This book, in 2007 terms, would need to have cost you $20 retail. No wonder publishers were getting broke off lovely back then—and why they are so mad now.

For five dollars more than the eBook version, you get more content in this version because I am an old school believer that you should get more for what you pay for. That will never change.

Anyway, here we are in 2012 and Worldwide is out and available to you. A great feat of personal triumph and dedication to see it get done. No matter what happens to me moving forward, I did it and I hope the story is just as good and better than the first Butta' adventure. Early reviews from friends—friends not afraid to tell me it would suck—tell me it's wonderful and they can't wait for the next novel. I have to go by that indication because I can't get my books reviewed by professional reviewers for some reason. I've been submitting emails to many of them—some of them with repeat emails—with no response or simply being declined.

It will never EVER fail to amaze me that my work gets reviewed well, when it does get reviewed—but I'm treated like a new jack every time. I don't understand it and that's when I feel like I need a literary agent.

Not complaining though because this is the path I decided for myself when I decided to work this alone. The pledge at the front of every book I publish is the truth and I honor it—provided you register. If you don't register, I won't know you have the book or the eBook and I can't replace it. It's a lifetime warranty.

When I was originally certain Butta': Worldwide was going to come out, I arranged a huge photo shoot with some of the most attractive people in the industry that I thought resembled as close as possible to the characters of the story.

Naturally, first on the list was friend **Samantha Murdock.** She already came with me to events to be the 'sexy spokes model' during the first novel. She helped sell MANY books. Samantha Murdock owns a fashion boutique in Long Island and occasionally continues her modeling work from time to time.

So, I flew her out to Georgia during one day in late 2009 and already cast for the other characters with the help of photographer **Kim Cantey-Davis**:

Doris Morgado was NOT supposed to be cast. I thought she was devastatingly gorgeous and she literally re-wrote the character of Marigold based on how she looked alone. The original generation of Marigold wasn't even named 'Marigold'. The original character was older. Then I met Doris and I even wrote in that the character had the same mole as she does. Doris Morgado can be seen on Army Wives and a host of other programs.

Haji Abdull is well –known here in the actor's field and can be seen in MANY high profile films shot in Atlanta including The Blind Side where you'll catch him sitting directly next to Sandra Bolluck in one scene. I thought he was perfect as 'Munch' could be even though Haji is clearly way taller. Still, Haji is a great friend and cool guy.

Kandiss Lewis is a breathtaking model and has since moved to Los Angeles (or Florida) practically right after this photo shoot. She continues to do great works out there and showcases her phenomenal body. Because of her I changed Kasey's hair from blonde to brunette. I think Kandiss' hair is brownish-gold, I think.

Kida Davis is a local Atlanta model who was the perfect size and look for Trigger.

Christina Boykin as Crystal Munch's daughter.

Roxzane T. Mims as Ellen whom had the right EVERYTHING to whom I thought Ellen would be.

As much as I would have loved to do the whole cast of characters, money just wouldn't allow and the goal was to shoot images that I would create with effects to replicate scenes from the book.

Included in this book (and not the eBook version) are the images that didn't get complete coverage at the time as I would have loved. Some of them are shots prior to removing the green screen. Some with effects that I was testing out. Various photos from that day that really need to be seen. I had a great time that day.

Now, a few words about many of Kandiss Lewis and the LACK of photos.

Let me tell you. I LOVED her. She was my 'Kasey' in every possible way except height. I envisioned Kasey as taller, but whatever. She was as close to perfect as I could find. However, I think the makeup applied to her that day did not do her justice and it just went downhill when it came to editing the special effects. Could just as well been a cultural thing because the Black actresses had great makeup. Obviously, applying makeup across cultures is a skill that isn't mastered by all.

That I regret the most. I really wanted the whole crew to stand out and it didn't happen as I liked.

But then again, a few short months later, the book wouldn't be coming out any way so it didn't matter.

Between 2009 and 2010, I did keep trying to do it myself but it just didn't happen. So from time to time you'll see promotional posters with different dates on them. It really got pathetic until 2011 when I said I would re-do the first book as an eBook to start the series fresh.

January 2012 – **Butta'** debuted.

May 2012 – **Butta': Worldwide** finally released.

January 2013 – **Butta': Cream** will be released.

The idea is to stay consistent with release dates. January and May of each year, drop two Butta' novels. At this rate, with twelve novels to complete, I'll be done around 2017 with the series.

Yes, there are twelve stories because it's supposed to come full circle to the second script I ever completed when I was around fifteen-years-old. It's called "Times 12" and it featured a character that will show up in Butta' novel book #5.

I know—a lot of planning and forward ideals yet to manifest. But look at it this way, back in 2007; I didn't think I would do another book more than 'Butta' and the Tower of Bling'. And then in 2009, I didn't think Butta: Worldwide was going to come out at all.

Never give up.

Guest novel excerpt from Author Joyce Stewart's
The BBQ – Fireworks Spark

Chapter 1 – The Intro

Monica stood in the kitchen while her mentor, Leslie, talked on the phone to Pastor Richard (Monica's Godfather). Leslie's husband, Charles was in the living room glued to the television's marathon of Law and Order (Special Victims Unit). Monica lived about fifteen minutes away from Leslie and stopped by her house to drop off Leslie's birthday gift.

The perfume was her favorite, "white linen" by Estee Lauder. By their conversation, it was obvious that Leslie and Richard discussed things that God showed them about her life.

Now ending her phone call, Leslie turned toward Monica.

"Pastor Richard says that he expects to see you today, so please don't disappoint him." Though Monica felt like a kid dragging her feet, she hugged Leslie goodbye and yelled goodbye to Charles and then began her road trip to Pastor Richard's house.

July 4th Independence Day

Monica sat in traffic impatiently waiting to merge onto the Palisades Parkway. Monica despised any driving that was more than twenty minutes travel, but for the sake of her mentor and Godfather she agreed to go to the Barbeque. July 4th's well recognized, Grand Finale of all Barbeques of the summer, but to Monica it may well end up being just another religious function.

Cars were literally at a standstill and she just took a long sigh. Even her favorite music couldn't suppress Monica's inward road rage from asserting itself into her otherwise peaceful personality. Monica swooped her car around a disrespectful man driving a Jeep Cherokee.

She saw him coming on her right hand side trying to cut her off to merge onto the palisades parkway. Monica blocked him and continued on her merry little way. Monica promised to call Leslie to advise her when she was near her destination. She dialed Leslie.

"Hi, just wanted to let you know that I'm only a few minutes away from crossing into New Jersey, but the traffic is overwhelming." Monica wished she could just turn back.

"Well dear, sometimes when you're very close to receiving a breakthrough – you have to do things you don't always feel comfortable with. You are in an important season in your life Monica," Leslie said. Leslie felt that Monica needed to remember "the promise". Monica was completely aware that Leslie was gifted with wisdom, but at the moment she wasn't feeling very spiritual

Monica debated on what to wear for nearly a week and even today she struggled. Knowing that church folk, strangers and people in general would be checking her from head to toe, she had to look her best. She thought, it's funny how men didn't have that pressure.

They could wear overalls and beat up sneakers - no one would care less. However, women had to shine like a peacock. She had a few choices: A halter top denim jean jumpsuit, a beautiful floral ankle length sundress or Baby Phat- leggings with a cute powder blue V-neck mini dress. She decided on the jean jumpsuit since it was cool and sexy combined with 3 inch cork heeled denim sandals. Monica stood petite at 5' 3 with an hour glass like physique.

Her face was very appealing as her features resembled a Native American woman with defined cheekbones; eyes were brown and naturally arched eyebrows and a pronounced nose with long hair that was worn straight or curly depending on her mood. Monica's built in navigation of her 2011 Chevrolet Malibu viewed her three minutes away.

The directions were great and she was turning onto the street. The final destination is 409 Llewellyn Circle, Englewood, New Jersey and she just passed 405. Seeing the cars lined up, she hoped there wouldn't be a long walk.

"Great!!! Someone's moving out of a space – perfect!" Monica said out loud. This was her first time visiting Pastor Richard's ranch style home. It was huge and definitely suitable for large gatherings.

The small shrubs on the land swayed with the light breeze and she looked at the temperature gauge in the car that read 85 degrees. Monica sat in front of the windshield mirror to do her last application of chocolate lip liner and peachy toned lip-gloss, then she checked her thin black eye liner and hand combed her soft waves of curled hair – now satisfied that she looked presentable enough.

Monica thought if nothing else the food would be a highlight. After all, who could resist southern barbeque cooking?

Coming out of the vehicle, her eye caught view of a few menacing clouds that lingered above. Monica rang the doorbell and waited for an answer.

"Hi Sis, come on in, the parties in the back." Shelton smiled as he led her through the house to the sliding doors. Shelton was a very handsome guy from her church. She followed him and observed the details of the shiny waxed hardwood floors and every room that she passed had a minimalist homey feel to it.

The house had a rustic with country style blend of taupe, green and reddish browns in the furnishings and décor. True to most old school black homes, a rusty-brown toned lazy boy sat in the living area along with an L-shaped taupe sectional couch. Scanning the huge yard she saw a crowd of about 45 of Pastor Richard's family, friends and church folk – she assessed.

As usual, she felt that same feeling most women must get on arrival of an event like this one. There were some who looked because someone new just walked into the room and then there were others, women and men alike sizing her up. A smile arose as Monica recognized a familiar face come up and hug her and brought a sense of relief.

"Hey Girly Girl," Monica said and embraced Regina's warmth.

"Hey Monie." Regina called her that for short. "Come let me show you where the food and stuff is."

Monica gladly followed Regina seeing she hated to come into any event feeling awkward. Her and Regina fellowshipped at her church and were intercessors for the pastor's wife. They arrived near the grill and she saw her God Father and went to greet him and his wife. She searched the surrounding area and a peculiar feeling came over her and she felt like butterflies had entered her belly.

"Hey YOU!!!" Pastor Richard reaches to embrace Monica.

He was a man that was huge at 5' 10, but weighed about 295. Monica is sucked in by his bear hug and waves at his wife, Colleen. Once she breaks from the hug.

She quickly goes to hug her as well. Colleen was maybe 5' 6" and not petite, but thick as some would call it Still not certain of where this strange unexplained feeling was coming from, Monica just smiles and looks onward.

Monica looked for Regina and saw her speaking to a tall gentleman wearing a blue short sleeve shirt and dark jeans. Monica stood stationary, not wanting to interrupt - they were standing such a short distance from her.

Monica could determine by his persona that he was a man of class. Regina's back was slightly turned away from Monica and the tall gent seemed to want to break away from their conversation.

Monica decided to walk towards the table filled with 4th of July favorites while contemplating where she should sit. Out of her peripheral vision she saw the two of them watching her as she moved. Monica could feel someone behind her. A hand slid across her shoulder.

"Monica, I want you to join me over there when you're done, okay?" Regina said. She pointed at a table that had four chairs where Shelton was seated.

"Sure, sure…I'm just going to get a few things and I'll be right there. Monica said."

By viewing the vast menu, it was plain to see that the Richard's spared no cost for this barbeque. The spread included: Richard's famous barbeque ribs, Colleen's mouthwatering potato salad, corn bread, corn on the cob, t-boned steaks, macaroni and cheese, fried chicken, baked beans, wild rice, hot dogs, hamburgers and desserts galore, etc.

Monica took a minuscule portion of Mac and cheese, corn bread, potato salad and fried chicken. Looking towards Gina's table she moved in their direction. Monica was still curious about the guy that Regina was speaking with moments ago but she wouldn't dare turn to see which way he went. She tried to keep focus and put her plate on the table and sat opposite of Shelton. Regina was engaged in a conversation with Shelton and they were making jokes as usual.

Realizing that she forgot to get a drink, she was about to get up, but before she could. She saw the shadow of someone sitting next to her on her left hand side. Wow!!!! That brother is absolutely gorgeous! Oooo we! Monica felt like the sun, moon and stars had just sat down beside her and she needed that cold drink now!!!

"Hello, my name is Shawn." The tall gent spoke.

"Hello." Monica answered trying to sound normal

**For more from Author Joyce Stewart, visit
outskirtpress.com/bbqfirworksspark**

The Humor of God
Coming Fall 2012
By Corey A. Burkes

Before Life Changed …

The Earth.

Constantly at war, an astronaut could hear the anger in orbit regardless of the peace they often swear it brought to them. The Earth is an angry globe with angry in habitants—turning endlessly and on precision time. Such perfect time, it's a wonder how anyone could doubt a higher being managed such an incredibly synchronous thing and include living beings of various sizes as a bonus.

But they do. More than half the inhabitants do.

So, the majority of sentient creatures, called 'humans', along with the rest of the mammals, fish, birds and things that creepth, go about their daily lives and, for the most part, ignore who put them there. Though it will always be uncertain if the bugs and animals connected with a higher deity—it's historically proven that man and woman have been seeking and rejecting equally—in faith or at war—the existence of a God.

Over the centuries, there has been a wide variety of gods to claim top billing. Some short and round. Some invisible. One or two coming in three's or fours. More in the form of man seated on thrones in the clouds. Oddly enough, the alternative evil version tends to come in one form and almost always is underground. Regardless of the wording, position and placement, man and woman have always needed someone to pin their troubles on; an invisible force to blame for the rights or the wrongs of their existence.

A heavenly scapegoat.

When man realized that he can use the name of God to justify his or her actions—and receive full pardon and understanding for those actions—life truly kicked into high gear. Who would *dare* challenge anyone who was doing the work of God himself. Since no one actually seen or heard from this faceless being, who can counter the slaughter of millions when it was said to be 'the work of the lord'. Millions of murdered Islamic followers during the Crusades can't return from the dead to say otherwise.

What has changed through the ages is the reason for fighting. While smaller skirmishes and coordinated genocide continues in places that the majority of humans don't care to intervene in; for the most part, the big Alexander the Great level wars went out with World War II. The Cold War, Afghanistan and Iraq aside, there has not been a global threat for a very long time. Just people terrorizing each other in small scales that seem big to one another individually as the human race weeps every 9/11 or Memorial Day that comes about annually. Sure, how they love to *never forget* the injustices they do amongst themselves—but they forget who put them there almost every second of the day.

Church? Worship? It's all unbalanced lies of hand-me-down text from one liar to another. Mankind can barely tell themselves the truth in a common interview on national television. How could anyone trust the text of what they deem as holy bibles or Koran? The same text that lead both Christians and Muslims alike to slaughter one another with craftily worded text that could mean one thing to some and another to others.

Faith. That's the ticket. If man or woman believes in what the words of their respective holy anything says, then everything will be alright. Gather multitudes of people who believe in the same thing and it's called a religion. With more people walking the same path, the greater the numbers, the more 'real' that faith must be. Look! That religion has billions of followers of that one called Jesus Christ. He must be the right God to follow.

Then comes the misinterpretations. The confusion. The trinity. No, there's only one God and a holy spirit. No, Jesus was God and man at the same time. No, but the text says "WE" and "US". No, that's impossible because this, that and the other thing. The infighting goes on in *every* faith.

But mankind keeps on going with the collective inner faith that they call can agree on: they will one day die and get the right answer for themselves.

Until then, it's mankind's sworn duty to hate one another with an annual desire *not* to every Christmas. At the fourth quarter of the year when it's time to get presents, it's a better time not to hate your neighbor if you want to get a gift. Besides what, it's winter and fighting isn't very good for the health during that time of year.

This is the sort of rampant arrogance that made God angry, as he reviewed the Earth and his inhabitants. No, he wasn't going to speak to them and he had no intentions to *ever* speak to them. Not individually, not in groups and, *him* forbid, from the clouds with lightning and thunder. This was a game of *respect* and they're all failing miserably.

The Earth.

He built it. He keeps it running. Like clockwork and he even keeps the meteors from taking them out in one fell swoop. Black holes, super novas—these ungrateful beings have it good and the last thing he remembered telling them all was to live long and prosper.

He always did like that quote.

So the reviewing went on. He studied the hate. He studied the fears. He studied the terrible atrocities. He studied the confusion. He studied the utter anguish and the foolishness. He studied the bitter tears. The stupidity. The wasted genius. The selfish. The forgotten. The lost. He studied them all and a few months before winter, he had enough and considered bringing to the Earth the worst plague it has ever encountered. Probably knock out a quarter of a trillion easily. *Now what will you do? Oh, look whose calling lord, lord now?*

He thought these things almost every day so this day wasn't new. Of course they have bitterness and hate. *He* gave them everything he *himself* is quite aware of.

That's when *he* often fell back and felt compassion. Yes, they are only living what he gave them.

There will be no plague this day. Not this time. He'll continue as planned and let HIV do its thing. Not really the killer *he* knew how to provide, but it brought them together. Which was the point of each and every plague and they never seem to get it.

That they were no different. Each woman was the same as the next woman of any color or location. Every man was the same as the next. Location and culture choice separated them and it was a very thin excuse to spend eternity as either better than the other culture or race when, in God's eyes, they were all the same dust he whipped up so many millennia ago. They don't get it. They'll never get it. They only get it when a common threat is upon them.

So he amped up the HIV scourge a little. Not by much. Just enough to keep things interesting.

Gays? Homosexuals? *He* saw dust. There were no division. One confused heterosexual was no different than a homosexual and to *him*, they were all walking bags of flash, bone and stupidity. Higher thinking just wasn't in the cards for them and he didn't think it would ever change. How could *the dust* argue and fight about sexuality when people were hungry or poor? Children were dying and they had the capacity to solve all problems. He made it so and left clues everywhere for them to be self-reliant. But oh no. They'd rather hunt down and slaughter many for being of another faith, race or sexual preference when, according to *Him*, when you start thinking higher, those things just don't matter.

They were missing the wonders of the universe and receiving his gifts at a dripping faucets pace when they could have conquered the universe collectively by now.

Heck, they could have even walked with him in the cool of the day through another Eden he had prepared for them. He would have loved to have spoken to them all as any father loves talking to his children. Openly without reservation. Intelligently without fear. They were supposed to love and respect *Him* and he would be able to share and love them back openly as he planned.

Could have. Would have.

In short, they screwed up his ultimate goal and he often could care less if one or a billion of them returned to the dust they first came.

When the days went on like this, and they went on like this often, *His* angels usually left him alone. They, too, had direct orders not to go to Earth and interfere for any reason whatsoever. Those days were long dead and anyone even entering the atmosphere would perish with extreme prejudice. The dust can think all they want of seeing angels in clouds and long dead virgin images in trees—the demons love to mess with them and so be it.

Oh yes, the demons. He has them under wraps too and the occasional wonton devil is so scarce, it's a wonder why it's so prevalent in dust culture. Possessions and ghosts and goblins; all of which a mix of stuff that *He* prevented long ago and enhanced fiction. If he were to let every demon and angel pop up and down as they pleased, it would seem as if he had no control whatsoever and a new religion would pop up for each and every demon as they have for almost every angel. That would not do, but the dust keep making things up as often as they can.

Why? Because they all want to be lead when he specifically made them to love *him* but lead themselves. Free will. They don't see it and it's so obvious. They give birth to children. They expect their children to love them, respect them but lead their own lives and grow and lead their own families. Word for word—encoded in their DNA—this is what *He* expected of them to return to him: a parental reverence.

But they think they came from the bogs. From fish and started walking in that half-knowledge evolutionary thinking. That insults him the most. Totally excluding billions upon billions upon billions of exact timing and planning that brought them to this very moment and time. To breath air and think and create things and build things. Art, great literature, love and to dream things and actually make those things.

Just like *Him*.

But they evolved from monkeys, they say.

Monkeys.

His anger was seething when he suddenly stopped in mid-preparation of sending a variant strain of the HIV virus that would confound them for a few years.

He had a new idea.

With all the planning already done and he just about knew where everything was going and when it was going to end, a new concept was fairly rare in *his* work. He usually just lets the plan for the mankind move gradually towards its sum. What he was proposing was radical, even for *him*, but it kind of stayed within the guidelines he designed but also changed the whole story.

The more *he* thought of it the more *he* loved the idea. The more *he* loved the idea, the more *he* was certain this would solve *everything*. What's more, he would finally—after all these years—get a good laugh out of it.

Oh, this was going to be good. He didn't have to wait for any specific time of the year. Didn't have to wait for anyone specific to be born and try to claim 'god status'. This was all him and he was going to have fun at the expense of the dust, teach them a lesson and finally get them back on track toward what *he* felt was the way of life *he* intended.

He was aware of their makeup and design as a mother knew her own child. The universal order he deigned always came back to 'when its time' as an answer to when things had to happen.

And that time was …

Corey A. Burkes

NOW

Queens, New York
September (Fall)

The story of Latonya, from the Gun Hill Road section of the Bronx
and Camden, from East Babylon, Long Island didn't begin right
away. Like all chemical things, a catalyst was required to draw two
distant, unrelated, unknown beings together to be the center piece of
a future struggle. That catalyst; or subject to cause a reaction, began
at a White Castles in Queens off of Union Turnpike on a Friday
night at around 1:30am.

The clubs in Manhattan were just starting to get hot and 18-year-
old Eric was usually late picking up the gang in the Castle parking
lot after snagging the keys from his mother's purse. She worked the
second shift and almost always came in dead tired by 12:30AM—
conking out till late Saturday morning. More than enough time for
Eric to party with friends to the city and back with a full tank of gas
to make him look like a good boy to his mom.

Eric's family was from the Ukraine and he liked to brag he had
ties to the Russian mob. Very much like his Italian friends who knew
a Gino or a Tony or an Uncle Louie who were all connected, Eric
carried that swagger with a badge of honor everywhere he went.
After all, ex-KGB Russian mobsters trumped La Cosa Nostra any
day.

Whether it was the truth or not.

The *gang* consisted of Monica, who would die shortly from a
bullet to the head ... Robbie, who will have three ribs broken and
need six stitches ... Frank, who will be the only unscathed survivor
of a forthcoming attack and Paul, the only one among them with
actual Italian ties that will escalate the following events.

But Paul will be dead from being hit multiple times from a
baseball bat so he wouldn't be available to verify end results.

For now, late as usual, Frank arrived in his mother's '89 Buick
LeSabre; with the Police car-like speed of an eight-cylinder engine
that flung the vehicle through the Grand Central like a brick on
rocket fuel.

Somebody in his mix always carried a Policeman's Benevolent badge to bypass speeding tickets and such. Somebody in his gang of all European, happy and young Caucasians would never have to worry about the cops in one form or another because this was New York, and fear of the police or being pulled over for no reason wasn't even a passing thought to them.

Maybe to others, but they weren't the *niggers* or the *spics*, so what did it matter? Well, it mattered to Monica because she had one or two niggers as girlfriends. Which is where the beginning of the end … *of the beginning* starts.

The club they intended was in Manhattan and on the way to the Triboro Bridge, a call came through to Monica's phone that her girlfriend was currently being roughed up by her boyfriend and she needed to get as far away from him as possible.

The girlfriend, Sherri, lived in Jamaica, Queens (a primarily Black community) that Eric did not feel comfortable venturing to. However she was at her boyfriend's off Ditmars Blvd, a notably Jewish and Russian-Jewish community, whereas Eric was more than willing to detour to. How Sherri would get home after this voyage would be her own problem. For one, Eric did not want to travel back thru Queens to drop any nigger bitch off in *spook* land. For two, he was in the mood to go clubbin' and would only do this mercy rescue mission because Monica gave him some head the other day.

They arrived at Ditmar's Blvd and had only about seventeen blocks to go before arriving at Sherri's boyfriend's house. She was that kind that dated White boys and now shit was hitting the fan. Eric had no problems letting his little clique know the politics and ramifications of mixing races—using tonight's problem as an example.

While the others weren't classic case racists, they had no love for voicing openly the black/white issue as Eric would whenever he could. Regardless if he thought Sherri's ass was to die for, he could never see himself communing with the niggers and that was that. This here … this pick up was a favor for a friend.

By the time they were fifteen blocks away, what they weren't aware of was Sherri's issues with her boyfriend had escalated. To ensure she did everything short of calling the cops, Sherri also called her brothers—Mark, who will suffer lacerations and a broken arm … James, who will be shot by the police, linger for a few days in the hospital and die from internal bleeding and Trevor, who will hunt down Eric and kill him.

Sherri will survive and betray them all.

Two of her brothers were United States Marines on leave for a family reunion and Trevor was the more street savvy blue-collar worker of them. All three were loaded up in the car with a backup of two van-full of heavy friends and family for extra muscle; at the *least* to flex as a show of force. They were heading into White territory and it was best to be prepared. Everyone and anyone in New York, if you are worth your weight in New York culture, will always remember Yusef Hawkins, Michael Griffiths and Willie Turks.

Sherri's brothers were fifteen minutes from Ditmar's. Eric and the gang arrived to see Sherri walking out of an apartment building with an arm full of clothing; mascara smearing her face from perpetual crying. The Fall weather wasn't crisp yet and to most people it was considered unseasonably warm still.

Most people, anyway. Some, like Sherri, have mentioned recently it was actually a little unseasonably chilly for an Indian Summer.

Because of the warmth of the air, most of the people around this section of Queens were outside and would be witness to what would happen in under ten minutes.

Sherri's boyfriend, Hedrick, a hulking 3rd generation German best known for bench-pressing 280, getting left back three times and next-in-line to some German factory business of vague description, was also known for knocking girls around whenever they mouthed off to him. Usually, most girls got in line and knew their place. Black girls didn't, though. Always something to say and tended to fight back.

A challenge that often was met with 280 bench-pressing pounds of returned force. Such as the case with Sherri. A great lay, without question. Regardless, the bitch needs to k now who was in control.

The last thing they both remembered was arguing about what club they were going to and the next thing they were going for blows. Deep in his subconscious, Hedrick knew enough to hold back not to fill out a police report, but this nigger bitch wouldn't stop talking and when she through the water bottle at him, it was on.

People rushed to break things up. She kept challenging him. She said she was getting her things and leaving. Nobody leaves Hedrick so he tried to stop her. People in the complex who didn't need police intervention either way tried to stop him and that kicked off one fight after another. Sherri made one call to Monica who was in the area conveniently and then another to her brothers when Hedrick was losing his mind and threatened to kill her before he let her go and Sherri scooped up her things and marched out in time to see Eric's Buick double-park outside of the building.

Monica jumped over her friends from the backseat, opened the door and got out to meet her friend. "Sherri! What happened?!"

"What the fuck you think happened?" She cried. "Get me the fuck out of here! I'm done with that mother fucker!"

Eric turned to the back seat to look at his friends. "See how these nigger's talk? That's a friend, huh?"

"Alright, alright. Let's go. Eric's going to take us …"

"Eric?" Sherri stalled, looking into the car, then at Monica. "What the hell, Monica."

"What? You called me. You needed help. I got you help."

"But *Eric*? I told you his ass is a racist sonovabitch."

Eric, naturally, heard that. "Hey! Go fuck yourself. I didn't have to come here."

Sherri turned on her Sketchers and high-stepped it away from the building. A commotion was heard in the foyer from a distance and Monica had a few choices to make that she wasn't aware of. Hedrick was coming and this would be where the death and mayhem began. If Monica left her friend and let Hedrick catch up with her, this evening would have concluded with just the death of Sherri, found beaten, raped and bloodied in some bushes days later. Her brothers would not have arrived on time, only five minutes away, and Eric would have had a full tank of gas in his mother's car by morning, none the wiser. Down the line, the police would have questioned Hedrick a billion times with denial after denial until trace evidence would finally turn up and he would be convicted of ten years, angering Sherri's family and upsetting the Black community that he got off easy and they lost a daughter and sister.

He would even escape the charges by skipping bail and running his father's company in Germany somewhere.

That would be a timeline not meant to be for Monica took the high road and followed her friend in order to convince her to get in the car. Eric, coached by his intrepid friends and with sound reasoning that he would get another blowjob from Monica as a reward, followed against the curb in the car.

Just in time for Hedrick to push past people trying to keep him away from Sherri …

… just in time for Sherri's brothers to arrive at the apartment. Two cars full of more African-American's than this part of town was ever use to.

Now THAT was enough for someone to call the cops. Their best time to this part of town was three minutes. In two minutes, Hedrick would be stabbed by James.

Hedrick caught up to Sherri, grabbing her by the arm viciously, pushing Monica to the ground. Eric and the boys got out of the car to *vocally* disagree with that action. Let's face it, Hedrick was a big guy so maybe they could reason this out (as cowards do).

Sherri's brother's weren't inclined to talk anything over and rushed Hedrick immediately. Hedrick took on two of the brothers while one comforted Sherri. The police could be heard on the way and the bulk of friends that came with Sherri's brothers advised an immediate evac to no avail. Mark and James were in full beat-down mode, but not exactly winning against the more angry and semi-skilled, wild MMA-wannabe Hedrick. Shirts came off and bare knuckle wrestling began in the streets drawing everyone outside.

James pulled out a knife with every intention of ending this rapidly by flashing it to calm the White boy down. Instead, Hedrick charged him and Hedrick was stabbed in the abdomen. Not enough to slow him down, but blood spilled and Hedrick's rage was uncontrollable.

Shoving and pushing in the crowds of people telling the Blacks to go home and scuffling began. One police car arrived and they already knew this was out of their control and back up was called. One officer, without rhyme or reason, jumped out of his car and pointed it at the first Black people in range, threatening them to get on the ground: Trevor and Sherri.

This incensed the crew that tagged along with Sherri's brothers and everyone yelled at the police while the Hedrick, James and Mark fight continued down the street relentlessly. Hedrick got the best of James and took the knife from him, then struggled with Mark who was closer to his equal. Hedrick managed to slice rapidly at Mark, severely cutting his face, neck and chest.

More police arrived at the same time the friends that came with Sherri's brothers felt they needed to defend themselves, breaking out the bats and poles from the van. In their mind, no Black man would be safe out here regardless of the mission.

When the makeshift weaponry was seen by the locals, the men of the area came out in droves and before anyone could breathe, a mini-race war shut down Ditmar's cold. Police were called in from all points and the night was lit up with helicopters and gunfire.

Gunfire that would strike Monica, in the confusion, once in the head: dead … and James twice in the chest … to die later.

Eric took this opportunity to let go some excessive hate and took it upon himself to batter anyone who was Black to aid the police in the round up. Within all of the confusion, he even took a cheap shot at Sherri, smashing her knee and moving on to be undetected in the masses of combatants. The problem was, Eric only took cheap shots at anyone who wasn't prepared for a blow from behind and had a little trouble confronting someone who saw him coming: Trevor.

Trevor who also saw him attempt to cripple his sister.

Eric was not a fighter by any means and ran for his life with Trevor in hot pursuit. Meanwhile, police swarmed the neighborhood battering all people who wouldn't stop fighting. The last gunshot fired was at Hedrick, through his head by a recent graduate, Officer Latonya Walker of the Bronx. Hedrick had broken Mark's arm and had every intention of gutting him like a fish. Latonya ordered him once to put down the knife, he refused and he was finished.

Welcome to the job, Officer Walker. Nothing like discharging your weapon for the first time, taking your first life for the first time, on your first patrol, just days after graduation services. She barely finished her congratulations cake.

Camden, Hedrick's equally large and equally angry brother watched with handcuffs on a few yards away. He and about fifty other people were being swatted at, stun gunned and beaten by the police to maintain law and order. His helpless, blood curdling howl could be heard through time and space. All Latonya could hear, between her dipping consciousness, was something about her killing someone's brother. Repeated over and over again. And over again.

She would be in the shower and dead asleep and will never get his hate out of her head for what she had done.

Elsewhere, streets away, a very tired Eric had no choice but to turn and fight Trevor in the empty Queens' neighborhood. He would regret not truly knowing anyone in the Russian mob, or learning to fight, spending most of his lifetime that ends shortly talking shit and acting tougher than he actually was. He would even regret not getting his car back to his mother.

Trevor's only regret would be he should have brought a knife of his own. So, the broken Heineken bottle on the curb would have to suffice. The younger Eric would take two blows to the jaw and chest, followed by three stab wounds to the gut with the broken bottle, followed by two kicks to the face as a final reminder.

Eric would be dead before Trevor could return to the fray.

Lives would be changed forever.

The Humor of God
In Production Now

Only from DesktopEpics
Stories You Can Feel